# SPIRIT
## OF THE
# RAVEN

# SPIRIT
## OF THE
# RAVEN

## AN ALASKAN NOVEL

Bob Cherry

**PiCARO PRESS**

Seattle/Denver

This book is a work of fiction. Names, characters, places and events are products of the author's imagination or are used fictitiously. Any resemblance to actual events, locations, or persons, living or deceased, is purely coincidental. We assume no responsibility for errors, inaccuracies, omissions, or any inconsistency herein.

The poem JOURNEY is used with permission of the author.

First printing 1999

ISBN 0-9665430-0-9

LCCN 98-93373

ATTENTION UNIVERSITIES, COLLEGES, AND PROFESSIONAL ORGANIZATIONS: Quantity discounts are available on bulk purchases of this book for educational purposes. Special books or book excerpts can also be created to fit specific needs. For information, please contact Picaro Press, 700 N. Colorado Blvd., Suite 124, Denver, CO 80206, phone 800-247-6553, url: www.picaro.com, e-mail: order@ bookmaster.com

*for*
NORMA
*and for*
PERRY
*who both believed*

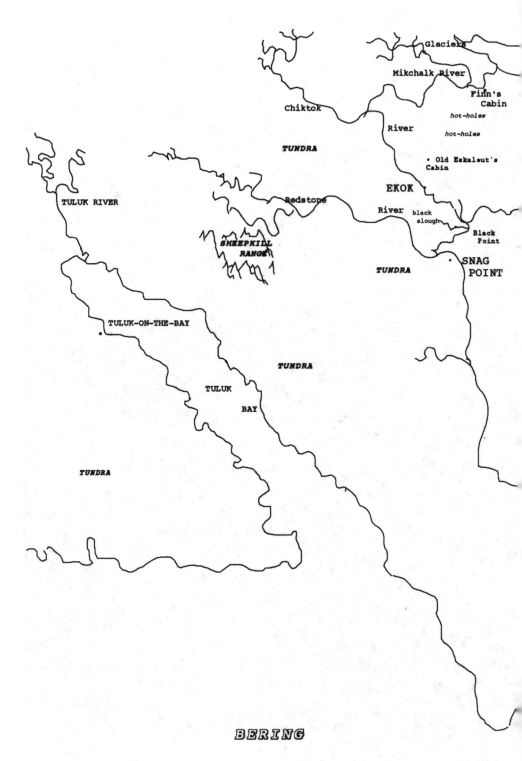

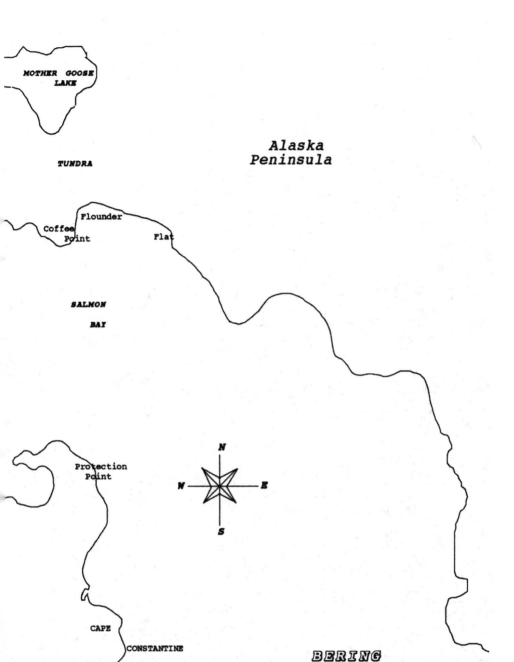

# JOURNEY

*I have been to a sky*
        *where Raven speaks in a thunder tongue*
*For I have called through beaded black eyes*
        *in my Sister's speech*
*And heard her answer with the voice of the*
        *hollow drum.*

*Smiling a crooked smile,*
        *my Sister holds a feathered secret in her beak.*
*She envelops me in the space held*
        *between sea and sand, between wind and fire,*
*And quickens my breath to the speed of winged*
        *heartbeat.*

*My bones become wands of light,*
        *hollow, and slim.*
*The sound of night wind like rushing water*
        *sings in my ear.*
*We merge into a single note*
        *and enter the East wind.*

—Tima Priess

# ONE

When Hjalmar the Finn broke his snowshoes free from the tangle of alders and stepped into the clearing he noticed the axe handle. It stood erect against the whiteness of the small frozen lake, a spectral finger pointing at a hard sky. At first he thought the head of the axe had been frozen into a mound of ice, but when he got close enough Finn could see a wool Mackinaw coat beneath the fresh skiff of snow. Half the double-bitted axehead was buried between the shoulder blades of the body lying on the ice.

Finn hunkered down beside the man and rested his butt on the back of his snowshoes. He listened to his breath in the stillness and he wondered for a moment if he could sew up the split and salvage the Mackinaw. Then he shook his head, scolding himself. "That's a godawful thought," he whispered.

There could be little doubt who the man was but Finn considered the Mackinaw for another moment. He shook his head again. "If it's Swede," he muttered, "the coat's too goddamn big for me anyway."

Finn stared at the corpse for a long while and let his eyes go out of focus until he was not seeing it anymore. Even though he had relaxed his body he was aware of the demands he would soon have to make on it. The ice on the little lake snapped like a dogwhip under his snowshoes. It was enough to bring Finn out of his trance—a sound that in early fall would have galvanized him, prepared him for an icy bath. But in the Alaskan bush in November it only reminded him that eight inches of ice could become twelve inches of ice and twelve inches could

1

become two feet and it always cracked and complained and sputtered each time the temperature dropped again.

He stood and removed a mitten and used it to sweep the snow from the back of the man's head. The face was hidden, frozen into the snow where it had melted a cavity while the flesh had still been warm. Finn thought about the ravens. At least they had not been able to get to the eyes but he knew they would be there somewhere and eventually they would take over if he did not. The ravens were always around, the only birds that did not fly south.

He struggled to turn the body but because of the axe he could not get it over so he grasped the handle and shook it vigorously, trying to dislodge the axehead. It was frozen in the corpse. Finally he stood on the man's shoulders and dropped his hundred and forty pounds against the handle, snapping it off next to the axehead and then he turned the body over on its back. He kicked the crust of ice away from the face and checked it just to be certain. "No sense dragging the goddamn thing if ain't him."

It was him. Finn saw that the foxes had been working on Swede's ears. One was chewed off and except for the protection of heavy coat and boots and beaver mittens he figured there would not be much left of the body in a few days to take back to Snag Point. He would have to get Swede back now. He would have to notify Delbert Demara, Deputy Marshal of the Territory.

Deputy Delbert Demara. Finn thought about him. Delbert would no doubt be warming his skinny ass right now in front of the fat little stove in Yael Feldstein's General Store. Delbert, the man with the questions, the man who would have to know, and the man for whom Finn had never had warm feelings. He focused on the body again. It was certain nothing here was still warm except perhaps a tiny part of the ambivalence he felt toward this partner prostrate in the snow. "Dumb Swede. Big dumb bastard."

It was the only eulogy he had time to offer but Finn wanted to say something, wanted to hear a voice. He opened his packsack and dumped the beaver traps onto the snow, ridding himself of the excess weight. It would be tough enough pulling the body ten miles down the frozen river without carrying another twenty pounds of spring steel. He squatted and picked up the feet and positioned himself between the legs like a draft horse. It was no good. Finn's snowshoes made it too awkward. He would have to tie Swede's feet together first and drag him through the alders to the riverbank where he could skid him down the slope to the river. From there it would be easier to pull him on the ice.

Finn removed the chains from the beaver traps and attached them to Swede's legs and encircled his own chest with them like a harness. He could move him better now so he leaned into the rigging. The body moved only a few inches at first then he felt it break loose and slide easier along the snow toward the riverbank. His breath was coming in grunts and he cursed each time he sucked in the cold air through his teeth. He lunged against the weight and rocked his body first backward then forward his eyes focused on the snow in front of him. He glared straight ahead as if anger could give him the extra strength he needed.

"Goddamn you, Swede." He leaned into the harness. "It's just like you. Leave the whole damn trapline for me to work." He pulled. "Your half of the wood to split—" He jerked. "And your pelts to stretch—"

And then Finn let his thoughts flow, remembering the half bottle of whiskey in his cabin on the Mikchalk River. He would not have to share it with Swede now. He and Swede had argued about it.

"I say it's half empty," Swede said sloshing the contents of the bottle. "I think we ought to just stick it away for the next blizzard."

"Screw you," Finn said. "I say it's half full and we could be dead by the next blizzard. I think we ought to drink it. Right now."

But he had let Swede have his way and now he was happy about that. He thought about the cache too—the one he and Swede had built last summer in the spruce thicket, filled now with two hundred and fifty illegal beaver pelts.

"Well, is this half empty too Swede?" he remembered saying as he leaned against one leg of the elevated cache. "Or half full?"

But Swede had not argued with him this time. He had not answered him at all. They both knew the cache was full and Swede had smiled and worked his eyebrows up and down just like he had always done when he talked about Nellie.

Moonface Nellie. She would be alone in the village of Snag Point now with Swede gone and the weight of Swede's body seemed easier to move as Finn thought about Nellie. The focus went out of his eyes again and they were steady. He set himself to his task with a numbness that allowed no thinking at all, no anger, no pity.

There was no fear either. As long as he did not linger on the thought of the axehead still in Swede's body there would be none of the fear that had been there two winters ago with his other partner No-Talk Owens. That was the kind of terror which could rise and cloud thinking like thick smoke if he but loosed it from a subconscious where it teased his mind more than he dared admit. But he ignored it like one might ignore a random shadow crossing the tundra under a full moon. Finn kept his eyes straight ahead.

*But other eyes watch Hjalmar the Finn from the spruce trees on the far side of the river. These eyes are not steady like Finn's. They are dark and restive and charged with their own brand of live and enduring fear. The wild terror in these eyes is as much a part of the man who watches as is the heritage which sets the cheekbones high on his round face. The heritage comes as a tenuous gift. But it comes free along with the ancient skill which commands his snowshoes through the confusion of trees.*

*And within these eyes is an anger which pits his lean body against an insidious cold, against hunger, against everything that would have this man who watches Finn dead too. These eyes see the world of Finn and Swede and they defy that. They see the watcher's own world and they defy that also. They see in the shadows and seek to create within them a separate province of darkness where no other man cares or dares to go, a place where this man moves without challenge or threat, like a spirit with a compulsion, not to protect or defend but simply to remain elusive like the bitter memory frozen in his own subconsciousness.*

*Keetuk spits into the snow. He hears the saliva sizzle in the coldness. Then he spins his body and in one fluid motion swings his snowshoes around and silently disappears back into the trees. Like a random shadow.*

Finn was on the ice now. He could rid himself of his snowshoes. He removed them and then buttoned them inside the front of Swede's

Mackinaw, the curved birch tips arching back over the head of the corpse. The rawhide webs covered the frozen face in a macabre game of peekaboo. He was able to move the body much easier now so the numbness in his arms and shoulders was slowly giving way to feeling. He began to think about time and the short daylight and when he might expect to reach the main branch of the big Chiktok River three more miles further near the small village of Ekok. Seven miles below Ekok lay Snag Point positioned on the high ground. It was a larger settlement and a central trading point for the trappers in the winter, the panners and gillnetters in the summer.

Snag Point overlooked the confluence of the wide muddy Chiktok and the narrow glacial Redstone River which drained the southwest slope of the Sheepkill Range. It was here the Alaska Peninsula joined the main body of the Territory like a giant curving tail. But the people in this wild and forgotten part had chosen not to join or to do so with their own brand of ambivalence.

They were the people like Swede and Finn and dozens more who had come up from Seattle or over from the old country, jumped ship from the three masted whalers and freighters and stayed to trap the beaver and to gillnet the salmon and to dream of the gold. It was here the clear water from the vast web of lakes and rivers finally turned murky, boiled over the mudbars in the summer with the giant ebb tides, rushed through the shallow channels of Salmon Bay and on out into the Bering Sea. There it became jade green and mysterious, filled with ghost ships cracked loose from the Arctic icepack, nameless vessels with sails of jagged ice, unmanned except by spirits the *Yup'ik* Eskimo people called *Inua,* the ancient ones, the true people.

It was here along countless and unmapped rivers that one from the outside could lose himself and his past, reinvent himself, become whatever he wished or dared just as Hjalmar the Finn had done.

Hjalmar the Finn. He had tapped a thin ethnic strain somewhere in his Irish-Scandanavian ancestry and assumed the name or acquired it by default. Finn did not remember. It was certain he was no longer Phineas Farrow, boss of a section crew repairing lonely stretches of railroad running west from Fort Worth, Texas.

Finn's hasty departure from that period of his life had been a lesson in bankruptcy, both economic and emotional. He had ample time to reconsider himself and his future as he and Marvin G. Crush and the boy with them, each pursued by separate demons, rattled inside the boxcars of a hundred different freight trains as far as they could go west and northwest and then even further, at least for himself and Marvin. But not the boy. Not a thirteen-year-old, screwed-up kid who had been an uninvited companion at best and who in Seattle had paradoxically fallen in with what Finn could only describe at the time as a babbling pack of religious zealots far too much like those from whom the boy had narrowly escaped in the first place, the only exception being that these new influences on the young man had chosen to walk into their starched white collars rather than back into them.

But for Marvin G. Crush and himself the journey had not exhausted itself for several more long weeks aboard a three masted ship sailing north as far as they could flee in that direction. Swinging in his hammock inside the dank creaking belly of the ship, Finn had envisioned himself returning to Texas someday in triumph having parlayed the small sum with which he had managed to escape into great wealth from beaver trapping or gold panning or both.

But all that had faded with the last few coins inside the leather pouch from which he made the down payment to Yael Feldstein in Snag Point for his first winter's grubstake, leaving the remainder he owed on what Yael had called a contingency account against beaver furs. Finn had signed his name then in Yael's big ledger not as Phineas Farrow but as *Hjalmar the Finn.*

And so he had become the Finn and most of the others he was sure had done the same. Swede was no more Swedish than Finn was Finnish but Swede was huge and strong and predisposed to wearing wool watch caps and so the name fit. And there was Roman Putvin, the Dago, because of his first name. Never mind that the surname was Russian. This nationality did not fit the man. But Italian did, Dago did, and so he became Dago and had done a good job of assuming the accent.

And of course there was Marvin G. Crush now *Starvin'* Marvin not by choice but only because the name fit both his rail thin body and a slowly atrophying personality. And No-Talk Owens and Hard Working Henry and Chubby and Karl Erlich who had opened Heine's Cafe and who was probably the only one with his original name and accent, that is except Yael Feldstein. But Finn was not even certain about Yael. The name just seemed to fit him too like the others, like Delbert, Deputy Delbert Demara, a name inviting by its sheer pomposity a mocking pronunciation but not to his face, never to Delbert's face. And all the other people who had stayed in Snag Point or moved up the Chiktok River and created their own identities, became their names, too many for Finn to consider right now.

Upriver from Ekok he would keep to the ice where it would be smooth until he got past the village and then on down to the bluff below Black Slough. There the ice would rise in a long sharp pressure ridge opened in the center of the river like the spine of some prehistoric animal in a jagged rip all the way from Black Slough down to Snag Point. The continuous movement of the tides heaved the ice upward forming warehouses treacherous and shalegray with mud. But the shifting allowed only a skim of ice in the places where the tide had pooled the water twelve hours earlier and where it had not yet frozen thick again even in November. At that point the river smoked and fumed at low tide until only a thin scale of rime ice coated the mud and waited for the next cycle.

He would have to wait at Ekok. He would overnight with Starvin' Marvin who occupied a cabin there and he would wait for the low water so that he could pick his way downriver avoiding the weak ice, thread his way through the slashes past Black Slough and on into Snag Point.

Everyone at Ekok would want to help get Swede down to Snag Point, especially Marvin but Finn would not allow it. He would tell them it was his duty, maybe even his mission now, and Finn was beginning to like himself for it as though cast into this role of regal messenger of grief, some tragic character in an ancient drama playing out his blind fate in an alien country. Finn would get Swede back down to Snag Point by himself because he would have to explain it to Delbert, tell his own story especially after what had happened two winters earlier with No-Talk Owens.

No-Talk was his trapping partner that winter and Finn had to explain that one too. But he had done it without benefit of the grotesque cargo he would show Delbert this time. This time he would show all of them his partner's body to gain their sympathy and distract their thoughts from No-Talk and any personal motives they might believe Finn harbored.

It had been difficult with No-Talk. Finn found only his fur hat on the trapline and nothing else and all the pelts had also disappeared. Finn had never elaborated but everyone in Snag Point knew he meant the others disappeared too, the illegal cache of pelts all the trappers took each season and which they all knew the others kept and bartered under the table in the spring when they sold their legal limits to Yael Feldstein.

But they had spoken about another thing in Feldstein's General Store. They had said it aloud to Finn's face, accused him of eating No-Talk Owens because Finn had run out of food. *Eating him!* But that was insane, that was ridiculous. Finn had made it back to Snag Point in the spring by sheer luck with a wild look in his eyes, terrified and half starved. "It's that goddamn native," he screamed out of his mind with fear. "That *Keetuk*. He's the crazy one not me. The bastard's looting caches and killing people and—"

In either case No-Talk had disappeared, just evaporated somewhere up there on the Mikchalk River and in that final twist of irony had become far greater than the reticent little wretch of a man that he was. His name had become both legend and spirit along with the name of that savage who was certainly the source of his demise at least in the minds of the villagers who spoke both names now in hushed mutterings up and down the banks of the Chiktok River. And every time the two names were uttered the terror and the tale and the spirit of both men were each magnified in a curious way, feeding on one another.

No one had budged an inch to look for Keetuk. Not even Deputy Delbert Demara who sat with his ass turned to the woodstove and said he could do nothing without a body. And no one could prove anything about Finn so they soon had to believe his story about the showshoe tracks which simply stopped dead in the center of a frozen lake. The only trace left of No-Talk was the beaver hat with no blood no sign of struggle no corpse like Swede's. And when Finn told the story again and again on long winter nights there was a small almost imperceptible shudder which would run its course through the crowd sitting in silence around the fat stove in Feldstein's General Store and then there would be the soft sputter of rolled tobacco burning with the slow sucking of air through a dozen cigarettes, the glowing embers rising and fading again in unison in the shadows and then the clearing of throats and the tense laughter and the passing of the bottle.

Finn stopped and the makeshift harness clanked to the ice. "No hurry," he said. "No use killing myself."

He sat down on the chest of the corpse and fumbled for the tin of snuff he knew would be in the pocket of Swede's Mackinaw. When he sat on the snowshoes which he had tucked inside Swede's coat the weight of his body forced the rawhide webs down onto the frozen face causing Swede's nose to emerge through the mesh. Finn flicked his mitten free and tapped the top of the snuff tin with his finger and removed the lid. The snuff was frozen but he scratched some free with a grimy fingernail. He packed a pinch between his lower gum and lip and started to replace the lid then observed Swede's nose sticking through the webs.

"You always did like to snort yours," he said and then he looked around a little guilty about talking to the corpse. It was alright to talk to oneself especially in midwinter. Everyone did. But a corpse—that was another matter.

"Hell, why not. It's the least I can do. Here—" Finn reached back into the tin and fingered loose another pinch and stuffed it into Swede's frozen nose. He stared at the palegray face behind the webs as if expecting it to sneeze. And he waited. And the ambivalence returned only this time growing warmer and friendlier as he remembered more of the good times than the bad. Finn saw himself again this time emerging from the last light of the bruised horizon above the riverbank, the thin winter sun reflecting from a silver breastplate, a plume in his helmet and a gold encrusted broadsword in his hand and he was avenging his friend—no, not just his friend, not merely a partner—Swede was now his *brother, his own flesh and blood,* and Finn was terrible and feared in his righteous vengeance. Finn thrust his thin shoulders back in defiance and raised his bony stubbled chin to just the right angle, noble and fierce. The dull yellow eyes sunken into the shadows of his forehead became coldblue clear fearless and proud, the kind of eyes that forced brave and honorable men to fall at his feet in quivering masses of cowardice.

Finn brought the broadsword round in a sweeping slashing blow at his unseen enemy but his numbed fingers lost their grip on the tin of snuff and it rolled out across the frozen river, slowed and spun to a stop like a coin on a tabletop. The tin rattled on the ice, the sound at first breaking but then returning the silence. He stiffened and looked around, once more aware of the stillness and the cold and the approaching darkness and the sounds which were not sounds at all but the absence of sounds. The hiss of nothing.

*"Keetuk!"*

He had spoken the word and in so doing Finn's fear had surfaced and now it set him into motion stripped of armor and weapon and courage, left with only the knowledge that to drag Swede down to Ekok would still require several hours work and it would have to be accomplished now in the darkness. Finn put himself back into the harness and pulled against his load with a sudden frenzy, leaving the snuff tin as an offering on the altar of river ice to whomever or whatever must be appeased. He lunged down the ice around the next bend in the frozen Chiktok River and disappeared into the dusk.

# TWO

The tiny settlement of Ekok was like a living thing. In winter it awakened when the late sunrise warmed the slab doors of its six log cabins. It cleared its head in the cold water of the Chiktok River flowing beneath the ice no more than ten paces from any doorway. The river was everything. It was access, it was isolation. It was subsistence and when necessary it was escape, for no one who came here, trapper nor panner nor *Yup'ik* Eskimo nor missionary knew why he stayed even briefly in this puny pocket of space, this sad and weathered string of squat log structures without a history, without a single bonding past. Perhaps one transient would linger awhile simply because Ekok needed a new arm. Perhaps another would pause because it needed a new head. Yet another might visit because it needed a conscience, a soul. And at this moment in its mutant history Ekok had a soul. Ephemeral as it was, Ekok did have a soul.

It arrived once a month the date circled boldly on the calendar left nailed to the inside wall of one of its cabins, the only structure with a genuine door, one which had traveled all the way from Seattle on a steamer. It was the only door varnished each summer against the weather and it was carved with The Cross against evil. And this soul of Ekok brought once a month the news from downriver villages, perhaps a letter for someone, some tobacco, some coffee, some comfort. And it brought The Holy Word, the written and spoken and only word permitted now. It brought the consultations to those devoid of all other means of coping, those who had come down to Ekok from the Mikchalk River or from the village of Tuluk-On-The-Bay or from some other unnamed river or village in despair for few here used The Word except in a final and desperate attempt at redemption. And this soul of Ekok, this keeper of The Word, arrived on that date in the form of one Father Felix Manguson.

Behind the door with the carved cross Father Felix struck a match and held it near his face. In the darkness of the small cabin he allowed the orange brightness to wash over his face, flicker across his features, which were neither young nor old but rather a strange amalgam of youth and wisdom which could in chameleon-like response perform in whatever way the audience in attendance might require. His audience of two on this night required both youth and wisdom and therefore the black in his hair had been combed into the streaks of gray, smoothed back over the balding area away from the full eyebrows which grew as a single line of coarse hair without the normal break. The brows continued across his forehead above the dark eyes, a thick heavy line lending a fierce authority to his face. Felix parted his lips and ran his tongue across them, just the tip of the tongue in a slow and sensuous manner and he wondered if the teeth had shone in the matchflame. Then he set the lips, a small smile of confidence and satisfaction hidden beneath his carefully structured beard and mustache.

The flame had worked itself down the matchstem, and Felix held it poised above the candle he had set into a pool of melted wax on the small table. Above this, suspended from a nail driven into an overhead log beam, a chainswung crucifix twisted slowly. Felix waited until the urgency of the flame next to his fingers brought from the other two a sharp and anticipated intake of air and then without haste he touched the flame to the taper, held it to the wick until it caught and began to fill the corners of the cabin with light. The orange glow spread over the Spartan furnishings, pushing the shadows across the narrow bed, which in mock privacy was secluded behind a thin blanket hung from the rafters in one corner.

Then as if finally discovering her the candleglow revealed the native girl, her adolescent face in relief against the shadows, her hair reflecting the light like a raven's wing. But it also distorted the features of the girl who for these past two years had come down to this cabin with her grandmother for Father Felix's teaching. The girl and her grandmother had been students and yet the girl had been more than simply student.

Instead of blowing it out Felix merely released the match, allowed it to fall to the floor knowing it would extinguish itself at the last moment and would again cause a quick and involuntary intake of breath from the two watchers.

And Father Felix saw that it was all very good. "We'll need to kneel and pray." He dropped slowly to his knees, arched his back and tried to flatten his large belly so that his body would be straight and youthful for although his hands clasped the book with The Word to his chest in reverence and his eyes were closed Felix knew the eyes of the two were still on him. The old woman Maruluk knelt next to him and watched him lower his head. In desperation she had requested he do this thing for them and now she waited to be certain his lips were moving silently before she finally did the same.

Mi'sha, the young girl sitting on the bench against the wall did nothing, said nothing. She watched her grandmother in silence knowing this act of penance should not be the old woman's alone and that her grandmother's true belief was not with this man and his candles and his cheap scarlet sash. Despite his monthly lessons and condemnations of their ways she knew her grandmother's true belief lay instead with the old ways of her own people but the old woman had been confused by the teachings of the priest. Maruluk was respected in her village of Tuluk-On-The-Bay as a *Shaman*, a link with the past and the spirit of Raven, the one to whom they turned in times of their own desperation despite the admonishments of Father Felix that it was a false and pagan thing to do.

Not yet fifteen Mi'sha had believed in nothing except the old woman herself. She had been her only family since the influenza had taken first Mi'sha's mother, then her father and then in turn each brother, each sister, until finally it had stopped short of Mi'sha herself, leaving her scarred with the permanent reminder of her vulnerability. It was a warning now reinforced by her mentor with his continuous requests that she must kneel close to him and pray, give gratitude for her salvation.

Mi'sha knew that although she might have some discomfort she could kneel with this man on this evening in November and not have the same problem he was having with the large stomach protruding over his belt. She was also aware that by April her own belly would be thrust out and upward.

Mi'sha watched the mouth of the man move in silence. She watched the tongue dart out and wet the lips with its pink tip, slow and repugnant and she turned her eyes in disgust from Felix and stared at the blackness outside the window. She closed her mind to this place of dark memories and let her thoughts flee to the warmth of a spring day. She saw herself on the spongy muskeg of the tundra near her village of Tuluk-On-The-Bay.

She was with Alexie Napiuk, also from her village, and she saw Alexie's body as young and sinewy. They frolicked across the hummocks in pursuit of each other. And then together they chased an elusive flock of ptarmigan still halfplumed in clean winter white. But just as Mi'sha knew she was changing she saw the tips of the feathers on the ptarmigan were also changing to a tarnished brown matching the summer tundra. Mi'sha and Alexie laughed and called to each other in their own language and rolled in the tiny blossoms on the soft muskeg and put their faces together and their bodies were young and close and warm like the day. And they laughed again. But this time Mi'sha heard only her single laughter, hollow and foreign as it broke the silence inside the cabin.

Felix rose from his knees and scowled at Mi'sha and her irreverence. He nodded to the old woman and said, "You must take her downriver into Snag Point to have the child. We can watch over her more closely there for any problems which might develop. It will be necessary to watch closely if she is to achieve salvation now." Felix sought the eyes of the girl in the shadows but she would not look at him and the hidden smile beneath his beard returned as he spoke in soft condescension to the old woman without turning his eyes from the girl. "And we can only pray that the father of the child will come forward and do what is right and I have done this thing for you tonight, I have prayed for this to happen."

Mi'sha jerked her head around, her eyes aflame with terror and hatred.

"But I give it little hope," Felix sighed.

"She must not go into Snag Point," Maruluk begged. She rose and placed her short round body before him, calling forth all her courage in protest.

"And why?" Felix turned from the girl and bore down on the old woman with all his authority.

"The shame will break her spirit," she pleaded. "The *kassaqs* will shun her just as our own village has shunned us." She moved to the girl, stood over her and pulled her head against her cloth *kuspuk*. "This shame is none of her shame. But I know they will not let it be. She must stay with me. We can go even farther up, all the way to the Mikchalk River to have the child. Perhaps then all of them will see her courage."

Felix turned away from them. He stood in front of the suspended crucifix and saw that it had ceased to twist but now hung with the Christside away from them, away from the light. "And the father of the child?"

Maruluk was silent. Mi'sha felt her stiffen.

"Perhaps we should find out who he is, make him responsible?" Felix reached for the crucifix and turned the figure again toward the light but when he released his grasp it began to twist once more.

"No one knows," Maruluk said and she furrowed her brow, puzzled by the priest's words. "Not our people nor the whites, the *kassaqs,* no one knows I swear it. I have said nothing."

"But we know don't we, old woman." Felix went to the table and removed his red sash, kissed it and placed it next to the candle and saw that the crucifix had stopped twisting, its back once again toward him. "What if I could call his name to you right now?"

His voice was low, deliberate. He reached up and lifted the gold chain from the nail and sat on the edge of the table, cupping the chain and the crucifix in his hands. He studied it as he spoke. "What if I could spread his name all along the Chiktok in shame, force him to come forward and do what is right by this child here?" He looked up at the girl. "And also the one she carries?"

Mi'sha's eyes widened with fear and confusion. She started to rise and rush him but the firm hand of the old woman quieted her.

"But I don't understand," the old woman said. "What do you mean, 'Say his name'?"

"I know his name," he said. "Don't I, Mi'sha? I have counseled you in private, spoken to you alone just as I did in bringing the sacred word into your heart and our secrets to you. Salvation cannot be achieved without truth between us. Is that not so, Mi'sha?"

"Then you must speak and set it in motion," the old woman pleaded. "One of you." She looked at Mi'sha then back at Felix. *"Both* of you must say it, release the spirit to do its work, to do the good that it must. Only by confession can salvation be good. You have said this yourself…"

The old woman brightened. The truth which in her heart she knew more than anyone would finally emerge. The truth she had herself concealed these past three years in her shame, fearing the villagers would condemn her as they had done to others who broke the ancient taboos. But for a *Shaman* the punishment for indiscretion would mean certain death for she had tried to meld the old with the new, the word of the *kassaqs* with the spirit of the *Inua*. And in so doing Maruluk had sacrificed her own granddaughter.

"Salvation?" Felix said. "Spirit? And which *spirit* is that, old woman? There is only one good and true spirit and it rests here." He thrust forward his cupped hands and opened them exposing the face of the crucifix as its gold chain slithered between his splayed fingers like something alive. "You must give up this childishness you speak of. How often must I come here and tell you these things? These are only fantasies of the wind which trick your mind and the minds of your people. Give them up, old woman, as I have urged you. This spirit you speak of is evil. And I'm afraid it lingers also in the heart of the one whose name I can speak."

Maruluk was confused more than ever. Did the priest intend to confess that his own heart was evil? This was more than she had thought possible. Perhaps an honest and complete cleansing would be enough to reinstate her and Mi'sha into their village of Tuluk-On-The-Bay, restore some of their pride among their people. Maruluk was certain it would be the only way she could keep her honor as a *Shaman*.

But then Felix abruptly closed a fist around the crucifix and turned his back to them. He positioned himself in the candlelight again, allowed it to play across his face setting only shadows where the eyes should have been. He had sensed that the girl was about to speak but he would not allow this.

*"Keetuk!"* The word boiled out of his mouth and the two stood stunned before him for they each knew the man of whom he spoke. The old woman looked into the eyes of the girl and saw the fear and she thought about the man whose name had been uttered, the man who had often shared their cabin at Tuluk-On-The-Bay in a strange and silent manner as a friend. She smiled at the girl and touched her black hair and her own eyes filled because she understood what Felix was planning. She knew this man, this Keetuk, and she alone as *Shaman* to her people knew the dark secrets he held locked away even from his own knowledge. And Maruluk's recognition hardened her for what she must do to make up to the girl for her blindness.

"We will sleep now," the old woman said. "And tomorrow we will go into Snag Point with you, Father."

The girl stiffened. But when she saw the old woman's eyes with this new resolve she was quiet again.

Felix frowned. It was a sudden shift for the old woman and though he wondered about it he was pleased. "Good. It is best this way, best that I can be near the girl for meditation." He reached out and placed his fingers on the girl's arm. "And counseling."

Mi'sha shut her eyes and tightened the muscles in her cheek as if his touch were hot metal. She turned quickly away from him and went to her bed. Felix sighed and shook his head. "It will take much work to solve this," he said to the old woman. "Salvation is a long trail to walk. But I have been over it and I know we must be strong, all of us."

Then he went to the hanging blanket and pulled it closed behind him to prepare for bed. The old woman stared at the blanket for a moment then went to the candle and blew it out. In the darkness she passed by her own bunk but did not stop. Instead she sought the bed of her granddaughter and stretched out next to Mi'sha without removing her clothing. The girl did not become still until the old woman rested her arm across her. She cooed gently into her ear and then Mi'sha slept.

Felix also tried to sleep, turning his body over and shifting from one side to the other of the small bunk. He did not know what time he finally gave up trying to sleep but the stark winter moon was high and the light filtered through the single window with its four panes. Felix lay awake and watched the light as it fell on the floor, segmented into four paleblue squares by the window frame. In Felix's eyes the shadow dividing the four squares became a crucifix and he began to ponder its meaning.

*Was it the wooden cross in the center of the window that caused the shadow on the floor? The Cross, a solid and tangible thing casting its image onto the real world? Or was it The Light itself from beyond this physical world which now lay on the floor thus giving definition to The Cross? The Cross cutting The Light into its foursquare form or The Light spilling through and thus casting a mere shadow of The Cross?*

Felix decided it was the latter. As much as he had always wanted The Cross to represent more of this world, something solid, it still remained a disappointing shadow, a reflection in this life of the things one must postpone until the next. Still this image of The Cross on the floor was a matter of perspective he thought, like the church and his relation to it. Had Felix Manguson defined the church or had the church defined Felix Manguson? Was the question itself a sacrilege he would regret?

Felix was certain he defined whatever there was of a church in Snag Point and he had even taken it upriver to the villagers at Ekok. He had brought the Word to the lips of the people and rebuilt the church in both substance and spirit, the infusion of his presence like a drop of blood in a vial of holy water, extending even to the distant village of Tuluk-On-The-Bay though he had never actually been there himself. And even his superiors in Seattle who had felt compelled to send him here for penance would have agreed that he had done more than anyone else for the territory. It had not been stated directly to his face but he knew that their sending him here was intended as exile more than penance. He knew it was their attempt to rid his soul of a stubborn blackness they felt had continued to manifest itself in acts like the purchase of unholy items with funds from the coffers of the parish in Seattle.

Perhaps the demons lay concealed inside his breast, not yet exorcised, lusting still for the things forbidden to Felix by his own grandmother and her fundamentalist friends all those years past in west Texas, that entire congregation of bigots devoid of either substance or light as far as Felix was concerned. And so he had fled, secreted inside the boxcar as the uninvited and unlikely consummation of a now fallen triumvirate which had included both Phineas Farrow and Marvin G. Crush. The three finally stopped in Seattle where Felix himself had been abandoned by the other two, just a boy, confused and angry and vulnerable to the magnetism of both substance and light in all its guises. And thus entering the priesthood had seemed for Felix the next plateau in a natural progression to absolute salvation.

But he could not dwell on his transition forever. The entire question of his salvation was one he no longer fretted about. Like Mi'sha, salvation had been thrust upon him too at an early age in his little hometown beside the railroad tracks in Texas. His Sunday school teacher had insisted that though some things might come together, the rails over which the trains ran never did. And just as Felix had not understood at that age how some things mesh in reality, if perhaps not always in spirit, he knew Mi'sha did not understand either. But she would someday. She would learn as he had finally recognized how humanity must bind itself in harmony regardless of race, regardless of religion or spiritual belief, regardless of ethnic origin. But as always, the more Felix tried to suppress it the stronger came the memories and he thought again about his own confusion all those years hence.

He saw the little frame church near that spot where other things had been joined near the junction of the Central Pacific Railway and the Southern Line there in the far western part of Texas and he heard the question in his own youthful voice, more a plea for understanding and enlightenment than sacrilege or even arrogance. He had shut his eyes tightly, straining to visualize this thing called infinity.

"But they gotta join up somewhere?" Felix was speaking to Timothy Raisin, his Sunday school teacher.

"They do," Raisin said. "Or did. Right outside town there, big celebration, Central Pacific from the west, Southern Line from the east, gold spike and—"

"No I mean the *rails* themselves come together," Felix interrupted. He opened his eyes and frowned at Raisin and pointed west. "Like they seem to do when you stand between them and look down them, hard. You know way out there on the horizon."

"Oh that."

"They gotta meet somewhere," Felix said again.

"Nope, never. Railroad tracks are just like parallel lines," explained Raisin, calling on his years as a school teacher for assistance of a less holy nature. "They're parallel too. They never come together. Ever. *Infinity.*"

"God could make them meet," Felix said. "My grandmother says God could make even railroad tracks meet."

"Well maybe so but then they wouldn't be parallel anymore, right Felix? Infinity's what we're talking about here, remember? Like salvation. It just goes on and on."

But Felix had never seen infinity and could scarcely visualize anything going on and on, even Raisin's salvation. It was not until some time later that Felix had experienced his own true salvation there in the little community. Nothing that Timothy Raisin nor the pastor nor even his own grandmother had done could persuade him until the call finally came in the way it did. And it was not even inside the church.

Felix felt it necessary to contemplate the incident only in those moments now of personal crisis when all else had failed. Salvation had come. It had been miraculous and mysterious and it had changed him forever. That was all that was important. He knew his mission now was to spread the same experience to others who were in need of cleansing. His own youthful catharsis would remain a bittersweet memory. He had attempted to purge the bitterness and leave only the sweetness when he had gone into the priesthood in Seattle, and he believed it was there he had secured salvation in a more permanent and official manner. He felt his offering of salvation to these primitive people, true salvation which took over one's entire being and spoke to one's soul as it had spoken to his own as a boy, would someday emboss his name in gold inside the Book of Holy Crusaders.

Felix thought about the girl, alone and confused and surely in need of comfort again in her bed. He listened for her breathing and held his own breath to see if there was a sign, some small signal for him, but he heard nothing except the faint whistling of the wind around the little cabin. He imagined it was her sobbing. He would go to her. He would move silently in the darkness across the room so as not to disturb the old woman and speak quietly to the girl in the darkness to comfort her, perhaps pray as they had done before.

Cautiously he slipped one leg free from the blanket and then the other. Cold. The floor was very cold. He was not hardened against the cold like the others but he would be warm soon as he had been warm the times before. Felix shifted his weight on each leg so as not to creak a single plank on the floor. He eased back the hanging blanket and made his way across the still room toward the bunk against the opposite wall. His breath quavered from the cold and the excitement and he had difficulty controlling it now that he stood over her bunk. He would have to move very carefully and not startle her. He reached out his hand in the darkness to place it on her mouth gently, ever so gently so as to awaken her but not frighten her. Easy, gently…

"*Wha—?*" he whispered and then aloud, "*Gone!*"

He flung back the blanket from the bunk. Nothing. He felt the bed. It was still warm. Quickly he went and stood over the other bunk. "Old woman!" he shouted. "Where is the girl? She's not in her bed!" But his shouts were useless for she too was gone and then Felix panicked and his thoughts went wild.

*What if he could no longer control her? What if they exposed him? Perhaps to Keetuk himself. He must catch them before Keetuk did, he must find her, he must bring her back.*

He burst through the cabin door and raced out to the river. In his frenzy he stumbled along the ice for some time before he realized he was clad only in his woolen underwear and he was without his boots. When the full grip of the cold finally reached his mind he curled his feet in agony on the sharp ice and cried out in pain.

Maruluk and Mi'sha heard the door slap open but they had moved quickly and were too far up the frozen Chiktok to see him. The old woman had been awake in the darkness of the cabin for a long while before making her final decision that she and Mi'sha must flee. She could no longer ignore the truth. But even then it had been only with the help of Raven that she had gathered the courage to break forever from this betrayal.

The sleepy protests of Mi'sha had made it more difficult and Maruluk had not expected Felix to pursue them so quickly. She feared he might use something evil to force them to return with him. She knew she could expose him to the *kassaqs* in Snag Point, even try to share the guilt with him, but they would never believe her. She knew her own village would condemn her after she had praised the priest and his new word, bringing it herself to them in a twisted version of their old beliefs.

As they moved along the edge of the riverbank Maruluk noticed in the moonlight a cluster of fresh spruce boughs propped against the cornice of snow. "Quickly, we must hide." She lifted some of the branches and shoved Mi'sha inside. Then she squatted and crawled in beside her and replaced the branches behind them. Between the limbs they watched the figure of the priest as he stumbled down the river ice, his white woolen underwear flashing in the light of the full moon.

Felix had stopped only a few feet away from their hideaway when Mi'sha, who was still not fully awake, lost her balance and thrust her hand out into the darkness to steady herself. It fell upon the soft bristles of a beaver skin. Slowly Mi'sha brought her hand down over the skin and felt the form of it as a hat. And then her hand came to rest on what seemed to be snowshoes. And there was a nose, cold and hard as a river rock, but unmistakably a human nose which thrust through the webs of the showshoes. At first Mi'sha would not let her mind conceive what her fingertips were telling her but there could be no doubt what she felt was human flesh. She whimpered and jerked her hand away. She made an abrupt move to stand and escape.

But Maruluk too felt the corpse. The old woman hardened her mind against this new evil by calling upon the Spirits again for courage. She clutched the girl to her breast and stifled the whimpering with her hand.

They heard Felix again, this time standing next to the spruce branches which shielded them. In frustrated sacrilege he cursed the raw coldness and the ice which had slashed his feet and then he turned and scrambled back up the riverbank. He fell twice before he could regain the top of the embankment. The frozen tundra above was no relief to the soft flesh of his feet, bleeding and numb from the jagged ice. Felix worked his way back along the riverbank and was nearing his cabin again when he slammed into a figure standing on the riverbank in the darkness.

"*Keetuk!*" he cried and covered his face with his hands.

"*Keetuk!*" the voice whispered back to him.

This time the voices were too far above the ice of the river for the two hiding under the spruce boughs to hear. Now that Felix was gone there was only the silence of the coldness, the mute presence of the corpse and the awareness that they were alone and at the mercy of the cold.

"We must go," Maruluk said.

"Where?" said Mi'sha.

"We will follow the river. We must not leave the river in the darkness."

"But the cold," protested the girl. "It's so cold."

"We cannot hide here in Ekok. The others will tell him we are here. We must go further up the river all the way to the Mikchalk."

"I can't. I'm cold and it's five days by the river. It's foolish." Mi'sha moved further back into the shelter and closed her eyes. "Just leave me with him," she whispered. "You go back to Tuluk-On-The-Bay alone. They will want you again if I'm not with you. I will go with the priest and do as he says. Tell them I wanted it, tell them I hate them, tell them anything. I don't care anymore."

Maruluk knelt beside the girl, encircled her with her arms. "Mi'sha you must not think this way. Think only of what we must do to prepare for the child. Do not let it destroy you. Even if it was treachery which brought this we cannot let it fill us with bitterness."

"Deceit is what fills me." Mi'sha twisted away from the old woman. She pulled her knees to her chest and sat next to the corpse though it repulsed her. "Then leave me here with this, whoever it is. They'll find us both dead and then it will be finished. Let them think what they will. You can be free of me."

"But you were tricked and I was tricked. Do you not see this?"

"I should not have been so stupid."

"Listen to me, Mi'sha. Turn away from this," the old woman said. "I too was stupid but this is death. What you hold inside you is life and you must not think this way."

She shook the girl and there was the old strength back in her voice and now there was anger Mi'sha had never heard.

"Lose yourself in pride not in this self pity," Maruluk said. "You do not need this. Look inside yourself and strengthen what you are and come with me. Together we can do this thing."

Mi'sha sought her grandmother's eyes. She found only shadows, for Maruluk's head was silhouetted against the moon outside the branches. But Mi'sha did not need to see the face because in her heart she knew the courage was there. It was the same quiet strength that had been near since Mi'sha had lost her family to the influenza. It was the face that had touched hers when the loneliness had overcome her that first long winter in the village without her family, the old face that had warmed even the coldest days with the stories and the legends and the tales of Raven and how he had made the world and how the Spirits now inhabited all the animals and forests and rivers.

Then Mi'sha saw a face glowing like candleflame inside the hood of the old woman's parka but it was the priest's. She pulled away in fear and confusion. Had this same old woman not been the one to ask the priest about his word and the new ways? Had the old woman not been the one who had made the mistake in the beginning and brought his word back to their village, the one to permit the priest to counsel Mi'sha? Whose betrayal was this? Whose salvation was she seeking now?

Even with new bitterness Mi'sha could not accept this for again in her heart she knew the old woman had also been betrayed. There would be little Maruluk could do to convince the villagers of Tuluk-On-The-Bay she had been tricked. Maruluk had been the one to urge the changes and that could not be reversed now without severe punishment for the old woman. Had the old face truly been replaced by this new one glowing in that strange blend of firelight and darkness as Mi'sha had just seen inside the hood of her grandmother's parka?

In her heart Mi'sha knew the old face was right. She realized with truth she could try to do what Maruluk was saying. She sat up and reached a trembling hand into the hood of the parka and suddenly the fire was gone and only the warmth of the wrinkled skin remained and she knew it was the same. "I will try," she said. "I can only say that I will try."

Maruluk pushed the branches aside and together they crawled out, leaving their grim companion to the night. Mi'sha pulled the hood of her parka tight over her head and helped the old woman to her feet and together they shuffled up the frozen Chiktok River arms locked like a pair of phantom dancers.

As they moved along the river in the darkness Maruluk struggled to remember the location of cabins built by trappers over the years but now forgotten. She knew it would not be long before the priest or someone would come again to look for them. They must not find them yet. She would need solitude and seclusion to bring herself and Mi'sha through this difficult time and she would need the months to think about the best things for both the girl and the baby. Maruluk forced herself onward despite the cold, despite the aching in her legs and feet and she called again upon the strength of Raven to carry her, to help her find a place to hide.

The gray of the early morning light had turned the shadows along the riverbank back into tangled alders when the girl fell. She had stumbled and fallen several times throughout the cold night but this time she lay still on the ice breathing deeply.

"Get up, Mi'sha," the old woman said. "You must keep moving."

"My legs will not move. They're numb." She pulled her knees up to her chest. "I have to rest."

"But you cannot stay here on the ice."

"I'm warm here. Please let me sleep."

"Mi'sha, this is not sleep. It is false. This is not true warmth you feel but the trickery of death. Get up." Maruluk tugged at the girl's arms but she could only drag her a few feet across the ice before she too slipped and fell exhausted. "Please. You must try."

But there was no strength in her voice either. She crawled to Mi'sha and pushed the girl's body into a sitting position and again enclosed her in her arms. Then she rocked gently back and forward cooing the ancient lullaby she had sung to the girl as an infant. And she thought about the Ancient Ones and how it had been with them, how it was when someone was old or useless or too young to hunt and the food was thin and the bellies were empty through the long winter darkness. She remembered how the wisest and eldest like Maruluk herself would take the youngest female infants and go into a blizzard or set themselves adrift on the ice and allow the coldness to take them so they would no longer be a burden and the others could survive.

Maruluk thought about spring when the river ice would break and their bodies might be seen drifting downriver on a cake of ice past the church on the bluff at Snag Point, past the fish camps along the beaches of Salmon Bay and on forever into the Bering Sea. She saw how the people stared through the long glasses at them, wondering if it were a single body or two. And then her mind turned to the third one, the unborn one and she saw it as a boy and she knew that the men in her village would be angry if they knew. But she had no strength to try any longer. She had been blind to the trickery of the priest and she made no effort to call on the mockery of his word. But this time she made no effort to call on her own Spirits either. She simply moved their bodies in unison, the girl limp and frail, their two sealskin parkas appearing as one in the first rays of the morning sunrise which inched across the ice.

*And the same sunrise selects out of the gray morning another sealskin parka, this one on a musher who cracks the whip above the tails of the dogs. The animals are fleet and lean and they move also in unison with the musher, a single determined machine skimming the ice of the Chiktok. He rides the runners of the sled with an agile sway, his feet never touching the ice itself never once assisting the animals with the classic kick and call. This musher saves his energy, hostile and wild and tensed like the spring on a beaver trap. He holds it in check for the things he must do but cannot explain even to himself. And he cracks the whip again and in the ragged morning air the sound echoes from the banks of the river like a rifle shot and then it dies. And the only sound breaking the silence is that of the runners on the ice hissing like a knifeblade drawn through a windpipe.*

# THREE

Finn spent several tense moments trying to decide who the figure was standing before him on the riverbank in front of the village of Ekok. Finally he composed himself enough to speak. *"Keetuk?"* he whispered again and then, "Felix? Is that you, Felix? What the hell you doing out here this time of night? Where's your clothes?"

"Oh...*ooh!*" Felix took his hands away from his eyes and fell to his knees. "Thank God it's only you Finn. Oh, thank God." He put his hands over his face again and spoke into them. "They've gone. Disappeared, just gone."

"Now hold on, Felix, calm down. Let's get you back inside. Them bare feet won't be worth a tinker's damn if you don't. Now get up." Finn helped him up but Felix could not stand alone on his torn feet.

"Thank you, my son. God bless you, my boy."

"Here, just lean against me now. Easy. And stop calling me son. Hell's bells I turned fifty two last winter. I'm at least ten years older than you are Felix. Easy now. Here we are." Finn shouldered open the door to the cabin and helped him to his bunk. "Now you just relax and let me get some light in here."

He covered him with the blankets and struck a match to the candle on the table. In the light he saw Felix's bloody feet protruding from the blankets. "My God, Felix, look at them feet. You'll lose a couple toes for sure." Finn tapped his finger against one of the big toes. "Feel that?"

"Unh..."

"How about this?" Finn held the toe and wiggled it vigorously. Felix cried out in pain.

"Good," Finn said. "Long as you can feel it you'll most likely not lose it. What the hell you doing out there anyhow?"

"That old woman Maruluk and the granddaughter, you know them?"

Finn knew them.

"I was with them here yesterday and last evening," Felix raised himself on one elbow. "We, that is *they*, have a problem and I'm helping them with it. We prayed, went to bed, something woke me. That's when I discovered them missing."

"Yeah?"

"Yes gone, vanished," Felix said and then neither man spoke for a long while, each weighing the possibilities.

"Well," Finn finally said. "You'll just have to wait 'til morning and see what happens I guess. I'll be going on down to Snag Point tomorrow. I could tell that deputy they're missing, that is, if you think it's serious. It probably won't do a damn bit of good but I could tell him. If you want me to."

"Take me down with you," Felix said abruptly.

"On them feet?"

"I can make it, I'll be no trouble."

"I dunno. I got troubles of my own." Finn thought about his other burden, the frozen body of Swede with the snowshoes stuffed into the Mackinaw. "Where you figure they went?" Finn was not really interested but he liked hearing another voice besides his own.

"With him. He has them I'm certain of it. Please take me down with you tomorrow."

"Who has them?"

"Keetuk. Please, it's not safe for me."

"Why?" Finn was suddenly interested and then he thought about Swede and how it had not been safe for him either. "Yeah maybe you're right. Maybe it's not safe now for any white man, any *kassaq* after what's happened to Swede."

"Swede?"

"Yeah, he's with me. Sort of."

"Where?"

"Well, he's down on the ice next to the riverbank. Dead. Frozen stiff."

"Oh my God. Froze to death." Felix collapsed back on the bunk and closed his eyes. He crossed himself and muttered some words in a language Finn could not understand. Finn shook his head but waited for Felix to finish.

"Yeah, well he ain't feeling pain no more, Felix, which is more than I can promise for you and me. But he didn't freeze to death. I think Keetuk got him too. He's okay now though. I covered him with spruce boughs so's the foxes can't get back at him."

"Why Swede?"

"Dunno. Maybe he had pelts with him. He was running one of our lines. We teamed up this winter you know, partners way up on the Mikchalk working out of my cabin there. Maybe Swede was just in the wrong place at the wrong time or maybe that native's just looney as a peach orchard boar like they all say. Anyway he put an axe in Swede's back so I'm dragging him down the river to Snag Point to show Delbert and then put him in the ground and have some words spoke over him you know."

Felix shut his eyes again and shook his head. When he opened them they were wide with terror. He sat up once more and took Finn by the shoulders.

"You've got to take me with you, Finn. Tomorrow. I beg you. I can help you with Swede and I can help with the funeral I can...*please*."

"I took you with me once, Felix. All them years ago. Me and Marvin. And stop pretending you don't remember even if you was just a kid. How old, twelve?"

"Thirteen," Felix corrected.

Finn had caught him off guard. Felix looked at him for a long while remembering he need not hold to any formalities. The stiff language of priesthood would gain nothing with Finn, so he dropped it. "And that might as well have been a thousand years ago, Finn. This is different."

"Well, it don't matter. I wasn't much older myself and running too. Me and Marvin both."

"And you didn't take me with you," Felix corrected again. "I was already in the boxcar when you and Marvin sneaked aboard."

"Well maybe. I don't remember and don't especially want to talk about it. Anyway I kinda need to do this thing now by myself." Finn looked at Felix and saw that his face was full of pain and fear in the dim light. "That native, he must have something good on you, Felix. What have you done to him?"

"He's been here in Ekok often. I know. The girl's been here also and he's been with her. He's the one who—"

Felix looked at Finn to see how he was reacting to all this. Then he looked down at his throbbing feet.

"She is—" he continued and then paused, adding as much drama as he could manage through his pain. He slowly brought his eyes back up to Finn's. "With child," he said softly but Finn noticed he had his priest voice back. "I know this. And I know he is responsible and he knows I will not keep the secret."

"The girl?" Finn said. "You mean that old woman's daughter?"

"Granddaughter. Mi'sha," Felix corrected and once again he dropped the formal language. "And that's why they left, to escape him and maybe the shame of it all. I think they've gone up there to the Mikchalk to have the baby. I'm worried about them. That's why I went after them so quick Finn without my clothes but—" He groaned and fell back on the bunk and covered his face with his arm. Finn watched him and began to feel a little sorry for him although it was none of his affair.

He had known Felix for more years now than he cared to remember and he considered the possibility, even the probability, he was lying. But perhaps they were brothers in a sense like himself and Swede and Marvin and the others all displaced in one way or another and he began to feel that same ambivalence toward Felix he felt toward Swede.

"Okay," Finn said. "You can come along tomorrow. But don't give me no problems, hear? And talk normal, goddammit."

Felix stopped the groaning. He rolled over into the blankets turning his back to the light and Finn. With a sigh of relief and exhaustion he buried his head in the shadows. Finn stood and stared at Felix's back for a moment then with his tongue wet his thumb and forefinger and touched the wick of the candle. The moonlight was no longer in the room so Finn groped for the door in the darkness and found the latchstring and opened it. He stood for a moment silhouetted against the pale sky listening to Felix's labored breathing.

"And like I told you before, I ain't your son neither." Again Finn waited for a response but Father Felix Manguson, soul of the village, was already asleep.

# FOUR

Finn left Felix and moved into the night toward Starvin' Marvin's place at the far end of the settlement, threading his way around the other cabins on the riverbank. He thought about Ekok and how it seemed different from other villages, a mere cluster of cabins and somehow not a community at all. Each dwelling existed as simply an island of crudely assembled logs alienated from others by the stubborn eccentricity of its architect. But each structure betrayed by its very proximity to others that curious paradox among trappers and transients expressed by a craving for companionship and yet a fierce desire to be left alone.

It had not been this way with him and Swede. They had been partners sharing Finn's cabin on the Mikchalk River fifty miles further up and away from the main branch of the Chiktok. Even so, they too had deliberately segregated themselves from curious eyes which might covet their full cache of pelts. Finn thought about other native villages as he walked and about the sounds of the dogs, the laughter, the children and the open doors in summer despite the droning swirl of mosquitoes. Dogs. That was what Ekok did not have, dogs or children, though no village had ever escaped the inevitable plague of summer insects.

Perhaps it was laziness or perhaps it was simply a distrust of anyone or anything except one's own legs and feet and handmade snowshoes but the people who came and went at Ekok did not keep dogteams. Just as he avoided the thought of summer bloodsuckers Finn did not like to think about children either. And like the others here he certainly did not trust dogs so he was glad there was no chorus of yips and squeals and barking when he pounded on Starvin' Marvin's door.

"Marv," he called and cautiously stuck his head inside the cabin door. "Marv, you here?" He went inside and struck a match expecting to see his old friend asleep on the bunk. But Starvin' Marvin was gone. He set the match to the wick of a kerosene lamp on the table and then fumbled in the single shelf for coffee. Nothing was there except a few pieces of stale hardtack which even the mice had abandoned. He peeked into the huge stewpot on the woodstove but flared at the greasy mysterious mass frozen in the bottom. He removed the lid from the blackened coffee pot and held the vessel up to the light. A caked residue of soured coffee grounds clung to the bottom.

"Shit," he said and then noticed the object round and gleaming lodged in the grounds. A glass eyeball. Finn smiled and reached in and dislodged it. He held it up to the kerosene lantern for inspection. Then he rubbed the eyeball against his Mackinaw and went to the door. Outside he banged the pot against the logs scattering the grounds over the frozen muskeg and went back inside. There had to be some coffee hidden somewhere in the cabin he thought. But then he remembered how it was when Marvin left his cabin unattended like everyone else. What few provisions he managed to acquire had been stolen so often now that when Marvin left he always placed his glass eye with his most prized possessions as a warning. He claimed it would be a curse on whomever or whatever would dare defile his cabin. Finn thought about the grounds he had dumped outside.

"Shit," he said again. "The eyeball was in the *coffee* for chrissake." Finn decided he would have to deal with Marvin and his curse later. Maybe he would not miss the coffee grounds. Right now Finn's body ached so he went to Marvin's bunk and without removing his parka or his boots collapsed on it. He thrust his hands in his parka, the glass eye warming in one fist. He was thinking about dogs again as he drifted into sleep.

But in Finn's dream the dogs were not the same small working mongrels from the villages. These were huge and fierce, halfwolf and halfdog and they foamed at their mouths and strained in the harnesses ahead of a sleek and swift dogsled bearing a furclad spectre whose long whip cracked above their heads in a blinding electric flash. And when the light died the whip became a golden double-bitted axe which the phantom musher hurled end-over-end at a stumbling figure in a Mackinaw, a terrified victim struggling to escape in the deep snow. And then Finn felt the axe slam into his own shoulder and carry his body forward.

"You sonuvabitch, you better have some coffee with you," the voice said. The grip on his shoulder shoved him again. Finn buried his head in the sweatsoaked blanket and pressed against the wall. "And where's my goddamn eyeball, you dried up little bastard?"

Finn turned over and blinked awake. *"Marv..."*

"Don't Marv me, get up." Starvin' Marvin pelted him with the beaver hat he held in one hand as he shook him with the other. Still not fully awake Finn raised his arms for protection. Finally he rolled off the bunk and crouched in a defensive stance on the floor still wrapped in his parka, a ratlike ball of fur under the towering height of Starvin' Marvin inside the bulk of his own parka appearing more massive than just tall.

"Hold on, Marv," he pleaded. "Geezus man, gimme a chance to explain."

Marvin ceased the flailing, which had been only half hearted anyway, a feigned anger and even that restrained by sheer joy at seeing another human, even Hjalmar the Finn.

"It better be good." Marvin sat on the edge of his bunk breathing hard and glaring down between his knobby knees, his one good eye focused on Finn still cowering on the floor. "I'm out four days in the goddamn cold, no coffee, no tea, no booze, no luck on the trapline, come home to find some worthless bastard's throwed out the last of my coffee grounds. Didn't you see it, you stupid shit? Didn't the evil eye do a goddamn thing to you?"

He threw the hat at Finn who dodged it. Finn held out Marvin's eyeball as a peace offering.

"I wouldn't do something like that would I Marv? Here. I found it outside when I come in. Them grounds was already dumped when I got here."

"Yeah sure and I suppose my stew was gone too?"

"No honest, I never touched that. It was froze solid on the stove so I just collapsed, plumb wore out from yesterday and last night and sick with worry about what happened to Swede and all…"

"Well, at least my spell worked on something I guess. That is if my stew's still here." Marvin took the eyeball. He stood and walked to the stove to check the stewpot. Then he inspected the glass eye in the scant morning sunlight which a sooted window spitefully allowed into the cabin.

"Evil eye," Marvin mused admiring the eyeball. "Keeps some of them at bay, some of my demons." He reached inside his parka and polished the eye on his wool shirt and started to replace it in its socket when he noticed Finn staring at him from the floor. Marvin turned his back so Finn could not watch as he put the eye in his mouth to warm and wet it and then return it to the socket. It was a small show of defiance, one of the last acts of privacy and dignity to which Marvin G. Crush clung.

Finn strained to watch but then averted his eyes in a sudden realization that he might be imposing on some kind of special and secret ritual. He felt even more drawn to Marvin whom he had thought of all these years since they had left Texas as something of a philosopher anyway. Those had been turbulent years but Finn had come to view Marvin as someone who would one day reveal to him and all the others the secret of life and maybe even the Glory Hole, the Mother Lode which Marvin surely must have found somewhere even though he lived like a pauper. It was certain Marvin was no trapper, at least not a very good one.

"Well, what's this about Swede?" Marvin said his back still to Finn. "He fall through the ice again? Big dumb bastard ought to lose some weight."

"Dead," Finn said.

Marvin turned to him and studied his face to see if he were lying again like he knew Finn had done with the coffee and a million other times over the years. But Finn was serious this time and Marvin spoke softly, "How? When?"

"I dunno." Quick to notice Marvin was moved, Finn kept the conversation away from coffee and stew and evil eyeballs. "I mean all I do know is Swede went out to run the traps on that slough, you know the one that forks off the Big Bend of the Chiktok?" Marvin nodded though Finn doubted he had ever been up that far.

"Anyway that was a week ago," Finn went on. "He never come back so I went looking. I found him on a beaver pond with his own axe in his back. Can you believe it, Marv? Killed with his own goddamn axe."

Marvin took six paces across his cabin. He shook his head and took the six paces again with the familiarity of a convict in a cell but this time he picked up his beaver hat from the floor. He stared at it a long while before speaking. "See this? Who the hell am I fooling? I never even took the pelt in this goddamn hat. Swede give it to me. What the hell am I doing here, winter in winter out?"

Finn lowered his eyes, embarrassed for him and a little set back by Marvin's sudden show of humility. And he was beginning to like Swede even more himself, more than he had ever thought possible.

"Who woulda done it?" Marvin said.

"Well like I said, I dunno but I got a pretty good idea and so do you. That is if you think about it."

Marvin looked at him with his goodeye, as cold and hard as the other. *"Keetuk?"*

Finn would not repeat the name. He nodded.

"Where is he?" Marvin said.

"How the hell should I know. How the hell does anybody know? I'm telling you he ain't all there. He's like a ghost, comes and goes and does this stuff and leaves like a spirit."

"No, I mean Swede. Where's Swede?"

"Oh, I got him down on the river. He's okay, stiff as a log. I hid him under the edge of the bank with some spruce boughs so the foxes can't get to him again. He ain't never been too pretty anyway but he's really something now. You should see him."

Marvin was not interested in seeing him but a few formalities would need to be followed. "Well, let's get out the picks and put him in the ground. If we start now we can have a hole chipped out by dark. I think Felix might still be here. Sonuvabitch won't dig but maybe he'd say some words. It's the least we can do, Finn." He set his jaw and moved toward the door.

"No." Finn stood with his chest puffed a little and tried to raise himself to Marvin's shoulders. It was easy to appear wider but impossible for him to stretch tall enough to look Marvin straight in either eye, good or evil. "I'm taking care of him by myself."

Marvin turned back and frowned down at him.

"This is something I gotta do, Marv, just me."

Marvin started to protest and then he remembered No-Talk Owens and knew Finn was still living with that from embarrassment if not conscience. "Yeah, I understand, Finn, but you'll never get it dug by yourself."

"I ain't burying him here. I'm taking him down to Snag Point for that deputy and all them others. I want them to see a real body this time—not like before with No-Talk." He squinted up at Marvin. "I ain't done this thing to Swede. You believe me don't you, Marv? And I didn't do it to No-Talk either."

"Sure, Finn, whatever. But how the hell you going to get him down there? There ain't no dogteam here, no sleds."

"I'm pulling him down the river. He moves okay on the ice. I broke the axe handle off but I couldn't get the head out. It's still in there. Swede skids along fine. Works sorta like an ice skate." Finn smiled at his ingenuity and then pursed his lips. "Felix wants to come along. Says Keetuk's after him too."

"He is here then? You seen him?"

"Last night out there in his longjohns. Cut the hell out of his feet but claims he can make it."

"In his longjohns?"

"Yeah, chasing that old woman and her granddaughter. You know, them two that's always meeting him here for—how does he put it—*counseling.*" Finn showed his snuffstained teeth in a grin. "Guess they got enough of that holy word. Run off in the night. Felix thinks that crazy native might have them."

"Well. Felix always was a little strange ever since he was a kid back there in Texas." Marvin paused and looked at him. The subject had not come up in years and this thing with Felix was no affair of Marvin's.

Anyway, a man did not interfere with someone else's business, especially if it was corrupt. He looked away but continued speaking. "Hell, you remember. A kid grows up with a screwball granny like Felix did and around all them other oddball thumpers in her church and well it's bound to make him a little wacky just like them and then all that other shit that happened—" He paused again but then to end it said, "Anyway, if you're gonna drag that load all the way down the river you'll need something to eat."

He moved to the woodstove and lay the kindling and lit it. Then he inspected his stewpot. "Ain't too much left in here. Maybe I'll just add a little sidemeat, enough to make a longsplice out of it, you know, and then heat it up. Nothing like a good stew huh, Finn? Nothing like keeping a good stew going on and on and on, one longsplice after another. Throw in a little beaver meat here maybe some rabbit or sidemeat there if you got it." Then he added bitterly, "Too bad we ain't got no coffee."

Finn did not respond. Nor did he relish the thought of breakfast from the mystery pot but he never questioned food when offered, especially when on a mission of such importance. He would need all his strength to pull it off. And besides, filling their bellies would give them a chance to discuss another matter of even greater importance, one Finn was very reluctant to bring up.

He watched Marvin working at the stove and heard the spruce twigs snap inside the firebox and though he could not yet feel heat inside the cabin Finn savored the warmth of old companionship. Marvin was different now, moody sometimes and certainly nothing exceptional on the trapline, but unlike many of the others, he had acquired over the years a solid fearless air about him. Finn thought sometimes it bordered on grim indifference to fate.

"You ever think about her?" Finn's question was abrupt, out of order and he knew it instantly. Marvin stopped stirring the stew. Of the things the two did not discuss any longer the topic to which Finn alluded was the most forbidden. But Marvin felt no anger, only a slight contempt that Finn would break the silence of all those years.

"Hell no," he said. "Not after thirty years. Why?"

"Nothing, just wondered. No offense?"

"No offense."

Finn turned away and was silent figuring he had said too much already. Marvin looked into the stewpot and watched the steam rise from the swirls of dark liquid.

He had lied. He thought often about Stella Villard. For the first few years in Snag Point and especially after he had moved upriver here to Ekok, every evening Marvin had looked at the old photograph he kept hidden in its leather folder. But now he rarely removed it from its hiding place. On those occasions when he was especially down he would take it out and stare at the images and think about the narrow escape.

Finn continued to stand in silence, worried he had opened up the old wounds, perhaps even offended Marvin, and he might not go along with the deal Finn had to offer. He decided to pursue it before Marvin had a chance to change the subject. "You ever think about getting out? Saving up a poke and booking passage south on the last ship some summer?"

It was another question on the fringe and once more Marvin stopped stirring. He continued to stare silently into the stewpot, contemplating the subject of escape again, and he gave proper note to the irony.

*Escape from my own escape?* And then Marvin noticed the object that had floated to the top of the liquid, which he recognized as a dead mouse. He closed his one eye for a moment, not to shut out the thought of eating something into which such a critter had fallen—he had long since learned that one did not become squeamish about what might turn up in a trapper's stew—but he closed his goodeye to erase from his mind everything but this rodent. He focused on how its last futile and desperate efforts at escape from the stewpot must have been.

*Why was it even there? Had it been fate, greed that lured it? Or just a burning need for survival? Rambling fever? Did it leap in of its own free will? Did it cry out in agony? Did its lover mourn or did she even care?*

Marvin glanced at Finn who was still turned away and suddenly he was embarrassed by this silent melodrama in which he had indulged. He lifted the mouse out of the stew by its tail. "Getting out? Escape is what you mean isn't it, Finn?" Marvin dropped the mouse behind the woodstove. "It comes in different ways I guess."

"Well, why don't you just pull out some of that dust you got hidden and leave then?" Finn turned and brightened at the thought of gold.

"Dust?" Marvin laughed.

"Sure. Everyone knows Starvin' Marvin don't survive on trapping." Finn studied Marvin's reaction. "Where's the gold, Marv? Why don't you let some of us in on it?"

"Number one," Marvin began, "if I had some color I sure as hell wouldn't be hanging on here. Number two, if I had some color I sure as hell wouldn't be telling the likes of you."

It was almost an accusation. Marvin wondered if perhaps he had said too much, breached the code himself. He could feel the stove so he took off his parka and retrieved two tin bowls from the shelf, wiped them out with his hand and filled one of them. "Here try this. Maybe it'll get your mind off gold and escaping and all that Keetuk bullshit."

"Well, the Keetuk stuff ain't bullshit." With the warming of the room Finn finally shucked his own parka. He wiped his grimy hands on his shirt and then held them up to the light. Satisfied it was the best he could do without hot water and soap he took the bowl of stew and sat at the table. "I know he done it, but why? How do you figure it, Marv? It ain't like breaking into a cabin and stealing sugar or something like he always does."

Marvin sat at the table and watched Finn go at the stew like a starved dog. He looked into his own bowl and thought about the mouse, hesitated a moment, then began to eat.

"Keetuk?" he said around a mouthful. "Well, they say his old man was a Swede too. But you knew that, a big guy."

"Yeah, I guess I did but I never give it much thought."

"They say he was brute strong like Swede only meaner, evil mean," Marvin continued. "Like he'd beat the mother something terrible and kept her like a slave. She had the kid Keetuk by him but that just made him worse. He saw the kid as a half breed they say, his blood tainted with hers or something so he beat her for that too and finally he just left her and the baby alone up there on the Mikchalk somewhere. I guess she just lost it, finally went berserk and did terrible things to the kid before the villagers found out and took him away from her."

"What happened to the old man?"

"Nobody knows for sure. Some say he stowed away on a freighter. Some say he boozed up and froze to death." Marvin looked up from his bowl and over at Finn who had slowed his eating, engrossed in the tale.

"That was over forty years ago," Marvin continued but he was whispering now to make the story sound more mysterious. "Ten years or so before you and me dumped Felix in Seattle and jumped ship down there at Snag Point. Some say he still lives in the spirit of his son this Keetuk, bloodevil and mean, the old man's blood mixed with the native blood of the woman's people sorta like a curse he can't shake. Maybe he seen Swede as his old man or something."

Finn stopped eating and looked up over his spoon. Marvin's glass eye was hard and cold and dead but the other one flashed.

*Bullshit,* Finn said. "I don't believe none of that bullshit, not one bit. I think he's just a goddamn thief and murderer, crafty and mean like a wolverine. Anyway he's probably got them women now just like Felix said. No telling what he might do to them."

Marvin rolled some tobacco slowly without taking his goodeye off Finn. He lit it and inhaled deeply and exhausted blue smoke with a long sigh. "Maybe so. Except she knows Keetuk pretty good, I think."

"Who?"

"That old grandmother Maruluk. I helped her sometimes with firewood when she brought that kid down for them lessons with Felix. He sure as shit wouldn't cut none, not Felix, always inside the cabin with that girl, sending that old woman out to work wood by herself. Bastard. Hell, I felt sorry for her."

"Why didn't you say something to Felix?"

"Like what? Hell, he always brought me up coffee didn't he and—"

"Yeah sure, Felix always did have a way with you, Marv."

"Well anyway, she told me about Keetuk one day, that old woman. Guess she knew this Keetuk's mother pretty good. She said she was there when they took the boy away from her. Anyway she seemed to know all about it."

"She say what the mother done?"

"Just that she done evil to the kid. Guess he was too young to remember it but he knows he's different because of it, meaner. He won't live with nobody, at least in none of the villages. Comes and goes around here though."

"You seen him?"

"No. But I know he's been around Ekok."

"How?"

"Little things. Nothing big like what was done to Swede. Nothing that big. Stuff missing, sugar, coffee, snuff, things like that. Mostly sugar. Steals it from everybody."

"Yeah. Me and Swede always had sugar gone. Sometimes pelts too. Swede must of had pelts with him or something."

"Maybe." Marvin took another long pull on the tobacco.

"It ain't like it use to be," Finn said. "Use to be able to leave things out in plain sight. Leave your cabin full of your grubstake and pelts and nobody would touch them unless they were in serious trouble. And then they'd replace them soon as they could."

"That's a crock," Marvin said. "You know that's a myth Finn. Everybody always talks about the trappers and their honor and all that bullshit. What about Hard Working Henry? When's the last time you been in his shack? Hell, he's got enough lines and anchors to outfit a whaler."

Marvin laughed and then continued. "He may have ten pounds of your sugar. Or your whiskey. You may want to check it out, Finn."

"Well, Henry, he's different."

"Different hell. There ain't a trapper this side of the Brooks Range who wouldn't steal the shirt off your back given a chance. Takers, that's what we are, Finn, all of us. We take the gold take the fish take the pelts more than we need and some day somebody will probably take the land. And this Keetuk he just comes in real handy. Somebody's got to take the blame. It ain't them old native guys that I leave this evil eyeball for. They ain't the ones I worry about stealing stuff. Hell, they don't know nothing about owning land. It's like the land owns them not the other way around. If anything they're the ones getting taken. They were here before us."

"Yeah, but Keetuk, he ain't native."

"Well he ain't Swede neither. And I ain't even so sure Swede was a Swede. Or anybody is anything they say they are. Hell, even old Felix is phony as a lead dollar."

"I think he's a real priest alright," Finn sighed. "He just leaves a bit to be desired in holiness."

"Well, he wasn't a priest when we left his ass in Seattle all them years back."

"Hell, he was only a kid then but I guess he did go through all that official stuff later. I seen his papers once after he showed up there in Snag Point. He was trying to prove to Henry he was official and ordained and all that shit. He even tried to get Henry saved remember that? *Saved!*"

"I wasn't there, Finn. Hell, I didn't have time for all that monkey business. I was trying to catch a beaver or two."

"Well anyway, Henry wasn't buying," Finn said and paused. "How about me though? You trust me, Marv?"

"You? Hell, you been using an alias for the past thirty years. Hjalmar the Finn? Now who would trust some bastard uses an alias like that? And anyway how in hell did you ever figure that name had anything to do with Phineas Farrow? Shit I doubt you ever even seen a real Finn."

"Well the names just seemed right. Phineas, Finn, you know they just sounded close. But that ain't what I'm getting at. I'm talking about trust, Marv, like we had once before."

Marvin stood. He wiped out the bowls with a dirty rag and replaced them on the shelf. He touched the leather folder hidden behind the small stack of tin plates and he thought about the old photograph inside he had not looked at in a great while. "There you go again getting private with me. But if you'll remember I did trust you once and it cost me considerable." He winced, drawing the skin tighter around his glass eye. "You better hit the trail if you're going to get Swede down to Snag Point today. It'll be daylight by the time you get started."

"Well, it don't matter. I trust you, Marv. I trusted you all those years ago and I'd do again. It's been a long time but I got another deal for you just to prove it. Just to prove to you that I can make things happen. That other deal back in Texas was a fluke anyway, long dead. Let's bury it. Let's just bury it all.

"Bury it?" Marvin released a laugh. He brought it from deep inside and it surprised him. Laughter was the only thing he had been truly successful in burying all these years. But the laugh was hollow and filled with self-pity as he remembered the idea about using Stella Villard's stock certificates in a scheme which had been Phineas Farrow's and though they had argued about it the question had never been settled during the time they had spent around the village of Snag Point. Marvin and Finn had finally split, Marvin moving upriver to Ekok and Finn acquiring an assortment of other partners over their years here in Alaska.

Marvin G. Crush and all the others should have known better than to take part in the whole scheme Phineas had dreamed up anyway, a scheme which had finally forced Phineas and Marvin to make their hasty retreat.

Marvin had cautioned Stella against it. But then convinced by Phineas that Marvin himself would benefit by securing a promotion as stationmaster in the little railroad town and perhaps even the love of Stella for his boldness he too had acquiesced. Of course Phineas had claimed no interest whatever in Stella and though wary, Marvin had believed him. Phineas would simply reap vast monetary rewards, enough to say goodbye forever to ten-pound hammers and railroad handcars and the dusty little community to boot.

Stella had insisted a photograph be made to commemorate their partnership. It would be an historical photograph too, one of Marvin G. Crush and Stella Villard and Phineas Farrow all standing atop a handcar on the railroad tracks near the very spot where the tracks had been joined by her late husband's brilliant surveying.

And so the picture had been taken with the three in it and Stella had given Marvin a copy. But an indifferent Phineas Farrow had not received one. He had been too busy thinking up other ideas for Stella's railroad stock certificates and when his schemes for making them all even richer had backfired and Stella had lost all her dead husband's investments, Phineas and Marvin were forced to hop a late night freight train and skip the country. But even after all these years Marvin was certain Stella had forgiven him. It had simply not been a convenient time to hang around the community to explain it to her, not with the mayor and a drunken bunch of macho saloon lizards feeling that a widow of Stella Villard's stature had been taken advantage of, even if it was not true. Stella would understand.

And so Phineas Farrow and Marvin G. Crush had escaped in the same boxcar by coincidence with the young Felix Manguson, himself fleeing from a overbearing grandmother and her righteous congregation, the boy indoctrinated with his own twisted version of salvation, Marvin and Phineas saving only their asses.

But Marvin had also escaped with something else. He had guarded all these years his copy of the photograph Stella had commissioned. Stella had kept the other one and on those rare occasions when Marvin did look he found her face in the photo and saw how she had stood turned slightly toward him, Phineas Farrow on the other side and all of them on top of the handcar. Marvin wanted to believe Stella had loved him all along and would welcome him back if he were to come home to Texas.

If he still bore resentment, maybe it was because Finn had never accomplished anything, never gained Marvin a single dollar toward getting out of Snag Point and back to Stella. Maybe it was time Marvin did listen to Finn again. The irony was that going along with Phineas Farrow once more might be Marvin's only way to escape his escape.

"Okay, what are you scheming up this time?" Marvin moved the leather folder with the photograph deeper into its hiding place behind the tin plates.

"Pelts," Finn said. "Beaver pelts and lots of them."

Marvin said nothing.

"Mine and Swedes. We left maybe two hundred, two-fifty in a cache up on the Mikchalk."

Marvin sat again.

"I'd share them with you, Marv. I need a partner, someone I can trust. We could join up again, go back up to the Mikchalk River and stay through the spring, maybe trap some more of them."

Marvin still said nothing.

"Well what do you think?"

Starvin' Marvin was thinking back all those years. He was thinking about the fiasco and about Stella. But mostly he was thinking about the mouse in the stewpot.

"You're jinxed, Finn," he said. "That's what I think. You're bad luck. First Stella's money then No-Talk and now Swede. Besides that ain't legal."

"Legal? Them pelts? Hell everybody does it, you know that. You just take your limit of twenty into Feldstein in the spring and dicker over the others, make a deal under the table. He goes back up in a skiff for the pelts himself after spring breakup. No mess no hassle."

"Not everybody does. Hell, I ain't trapped two hundred beaver in the past ten years."

Finn was embarrassed again for him.

"Well I can show you how, Marv, teach you my tricks. You'd get better."

Marvin doubted that he even wanted to get better but he thought about making one big stake and getting out and it sent his hopes soaring. "You're just afraid that's all," he said. "You just want me to be around in case Keetuk comes after you next."

Finn tried to look brave but he knew fear showed. He was thinking about Swede secure under the lean-to of spruce boughs on the river. But he was also thinking about the axehead still lodged in the back of the frozen corpse. He scratched the stubble on his face. "Okay, that's part of it but I meant it about the pelts and helping you. Hell, a man here needs a partner. So do you. You've been too much of a loner anyway. Gets to your mind after awhile."

He was right. Starvin' Marvin was showing earlier each winter the signs of cabin fever and sometimes it showed even in the middle of summer. It was not good. Even if he did not make a stake it was time to join up with someone. He was fifty-four, thirty years of bringing up the dream each winter, fooling himself. Any day now he might need someone, not even a friend, just someone to drag him down the river like Finn was doing for Swede, to say some words and put him in the ground. And he did not even have half interest in two hundred and fifty beaver pelts to barter with.

Marvin stood again and walked the six paces across the cabin then turned and walked back retracing the steps he had taken thousands of times before. "Hell, I didn't even build this cabin." He looked at the dinginess. "I got nothing to hold me here. I guess you got yourself a deal, Finn."

*"Hot damn,"* Finn said. "We're gonna make a killing, Marv."

Marvin was not sure he liked the term but he took Finn's proffered hand and shook it. Then he closed his goodeye and shoved his face next to Finn's, his breath like a rancid fog.

"But you just remember this." He poked a finger into his glass eye causing Finn to wince. "Just you remember I didn't have this all them years ago in Texas. Maybe it was fate, I dunno. Whatever it was I wound up with this evil eye. And you just remember, Hjalmar the Finn, I always got it handy and I ain't particular who I use it on."

"I'll remember," Finn promised.

"Now get on with your 'mission' as you call it," Marvin said.

"You'll wait here for me?"

"I'll be here when you get back. Where the hell do you think I'd go?"

Finn put on his parka and beaver hat and pulled the earflaps tight around his ears. He turned to go. Marvin stopped him.

"Finn…"

"Yeah?"

"Say something over Swede for me will you?"

"Don't you worry none. I'll put old Swede away right, count on it. Felix is going down with me to say the right words." He went to the door. Marvin stopped him again.

"And Phineas." Finn turned back. In all those years since they had left Texas it was the first time Marvin had called him by his real name. "You better bring back some coffee, you sonuvabitch."

# FIVE

"What the hell's that all about?" Finn said to Felix who was kneeling beside the body of Swede. Finn had pulled it back out onto the river ice in front of the village of Ekok and Felix was muttering as he knelt. "All that hocuspocus on your knees?" Finn helped him to his feet but Felix lurched sideways when he stood. He tightened his face in pain.

"I have prayed for our safe journey," Felix explained. "But I am afraid that's all the assistance I can be, my son." He shook his head and looked down at his feet. He had donned a pair of skin boots, native *mukluks* which had been handsewn and presented to him by the old woman as a gift for his teaching. "I wrapped my feet with strips of blankets but they're not much good."

"No sweat, I ain't aiming to let nobody help anyway. This is my deal, Felix. You just stay out of the way and you can tag along." Finn glanced nervously around at the woods on the riverbank. Now that he was rested, the bravado of the day before had deserted him. "Besides I can use the company, I guess. Anything's better than talking to myself."

He bared his stained teeth and lifted the makeshift harness he had devised the previous day from the chains of the beaver traps. Finn leaned into it again setting the corpse in motion. Felix followed, stepping gingerly with his swollen feet as though treading thin ice. He grunted with each step waving his arms in the air like a tightwire walker.

"Not too fast now, Finn," he said and took a short hop to keep up. "Slow down, my boy."

Finn stopped. "Felix, you keep talking to me like that and I'll leave you sure. Why in hell do you keep laying on that phony talk? That's bullshit. I know it, you know it, Swede here don't give a shit now and them women ain't here to impress so just talk sense okay?"

"Sorry, my b—I mean, *Hjalmar.*" He caught up with Finn. "Well, what'll we talk about?"

Felix was trying to remember the accent from his youth in Texas. He realized he would have to keep Finn engrossed in conversation or he would outpace him.

"Suit yourself." Finn said and assumed his previous drafthorse mentality, suddenly preferring this to conversation with Felix.

"Well, how about salvation?" Felix offered.

"Salvation?"

"Sure, salvation."

"Whose, mine or yours?"

"Yours of course. You know you're not a spring pup any more Finn. And mine's relatively assured." Felix smiled but then winced again.

"You know, Felix, you always did have a way of starting conversation that ended conversation. Salvation? *Gee*-zus." Finn sped up and then slowed down again.

"Well, that's a start," Felix said pleased with Finn's knowledge of the word.

"I don't know nothing about salvation and I don't want to know nothing about it. Besides you ain't exactly my idea of a teacher anyway."

"Now look," Felix said indignantly. "I happen to be a fully ordained minister of the gospel."

"So? That don't cut no ice with me."

Felix saw he was not impressing him.

"Well, it might interest you to know I'll soon be gone forever from this godforsaken place. You may never have the chance again, any of you. Marvin, Henry, Delbert and for sure not Swede here."

"Gone?" Finn weighed the possibilities and thought about his options just in case Felix did leave. "Where you going Felix? Back to Texas? Gee-zus Christ everybody's going back to Texas. But then maybe a guy like you oughta consider it." Finn smiled. "I mean your *granny* being there and all."

"She's dead by now," Felix said flatly. "And I didn't leave anything else there, not like you and Marvin did. But then I could go back anytime I wanted. I don't have anything to fear like you two have. At least not back there."

The topic of getting out made Felix think about Texas again and his own exit. He would never admit it to Finn or Marvin but he did have some apprehension about returning though his fear was less tangible than theirs. It made no real difference where he was, his memories were the kind that stayed with him whether in Texas or some other godforsaken part of the world.

But Felix did not want to think about that final summer of adolescent innocence. The black woman Mattie and his grandmother and the entire congregation of the First Gospel Church were distant memories he only allowed himself in moments when he needed a true reference point for his fears.

Felix checked the trees around him. There might be plenty to fear right now on the frozen Chiktok River. He stopped and turned to look back, his eyes wide, scanning the width of the river and up into the alders.

"Yes I'll be leaving Snag Point soon," he repeated louder this time as if to make certain the trees along the riverbank heard him. All of the details of his departure from Snag Point had not been fully solidified but during the previous night as he had rolled in his bunk with the pain spiking up from his feet and through his legs, Felix had decided he would leave on the first ship south in the summer, at least as far as Seattle and his old parish. He would try once again to salvage something of his own soul and his own skin. When he turned back around he saw that Finn had moved down the river. He hobbled to catch him again and when he did he hooked his arm through Finn's.

"I've been, well, called away," he said. "They've given me a ministry in a huge cathedral on an island."

"An island?"

"Yes. In the Cayman's. You know them?"

"Nope." Finn started to outpace him again but Felix checked his speed this time by clinging to Finn's arm. He painted the scene in the air with his free hand.

"Well they're in the Caribbean Sea. Lovely white beaches with sunshine warm days and cool nights. And the people, ah the people Finn, lovely and gentle and kind and primitive and unspoiled," he said and then added sternly, "but they hardly wear clothes at all. They need much counseling and meditation Finn, much, much counseling." Felix thought about this and all the possibilities it would offer and then he continued. "And there are trees, real trees, not this scrubby spruce and alder but real trees with huge palm leaves and, and...*fruit.* Oranges and coconuts and bananas."

Finn adjusted the chains around his shoulders. He thought about freeing his arm from Felix's so he could concentrate again on pulling Swede but he found himself being drawn into the fantasy. He moved on slowly. "What about the cathedral?"

"Cathedral? Oh yes, the cathedral. *Magnificent.* Gold everywhere, Finn. Everywhere."

Felix was almost in tears as he pictured it. He saw himself fully forgiven now for any earlier transgressions, kneeling before his superiors as he accepted the purewhite silken robes of his new assignment. And then Felix was standing before a carved mahogany altar covered with gold vessels atop a sacred scarlet tapestry woven with puregold threads and above him on the enormous domed ceiling were priceless paintings of sheltering angels and seraphim moving in living color about the clouds of heaven. And a choir of vestal virgins surrounded him singing in voices so serene and sweet that the entire throng of people who had come for his service was stunned into silence, their eyes filled with tears of joy for his holiness *Cardinal* Felix standing before them raising his arms in benediction. And then the bells began deep and resonant and authoritative ringing, ringing, ringing...

*Clang!* Finn stopped and dropped his harness of chains to the ice, abruptly bringing Felix back to the Alaskan bush. "Yeah, that's all great, Felix, but there ain't no bananas here. I gotta rest a minute. Black Slough's just around the corner and then maybe two more hours into Snag Point." He looked down at Felix's feet again. "How are they?"

"Bad. Throbbing." Felix had managed to ignore them in his reverie but now they came to life again in full fury. He doubled over and grabbed the calf of one leg with both hands trying to choke off the pain. He moaned. "I don't know if I can make it."

"Hmmmm…" Finn looked at him and then down at Swede's face behind the snowshoes and he wondered how Phineas Farrow, alias Hjalmar the Finn, manage to get himself into these goddamn predicaments. He briefly considered leaving Felix but then he would have no one to say words over Swede's grave, no one except Yael Feldstein. But Yael was Jewish. Finn didn't know for sure what Swede was but it was damn certain he was not Jewish. Felix would have to do. Besides it must have been providential their being brought together again like this, some kind of sign or omen that Finn could not just shrug off. Finn had avoided Felix as much as possible in Snag Point. There was no way he could ignore him right now.

"Look, you're going to make it, Felix. It ain't far now, you gotta try."

Felix tried, stumbled and fell, got up again. "I don't have much left," he said and then thought about the body and the harness and Finn pulling like a draft horse. "Finn, maybe you could pull me too?"

"Pull you? Hell, I'm barely making it with Swede. How the hell could I pull you too?"

"On top of him. I could sit on his chest on the snowshoes and you could pull us both."

Felix brightened. Finn's mouth dropped open slightly, a thin dark trickle of tobacco juice escaping from one corner into the stubble. He stared at Felix as if confirming what he had suspected all these years but thus far had ignored.

"You'd do *that?*" Finn blinked at him and shook his head. "Yeah, I guess you'd do that alright. Defile a dead man's body and then talk to me about salvation and all that bullshit." He spat a long string of black liquid barely missing Felix's feet.

"Now, Finn, don't get upset. Listen, you'd forever be etched in the sacred book right along with all those others throughout the history of Christendom who assisted a holy man in his time of need."

Finn thought this sounded like the beginning of a sermon. He looked at Felix with skepticism.

"You see," Felix continued. "Swede here would become like a saint, a sacred chariot of a sort in the service of heaven. Don't you see?"

"Yeah I see." Finn turned and quickly got into the harness again and started off at a faster clip.

"Finn, Swede won't mind," Felix called. "I swear it. I mean after all, there are things about Swede that maybe you don't know and well, things that—"

Finn paused, looked back. "What do you mean, *things.*"

Felix caught him again. "Things I know about but well I guess maybe they were confidential and anyway it won't matter with Swede now and—"

"Bullshit. Ain't nothing confidential between a man and his partner, big and dumb maybe but a nice guy, always was."

"*Was* your partner, Finn, that's right. But he wasn't always just that big easygoing brute you believed, especially to Nellie."

"You're just bitter 'cause he beat the shit out of you that once, Felix. And I didn't blame him neither."

"It was her he was beating. I just came up and tried to…"

"Everybody knows what you was trying to do. And it was Nellie you was trying to do it to. Swede just caught you there under the dock. Admit it. Maybe you and Nellie both deserved it just like Swede said. Anyway I don't really give a shit. You just want to get even now that he's dead."

Finn turned around and began pulling the corpse again.

"Don't leave me, Finn. Please, my *feet.*"

Finn kept moving.

"The *pain.*"

Finn continued.

*"Keetuk!"*

Felix knelt on the ice, whimpering. Finn stopped. He looked straight ahead for a long while and then pursed his lips. Finally he dropped the harness again and went back to Swede's body. He unbuttoned the Mackinaw, removed the snowshoes and returned to the priest. He looked down at him sobbing there on the ice. Even though Felix repulsed him, Finn could not leave him.

"Look, Felix, stop it. Now you see that bend up ahead? You know Black Slough is just around the corner, right?"

Felix turned off the sobs. He looked up at him with his most pathetic expression. He nodded.

"Alright. Now you take these snowshoes and put them on. If you stay on the river it's maybe two hours on into Snag Point. But if you was to cut through the trees right here you'd come to a big clearing. Soon as you get through that you'll break over the hill then it's just a bit on into the village. That'll cut at least an hour off your time. What do you think?"

Felix look up in him, gaining a semblance of strength and composure from Finn's optimism. He glanced at Swede's body again but realized Finn could probably not be persuaded to let him ride.

"I'll be all alone."

"Yep."

"I might lose my toes to the cold."

"Yep."

"And I'll die if I stay here…"

"Yep."

"You'll not let me ride Swede?"

"Nope."

Felix looked around again at the shadows in the spruce trees and at the eerie images created by the twisting lines of bare alder branches. He sighed. "Give me the snowshoes."

Finn watched him fumble with the bindings getting them all wrong. Finally Finn bent down and attached the webs, tightened them until Felix protested with the pain. Then he returned to his task with Swede. As he started down the river Finn heard the grunts and huffs and the moaning sounds behind him as Felix struggled up the riverbank toward the line of spruce. Finn glanced back and watched Felix stagger along and finally disappear into the trees.

"At least I did give him the snowshoes," he muttered. "At least I didn't just leave him out here to freeze to death right?" He looked down at the corpse, puzzled with what Felix had said about Swede and Nellie. "Maybe I should've, huh?"

But Swede was having no part of this conversation and like Finn had said, it did not matter now anyway. Whatever Swede and Nellie might have had it was certain they had it no longer. And as much as Finn had wanted no part of Felix's problems in west Texas he wanted even less of it here in bush Alaska. Still he wondered about all that salvation business Felix kept bringing up. And Finn thought about his name in that big book.

# SIX

*"Oh, the first mate he got drunk…"* Hard Working Henry was singing. He picked his way around the icelocked piling under the dock at the Scandinavian Cannery. His condition made it difficult for him to stand on the ice and at the same time try and remember the words to the song. Too many years had passed since Henry had sung the chanteys as a cabin boy on the threemasted whalers. He had memorized the songs throughout those long months at sea before he finally jumped ship right here at Snag Point on a drunken adolescent impulse. Henry started the song again, this time humming in the places where the words would not come to him.

*"Oh, the first mate he got drunk…hmmm…broke into some people's trunks…hmmm…"*

He had been in worse condition under the dock many times. That was with his friends who gillnetted for salmon. But that was also in the summer months when they could sleep off the whiskey and not worry about freezing to death. Even in his present state Henry knew he could not stay too long in the cold. He would have to tend to his business, find the bottle he had hidden under here and get back to the cabin he and his friend Roman Putvin had built last summer at the edge of the cutbank.

Henry thought about his cabin and how Roman had helped him. Some of the others had promised help but Roman, whom everyone called Dago, had been the only one to help. That is, except Felix. "But that wasn't really *help* help," Henry grumbled but then he smiled.

57

"Moral support maybe. If you could use that word, maybe stretch out the meaning a tad."

Dago did not look Italian. But then in all his sailing days Henry had not known any real Italians anyway. "Last name sounds Russian to me," Yael Feldstein had said when Roman Putvin decided to stay in Snag Point. "I think the sonuvabitch is Russian and I don't trust Russians. Let's just call him Ruski or something like that, then everybody can be warned about him."

But the name Dago had been okay with everyone else. Yael could write anything he wanted in his big record book next to the amount a trapper owed him for grubstakes and whiskey but Henry figured people could use any damn name they pleased with their friends, as long as the friend did not care.

Sometimes even Finn had offered advice with the cabin when he was not too busy figuring out ways to get to Yael Feldstein. Finn never lifted a hammer or a handsaw or anything like that but he had stopped by when Henry and Dago stalled and did not know what should be done next, but it was Dago who brought up the topic in the first place. "Henry, you need a cabin." He spoke with his accent and his palm-up Italian gesture. They were sitting under the dock in midsummer drinking whiskey. "Drinking under here's okay in summertime but you need a cabin in the winter, Henry."

"But I ain't ever in Snag Point in the winter," Henry lied. "I'm a trapper. I run my lines, I skin my beavers. I bring them in to Snag Point, I sell them to Yael. I'm a trapper."

"Yeah, sure, Henry," Dago said. "But just the same you need some place to flop. Winter's a real bastard under the dock. And it ain't always so nice under here in the summer either. Hell, look around you."

Dago gestured at the pilings and the mud and the water dripping through the cracks overhead but would freeze into icicles in a few months. "I say we build it," Dago continued. "I say we get the stuff and build it right out there next to the edge of the bluff, and I say we call it *Henry's Cabin.*"

"Well that's okay by me," Henry conceded. "But all you other guys can use it too alright? Marvin and Swede and Finn and—" Henry thought about who else should be allowed to use it. "And No-Talk," he continued and then he shivered a little when he thought about the disappearance of his old friend. "If he ever comes back. And all of you other guys can use it too except Yael. Yael can't use it. Not Yael. And not Felix either. He'd just want to do some kind of religious bullshit in it or something."

Henry paused again and nodded. He was pleased with this arrangement so he took a long draw from the bottle and passed it around the circle of friends who nodded their heads in agreement. "But I don't think we ought to call it Henry's Cabin."

"Well shit Henry, we can call it Delbert's Cabin or Nellie's Cabin or even Father Felix's Cabin if you want to," Dago said. "But it's *your* cabin we're talking about."

"It ain't *whose* cabin that's bothering me. It's just that I don't know if it ought to be called a *cabin.*"

"Christ, it ain't even built yet, Henry. But I don't know what the hell you're talking about. If it ain't a cabin then what is it?" Dago had dropped the accent. He always forgot to use it when he got riled.

"Well maybe it's a shack or something like that," Henry said. "But let's don't call it a cabin. A cabin's something you'd use on a trapline or upriver. A cabin ain't something you see around here in Snag Point. I know a cabin when I see one."

He looked at his friend and waited. Neither could think of anyone who actually had a real cabin, not one made of logs anyway, but Henry wasn't sure he had made his point because none of the men in the circle offered any comment one way or the other.

"I mean I was a cabin boy on a whaler once," Henry went on. "Lived at sea for months in what I'd call a real cabin. But what you're talking about ain't that at all."

"Okay then we'll call it a shack, Henry. Henry's Shack. Hell, it don't make a shit what we call it let's just get the stuff and build it!" Dago stood and tossed the empty bottle against the back of the rock bulwark. It shattered and fell on top of the remains of other empties. All the others watched this with sad faces and then looked back to see what Dago would do next.

"Let's go," he said and reached down and took Henry's hand pulling him to his feet. "We'll need hammers and handsaws and nails and planks, all that stuff."

"Okay," Henry said. He brushed the sand from his trousers and looked around the circle of friends, waiting for them to all get up and help. No one budged. "And whiskey."

This got the attention of a couple of the others but even this was not enough to cause interest in real work so Henry gave up on them. "Yael might let us have all that stuff on grubstake cause it's kinda like trapping supplies we'd be using. Ain't it, Dago?"

"Right."

"Wrong," Yael Feldstein said when the two waltzed into his general store reeking of booze and demanding to see what he had in the way of building materials. "Ain't no way building supplies is trapping supplies. Now you deadbeats waltz right on out of here. I'm busy."

Yael stared at the two, spat tobacco in an empty tin can on his counter and turned back to stocking his shelves.

"I guess it'll have to be logs, Henry," Dago said outside. "And that means going upriver, cutting them down, bringing them into Snag Point, trimming them and hacking out the corners and stacking them—"

Henry sat down on the boardwalk in front of Feldstein's, tired already. "I don't know. Maybe we should just forget about it for now, Dago. Maybe we can do it sometime when we got cash or pelts and Yael's in a better mood to dicker."

"Yael ain't ever in a better mood to dicker," Dago concluded and that would have ended it that same summer except that Finn had walked up and joined the two on the boardwalk.

"Well, it seems to me you guys are trying too hard," Finn said. "Hell, there ain't even logs close enough to drag in by dogsled in the winter much less bring downriver in the summer."

"Yeah," Henry agreed.

"And you guys are too damn lazy anyway to build anything except a big debt on Yael's liquor tab."

"Well it ain't my idea anyway so just forget it," Henry said. "And speaking of lazy all you guys want to do is talk about it. Talk, talk, talk. What I want to do is forget about it."

"Okay, Henry," Finn said. He decided it was time to tell the two about the *Tebinkoff*. "What if you was to have one already made?"

Dago showed some interest at this but Henry sulked.

"What if I could show you two right where there's a cabin already built? All you got to do is take over."

"There ain't any," Henry announced. "I already been throwed out of every one that ain't lived in. Just because there ain't nobody inside one don't mean it ain't claimed. There ain't any."

"What about the *Tebinkoff?*" Finn said.

"The Tebinkoff?" Dago said.

"That old power scow?" Henry said.

"Sure. It's beached, been there forever, probably be there forevermore." The *Tebinkoff* was like a dinosaur and Dago was not sure how all this fit into the discussion. He waited for Finn to continue.

Henry was growing weary of the whole subject of cabins and shacks and power scows. His thoughts were turning to what goods he might have stashed somewhere as barter material for a bottle of Yael's whiskey. "Let's go back inside and see if Yael would stand us for a bottle, Finn, you know against next spring's pelts while we try to figure this thing out."

Finn ignored this. He turned away and walked down the street. "Come on. I ain't got all day to show you this Henry. Me and Swede's heading back upriver on the floodtide."

Henry looked at Dago who shrugged and stood. There was nothing he could do but go along. Sometimes it was just better to get swept in with the tide than to buck it. He got up and followed Finn and Dago down to the beach. The three walked below the embankment and around the corner of the bluff to an area where the currents had eroded the beach into a low flat shelf of sandy soil. Henry had not looked over the bluff here for some time because Felix had remodeled the old church on the promontory just back from the bluff and Henry avoided Felix and churches both like thin ice.

"He's always after me," Henry had whined to Finn one day after a close call with Felix. Finn had found Henry coiled up under the dock hiding from Felix. He was shivering more from the whipsaw teeth of a north wind than his hangover. "You know, talking about my soul burning in hell and all that shit. I don't want to burn in hell, Finn."

"Yeah, he does that," Finn had said. "But hell would be better than this wind, Henry. Come on out of there, let's go warm up inside Yael's."

"He's already throwed me out twice today."

"He won't throw you out if you're with me, the little bastard. Come on I'll stand us for a jug, I got some dust," Finn had offered and Henry brightened and followed him like a puppy.

So below the bluff now Henry was surprised to see that the eel grass had started to grow. When he saw the old power scow beached high and dry on the shelf he stopped. The vessel had run aground years ago and now it rested in the eel grass like some giant sea creature on a nest.

"It looks like she's nesting there," Henry said and he smiled. "Wonder how she ever come way up here Finn? How'd she get up this high?"

"Southeast wind, big floodtide," Finn explained. "Drunk captain, who knows? Maybe his ghost is still here."

"She'll never come off here," Dago said. "Even if she'd still float she'd never come out of the grass. I think she likes it there." Dago studied the old scow then he approached her and put a hand on her side as if checking for a heartbeat. "Man, I bet there's been many a bowl of chowder eat in this one."

Finn moved around behind the vessel and pulled a long flat timber out of the loose sand. He leaned one end against the gunwale of the scow and planted the other into the sand. "Come on up. Let's look inside her."

Finn walked up the inclined plank holding out his arms for balance. He stood on the deck looking down at the other two, their heads below his feet. "Bigger than I thought she was. Come on up. Let me show you something."

"That's okay," Henry said. He was thinking about the captain's ghost. "I can see from here."

"Well, I can't," Dago said. "Come on Henry. Let's see what Finn's got in mind."

"I dunno," Henry said. "Finn's always got big ideas. I don't like Finn's big ideas."

"It ain't a big idea, Henry," Finn said impatiently. "I got about an hour to show you what I was thinking and then I'm gone. You interested or not?"

"I think we ought to let her be," Henry said. "I think we ought not disturb a dead ship."

"It's no ship, Henry," Dago said and worked his way up the plank.

"And it ain't dead," Finn added. "You said so yourself, said she was just nesting. Come on up and I'll show you why."

Henry could see that he would have to listen to what Finn had in mind. And he would have to do it aboard the *Tebinkoff.*

"Ain't ever heard of any sailor walking up the plank," Dago teased when Henry started to inch his way up the timber. "Careful now Henry, there's sharks in these waters."

"Shut up," Henry said and then when he reached the deck, "How come I allow this stuff? All we're talking about is a place to flop. How'd it get to all this? A dead ship?"

"Stop grumbling Henry and look at this," Finn said. He was standing in the doorway of the combination wheelhouse, cabin attached to the deck. Some of the glass was missing and the old door leaned on one hinge but it was intact.

"You always said you wanted a ship of your own, Henry. Well here she is, dead or not." Finn bowed and gestured inviting Henry to join him. Finn went inside the old weathered wheelhouse and worked what was left of the ship's wheel back and forth making sounds as if he were the wind in the sails of a schooner. Henry was not amused.

"I don't think this is very funny. I don't think you guys ought to make fun about me being a captain some day and all. It's a dead ship I tell you."

Dago said nothing. He decided Finn had gone too far with his joking and he too was becoming angry. He did not want Henry to think he had helped Finn with his joke.

"Let's go, Henry," Dago said. He knew how Henry felt about having his own sailing vessel some day and now he too felt this was a dead ship. "This is about as low as you can get." The two started toward the makeshift gangplank without looking at Finn.

"I ain't talking about sailing her," Finn explained. He knew he would have to talk quickly now because he saw he was losing them. "But I am talking about floating her."

"Ha, floating her," Henry said and laughed, convinced Finn was playing a cruel joke on him. He started down the plank.

"She'd sink like a lead anchor, Finn," he said and laughed again. "Even you ought to know that. The *Tebinkoff* ain't never going out to sea from here. She's dead."

Finn moved quickly and stood in front of the plank, blocking the path of the two. Each time they tried to move around him he moved in front of them.

"I ain't talking about floating her out to sea, Henry." Finn was more serious so Henry and Dago stopped and looked at him. They would have to listen—but that was all.

"It's the cabin I'm talking about, idiots." Finn turned around and moved to the plank. He balanced himself on the top of the incline and then shuffled down trying not to move too rapidly but that was not possible. Toward the bottom end of the plank he let go and trotted down yelling back up to the two as they watched him bounce along.

"I'm talking about moving the cabin off her," he called back. "Just the cabin. Plank by plank." Finn stopped at the bottom of the timber, turned and pointed up to the edge of the bluff twenty-five feet above them. "Rebuilding it up there. And then you'd have a real cabin, Henry." Finn smiled. "Just like you been talking about. Ain't that what you always wanted? It'd be sorta like bringing her back to life. Right?"

Finn left the two standing on the deck of the old scow. He walked up the beach toward the cannery where the two skiffs waited to take him and Swede and their gear upriver. Henry said nothing back to him. Ordinarily he would have called after him, wished Finn luck, told him he would see him in the spring. But he did not know how to take what Finn had said.

Sure Henry wanted a place to flop when he was in Snag Point. He was needing it more often. And like he said it would not be just Hard Working Henry's Cabin. He looked around at the gray planks on the old wheelhouse and thought about it. Henry decided it would be nice living inside a real seagoing cabin again even one from an old power scow and not a schooner. Maybe what Finn was suggesting made sense.

Henry walked over to the wheelhouse and went inside. The paint had fallen from the walls and flakes of it crackled under his feet making a eerie sound in the empty room. Henry glanced around. He could see through the cracks of the planking on the walls and he saw the sky through the holes in the ceiling where the torn tar paper had long since flown away on the wind. But no ghosts as far as he could tell. He was becoming a little more comfortable with Finn's idea so he leaned out the port window and looked at Dago who still had not decided whether to take what Finn was saying seriously. "If a guy was to do it how do you figure he'd go about getting her up there, Dago?"

At first Dago had frowned at the idea but then he loosened a bit and walked around and around the outside of the wheelhouse stopping occasionally to rub his fingers across his mouth. Henry watched him from the port side then moved over to the window on the starboard and then back to the port following Dago as he circled. Finally Dago stopped and leaned through the port window beside Henry and inspected the insides.

"Plank by plank," Dago finally announced. "Just like the man told us to do, plank by plank."

Henry smiled at him and made a little noise like the wind just as Finn had done.

"Plank by plank," Henry repeated and looked back up toward the top of the bluff. And then his face fell as if suddenly horrified by the thought. He went over to the gunwale and sat with his feet dangling over the side and stared upward his mouth slack.

"What's wrong now?" Dago sat beside him.

"Can't do it," Henry whispered.

"Why?"

"Just can't."

"I thought you was liking the idea, Henry?"

"I was."

"Well?"

"Well, I was."

"Then let's just do it, let's—"

"It's too close."

Dago looked up. "We can set it back some. Hell, Henry, we don't have to rebuild it right on the edge."

"I don't mean that, I mean the church. It'd be too damn close to Felix and all."

"Felix?"

"Yeah."

*"Madre mia,* is that all?"

"It's enough. How'd you like to burn in hell?"

Dago considered this for a moment and he too fell silent not sure what it had to do with anything but it sounded serious enough. Neither spoke for a long while and then Dago leaped from the edge of the scow and walked away from Henry.

"Where you going?"

"Sit tight, Henry."

"Where you going?" Henry repeated but Dago did not answer until he was far down the beach and then he called back. It sounded like he said *To talk to the angels* but Henry was not sure if Dago was going to do that or if Henry himself should.

"She's a dead ship anyway," Henry called through palms cupped around his mouth. "Just forget it, it's just a lot of *bullshit."* Henry was almost certain that word was not in the vocabulary of angels. As far as he knew he would not recognize their language at all. He lay back on the deck of the scow watching the gulls and studying the shapes of the clouds trying to imagine what an angel might look like. That is, to someone who truly believed.

"Bullshit," he whispered again.

It was not an angel Henry saw that day when he sat back up though he thought it might be the Angel of Death the way it moved toward him on the beach, a singular figure cloaked in black flowing vestments. This angel's frock swept the beach with its feet—if they were feet at all—concealed as though this angel floated. And although this particular angel rarely wore that much religious garb and never in the winter Henry was not fooled. He knew it was Felix. He also knew he was trapped.

Henry looked around for escape. No use trying to get past the tide on the opposite end of the beach. He would just get wet though he considered this for a moment as preferable to burning. And he could not scale the bluff fast enough to escape upward. For all he knew Felix would just rise up anyway. Henry lay back resigned to his fate. He heard the feet on the gravel grow louder and then stop and then silence.

"Howdy, Felix," Henry said but he did not sit up. He continued to look for angels in the clouds or anything else that might swing low and save him from Felix.

"I done that once," Felix said and Henry frowned at the voice. It did not sound at all like Father Felix and he began to wonder if someone had run in a second priest to work on him. Henry bolted upright at the thought of those odds. He looked down, scowled. The voice seemed different but it was Felix alright.

"Done what?" Henry cocked a curious ear.

"Searched the clouds for angels."

"Yeah sure Felix. Now what'd you want?" Henry wondered how Felix knew he was looking for angels in the sky. "I done told you I ain't interested. And that ain't what I was looking up at, I was watching them gulls. What'd Dago do, put you onto me?"

"He said you were…distraught."

"Screw him. I ain't no such thing." Henry did not know what Felix's big word meant but it sounded like angel talk to him and not Dago talk. "Dago don't even know that word anyway."

"Well, he said you were struggling. And in pain. That's what I'm here for, Henry, to help people in pain."

"I ain't in pain unless it's maybe a pain in the ass which is what you are, Felix."

"I was in pain once myself," Felix went on ignoring Henry's comment. He moved to the incline and worked his way up. Henry noted he did this easily and without the assistance of wings.

"As a boy." Felix sat next to Henry, gathering his vestment up over his knees and exposing true feet with real shoes, which calmed Henry some. "I sought angels in clouds but I didn't find one either not up there anyway. I found her here on earth right across the railroad tracks where I—"

"As a boy?" Henry thought about himself and his years as a cabin boy and he brightened, relaxed a little more. "You were on a ship? You sing chanteys, Felix?"

"No ships in the west Texas sand dunes, Henry. And I sing in, well, in Latin now."

"Angel talk?"

"What?"

"Nothing, I just don't know much about that kind of singing," Henry said and then tightened again. "And I don't know nothing about hell either, Felix, or burning there and I don't want to know."

"That's the kind of pain I meant," Felix muttered and he looked at Henry. "And I'm sorry I said that to you, Henry. That's what someone said to me once and I just fall into that sometimes. I won't do it again."

"Well, it's what you do I guess," Henry said and he began to feel a little sorry for Felix and the job he had to do. "Forget it."

"Dago said you were looking to build something." Felix glanced upward. "Up there? A cabin?"

Henry shrugged. "Dago thought it up not me. It won't work anyway."

"Why?"

"She's a dead ship."

"Ship?"

"Yeah, this old scow. We thought maybe this cabin here could go up there but—"

"And why not?"

"Well it's—" Henry began and then remembered why he really objected to the whole thing and said, "a little close."

"To the edge?"

"Yeah, the edge, that's it, the edge."

"That'd be no problem," Felix said and looked straight into Henry's eyes. "That is if I blessed it. A lot of things exist on the edge and do just fine as long as they're blessed."

Henry frowned and looked back at Felix and suddenly realized what he meant.

"It would be like bringing it back to life, Henry. And that would be that, sorta like salvation for it. The cabin I mean. No pain."

"No pain?"

"Yeah," Felix repeated. "No pain."

Henry smiled.

And so they had done it, he and Dago. No one who came by for inspection had been sober enough to urge caution about it being so close to the edge and Henry did not worry about it. Now that he had his talk with Felix he had come to like living on the edge.

Yael was the only one who had said anything. "It caves off there every spring, you idiots. Only a matter of time 'til she topples over and floats away with the tide. Course, Henry'll be inside her to set sail so she won't ground out on a sandbar."

But even Yael had stopped the joking when he saw they were serious. Besides he could furnish the whiskey, on credit of course, and in a moment of weakness Yael had even contributed a few nails and hammers free of charge.

When they had finished reconstructing it Henry himself had invited Felix down from the church and asked him to crack a bottle of whiskey Henry had supplied, empty of course, on the corner of the cabin and say the words like a christening. And to Henry's everlasting amazement Felix had spoken nice words too and not a single one in Latin.

At first Henry had used the cabin only when he was not sleeping beneath the dock as he did during the late summer and into the fall. But now that everything was frozen up under the dock Henry was staying in his cabin almost every night. Dago had painted a large sign with white boatpaint on the outside of the old wheelhouse that read Henry's Cabin so now everyone knew it belonged to Henry. It also made it easier to find in the dark. That is, if the icefog were not hanging over the village like it was this very evening as Hard Working Henry tried to remember the words to the sea chanteys.

In the past Henry usually had found himself under the dock in the mornings after Yael Feldstein had sold him whiskey on credit and had thrown him out of the back room of his general store for being drunk. To Henry it did not make any sense for Yael to sell him whiskey and then get angry because he was drunk. But Yael did not like drunks sleeping back there on his dry goods puking all over them. The coal room was okay with Yael if someone needed to stay warm but his storeroom with the dry goods was off limits. But now Henry liked his cabin even better than the coal room especially since Felix had blessed it. Mice would crawl all over a guy in the coal room. Henry hated mice.

*"...constable had to come and take him away...hmmmmm..."* Henry continued singing pieces of the song as he stumbled around searching under the dock. "Now where the hell did I hide it?" It was already growing dark under the pier but Henry did not need light to find what he was seeking. In the shadows he could see the niche in the timbers above his head where he had hidden a bottle of whiskey, true Irish whiskey, at least that was what Feldstein had guaranteed when he had sold it to him last summer. Hard Working Henry O'Hara was Irish. Damn proud, too.

Henry groped for the bottle, felt it, brought it out. Then he uncorked and held it up, toasted his absent friends. Funny thing about whiskey, it never froze. It might get a little thick, a bit syrupy in the bottle when it was below zero outside, but it was always ready, like his friends, like family really all of them, all of his different kinds of bottles he had cached here and there around Snag Point and all of his different kinds of friends. He looked around then sat down. He would stay a few moments more. Even in the darkness and the cold of winter it was familiar under here and he savored it as he sloshed the liquid in the bottle, tipped it up.

*"Sheriff John Stone why don't you leave me alone...mmmm...I feel so breakup I wanta go home..."*

He could remember all the words to the song now so he squeezed his eyes tight to imprint them on his mind for next summer to sing with his friends. It was okay here even in winter especially with the cabin for a backup. But it was nicer in summer.

In the long daylight of summer the shadows under the dock shielded him and his friends from the eyes of Snag Point busy then with people coming and going at Feldstein's General Store and at the cannery. They were also hidden from the people sitting in Heine's Cafe on the downriver side. Since the cannery dock was located between Feldstein's and Heine's it served the needs of the fishermen well. And it also worked for the trappers in the spring when they made their deals with Feldstein. Yael always threw in a bottle of whiskey if the trappers dealt with him for their caches of illegal pelts. The other buyers, the transients who set up to buy on the beach sometimes, paid better but they had no whiskey to barter and they were not around in the winter to extend credit. Henry never did as well with his trapping as Swede or Finn so he always waited until Starvin' Marvin came in to barter. It was then he would throw his stack of pelts on the table next to Marvin's. It always made Henry feel better seeing his pelts next to Marvin's.

After trading with Feldstein they all took the bottles under the dock, drank it up, slept it off and then moved into Heine's for sidemeat and hotcakes and coffee then back to Feldstein's in the afternoon and cycle through again until all the fishing money or the trapping money was gone. Yael was crafty though. He kept an open tab at his store so the trappers could grubstake up for winter. He cursed and grumbled when he gave them what they needed and he swore he would never do it again on credit but there was never any conviction to it. Yael wanted their pelts again in the spring and he was always assured of getting them.

The whole thing was like bucking heavy tide and though it was slow coming through the Irish Whiskey, Henry was aware he was draining more than just the bottles. He had started coming down to Snag Point more often in the winter now.

"I just want to see who's staying around and who's not," he had said earlier that winter. "I want to see which of my fishing friends are here for the winter and which ones ain't. And besides I gotta check on Henry's Cabin too."

But even though he did not mention it to the others Henry knew this year's supply of whiskey would not last through the trapping season. Trapping was tough but it was better than gillnetting. If you were a fisherman the cannery owned your soul like it did with Willie and Skipper and Chubby and Dago and all the other gillnetters. But not Henry, not Hard Working Henry. No way.

"Nothing or nobody owns me," he was fond of saying and he thought about how he had even made a truce of sorts with Felix by allowing him to bless the cabin. It was not a trick on Henry's part but it was not salvation either, not the way Felix might have wanted. Henry would never fall for something so fleeting as that. Felix could have Henry's soul only if it came wrapped in the reality of Henry's Cabin with all its secret nooks and crannies with appropriate supplies for sailing long voyages to who knows where and Felix seemed curiously satisfied with that. "I got my freedom and I do as I please," Henry said. "And Felix knows it. That's just the way we are, all us trappers, me and Marvin and Swede and Finn and No-Talk, all of us."

He thought about No-Talk, how he had finally found freedom and about how often they had been together under here. "Sonuvabitch," he said lifting the bottle. "This one's for you, No-Talk." He drank long, not swallowing, just opened his throat and then released his breath and said, "Wherever in hell you are."

Then he looked through the pilings at the ice floes moving out with the ebb tide in front of the dock and he looked up the beach where the high tide had left a glistening sheet of rime ice. Though he could not see it he knew the hulk of the *Tebinkoff* was just around the point, naked now without her cabin. It would be slack water soon so he decided he would sit just long enough to see it change, see the ice cakes, some as big as the *Tebinkoff* herself slowly start moving upriver into the icefog which now had billowed in and formed a graywhite wall along the bluff.

The movement of the ice reminded Henry of spring breakup when the chunks drifted back and forth and seemed to take on lives of their own sometimes, beached like white whales at low water but then alive again with the next high tide, never going on out to sea, never quite completing an escape, just moving in and out with the tide in front of Snag Point until they had no more form or mass at all, just disappeared, becoming part of the bay itself.

*"I feel so breakup I wanta go home…"* Henry liked the ending of the song so well he repeated just that part. *"I feel so breakup I wanta go home…"*

Then he drained the bottle and tossed it toward the bay. It clinked against the ice and rolled down the beach and rattled to a stop. But the sound in Henry's head did not stop. He blinked at the bottle and began to worry about how much he had drunk. It did not seem like that much but he was not cold any more and he knew that was not a good sign. Henry decided whiskey played bad tricks on you, especially in the winter. He looked down to his left hand at the two fingers with their missing tips he had lost to frostbite the previous winter. But that had been a stupid mistake, he thought. He had been drunk then, real drunk, and that was the winter before he and Dago had built Henry's Cabin. Yael had kicked him out of the store and he had almost made it to Heine's where he knew he could sleep it off. But he had fallen in the snow and stayed longer than he thought, a painful lesson he did not intend to repeat now that he had his own place.

Henry looked at the bottle again, resting at the edge of the ice but strangely he heard the clinking sound as if the bottle were still rolling. Must be the ice, he thought, bumping around out there. Ice floes make strange noises when they drift into each other. Northern Lights make noises too but most people did not believe him. Henry had heard them though many times. The Northern Lights crackled. One just had to be still, hold his breath and listen. This was different though, this sound he was hearing now. Henry decided maybe it was just inside his ears, maybe he was just getting old.

"Stop it!" he shouted at the bottle. The sound continued. Henry staggered forward and drew back his foot to kick the bottle out into the ice floes. Then he saw the figure moving down the beach toward him, emerging from the wall of icefog as if stepping from some other world. At first Henry was relieved because he realized the clanging was coming from the figure moving rhythmically like a great shore bird feeding on the beach, dipping and rising, dipping and rising. And then he thought about No-Talk Owens again and he stiffened.

"Maybe it's him," he muttered. "Two years gone and he's come back maybe from the dead." He squinted into the fog. No, it was chains, it sounded like the dull rattle of chains. "She's weighing anchor," Henry called to the figure and this seemed to relieve him. "The *Tebinkoff*, by God, she's off to sea." But then Henry saddened. "Hell, she ain't got no wheelhouse. How's she gonna make it without her wheelhouse? And she ain't got no captain either. Or first mate or second mate or even a cabin boy."

This frightened him again. He looked at the figure still moving toward him. "Maybe it's her captain. Maybe it's the ghost of her captain come to get me for stealing his wheelhouse." And then he thought about No-Talk again and how he had disappeared without even a spot of blood on the snow.

"Or maybe it's that goddamn *Keetuk?* Oh Lordy—" Henry shut his eyes and put his hands over his face trying to remember that little phrase Father Felix had been urging him to learn about everlasting life and Henry regretted not knowing how it went. "It wasn't even Latin either. Shit I coulda learned it…"

He moaned and removed his hands and opened his eyes again just to make sure it was not the whiskey. This time the figure was gone but the fog had only closed in around it and when it reappeared the spectre was closer, moving steadily with the same jerking motion down the beach toward him. Henry whined and shut his eyes again. He would keep them closed longer this time, wipe this thing out for good if he could only remember. But he could not say the words and he knew the apparition was right on him.

"Hello, Henry." Finn dropped the chains of his harness onto the sand. "Drunk again? Probably didn't save me a goddamn swill did you?"

Henry opened his eyes and stood there voiceless.

"Well?"

Henry shook his head no and then changed it to yes. "Got some hidden in the shack, Finn," he whispered and smiled like a man stepping from a fiery furnace. "I mean the cabin. My cabin, Finn. Henry's Cabin."

"You done it, huh?" Finn said.

"Yeah. Me and Dago. Plank by plank just like you said." Henry spoke proudly and then he remembered how he had planned to surprise Finn with the news in the spring. "Yeah, last summer after you and Swede left upriver. But what're you doing back down here, Finn? It's the middle of the winter. You run out of whiskey, too?"

Finn turned to the corpse behind him. "It's Swede. Done in by that crazy native just like No-Talk."

"Swede? You're bullshittin'."

"See for yourself."

Henry bent over the body. Even in the twilight he could tell it was one of his drinking buddies. "How?"

"Shit. How come everybody wants to know all the details? Hell's bells, he's dead. Ain't that enough. What is this, a goddamn jury or something?"

"Sorry, Finn. Just asking."

"Well, you can hear all about it when I explain to that pimp deputy. Is he here?"

"Nope. At least not yesterday. He's on beaver patrol, I think."

"How about Felix? Did he make it across yet?"

"Ain't seen him neither."

"Hell, he oughta made it here by now." Finn paused for a moment, sighed.

"Across where, Finn?"

"Nevermind. Help me get old Swede up the beach Henry. Maybe Yael can give us a place to keep him tonight."

"Sure thing, Finn, sure thing."

Henry's head had cleared a little with the importance of the moment. He grasped one side of the chain harness and helped Finn tug the body up the slope.

"Now, let's see, Finn. First we can take care of old Swede for the night then we'll get you something hot at Heine's and then—"

"Yeah, swell."

"And then bunk down at my cabin."

"Fine, Henry."

"You must be plumb wore down."

"Un-huh."

"How come you brought him all the way down, Finn? How come you done that?"

Finn did not reply. He looked up the slope at the familiar silhouette of Feldstein's General Store, its false front crenelated like a turret on a castle. This first facade of the building had been constructed toward the beach, then later a twin face was added on the opposite end toward the village which had grown out and away from the beach front. Two faces, Finn thought, just like its owner.

There was the beginning of a main street parallel to the beach now. It ran between the new face of Feldstein's store and Deputy Delbert's jailhouse across the street. On down the beach was the cannery and adjacent to that Heine's Cafe. Scattered up the hill behind the small complex of buildings and around the tundra for a half mile radius lay the gray weathered shacks of the seventy-five other winter residents of Snag Point. In winter the village was colorless and still, frozen in time like a worn daguerreotype, black and gray and white with an occasional patch of brown where the northwind had blown the top of a hummock free of snow.

The only building in the settlement with any paint was Father Felix's chapel segregated at the peak of the bluff overlooking the bay. It stood out whiter than the snow, trimmed with green and red handcrafted latticework and in summer all the fishermen sailed past, even the faithless ones crossing themselves for luck on their way to the fishing grounds. It was then the cottonwood tent frames went up and the population tripled with other fishermen from Seattle and with the villagers who came downriver with their families to work in the cannery and fish the salmon run in July.

"Yael closed up yet?" Finn said. They were on the street side of Feldstein's now, dragging Swede down the boardwalk, his heels thumping into the cracks with a hollow sound. The street was deserted except for the icefog, which was beginning to fill it.

"I think so but I just left there a while ago. He's probably still inside."

"Well, this is serious," said Finn. He was beginning to feel unusually brazen with the importance of his mission. "We'll make the fat little bastard open up anyway."

Through the dingy window they could see a lantern in the back of the store. Finn pounded on the locked door. He paused and then hammered again louder this time and a few minutes later they saw the lantern move through the building toward the door. They heard the bolt slide. The man who opened it scowled at them and stood with the lantern raised above his head, casting the light out into the night and against the icefog which had now filled the street.

He was short, even shorter than Finn or Henry but solid, round like an oak cask and though he held it over his head the lantern scarcely came up to the faces of the two men outside the door with the corpse behind on the boardwalk, the three now standing in the lantern glow like a conspiracy of grave robbers. The man wore a white shirt with black garters around the upper arms of each sleeve and he had fastened suspenders to his wool trousers. The suspenders were for the image the man wanted and not a necessity for the waist of the pants cut into the roll of fat with a tautness that held them in place anyway. His appearance was enhanced with a beaver hat which seemed out of place with the rest of his clothing. It was stuck on the back of his bald head as an afterthought, announcing he was indeed in the fur business. The only hair aside from his thin eyebrows was a carefully trimmed goatee. Finn and Henry blinked, adjusting to the light in their eyes.

"Yael?" Finn shielded his eyes from the lantern with an upraised palm.

"Well, who the hell did you think it was, Santa Claus?"

"Get that goddamn light out of our eyes," Finn demanded. "We need to see you."

"Sure you do. You always do when the whiskey's gone." He looked at Henry but did not move the lantern.

"Now come on, Yael," Henry said. "This is serious and it ain't whiskey. Swede's been murdered."

Yael lowered the lantern and stood silent for a moment, weighing what effect this might have on his beaver pelt buying in the spring. Swede was a good trapper but he was dumb when it came to bartering. A bottle of whiskey on the table and mention of Moonface Nellie with her steambath always seemed to speed things up. Finn was tougher, craftier. But then Finn liked poker. And he played badly. "Dead, uh?"

Finn nodded and stepped aside so the light would fall on the body. Yael looked at it and wrinkled his nose. "Well, what the hell can I do? You shoulda took him over to Deputy Demara."

"He ain't here," Henry said. "He's out on beaver patrol."

Yael smiled and squinted at them. "Beaver patrol? Hope you guys ain't hanging out too far. Hope you got all of them hid good? You know old Delbert's been on a rampage with poachers this winter. One hell of deal. Seems he dropped over to Moonface Nellie's one evening for supper, had himself a nice steambath, ate a big meal of fresh moose, drank up all her whiskey and on the way out old Delbert seen part of that fresh moose hide draped over the woodpile," Yael said and then chuckled. "Know what he done then?"

"Come on, Yael, cut the bullshit," Finn said. "You gonna help us or not?"

"Well, old Deputy Delbert he went right back in and arrested her for poaching. Hell Moon ain't even the one that shot it, somebody just give it to her. Delbert fined her ten dollars and let her go but I think maybe Moonface cut him off after that. He's been real onery. He thinks he's some kind of Canadian Mountie with that goddamn dog and that whip with lead in the handle and that fur hat with a badge and all."

"Look, goddammit, we ain't here to discuss all that," Finn interrupted but Yael noticed that both men had glanced back into the darkness behind them. Finn spoke deliberately as if Yael had not understood it all. "I brought Swede down here to put him in the ground," he continued. "Say some words, show everybody that I ain't done this one neither. And maybe this time we can get something done about it."

"Yeah," Henry added. "Don't you think it's about time we put that guy away, Yael?"

"You mean Delbert?" Yael said toying with them.

"Knock it off, Yael. You know who I mean," Henry said. "That native guy that's doing all this stuff. That Keetuk."

"He done it?" Yael said.

"Course he done it," Finn said. "And he's done a lot more than that too. Stealing traps and pelts and sugar. He's even got a couple of women now, scared hell out of Felix."

"And don't forget about No-Talk," Henry reminded. "Remember old No-Talk."

"No-Talk?" Yael said. "You mean Owens?" He chuckled when the name prompted the familiar joke about Finn eating his partner. Yael leaned over toward Finn and bared his teeth, clicked them together hard a few times as if chewing on something tough and then chortled again.

"Knock it off, you little cracker," Finn said moving toward him. "That ain't funny any more. No-Talk never done nothing to you. If the truth was known what he did was donate his pelts to you every spring. I'm tired, Yael, and I ain't in no mood for your bullshit. Now you gonna help us or ain't you? I'm cold standing out here."

Yael became serious as though he might have overstepped the line with the joke about Finn eating No-Talk. If No-Talk had indeed been murdered maybe a little more respect was in order. But most of all Yael did not want to lose Finn and Henry's business in the spring. "Okay, okay Finn. What do you want me to do?"

"Well I can't leave Swede out here in the street. Dogs might get to him. Can I bring him inside?"

Yael looked at the corpse which was a bit trail worn by now. "I guess so. But take him into the back."

"He'll thaw out back there, Yael," Henry said. "I don't think you'll want him to thaw out back there on your dry goods." It was Henry's turn to wrinkle his nose.

"I ain't talking about the room with the dry goods, idiot. I'm talking about the coal room. I don't want the sonuvabitch in there on my drygoods. You should know better than that, Henry. Put him in the coal room. It's cold enough back there but you can open the windows too. That'll keep him froze."

He moved aside and held the light for them as they dragged the body through the store and into the coal room. A flurry of mice scurried into the coal pile as they entered.

"What about the mice," Henry said. "We can't just leave him on the floor with the mice."

"Mice ain't going to bother him now," Finn said.

"Well, just the same I don't think it's right to leave Swede on the floor," Henry said.

"You could put him on them sawhorses there," offered Yael. "He's stiff enough."

"Yeah," Henry said. "Let's do that for him, Finn. Get him up off the floor at least."

"Well, I've gone this far with him. Might as well finish the job," Finn sighed. "Make him comfortable."

They lifted the corpse and placed one sawhorse under his neck and the other under his knees. The body sagged a little but then lay stiff across the sawhorses like a suspended bridge.

"What are you going to bury him in, Finn?" Yael said.

"I dunno. You got a box or something?"

"No."

"Something we can make a coffin out of? Anything?"

"Nope."

"We could wrap him in a blanket," Henry suggested. "Swede always was cold. Let's just wrap him up warm in a blanket."

"Yeah, fine whatever." Finn was becoming very weary with the whole thing and wanted to end it, wanted to get back to Marvin and then on up to the Mikchalk River, check on his pelts and his own cabin.

"I'll help you dig tomorrow," said Henry. "Ground's frozen deep by now so you'll need some help."

"I don't want no help," Finn announced. "I just want a pick and a shovel and some words said." He paused and looked down at his frozen partner. "I ain't no good at words Henry. I wonder where that damn Felix is. You sure he never showed?"

"I don't think so," said Henry. "Leastways I never seen no candlelight in his church if he did."

Yael moved out of the coal room with the lantern. Henry followed him to the front of the store but Finn stayed for a few moments standing in the dark listening to the mice scratching in the coal and then he went toward the light in the front of Yael's store.

"Well, I'll donate a place for him tonight, even throw in a blanket to wrap him in," Yael sighed. "Carry you bastards in the winter, carry you bastards in the summer, carry you when you get married, carry you when you die…" Yael stopped and held the door open for them and the lantern above his head again. "But I sure as hell won't help dig no hole in this weather."

"Thanks, Yael," Henry said.

"Yeah, thanks, Yael," repeated Finn. "That's big of you."

They moved through the door and out into the icefog which swirled behind them and muffled the light from Yael's lantern. "And gentlemen," Yael said. "One more thing." They turned back to him but could not see his face under the muted glow. "I sure as hell ain't saying no words over him." Yael closed the door. They heard the bolt slide back into place.

"Screw him," said Finn. He moved off down the boardwalk toward the bluff. "Now you can show me that cabin, Henry."

Henry lingered for a few moments watching the lantern through the windows as it disappeared into the back of the store. Then he realized Finn was no longer beside him. Startled, he jerked around and strained to see into the darkness. "Finn?" He heard Finn's footsteps on the boardwalk but he could not see him.

Finn was at the end of the boardwalk but he did not answer. Although he was still angry with Yael he realized he could not show it. He could not go back and say what he felt for fear it would jeopardize his credit. The small pouch of gold hidden inside his shirt would not be enough. Finn would need extra credit from Yael for another grubstake when he and Marvin returned for the pelts this winter. Henry was the only thing handy for his ire so Finn stepped off the boardwalk and moved a few paces through the snow, stopped and waited.

"Finn?" Henry called again and listened. He tried to make his voice sound brave but he was not successful. When he did not hear the footsteps any longer, Henry shifted his feet and looked around into the night. He was thinking about Swede's corpse in the coal room and the mice and about No-Talk and suddenly he broke and walked rapidly down the boardwalk. "Finn, wait for me. What about Heine's?" He almost bumped into Finn at the end of the walk.

"What?" Finn said. "You lose your momma, Henry? Come on, I ain't hungry no more. I got a long day tomorrow."

Henry did not hold Finn's hand but he did keep their elbows touching all the way up to his cabin. "You could see the sign Dago painted on her," Henry said as they neared the cabin. "If it wasn't so dark and foggy. It's on this side of her right here."

Henry slapped the side of the cabin and moved around to open the door but the bottom had frozen to the transom. Henry kicked it and jerked. "Gotta fix this next summer. Me and Dago are going back over her next summer and make her nicer." The door finally snapped loose from the ice. "Well, come on in, Finn and have a look. Kick off them boots and make yourself at home."

Inside Henry put a match to the wick of his own lantern. He held his face next to the globe, the light working across the wrinkles and the red cheeks and the elfin features.

For Finn the light provided a semblance of warmth but it did little else for the place. There was a set of bunks nailed together from shipping pallets along one wall. In the center was a small table with a frayed oilcloth someone had contributed, once white and red checked but now faded and seared with black rings from a thousand hot coffee pots. Two wooden crates served as chairs. The ubiquitous oildrum fashioned into a woodstove for both heating and cooking squatted nearby. The end had been removed and a hinged metal door took its place. Outside one wall a rusted piece of corrugated tin had been nailed over an inserted brass port, its glass long ago shattered.

"Well, tell me how you got her up here, Henry," Finn said. He looked around the inside of the cabin. It seemed tight enough. No snow had blown through the cracks, which surprised Finn.

"Plank by plank," Henry said. "Just like you suggested. Only you never did say how we should get each plank up here did you?"

"Well, looks to me like you did it." Finn figured Henry was going to tell him all about it anyway so he said nothing else although he was hoping Henry might light the stove first.

"Yep. We sure as hell did," Henry said. He made no move to fire up the stove but strutted around the room holding the lantern up for Finn to see the inside of the cabin better. "What we done, see, was string a wire from the top of the bluff here to the bay side of the *Tebinkoff.* We buried it deep in the sand, tied it to some anchors."

"Yeah?"

"Yeah. Then we got a pulley and a harness and a lot of rope," Henry continued. "I had a lot of rope anyway Finn."

Finn nodded his head. He guessed Henry had more rope and anchors than anyone else in the whole territory. Henry had stolen anchors and rope from every fisherman in Salmon Bay at one time or another. It was standard procedure for gillnetters to check for missing anchors each time before they went out on the tide. More than once Henry had made extra whiskey money selling an anchor right back to its owner. The fishermen all grumbled and threatened to report Henry to Deputy Delbert but when the fish were running no one argued long with Henry. A fisherman did not go out in the riptides without an anchor even if it meant buying his own gear back from Henry.

"Then Dago stood on the beach and tied each plank to the harness and pulley," Henry continued. "I'd stand on the bluff right where we sit Finn and just tug each one of them up the wire to the top."

Finn nodded again. He had not had time the previous summer to work out the scheme for getting the cabin off the *Tebinkoff* and up the bluff but he approved of this.

"Not bad, Henry," Finn said. "Not bad at all." He thought that would end it and Henry would light the stove now. But Henry was not ready for that yet.

"Yeah," Henry continued. "And that ain't all Finn. You might have noticed how tight she is?"

Finn had noticed—tight but cold.

"Well, what we done was caulk her up just like the bottom of a boat. Everywhere a plank come together we stuffed her full of oakum and tamped her tight," Henry said and smiled. "Dago done all that, got the oakum and corking and hammers and stuff from the cannery."

Henry ran his hand over the plank surface of the wall. "She's tight, Finn. Tighter than the cheeks on old Feldstein's ass. Ain't a flake of snow made it through all winter." He rubbed the wall again.

"Tight," Finn agreed. "But is she warm, Henry? Even if they're tight sometimes they still ain't warm and they ain't worth a damn unless they're warm too." Finn was thinking about Moonface Nellie now but he was also thinking about Henry's stove. He had begun to shiver a little since he had stopped moving.

"But all that ain't nothing, Finn," Henry continued. He paced around some more. "Guess what else I done?"

Finn could see the stove would get no attention until Henry had it all out. And since he was responsible in a way for all this Finn would have to listen.

"What, Henry? What?"

"You won't say nothing?"

"No."

"You sure?"

"Yes, Henry, I'm sure. Now get on with it."

"Well it's this," Henry said. He went to one of the bunks and pulled from under it the remnants of the old powerscow wheel. He held it up to the kerosene lantern. Finn could see that he had been scraping off the moss and the gullshit.

"That's nice, Henry. That's real good. But what the hell are you gonna do with it?"

"You said you wouldn't say nothing."

"Well, I ain't said nothing Henry. Except ask what you're doing with it." Finn was losing patience now. He considered lighting the stove himself.

"I mean if I tell you, you won't say nothing to nobody else?"

Finn shook his head.

"Well, I plan to mount it over by that port, fix it up and varnish it and mount it over there so's I can look out the port and see off the bluff and out into the bay."

Henry took the old wheel and stood beside the tin covered porthole. He propped the wheel next to it. "Right here. I'll mount her right here. Course I'll need to fix the porthole some day, put some more glass in it so's I can see out." He turned around to Finn and smiled. "Well, whatta you think, Finn?"

"Great, Henry. That'll be great."

"And there's one more thing, Finn."

Finn was silent, waiting for the end.

"Promised you wouldn't tell, right?"

Finn nodded and sighed heavily.

"Well, Felix blessed her too."

"Blessed who?"

"My ship here."

"Oh…Felix?"

"Yep. But don't go jumping to no conclusions, Finn. I ain't gone over the bluff yet but Felix, well, he ain't so bad if you really get to know him and if he don't talk in them angel words and—"

"Angel words?"

"Yeah, that Latin stuff and all. He blessed it in English." Henry beamed.

"Yeah, sure. Texan I bet." Finn stood and went to the stove, bent down and swung the door open.

"I'll get her, Finn," Henry said. "You just relax."

Henry took the shipwheel and slid it under the bunk. He returned to the stove. Finn saw he was serious about getting heat inside the cabin but he decided he would move around anyway in order to stave off his shivering. Then Finn noticed a brass shipbell which waited on a shelf above the stove.

"What the hell you keep this for?" Finn immediately regretted bringing it up. He was not sure he could survive another description of future plans for Henry's Cabin. He lifted the bell by its leather lanyard and studied it while Henry tried to start the fire. Finn shook the bell trying to make a noise. "Hell, it ain't even got a clapper any more. Kind of like you, huh Henry?"

Henry was trying to focus on getting the match inside the oildrum and under the birch bark but the matches were damp and would not hold the flame. "What do you mean?"

"Well, you ain't got no use for a clapper anymore either," Finn said. "Except to filter booze through."

"Piss on you." Henry was becoming irritated with the wet matches. "It's a goddamn cinch I wouldn't put mine where yours has been."

"By the way, how is Moon anyway?" Finn smiled. He sat on one of the crates and placed the bell on the oilcloth.

"How the hell would I know? I don't have no truck with her. She's Swede's girl, at least she was."

"Maybe Delbert's taken over now."

"There she goes." Henry had taken a cup of kerosene and doused the stubborn wood. It roared to life when he touched the match to it, the old oildrum snapping and creaking with the sudden heat. His face brightened. He stood and laughed and danced a little jig. To Finn, Henry looked like a leprechaun.

"Grant me one wish, Henry"

"What's that?"

"Just don't burn the goddamn place down." Finn tapped the bell with his fingernail and wailed like a fire engine. "How come you keep this old relic?"

Henry moved to the table and cradled the bell. "This one come off the *S.S. Baranov,*" he explained. "You knew I was second mate on her? That was when she foundered off Cape Constantine. I saved nothing in the lifeboat but my own ass and this old ship's bell, took it right off the top of the wheelhouse." Henry rubbed the tarnished brass with his sleeve. "Can't remember what happened to the clapper though. I'm gonna replace it sometime then shine this thing up and hang it again right on the top deck of a whaler or a schooner or maybe even a steam freighter, something like that you know."

"How come you don't put her up here? Right on top of Henry's Cabin?"

"That'd be stupid," Henry said and Finn saw he was serious. "You know this ain't no whaler or schooner or nothing like that." Henry turned the bell slowly in his hands. Then he polished it some more on the front of his shirt and now he could see his face glowing dimly in the brass.

"I'll be the skipper and have a full crew." Henry was ignoring Finn, talking slowly to his reflection in the brass. "And a private cabin, one with a cabin boy that sings all day long, knows all the old chanteys like I used to know. And I'll have my own cook and sail the Pacific."

"Where to?" Finn said.

Henry didn't answer. He just looked up at Finn and then moved toward the door, reached above the jamb and retrieved a pint of whiskey. He brought it back to the table and gave it to Finn.

"All over," he said to Finn. He cocked his head and looked up into a corner of the room. "I ain't gonna wind up like Swede and the rest of you bums. I'm gonna sail all over. And I'll have women in every port just waiting for me. And not like Moon neither. I'm talking about fine and elegant young ladies that wear silk and lace and smell good."

"Ladies, huh?" Finn passed the bottle back across the table.

"Yeah." Henry swilled from the bottle and gave it back. "Ladies. That's something you wouldn't know about Finn."

"Ladies?" Finn said wistfully. "Only one I guess."

"Bullshit," Henry said. "Which one?"

Finn was thinking about Stella Villard, the second time in two days that she had invaded his mind. He remembered the way she had held her head in that regal fashion, the way her fresh clothes rustled when she moved. And he remembered how her creamysilk skin under all those clothes had felt against his own. He considered telling Henry about himself and Stella but he was afraid that in a drunken moment Henry might expose Finn's secret to Marvin. And all that was long past anyway. There would be no useful purpose in dredging up any of it especially now that he and Marvin were to be partners again. Let it die he thought, be buried for good this time. "Hell, you must be pushing sixty, Henry," Finn said shifting the subject. "What the hell would you know about women any more?"

"Plenty," he said. "We called at ports all up and down the West Coast, San Francisco, Seattle, Vancouver, you name it I been there. Women in them places Finn, lots of women. And I had all kinds."

"Yeah?"

"You bet. And I ain't intending to hang around here forever. You mark me. I'll have elegant ladies again Finn you'll see."

"Well that's great Henry. When you figure on leaving?" Finn yawned and thought about Felix and his island.

"Soon. Maybe even this summer." Henry went to the shelf and took down a can of sardines. "You sure you ain't hungry, Finn?"

"No, I'm gonna hit that bunk." He went to the bed and shook the blanket and stretched out. "Maybe you could spread the word about Swede in the morning while I start the hole. When Felix shows up we can have him say the words and put him away tomorrow afternoon."

"Yeah, Finn, you bet. We'll get a crowd up. Heine and Dago and Moon and all of them and I'll make Felix talk in English. He'll do that for me now." He opened the sardines and pulled one out by the tail. He tipped his head back and dropped it into his mouth and spoke as he chewed. "You know I intend to build up a pretty good cache of pelts this winter, Finn. Depending on prices and Yael and how we work it out I might have enough next summer. I figure on getting maybe seventy-five extra pelts. By God, I might just pull it off."

The lantern glow was growing faint so Henry had trouble seeing the sardines. He took out his pocket knife and stabbed inside the tin with it and hit the bottle between each sardine. "Yessir, I'm gonna have one of them wool captain's hats, the kind them Greeks wear with scrambled eggs on the bill and maybe even a pea coat with some kind of braid on it. Right, Finn?"

Henry turned around just as the lantern burned itself dry but Finn was already asleep. He stood and dropped the empty can onto the table and then looked around the room trying to remember in the blackness exactly where each object was, training himself like he had done when he remembered the songs under the dock. He needed to practice imprinting objects and their locations like he would have to do with maps and charts when he became the captain of his own vessel.

Henry reached out in the darkness and found the leather lanyard on the bell and picked it up. He tried not to stumble as he shuffled his feet toward the door. It was brighter outside with the icefog but it had consumed everything so he did not rely on his memory to imprint the location of Henry's Cabin. Instead he leaned against the reality of it, felt the rough planks with one shoulder as he relieved himself in the snow. When he finished he squinted into the fog, looked beyond the three masts, past the huge front mainsail and on forward over the bowsprit. His sea legs buckled slightly as the huge schooner lurched and bucked into the swells. Then he raised the bell and with his penknife, tapped two times on its side, paused and then tapped twice more, sending the warning into the fog. But no one rang back to Captain Hard Working Henry O'Hara. *"I feel so break up I wanna go home..."* he sang softly. And then he tapped the bell twice again, turned and stumbled back through the doorway of Henry's Cabin.

# SEVEN

When it chose to visit Snag Point, death was as devious as the citizenry. It could sneak in the back way as Finn had done with Swede or it could charge through the front brazen and unannounced. Death could select with cruel precision as with the inevitable winter stillborn or it could sweep through indiscriminately, leaving little time for mourning.

It had left no time at all for grief in 1913 with the influenza epidemic and it had visited in a similar fashion just this past summer of 1925. On this occasion a Southwest gale blowing eighty knots had trapped seventeen sailboat fishermen as they set their gillnets on the ebb tide at Flounder Flat. Four others this same season had simply lost their footing on a slippery gunwale and had been sucked into the riptide off Coffee Point. A death in Snag Point could be a mundane thing; a burial was quite another.

For this one Nellie Napiuk would select her wardrobe with care. She stood in front of the battered dresser in her full length parka, the one she had made years ago in her village of Tuluk-On-The-Bay, the garment she had crafted from the tan and gray fur of seventy parka squirrels. It was the parka that Old Suyuk had taught her how to make and into which Nellie had sewn the small pouch perfect for someday carrying a child close to her body.

Nellie could not see her head in the missing tophalf of the broken mirror so she had to stoop to see her face and hair. No, it was not right, she thought. The parka would do if she were to return to

Tuluk-On-The-Bay for the dancing or for a special potlatch but not here.

Nellie thought about the villagers and knew that even though they would accept the parka they might not allow her back in the village after what had happened to Old Suyuk. But the parka was wrong for Snag Point and Nellie had always recognized this. She was not like the others in her village now, limited in their knowledge of the world and naive to fashion. Nellie had chosen to live in Snag Point among the *kassaqs* and she had learned their language and their fashion and their customs.

Nellie removed first the parka and carefully returned it to the wooden box under her bed where it had rested for so long. Then she shed her gray laundry dress to try on the new one she had purchased from the rack at Feldstein's, a silken green print trimmed with false lace ruffles. Over this she would wear the heavy cloth *kuspuk,* the red outer shell with the hood and the full length skirt made to protect her legs from the cold. On her feet she would wear her *mukluks,* hand sewn from seal skin and leather and trimmed with her best beadwork. They were not as fine as the black leather boots worn by the teacher at the orphanage but even this educated lady had admired Nellie's skin boots. They were her only public connection to her people not because she wanted to display this but because she had no other winter boots. Satisfied her appearance would be appropriate for a burial she took these clothes off and placed them carefully over a chair and wriggled back into the gray dress.

With her broom Nellie worked her way around the one room shack, taking care to clean in the corners and under her bed where she kept the honeybucket. She averted her eyes and nose as she removed the full bucket and clapped the lid on it. Then she shuffled out the door with the awkward load and went to the edge of the bluff and there sloshed the contents over into the bay. Back inside she made the bed, washed and cleaned the coffee pot, scrubbed some of the grease from the top of the oil cookstove for she would not cook here this morning. She would take money and buy her breakfast at Heine's Café and wait there until time for the burial.

Her work finished Nellie removed the gray dress again and put on the green print and the *kuspuk*. She brushed her black hair straight away from the dark skin of her round face, fast and hard until it shone. She worked it into a single braid at the back and tied the end with a small red ribbon. With an eye attuned to the fashions of Snag Point, Nellie inspected the headless trunk of her body once more in the broken mirror. One never knew who would be at a burial.

At the door she turned to take in the room. Everything was in place. The window was washed, the plank floors swept as clean as possible and the big goosedown quilt was beneath the frayed bedspread. Tin cups and plates were in their places on the shelf. The skinned beaver tail, a delicacy ripe and warm, lay ready to eat in the pan above the oil stove. Yes, everything was tidy. One never knew who would visit following a burial.

Outside, the icefog was still everywhere so she had to pick her way carefully up the trail. She found the boardwalk and moved faster toward Heine's Café, pulling up her hood for she did not want the ice crystals to spoil the sheen in her hair. Karl Erlich was leaning on his counter when she entered. He was the only person in the small café.

"Morning," he said. "And how is Nellie?"

"Sad," she said and grinned at him. She sat next to the window to see who would pass by today.

"Yes," Karl said. "Too bad about Swede. Are you having breakfast today?" Karl spoke with the hard guttural dialect he had brought from the old country. His was one of the remaining true accents in Snag Point but even he knew how to speak without it when it suited him.

"Coffee. And hotcakes, big ones with syrup and butter," she said still smiling. "And bacon."

Karl worried a moment about the large order, with bacon even, and about the money to pay for it but then he remembered that Nellie always had money and this was a special day.

"Nice dress, Nellie."

Nellie grinned.

Karl brought the whole pot of coffee on a tin plate. He knew that when Nellie sat near the window at the front of the café she would be there all morning. It was not like the time when he had worked on a cannery scow. On a scow men ate and men went back to work or were so tired they left right away for their bunks. Nellie was like the people he had served in the old country at the sidewalk café in Hamburg leisurely sipping the wine or drinking the mugs of beer, timing their consumption so that they maximized the stay at a table and yet minimized the amount of money they spent. But here in his own café Karl did not mind. And besides Nellie had money and business was slow in November even with a burial and Karl enjoyed Nellie's company.

"Don't hurry," he said. "It will be awhile until the burial. Finn is still digging the grave by the chapel. Everyone is waiting for Felix. Finn says he is to say the words and—" Karl stopped abruptly, remembering the rumors about Felix and Nellie and what had happened between Felix and Swede and he wondered if Nellie would allow Felix to be there at all. But then Finn seemed in charge anyway.

Nellie smiled a little at this but shrugged and said nothing. Karl move to the stove to cook and Nellie wiped the moisture from the window by her table so she could see anyone who passed. As she waited she looked at the dead tops of last summer's grass scarcely showing now through the snow and between the cracks of the boardwalk. She thought about Father Felix and the late summer four years ago and how he had influenced what had happened in her village and that added to her confusion about Felix especially since his confrontation with Swede under the dock here in Snag Point.

Nellie saw herself warmed in the longgrass that summer, her black hair the only thing showing above the grass in the sunlight. She had liked being there at the highest point above the embankment which was down the beach from her village of Tuluk-On-The-Bay. Tuluk, named after Raven himself because as the legend went the founder of the village, Old Eskaleut, had been lost for days during a summer storm high in the Sheepkill Mountains. Cold and starving, the old man had finally collapsed under a spruce tree to die. Raven had come then to the top of the tree and had scolded him for giving up. And so with a great effort Old Eskaleut had struggled to his feet and following the flight of Raven he had emerged on the slopes leading down to the water which was now named Tuluk Bay.

Old Eskaleut had looked out over the surface of the strange bay and had seen millions of Coho salmon finning and jumping and crowding their way into the mouth of the river to spawn. And it was there he managed to survive on the bounty of the salmon and with the help of Tuluk, Raven himself, the creator of everything. And thus Tuluk, the village, was born and had grown into a place of true people without the intrusion of the foreigners who had come to Snag Point to live.

Tuluk lay north and west of the village of Snag Point. It was a reasonable distance to travel into Snag Point from Tuluk if one desired the things offered here: guns and ammunition and sugar and flour—and whiskey. In winter it was only three days by dogteam if the snow were not too deep to traveled through the saddles of the Sheepkill Range. It was easy then to move on down the frozen Chiktok River past the village of Ekok and on into Snag Point.

But by skin boat in the summer or fall it was said that five full days would be needed to round Cape Constantine and Protection Point and to make it on into Snag Point. And that was only if the weather held good for that long. No one could remember the weather in Tuluk-On-The-Bay ever being good for five consecutive days. And so when the villagers spoke of traveling by boat to Snag Point in five days everyone knew this was only an accomplishment to be wished.

To the southwest of her vantage point in the tall grass that summer Nellie remembered seeing the purple humpback of Crooked Island lying on the surface of the water like a foundered Greywhale. Though she could not see it she imagined the one small beach layered with the mahogany bodies of hundreds of great bull walrus who hauled out there in the summer sunshine. Only the males came to Crooked Island as if on a leisurely rest from their duties with the females.

Nellie had never seen them for it was the privilege—some of the older women would say the duty—of the men in the village to approach these docile beasts as they lay sleeping and kill them, take their meat for the village and their ivory for carving, take the walrus skins they stretched over new skeletons made of green birch branches. And then with their newly created *umiaks,* the skin boats which carried them back year after year, they would return to Crooked Island to attack the walrus again.

For two weeks that late summer Nellie had indulged herself in her own privilege, the gathering of dead grass along the embankment for basketmaking but now she paused in her task. The wind caught her hair as she shook her head and allowed the single braid to unbind itself and fall free. And then the wind teased the grass, pushed it flat against the tundra and released it then pushed it flat again when it struggled to stand. Nellie listened to the hissing the summer wind made in the grass. The only other noise was from the gulls as they called first near and then far and with their wings sliced the air on the downwind.

And in her head the basket Nellie would make had become a thing of delicate beauty. Over the years Old Suyuk had taught her well and Nellie would make this one in the ancient way, intricate and tight enough to hold water. She would embellish it with the *Inua*. She would capture the Spirits in the complex designs and in the arrangement of the dyed grass and the pieces of seal gut dyed with the juice of huckleberries and highbush cranberries. When they came to her cabin all the women in the village would envy Nellie's basket and she would grin at them—especially at Old Suyuk.

Nellie did not think of this as a duty either, the gathering of the dead grass in late summer, for the real work was finished now. All summer the village had been a riot of activity anticipating the arrival of the salmon which spawned on the shallow beaches in front of the village. But only a few silver-colored backs of the sockeye had finned the surface of the water by the first weeks of July and many of her people were predicting a poor run of fish and a poor catch and a hungry winter. And by the third week of the month of July the elders were talking of moving their gillnets to another bay to the north in hopes of better fishing.

"They will not come this late," Old Suyuk had said as she sat on the beach next to her husband Aiyut. The two watched the surface of the water. Old Suyuk was the eldest and most respected of the women even more respected than Old Maruluk who was herself a Shaman and who communicated with Raven and the other spirits.

"They have never come this late," she continued. "We have to do something or we'll spend a very hungry winter."

"Three days," Aiyut said. "I will wait only three more days and then take a group around the north point and into Nuna'vik Bay. The coho come into the Nuna'vik River to spawn but always later than the sockeye."

He turned and looked steadily into the faces of the others who listened but remained silent. "There will be fish there even this late," Aiyut declared.

Then he turned back to Old Suyuk and talked briefly with her about action. The two said nothing more for three days. Each morning they emerged from their log house beside the beach and they walked down the slope to the edge of the water. But they did not speak again. They sat alone on muskeg next to the beach like a pair of nesting geese and stared at the water without speaking, without eating and then after the closing darkness had left only a grey sheen on the surface of the water, the silhouette of Old Suyuk would stand first and return to the log cabin and then shortly after the shadow of Aiyut would follow.

The two old people had lived together as man and wife for over sixty years in the traditional bond arranged by their parents without the consent of the two youths. But like all of the traditions, many which had grown out of the necessity for survival of the people, there had been no questioning of the arrangement and the bonding had endured. It seemed to everyone in the village that they now communicated without speaking.

"The sockeye will come," Nellie's brother Alexie had said. "I think we should just stay here and wait. They'll come."

"But they are not coming," Aiyut finally said after three days of silence. "What do you know about it, Alexie Napiuk? When have you ever been right about it?"

Alexie recognized Aiyut as an important elder who had taken leadership from Old Eskaleut his dead father and the founder of the village. And Alexie also knew Aiyut as an *umialik,* one who owned an umiak, the walrus skin hunting and fishing boat. But more than an owner of an umiak Aiyut was the most knowledgeable hunter and fisherman in the village and like Old Suyuk he too could not be questioned. But also like Old Suyuk, Aiyut was stubborn. And when Aiyut made up his mind he seldom changed it.

But Alexie was stubborn too and when Aiyut convinced the other men to leave the village and search for fish, Alexie had stayed even though at sixteen he would be the oldest male to remain in the village with Nellie and Old Suyuk and Maruluk and the other women and children.

"Stay with the women," Aiyut had said to Alexie scornfully as he pushed his umiak away from shore with the help of a silent Old Suyuk. "You probably should make baskets anyway, Alexie."

For another two days Suyuk had sat on the riverbank staring in the direction that Aiyut and the other men had gone. Maruluk finally persuaded her to go inside her house. But no one could force her to eat and Maruluk became convinced she was possessed now with some kind of evil and so she cautioned everyone to avoid her.

But Alexie had been right those four summers past. Early in the last week of July the sockeye did arrive. More sockeye that anyone in the village had ever seen and Alexie had mobilized the children and the old women and had set out the older tattered nets the men left behind. But even with the old nets more fish were caught than the people could handle and so the nets had to be taken in from the river while everyone split the fish and draped them over the cottonwood racks to dry.

Everyone except Old Suyuk.

Old Suyuk had not picked up her *ulu,* her curved knife, to help. And she would not offer her *ulu* to anyone else and no one dared to approach her as she squatted on the tundra and scowled at the others as they worked the nets. It was as though Old Suyuk felt the women and children should not be doing this thing without the men of the village. She did not say this but word went through the village that without Aiyut, Old Suyuk thought the effort was cursed and somehow evil would come of it. And though Old Suyuk had not yet hindered the work she had not participated and the others felt uneasy about this also.

To Nellie it was a sad thing to watch, for Old Suyuk had been the most influential on her. More than anyone else, even more than her own mother who had borne eleven children and had not had time to show Nellie all the things she should, Old Suyuk had taught Nellie about her culture. Old Suyuk had shown her how to sew the small furs of the ground squirrel into a full-length parka using only the thicker skin of the backs.

"Which is tougher?" Old Suyuk had often said to young Nellie. "This part of the animal or this part of the animal?" She had pointed first to Nellie's back and then to her front, tickling her stomach with her finger until she laughed with delight. "That is why you use only the skin from the back," she repeated and Nellie understood.

Nellie had learned how to conceal the small pouch for an infant inside the warmth of the fur parka. And in time Old Suyuk had even told Nellie about how one creates the infant itself to place inside the pouch. Nellie had understood that too but she had ignored the suggestions of the older women about an arranged marriage.

"I can weave a basket tight enough to hold water," Nellie had said. "But I don't think I can weave a bond with a man tight enough to hold forever especially if I have no choice about which man."

But Nellie ached to fill the pouch in the parka. There was no way she could rationalize the emptiness both inside the parka and inside her heart. She wondered if she had ruined her chances for filling the emptiness by her carelessness in making the parka. Old Suyuk had warned her about mixing the skin of the land animal with the skin of the sea animal in her garments. She scolded her when Nellie would forget to wash her hands between handling the seal gut in making patterns in the baskets and then working on the squirrel parka. "It is bad to mix the work with the seal gut and the work with the squirrel skin," Old Suyuk said.

"Why?" Nellie had questioned but she asked in a polite way and would never consider disobeying Old Suyuk.

"Because the land and the sea are guarded by very different *Inua* and it is not good to blend the two," Old Suyuk had explained and that was enough.

But late that summer, which Nellie now remembered with much pain, she could not ask Old Suyuk the questions which came to her mind. She could not go to her for the advice about what to do with the problem she now had, for Old Suyuk herself was the problem. Ever since Alexie and Nellie and all the villagers had caught and dried the salmon Old Suyuk had shunned Nellie and had turned away from her now each time Nellie approached to talk. Old Suyuk had become the focus of the entire village and though no one spoke of her or to her it was agreed that something must be done.

"What can we do?" Nellie finally asked Maruluk standing at the old Shaman's door. Nellie turned her head, waiting for the invitation to enter before looking directly at a Shaman. Her eyes caught the movement of her brother Alexie by the river. Now that the volume of fish had dwindled, the work of splitting and drying them had slowed. But each evening that summer Alexie had walked around and around the full racks of fish, his pride in helping to fill the bellies for the winter beaming in is face. He would stop just at dusk and sit by the river and think but then his face would burn when he remembered Aiyut's final remark to him in front of the other men.

Alexie eagerly awaited the return of the men and he wanted to be on the beach when they arrived to watch their faces as they saw all the heavy fish racks. And he especially wanted to see the face of Aiyut, to see if it burned like his own because if he and the other men did not return with fish Aiyut would be disgraced and Alexie would be honored. Alexie did not like to think about it too long because it frightened him but he wondered if they might honor him as an *umialik* and even give him old Aiyut's boat.

"We can talk about her," Maruluk said to Nellie at her door late that evening. "Come inside."

Nellie looked at Maruluk and entered her cabin. She stood, waiting to be asked to sit. Nellie smiled and nodded to Mi'sha, the old woman's granddaughter who sat braiding her hair for bed. Nellie remembered the girl had stopped returning smiles and seemed to drift through the days. Even with all the activity of putting up the fish on the beach Mi'sha had not joined in the laughter and the chatter like the other children. Nellie decided it must be because she had entered her cycles as a woman and she remembered how she had been frightened herself as a girl. She had worried about the taboos for a long time after Old Suyuk had told her of certain restrictions she must now follow like the wearing of mittens outside during summer.

"Leave us, Mi'sha," Maruluk said.

The girl obeyed retiring to her bed in the darkness at the rear of the cabin as though she preferred that part of the room.

"She is a good girl," Nellie said to Maruluk as if apologizing for the girl's dour attitude. "And she is lucky to have you."

Nellie thought about how she too had been lucky to have someone. And she remembered the influenza and the death of Mi'sha's parents but she did not mention it. There had been many others who had endured the pain of losing loved ones—even some of Nellie's own brothers and sisters—but no one talked about the epidemic any longer for fear that the mention of it might bring it back.

"I do not know if she lives in the shadows or in the light," Maruluk said. "I worry about her."

"And I worry about Old Suyuk," Nellie said. "It is certain that she is living in the shadows now. She will not even speak to me."

"Yes and Suyuk also," Maruluk said to show that she did think about others besides Mi'sha but she did not offer advice.

"Do you have something which you can do? Some way to bring Old Suyuk back to us?" Nellie said.

Maruluk was silent for a long time, reluctant to answer Nellie's question. She did not know if she should tell Nellie that she had wavered in her own belief in the *Inua*. She did not know if she should discuss the sessions she had begun with Father Felix from Snag Point. She did not know how Nellie would accept the meetings she and Mi'sha had attended when they had traveled with Aiyut this past winter through the Sheepkill Range and down the frozen Chiktok to the village of Ekok. Maruluk wondered if she should show Nellie the words inside the black book she had concealed under her bed, words Father Felix had given to her saying they were far more powerful than the *Inua*. But Maruluk could not read the words and she needed the priest's help in understanding it all. She knew Nellie could not help.

"I could call on the *Inua*," Maruluk said, "and see if they would enter Old Suyuk and take away the pain in her mind."

Nellie said nothing. She sat looking at the Shaman, trying to show neither encouragement nor hesitation but secretly she hoped that Maruluk would do this thing.

"But perhaps we should just wait for the men to return. Wait and see what Aiyut and the council of elders say we should do as a village. She has done nothing yet which is serious."

Nellie's face hardened into desperation. "But something is wrong!" she cried and then regretted the outburst.

Maruluk assumed a look of tolerance, the look Nellie had seen and remembered on the Shaman's face years ago when she had been asked to help rid the village of the influenza. Maruluk had called on the Spirits then and most of Nellie's family had been wiped out. She had called on the Spirits again and Mi'sha's family had fallen to the epidemic. The Shaman had called on *Inua* again and again and still the people fell. Finally she stopped the pleading and simply told the village: *This is the way it is to be.* And the people had accepted it. And eventually the influenza had left them because that was also the way it was to be.

"Yes," Maruluk said finally giving in to the look of desperation on Nellie's face. "Yes, something is wrong with Old Suyuk and it is my duty to try."

Nellie said nothing further. She rose and went to the door but did not look back. She knew Maruluk would do as she said and Nellie would not be permitted to see how she did this.

Outside Nellie saw the silhouette of Alexie against the thin light of midnight, which now glazed the surface of the bay with a muted sheen. He sat by the edge of the water and Nellie went toward him and stopped behind him without speaking.

"I hope they come today," Alexie said without turning. He knew it was Nellie because he had seen her enter Maruluk's cabin and the other villagers had already gone inside for the night.

"The sky is clear," Nellie said avoiding the mention of Old Suyuk or of her visit to Maruluk or of the fish hanging in the racks behind them. She sat down beside her brother. "If they travel this way today they will have good weather."

"They'll see I was right," Alexie said giving Nellie the invitation to talk about something other than good weather. He picked up a flat stone from between his knees and dropped it from one palm and back into the other. Nellie said nothing. Almost twice his age she still honored the belief that men, even sixteen-year-old men, should be the aggressors and they should bring up topics of importance. Still she could not help but smile in the darkness at Alexie's youthful arrogance.

"Right about what?" Nellie teased.

"You know what," Alexie said. "And they will too when they see all the fish."

"And if they have fish also?"

Alexie had not dwelt on this possibility. For days he had seen himself in the bow of Aiyut's umiak with his own crew paddling out to Crooked Island to kill walrus, leaving Aiyut behind to make baskets.

"They won't find fish this late in Nuna'vik Bay," he said.

"You speak as though you hope they will not find fish Alexie."

He said nothing but he worked the stone faster from one hand to the other. For a long while Nellie too was silent, listening to the night waves come in softly on the beach and then she said, "Maruluk will help us with Old Suyuk."

"Help us?"

"She will call on the *Inua.*"

"Ha! That should be a great help," Alexie said and tossed the stone toward the bay.

It skipped across the surface—he counted four times—and then it sank into the black water.

"Was it truly wrong, Alexie? Is this what Old Suyuk is trying to say?"

"You mean to take the fish without the permission of the others?"

"Yes."

"How can that be wrong? Can it be wrong to put away food? Can it be wrong to do something for the good of the village even without the blessing of—" Alexie stopped. He felt his face burning again and this time the fire was spreading down his neck and gripping his throat. He sucked in the night air and spoke calmly again. "Did she say she would call on the book too?"

"The book?"

"Yes. The book she hides under her bed. The one she calls The Word. Did she say she would use it in trying to help Old Suyuk?"

Nellie did not know what Alexie meant so she said nothing, waited for him to continue.

"I have not been under Maruluk's bed if that is what you are thinking," he explained. "Mi'sha told me."

"Mi'sha?"

"Yes," he said and then quickly before Nellie could ask, "She has been following me."

"Maruluk has been following you?" Nellie teased.

"I did not mean Maruluk, you know that. I meant Mi'sha, she has been following me. She followed me again today all the way across the tundra into the foothills," he said and then added quickly. "I was checking my snares."

"And what were you snaring, Alexie?" Nellie said and grinned into the darkness.

"Mi'sha told me about the book," Alexie said ignoring Nellie's teasing but he was thinking about that day and how the sun had been warm on the tundra and how he had chased Mi'sha. And he remembered how she had been laughing and running and she had tripped and fallen and he had pretended to stumble also and fell down beside her. They lay close looking up at the sky for a long time before they talked and he smiled when he remembered the talk. But then Alexie scowled when he thought about how it had ended.

"And about the priest," he hissed. "She told me about the priest Father Felix and about how she and Maruluk have been meeting him. And she told me about the teaching. He gave Maruluk the book but she cannot even read it."

"Well, it does not matter," Nellie said. "Maruluk said she would ask the *Inua* to help Old Suyuk and I believe her."

"And then she cried when I ask her about the teaching," Alexie continued as though he needed to talk about it.

"Why?" Nellie said.

"I don't know. She would not say. She just said she hated the teaching and then she ran from me. Maybe she is afraid that Maruluk is believing the words. I don't know."

"Well, it isn't our concern," Nellie said and stood. "Maruluk is wise and she knows what is best for Mi'sha. And she knows what is best for Old Suyuk and the village also."

She looked up the slope at the silhouettes of the cottonwood racks heavy with split fish. "We were right in doing this, Alexie, no matter what Old Suyuk may be thinking. We just have to explain it to her and make her see that it can't be wrong even without the men and their blessing. Maruluk will know how to do this."

"I do not have to explain anything," he said. "It would be stupid to let the fish go up the river without catching them. Even Aiyut must know that though he will not admit it even if he returns with an empty boat."

"Well, he will not return in the middle of the night," Nellie said. "And besides the tide is leaving. If they do come tomorrow it will be on the afternoon flood. Come on inside, Alexie. You can sit here all day tomorrow if you wish. And the next and the next but they will not be coming tonight."

She waited for a moment and then turned and went toward the dark shadow of her own cabin at the end of the village, empty of brothers and sisters and father and mother now. Empty of all except Alexie. Nellie lay in her bed for a long while thinking first of Alexie and then of Old Suyuk. Just before she slept she thought she heard and owl outside but she was too drowsy to be sure. Maruluk would take care of it she thought and then she fell asleep. She was asleep a long time before Alexie decided to come in.

Sounds of excitement from the village awakened her the next day, loud voices which sounded like screaming and cheering. Nellie first checked Alexie's bed and saw it had been slept in but was now empty. She quickly dressed and went outside into the coolness of the morning air. No one else was in sight. At first Nellie thought the men must be returning and the other women and children were down on the beach calling to them as they approached. Alexie would be there waiting to see their faces.

And then she saw the tide was still ebbing, a long runout which was exposing the mudflat in front of the village. The men could not be returning yet she thought and she quickened her pace around the other cabins and toward the beach.

She saw Alexie first, standing silent and staring at the fish racks. Then she saw the crowd of women and children closer to the water but they had stopped their screaming and shouting and were staring toward the exposed mudflat. Nellie ran to Alexie and saw his body was immobile, his eyes locked on the fish racks Nellie noticed were almost devoid of fish. Only a few strips of dried flesh still draped like flags of defeat from the cottonwood poles. Nellie stopped beside her brother and stared.

"Gone," Alexie whispered shaking his head. "All the fish, all the work."

"But why?" Nellie said. "Where?"

"In the mud," Alexie said and laughed bitterly. "She's thrown them all onto the mudflat." He turned his eyes toward the others standing far down on the beach where the gravel became mud. Nellie did not ask who; she did not need to. She touched Alexie's hand and left him. She walked slowly down the beach toward the crowd. At first she did not look at the mudflat but instead searched the faces of the others as if the reflection in their eyes could tell the truth. It was there in each tired eye, in each drawn face, the disappointment and disbelief. But in some of the faces Nellie saw the shock was changing to fear.

All except Old Suyuk who stood smiling out at the mudflat which had sucked into itself the entire offering of fish that the old woman had tossed onto the mud. The slick sticky surface was pocked with hundreds of soft indentations where yet another dried salmon had first landed and then sunk below the surface. Nellie went to Old Suyuk. She knew there was nothing to be done about the fish now. There was no way to refill the cottonwood racks this late in the season.

But Nellie also knew what it could mean for the village, a winter without sufficient food, especially if the other men had not found fish. And Nellie knew the look she had just seen in the faces of the villagers and the look she had seen on Alexie. But she could say nothing to Old Suyuk. She stood in front of the old woman who swayed left and right and stared through Nellie and out toward the mud. Nellie watched her with a look of pity. The eyes she always knew as black and alive were now ashes in a face which showed no remorse, no fear, only an innocence Nellie now understood. She reached out and touched the old face with the tips of her fingers, ran them over the wrinkles and across the lips which were parting and closing in little silent puffs of air. Then Nellie took Old Suyuk's hand and turned her back up the beach toward the village. The old woman turned stiffly and followed Nellie's gentle urging as she shuffled her feet in the gravel.

But the crowd led by Maruluk had now moved down the beach. They stopped in front of Nellie and Old Suyuk and formed a semicircle blocking their progress.

"I have done as you asked, Nellie," Maruluk said. "I believe it was too late for the *Inua*. But the old ways can be strengthened with the new." She looked at Old Suyuk and Nellie saw something different now in Maruluk's face, a determination that had not been there the previous evening.

"And it is not too late for this," Maruluk said and she held up the book the priest had given her. "I have also consulted this and have been given direction. With it and with the strength of the *Inua* we can be certain." Maruluk opened the book and pulled it to her breast. She closed her eyes and murmured. The crowd watched her as if witnessing some secret ritual never seen before. Maruluk then began to move toward Nellie and Old Suyuk, the book still clutched tightly to her breast.

"Follow," Maruluk said to the others. She continued walking and murmuring to herself. The others kept the semicircle intact and followed Maruluk closing in on Nellie and Old Suyuk. Nellie looked at the crowd, into the faces of Alexie and Mi'sha and all the others and she saw them not as distinct and individual but instead as a collective image of a halfbeing, a *tunerak,* grim and angry. The image swelled behind Maruluk as though she were the head and the mind of this single beast of prey. Nellie dropped Old Suyuk's hand when the crowd finally stood surrounding them. There was no sound except the slapping of the floodtide which had begun moving toward the beach covering the mudflat and soon would cover the entire summer efforts of the people of Tuluk-On-The-Bay.

But then Nellie recognized the other sound which was close enough and distinct enough to understand, the voice of Maruluk whispering in the ancient language of their people.

*"Kikituk, kikituk, kikituk, kikituk,"* the Shaman chanted. *"Kikituk, kikituk, kikituk, kikituk."*

Nellie knew the word. She backed away from Old Suyuk. "No," Nellie whispered but Old Suyuk continued to stare as though unaware of Nellie or the Shaman or the villagers. Then Nellie pushed her way through the wall of people and stood on the beach above and behind them. She was outside the semicircle now but Old Suyuk was trapped in the center. "No," Nellie pleaded.

But the crowd moved toward Old Suyuk forcing her back toward the mud and the incoming tide. Then Old Suyuk stumbled onto the gravel. She forced herself up and backed away until she was off the rocks and standing in the soft mud. And still the crowd came silent except for Maruluk who continued to cling to the book and chant faster and faster, *"Kikituk, kikituk, kikituk, kikituk."*

Old Suyuk looked down at her feet in the mud and then turned her face up to Nellie who had dropped to her knees on the gravel beach. Nellie looked back at her but she knew it would do no good to get up. She saw Old Suyuk blink her eyes for the first time that morning. Then Old Suyuk lowered her chin and turned her back on Nellie and the others. She turned her back on her village of Tuluk-On-The-Bay. With a great effort Old Suyuk worked her way as far out into the mudflat as she could. When she was up to her knees in the sucking mud she stopped and stood silent and straightened her back to the people who watched her from the beach, watched and waited grimly for the water to lap first at her legs and next at her body, then her shoulders, her chin, her lips. And finally without so much as a whimper of protest from Old Suyuk the cold water of Tuluk Bay covered her head.

One by one during the floodtide the villagers turned and walked back up the beach to their cabins. One by one they passed Nellie, paused and looked down at her sitting on the gravel. And in each face Nellie saw contempt except in the eyes of Maruluk and Mi'sha where she saw only confusion. The faces of the other villagers showed no remorse for Nellie. She had not joined them and their scorn would never leave her. The only way Nellie could ever escape it would be to leave the village herself.

The last to come away from the beach that day was Alexie. He stood watching the water, which now concealed the old woman and covered the hopes of his early rise to a place of importance in the village. When he passed Nellie sitting on the beach Alexie did not stop or even look at her.

"Alexie," she called after him. "Why don't you skip some rocks, Alexie? Across the water. Why don't you see if you can reach her with the flat stones, Alexie? Maybe you can skip them over her head now?"

But Alexie Napiuk did not answer his sister. And as he had hoped the men returned on that same floodtide. But their boats were heavy with fish. And though Aiyut had wailed and cursed when he found out about Old Suyuk he knew he could not direct his anger at Alexie nor Maruluk nor any other villager. He knew that anyone—even himself—who threatened the survival of their people should be punished severely. And as Maruluk had said about death and about that other floodtide, the influenza which had covered her people once before, *This is the way it is to be.*

And so this was also the way it was to be for Nellie Napiuk. She no longer felt a part of Tuluk-On-The-Bay. She no longer dealt with the splitting of fish and the making of baskets though she still thought of gathering the grass and dyeing the sealgut in the way Old Suyuk had shown her.

And since the killing of Old Suyuk she had not thought about death, only about burials like the one which was about to take place now in Snag Point. And rarely did she think about filling the small pouch in her fur parka because she no longer wore the parka. Like the birth of a child the trip back to Tuluk-On-The-Bay was a fantasy Nellie allowed herself only on those rare occasions when she did look at the parka in its wooden box under her bed. Death and birth, birth and death: Nellie had come to view the final act of living the same as she did the first, each simply the movement from one darkness into another.

And now in Heine's café as she looked at the tops of last summer's grass above the snow, Nellie wondered about Maruluk and Mi'sha and what had become of them and the teaching. She wondered if they had worked out the difficult parts of learning the word and if Mi'sha had brightened with her full growth into womanhood. And she thought again about Father Felix and wondered if it had truly been his teaching that had influenced the killing of Old Suyuk. Perhaps it would have happened anyway even without Maruluk and the book pressed to her breast. Perhaps it would have been the same a thousand years ago.

But she remembered how fierce was her hatred for Father Felix on that black morning when she first arrived in Snag Point, self-exiled from Tuluk-On-The-Bay. Old Ayiut himself had carried her all the way through the mountain pass in his dogsled. Nellie had bundled her native sewn clothing and stuffed it into the infant pouch inside the parka and left the village on snowshoes soon after the first heavy snow. She was determined to walk all the way over the mountain pass and into Snag Point. Old Ayiut knew Nellie had not participated in the killing of Old Suyuk and when he learned of her disappearance he feared she would die in the mountains without shelter or food so he harnessed his dogs and caught her in the pass. But she refused to return with him because she knew no one but Ayiut wanted her there anyway. He finally urged her into the sled and removed her snowshoes and covered her with a caribou skin, promising to take her into Snag Point. Even in the darkness he made his way through the mountains. But the old man stopped the dogs on the rise just outside Snag Point and without a word, gestured for Nellie to get out. Confused, she said, "Have you become angry?" But Old Ayiut only shook his head. "Then why here?" she said.

*"Kassaqs,"* was all he said and pointed to the structure just below where quivering orange rectangles of candlelight fell like fire through the windows and onto the snow. Nellie looked and understood. Other firelight from a late dawn cast their long shadows onto the snow as Old Ayiut tied the snowshoes again to Nellie's feet and stood. She moved to him and tried to speak but nothing came so she reached into his hood and touched his cold cheeks and for a few moments warmed

them with her palms. Without further words the old man turned his team and left Nellie to whatever fate she had chosen.

And so it was Felix himself who welcomed Nellie into Snag Point on that dark winter morning four years ago. Inside the ancient chapel he knelt beneath the altar he had rebuilt with his own hands. In the earlier hours of that morning he had risen from his bed and paced the floor, awakened from the same old nightmare with fire inside his mouth and ears and erupting from his eyes, fire inside his mind, fire consuming his garments and sputtering against his flesh accompanied by a cacophony of laughter from Timothy Raisin and the entire congregation of the First Gospel Church and even his grandmother, a horrid and feverish cackling from the old woman and then a sudden silence broken only by the clicking sound of her breath entering and leaving her throat as she slept in her rocking chair with the big Bible in the center of the doily on the little oak table against the wall where the boy Felix had abandoned it that final day having read her to sleep.

Only the altar wine could extinguish the flames when Felix awoke like this. And so he had quickly drained one bottle and opened another and in the darkness filled his entire collection of candelabra with votive candles which he then ignited one by one filling the little chapel with fire he could see, the substance of light Felix knew he could control if he chose. And in his hands he held the painted wooden panel no larger than his grandmother's Bible, an icon he had taken from the church in Seattle and secreted among his other religious artifacts like the trunkful of golden candelabra. As he knelt he spoke to the images on the panel, the painted flesh of the child, yellowed and cracked with age but still cherubic and naked and cradled against his mother's breast rising and falling with her own breath in the candleglow, sweet holy breath of each. Felix kissed the painting, his eyes misting. When he lifted his lips he reached to touch those of the Madonna and was startled by the wetness of her cheek, her own tears flowing miraculously from the wood.

He rose and clutched the icon to his breast and spun round and round dancing with the sheer ecstasy of being both inside the fire and outside the fire. At the door to the chapel he stumbled and caught himself against the jamb, nauseous from the twisting roomful of smoking wicks and the cheap port inside his belly. He propped the painting against the wall, slapped opened the door and sucked in the cold morning air just as Nellie had reached the corner of the chapel outside. Startled she stopped and jerked around.

Felix wavered in the doorway, his image cut from the opening by candlelight which projected his silhouette onto the snow in front of her. Nellie raised her arms, pressing to her breasts the bundle of clothing she had stuffed inside her parka.

"A child?" she heard Felix whisper in amazement as she leaned away from him. "I have seen visions tonight but this is not what I expected, this is truly a miracle from the blackest of nights. Come in, woman, bring your child please, warm yourselves inside."

Though she had never met him she knew immediately who this was. Nellie tried to step backward but lost her balance on the snowshoes and fell into the snow. Felix was immediately on her, trying to help her secure the child. Nellie panicked. She screamed when she felt Felix's hand probing her parka.

"Hush," Felix hissed. "You'll wake the whole village. I'm only trying to help with the child, don't you know I'm the priest, I'm—"

"Get away from me!" Nellie cried and she could smell the wine on his breath and the smoke from his clothes as if he had stepped from a pit of fire himself. "There's no child, there's nothing for you to touch. I want nothing of your words."

"But who—" Felix stepped back confused and startled by the hostility of this strange woman lying twisted in the snow. He moved back and stood leaning against the wall of the chapel. The light now flooded her face and he could see her hatred. Nellie reached inside her parka and pulled out the bundle of native sewn garments.

"And I will wear these no longer." She spat on the bundle and tossed them at his feet. "You cannot trick me like the others who wear them." She turned and left Felix standing bewildered in the darkness.

It was soon afterward that Nellie found her own place in Snag Point but it was without the assistance of clergy. She had hidden the parka under her bed and like all the others in Snag Point assumed her own identity and her own way of dressing.

Still Nellie could not hate Felix now as she did then, not after what he had tried to do for her with Swede. And she thought about Alexie but she was past her bitterness toward him too. She longed to see him and know he was well and happy. And she smiled when she thought about Alexie and Mi'sha chasing each other across the tundra.

Karl worked at the stove behind Nellie and she smelled her breakfast in the tight air of his cafe. The bacon hissed and spattered grease on his arm as he worked it with the spatula. Nellie shut her eyes and imagined the hissing sound as the wind in the deep grass at Tuluk-On-The-Bay.

But Karl did not know this sound. Instead he heard it as the white sound of a thousand cheering voices. He remembered it from the time following the great World War when he had visited the arena at Barcelona. Like a *muleta* Karl draped the dishtowel over his arm to protect it from the sputtering grease and then moved aggressively back to the stove. It was the moment of Truth. Lining it up with a squinted eye Karl sighted carefully down its full length and then stabbed at the bacon with the spatula. The crowd roared again and he stepped aside, the horns passing only inches from his stomach, hard and flat inside the silken *Traje de Luces,* the Suit of Lights. Defiant he turned his back on Death and then as if he commanded the huge chorus of voices, Karl held one arm up to the crowd with his palm arched gracefully upward as he slowly made a pirouette, the screams rising and then fading in the wake of his hand as it passed along the perimeter of the grandstands. Then with his shoulders still thrust back in victory Karl strode like a ballet dancer to Nellie's table and placed the bacon and hot cakes before her. Instead of the small dab he usually put on a saucer for the breakfast customers he put the whole can of butter in front of Nellie next to a large tankard of hot syrup. One could afford to be generous in victory.

Nellie looked at the dead grass through the window and ate slowly, remembering, remembering. Karl sat at the counter and watched her. He wondered how she ever managed to eat with the grin. It never left her face. He had even tried it himself, tried to chew and swallow hot cakes and syrup without once touching his lips together. Impossible. He always drooled down his chin when he tried. How did she do it?

Look at her, he thought. She even smiled when she drank coffee from the heavy mug. Nice gal that Nellie, always smiling. Even when she was grieving.

# EIGHT

It had been dusk when Felix stumbled up the bank from the frozen Chiktok River and into the trees. Even now in the failing light he could see that soon he would break out into the clearing Finn had mentioned. From there Finn had said it would only be a short distance over the ridge and into the village of Snag Point. It made the pain in his feet almost bearable when he thought about being in his own cozy little chapel on the bluff above the village. He thought about washing his shredded feet in a pan of warm water, perhaps having a little wine and he wondered if Finn had made it past Black Slough and on into Snag Point with the body of Swede. He grew a little angry when he thought about the possibility of missing a funeral.

The whole plan to take The Word upriver into the villages had been a mistake to begin with. Felix decided he was not meant to be a traveling man of God. He knew nothing about the trails and the ways of surviving. He knew only about The Word and the language and teaching salvation. They should have been coming downriver to him in Snag Point. But once he had begun, it had been like a drug, especially with the girl.

The snow was deeper in the trees and Felix began breathing hard, fighting the snowshoes which tugged and twisted his feet. "I have to rest." He stopped, gasping for air. He looked around for somewhere to sit. Just ahead, a deadfall blocked his path. He struggled toward the inclined tree and then reached up and pushed on it but it would not move. Felix turned around, dug his snowshoes into the snow, crouched and raised his back against the dead tree. Suddenly it gave way and crashed into the snow with Felix lying backward astraddle it, the tails of the snowshoes driven deep into the snow. He could not move. He struggled to free his feet but the pain became unbearable and he was wet with sweat.

"Got to stop," he wheezed. "I'll be okay if I just stop and rest first." As he did this Felix thought about the island and the fruit and the cathedral again and he became warmer. But then he thought about fire and burning and even in this cold he could feel all the heat of Texas again. He would never admit it to Finn or Marvin but he did have fears about ever returning. It made no difference where he was, Felix's memories were with him whether in Texas or some godforsaken frozen part of the world.

He remembered Timothy Raisin and the congregation and his grandmother and even though his salvation had come outside the walls of the First Gospel Church he wondered how much they had all been responsible for his final plunge. But more than Raisin or the parishioners or even his own grandmother it had been what happened with Mattie across the railroad tracks that finally opened up the mysteries of true salvation for Felix all those years ago in Texas.

He had delivered the newspapers to Mattie. It was a route he had taken over from her nephew Verily. "I'm gonna win me a train ride," Felix had boasted to Verily when he had taken over the route.

"What ride? There ain't no train ride," Verily said, trying to sound blasé but he was beginning to wonder if maybe he had been too quick to give up his route.

"The *Fort Worth Times Herald* is giving a free ride on the Texas Line to the kid that builds up his route the most by Christmas. A free ride all the way into Fort Worth for a whole weekend to see the circus Verily. They got a real mummy there at the circus."

"A mummy?" Verily said.

"Yeah. He's on display there and I'll get to see him. Marvin Crush at the stationhouse told me all about it when I picked up the papers last week. Winning that train ride is why I need this route."

"Yeah, sure, and you'll probably win a couple horses with silver saddles and a big stable to keep them in too. Ain't no such thing in this world as a free ride, Felix. I'll ride these," Verily had said lifting one foot to show his shoe. Felix remembered Verily always wore shoes during the summer even though none of the other kids did. No socks, just shoes.

"They're paid for," Verily said and stomped off down the street happy to be rid of the route.

Each time he crossed the railroad tracks to deliver Mattie's newspaper Felix remembered to look down the single set of rails which stretched without curving straight away into the sand dunes as far east as he could see. He imagined them terminating at Fort Worth, finally coming together there somewhere in that city he had never seen. But Felix would see it soon enough and the circus too just as soon as he won the ride. Felix also had begun to think more about Raisin's theory of parallel lines never coming together. "I could just take that free ride down there right now and prove it to old Raisin," he remembered muttering to himself that day. "If I was to win it. And if old Raisin was here."

But Felix did not have time to test his theory against Raisin's because it was getting late by that part of his route. He did not like going across the tracks in the dark. Felix named this part of his deliveries the Trainride Route; Verily said it was niggertown.

Felix collected from Mattie each Saturday and he had explained about the circus and the mummy. Mattie believed he would win and he had grown to like her very much because he knew she also read the newspaper. That made him feel important. He suspected the others across the tracks did not read the paper though several of them were on his route. Mattie had finally felt secure enough to tell him about her neighbors on one Saturday afternoon when Felix had come to collect. "Ain't a one of them can read and ain't a one of them gonna pay for them papers once they get them. You better collect in advance Felix," she said. "Or you ain't never gonna win that train ride."

She was slipping Felix a quarter through a slit in the screen door as she spoke. Felix took the quarter and gave her fifteen cents back through the hole. Mattie was hidden by the dusty screen and Felix was feeling a little brazen because he could not see her face. "Mattie, you saved?"

Mattie said nothing.

"Well, are you?"

"Course I save, Felix. I got a sock full of bills and a jar of gold coins buried in the back yard."

She laughed. Felix frowned and wiped sweat from his cheek. "No, I mean *saved*, you know by the Lord and all."

"Oh, that kind. Well, sure I am, ain't you?"

"Well, I'm thinking about it but—" He pocketed the dime and thought about Raisin and he looked at his bare feet. Mattie waited for him but he did not finish.

"Hey, Felix?"

"Yeah?" He did not look up. It had become hotter, encouraging the chorus of cicadas in the mesquite trees.

"Sure hot out there ain't it?"

"Yeah, but I guess it ain't so bad."

"Well, I think it must bother us more than it does you. Why don't you come on in anyway, have a glass of cool water, talk." Mattie eased the screen door open and held it. "Besides you ain't gimme my paper yet."

Felix looked up at her and then down the road at the other shacks and he imagined movement in each one behind the tattered curtains. "I dunno."

"Aw hell, ain't nobody gonna say nuthin' about old Mattie and a white boy. You can come on in."

"I better not. I gotta go." He started to leave.

"Would it help if I told you I was a minister? A fully ordained minister of the gospel?"

Felix looked at Mattie for a long while and then smiled. He wanted to chuckle but he decided Mattie might not be joking. She stared back at him, her eyes calm.

"Well okay just a while," he said and handed her the paper. She moved aside and Felix walked in, his eyes slowly growing accustomed to the dark room. Mattie stepped away from him and he lost her gingham dress in the shadows so he followed the *snap-snap* of her slapback shoes on into the room.

"Don't look out at the sunshine or you'll never get used to the darkness," Mattie said but he wasn't sure she was talking to him. "I like it dark in here. Cools it off."

He heard her splash some water into a glass. "You really a preacher?" Felix took the water and sipped.

"Well, I really ain't any more but I sorta was once. I know all about the Bible though. Heck, I'm the one that give Verily's momma that name when he was born. It's from the Bible. You know that part don't you Felix? It goes *Verily, Verily I say unto you, go on down into Egypt and…* well you know the rest, Felix."

Mattie sat next to him on a faded lumpy davenport which had once graced a pullman car belonging to some wealthy railroad baron. She was a large woman and the cushions flattened under her so Felix had to lean away from her to keep his balance.

"I know all about savin' too," Mattie continued.

"Oh yeah?"

"Yeah."

"Well then what's it mean?" Felix said.

"Well it don't mean a lot of things that folks think."

"Well what's it mean to me then?" Felix decided she was evading him.

"It means different things to different people Felix but the main thing is good and evil. That's all, good against evil."

"And that's it?" He was a little disappointed. He had been under the impression from Florence and Raisin that it was far more than that.

"Sure. But you gotta decide for yourself. I mean savin' ain't really something somebody does to you, you gotta make that final leap yourself but it takes a person what knows the difference to help you over the hill."

She fanned herself with the folded newspaper. Felix felt the wisp of air mixed with her body odor and strong perfume. Mattie was quiet. She sat there in the shadows with a secret smile fanning herself and finally she said, "I could do it for you, help you I mean."

"You?"

"Sure, they all come to Mattie." The smile was a grin now full of stained crooked teeth. "Sooner or later."

Felix was not sure what she meant or whether it would be exactly legal for a black woman to save a white boy but it sure would make it easier, just get it over with, get Raisin off his back.

"If you wanted me to," Mattie said.

"Why should I though? I mean even if you could, why should I anyway?"

"Good and evil. Good against evil, Felix, that's all. But you gotta really want it first."

Felix sipped at the cool water and stared out at the sunshine. Long shadows now spilled onto the dirt road away from the shacks. A solitary fat fly buzzed and thumped against the four panes of the single window inside Mattie's shack seeking the brightness. Felix looked back into the room but his eyes could only adjust to the sunlight on the floor of the shack. He saw it was divided into four squares by the shadow of the wooden cross separating the glass panes in the window.

He decided he really did want it, this salvation thing but he was not positive the Lord really wanted him. When he looked back at Mattie he could not see her in the darkness except for the white of her eyes.

"I gotta go," he said rising.

"You sure?" Her voice was gentle, inviting. She sloshed the water in her glass. Felix moved toward the screen door but suddenly stopped.

"Okay then," he said abruptly. "But what do I have to do?"

"Well, first we gotta pray, we gotta kneel down and ask the Lord to accept you." She moved quickly now grasping his hand and pulling him to the center of the room. Before Felix could change his mind she had knelt on the floor and grabbed his other hand, pulling him to his knees facing her. "Now close your eyes and we'll pray. Wipe everything from your mind, everything, and just let it come to you."

Felix shut his eyes and squinted hard to erase his mind.

"Lord, take this child and save him," Mattie whispered. She squeezed his hands hard. "Lord, save him, save him."

She repeated it over and over, her voice rising a little each time until finally she was screaming the words. Just as he had often done in his church Felix opened his eyes to take a peek. If salvation were going to come he wanted to see what it looked like. Mattie had her chin pointed heavenward. Her eyes were closed and sweat dripped from her black glistening chin, trickled down across the tops of her large breasts and disappeared into the top of her gingham dress. A dark patch of moisture stained the front. The breasts were heaving up and down with each chant and finally in a frenzy she dropped his hands and groped for Felix in the shadows, pulling his body against hers. Felix tried to resist but he lost his balance and found himself trapped against her body, his cheek pressed against her bosom as it continued to rise and fall with the words.

"Lord, save him, save him, Lord."

The words echoed in the room. Felix decided that he had better shut his eyes. He would try very hard to picture salvation. But the only vision he could conjure was that of the railroad tracks which were flashing in sunlight now, shining like the chrome cowcatcher on the freight train and Felix saw his own body floating over the crossties which moved in a blur under his feet like spokes on a wagon wheel. He sped over them far faster than he could have run. Still he was being forced and he watched helplessly as they accelerated beneath him and when he looked up, the tracks had stretched to the horizon and beyond endlessly.

Mattie pulled him closer, squeezing him so hard that he was losing his breath. She had one large thigh now between Felix's legs, rubbing against his trousers as she rocked back and forward screaming. Felix wanted to push himself away and breathe but he could not. He felt himself breathing hard as he ran down the tracks, trying to bring them together. Mattie continued to rub against him harder and faster and Felix felt her hot breath on his neck. And then in a blinding flash he felt a tremendous release and behind his eyes he saw railroad tracks come together in an explosion of metal sparks.

With a great effort Felix pushed himself away from her and stood, drained now of his strength. She stopped the chants and sat back on her heels with her eyes still closed, her breath coming in short gasps.

"Mattie?" Felix reached out his hand to help her up but she continued to sway back and forth on her heels, moaning low. "Mattie, you okay?"

Her heavy breathing subsided and she opened her eyes and looked at Felix standing in the sunlight which lay in the four angular squares, distorted now across his body. He saw her eyes drop and slowly Mattie brought her hand up and pressed the tips of her fingers to the sticky dampness that Felix felt soaking the inside of his thigh and running down his trouser leg. He jerked away from her hand, embarrassed.

"Sure, Felix," she said. "I'm okay." Her voice was weary with what seemed like a great sadness to him. "You saved now, boy."

Mattie labored up and moved into the back room without another word. Felix heard the springs of her bed creak and the low moaning continued as if she were in agony. He left her alone, closing the door gently behind him.

Outside, Felix remembered, he had been startled by the lateness. Mattie's sweat had dried to a stiffness on his cheek but he still felt the dampness of his trousers against his leg. He did not look down the tracks when he went back across.

A short time later Felix made up his mind he would leave and he found himself by chance inside the same musty boxcar rumbling north on the Missouri-Kansas line with Phineas Farrow and Marvin G. Crush, all three fleeing from the fire of their separate demons in Texas. Felix had begged and stolen his way across the Northwest, finally stopping in Seattle with Phineas and Marvin because that was as far west as the three could get without a passport. But the other two had deserted Felix there, rid of him for good, or so they believed, until he had sauntered into Snag Point and back into their lives with salvation glowing from his face.

But now as he rested atop the deadfall Felix thought again about Mi'sha also fleeing and he wondered if he had helped her purify her soul. He hoped he had helped her see salvation the same way Mattie had helped him to see the light and he wondered if Mattie would be pleased.

But Felix shoved Mattie and Texas and railroads and salvation from his mind now. He had more critical things to consider, like surviving. He needed to get himself unstuck from the snow, conserve his energy and his wits and walk on into Snag Point. He began to wriggle his feet and though the pain was excruciating he was relieved to find that live flesh was still there. He rocked left and then right and finally fell from the dead tree, freeing one foot as he tumbled into the snow. By the time he worked the other snowshoe free Felix was breathing hard again and sweating even more. He began to shiver a little, every muscle twitching with his effort to keep moving.

He had broken out of the trees and almost crossed the clearing when he saw the dogteam. It appeared at first as a thin line of black dots emerging from the icefog which was moving up from the river. He sucked in several short breaths of cold air almost sobbing when he recognizing it as a dogsled. As it neared he saw the arm of the musher rising and falling with the dogwhip but he could not yet hear its snap. His pulse livened at the thought of riding in a sled, warmed in the basket, perhaps wrapped in a caribou skin. No one could refuse a man of god no matter how much the sled might be loaded.

But the angle of its approach was wrong. Perhaps the musher did not see him. Perhaps he would not stop. *He must make him see.* Felix lifted his arms above his head, shouting in a rasping unintelligible cry. He lumbered toward the dogsled, his lungs aching from the cold. And then in the twilight he saw a curious thing happen. He stopped and watched the dogteam swing in a long arch around the perimeter of the clearing. At first he thought it was coming directly for him but then he saw it continue the arch as if making a huge circle around the edge of the clearing and around himself standing alone in the center. Slowly he pivoted his head and followed the team until finally he had to moved his whole body around in a complete circle to watch them. He had stopped waving his arms because he knew the musher must have seen him by now. Then one of the dogs seemed to break loose from the pack, separate from the others as if he had not been harnessed to the sled. He came straight for Felix who was now backing away from where he stood, stumbling with the snowshoes. Felix finally turned in terror and forced a single word, deep and hollow from his chest. *"Keetuk!"*

He ran as best he could but the tips of the snowshoes caught the deep snow with each step. He imagined the lone dog behind him as a Hound of Hell salivating through its horrible fangs and breathing fire on his neck with his fierce master close behind in pursuit. And then Felix fell and fell and as he did he remembered the panic he had experienced with Mattie and the railroad tracks and he knew he had finally plunged through all barriers and into that black infinity of which old Raisin had spoken, devoid of all hope for true redemption. His lungs were stinging and he saw the tracks with flames licking between the crossties, rushing beneath his feet now tortured with fire instead of ice. Just as Timothy Raisin had predicted, the rails were separated forever and between them, caged for eternity behind the crossties and locked within the flames he saw his own face as a boy, twisted in agony as the skin melted exposing his bleached skull. And then his skull reincarnated into the likeness of the girl Mi'sha but her soft flesh soon withered too and fell from the skull and it became Felix again and then Mi'sha and then Felix once more, the interchange recurring over and over until he could stand it no longer. He wheezed and released a final moan, brought his knees up to his chest and curled into a fetal position. And then Father Felix Manguson lay still.

Tinney, the constant companion of Delbert Demara, was licking the face of the man on the snow when the deputy finally brought his dogteam to a halt.

"Heel, Tinney," he said. "Whoa, you mangy bastards." Delbert kicked at the dogs as he stamped past them toward the figure on the snow. Like Father Felix, Delbert had a peculiar fondness for dramatic entrances and exits.

"What's happening here, Tinney? Good dog. Sit. Stay." Delbert unsnapped his holster and moved his hand toward the pistol butt. Then he cautiously knelt by the figure still motionless in the snow. "Hey, Tinney, it's that preacher Father Felix. Get up, man. What are you doing out here, you'll freeze. Get up." He tapped Felix on the arm and bent closer to see his face in the twilight. "Felix, it's me Deputy Demara. You okay?"

But Felix did not stir. Delbert removed first his mitten and then his black skintight leather glove and put the back of his hand next to Felix's nose. Then he pressed his fingers to the priest's neck, moved them around, felt again. Nothing. "This man's dead, Tinney." He stood and removed his fur hat. "Heart musta give out."

The dog whined.

"Now what the hell was he doing out here?" Delbert put his hat back on and snapped his holster shut. "Poor bastard. Musta thought I was after him or something. Hell, I was only making a quick circle, cooling my dogs down a bit." Delbert sniffed and stared at the body for a moment and then turned to the dog. "Right, Tinney?" He gave the dog a smile and a friendly scuffing of his ears. The dog returned the play with a growl and a mock attack on his master's hands and arms.

"Okay, okay. That's enough." Delbert turned back and looked down at the figure again and shook his head. "Goddammit. Of all the bastards around here, I gotta go and scare hell out of the only preacher in the territory. Look at that face, Tinney. My god you'd think he seen satan or something."

Delbert stared at the body. "Well, ain't no use moving him in the dark." He sighed and looked out toward Snag Point and the spot where the two rivers joined and he thought about the warmth of Heine's Café and about Yael Feldstein and Hard Working Henry probably drunk by now and all the others there. Delbert wondered what they would say about Felix being dead. Then he thought about darkness coming and about crossing the ice. "Icefog's moving in along the river, Tinney. Tell you what old buddy we'll just make camp here tonight and take him down in the morning. What do you say to that, huh?"

He knelt beside the body and scratched the ears of his dog and then he looked at Felix again. "Look how he's just laying there, Tinney, all curled up like that. Now you reckon that's what they call the missionary position?" Pleased with his wit, Delbert chuckled and scratched the dog's ears again.

# NINE

Up on the slope near the chapel Finn stood to his shoulders in the grave. He alternated the use of the pick with the shovel as he labored against the frozen earth. Henry had retrieved a pint of whiskey hidden below the doorstep of the chapel. He was sitting on a small box next to the hole giving encouragement. The fog hung on their shoulders like a shroud. "You sure you don't need no help?" Henry said.

Finn tossed out a shovelful of frozen clods, stopped and leaned on the edge of the hole. He stared at Henry.

"You sure?" Henry repeated and held out the bottle.

Finn shook his head, refusing both. "I told you last night this job was mine. Swede was like a brother to me. It's something I gotta do by myself."

"You know, Finn, I just don't remember you two being so close. I mean not like you and No-Talk."

"Swede and me was close too," Finn said. "Real close. We talked a lot about things."

"What kind of things?"

"Well, things like life and what it's all about and—" He swung the pick.

"And what?"

"And death." Finn crawled out of the grave and sat on the frozen ground with his legs dangling into the hole. Henry joined him on the edge of the grave and offered the whiskey again. Finn took the bottle this time and drank. Both men stared into the hole.

125

"We talked about death and what it would be like to be dead," Finn said.

"What did you decide?"

"We decided it's black over there. That's all."

"Well, maybe it ain't so bad, Finn." Henry hopped down into the grave and sat with his back against the dirt. He looked up at Finn. "Hell, maybe it ain't too bad at all. What made you and Swede discuss it anyway?"

"Well, it was like he knew something was wrong, something was going to happen," Finn said.

"Maybe Keetuk talked to him or something, threatened him," offered Henry. "Or maybe it wasn't even Keetuk at all. Coulda been somebody else for all you know, Finn."

"I don't think so. I think Keetuk just got pissed seeing Swede take all them beaver or something. It's like Keetuk thought they were all his, like he owned this goddamn territory or something. Maybe he just didn't like Swede's looks either. That's what Marv thinks but I dunno. Anyway we talked about other things too."

"Like what?"

"Things. Now come on, get the hell out of that hole. You're making me nervous."

"What kind of things?" Henry persisted and crawled back up to the edge of the grave.

"Things like Nellie. He liked her a lot."

"Nellie?" Henry snorted. "Moonface Nellie? No shit?"

"No shit. He was pretty attached to her. Talked about her all the time. About how he was going to save up a stake and quit trapping and take Moon out of here."

"Where?"

"He never said. Just take her out of here somewhere, anywhere."

"Marry her?"

"No, not that. Leastways he never said marry her. I think he just wanted to get out and he figured Moon needed to get out too. Thought maybe she was being used, being kicked around too much or something. And then all that shit everybody was saying about Felix with her and—"

126

"I think Moon likes it." Henry drained the bottle.

"Likes what?"

"Being kicked around. I seen it a couple of times under the dock. Swede himself was knocking her around once, both of them drunk. She just kept on grinning you know like she does, just kept on grinning and Swede just kept on hitting her and hollering. She finally started crying. At least tears was coming down her face but I'm telling you, Finn, I think maybe she loved it. Anyway, she just kept on grinning all that time."

Finn remembered now about Keetuk's father being a Swede too and Marvin telling about how he had beat the mother.

"Swede done that?"

"Yeah."

"And Nellie just kept on smiling?"

"Yep."

"And he kept on hitting her?"

"Yep."

Finn took the bottle, turned it up. When he saw it was empty he threw it against the bottom of the grave.

"Bastard."

"Hey, I'm sorry," Henry said. "I got more hidden, don't get so riled up."

"I ain't cussing you. Swede actually done that to Nellie, knocked her around like that?"

"Yeah. Lot's of times I think. Only slowed down that once."

"What do you mean slowed down?"

"Well, that one time I'm telling you about, he never finished her off because of Felix."

"Felix?"

"Yeah. Felix saw it and come down under the dock and tried to stop Swede. I was the only other one down there, you know, sorta back in them shadows. See I'd run completely out of whiskey, Finn, and I was looking everywhere under there, scratching around in the dark and—"

"Wait a minute, Henry, wait a minute. Felix stopped Swede?"

"I said he tried."

"What happened?"

"Swede turned on him, beat the shit out of him and all the while Nellie trying to stop Swede from doing it and finally when he was done with Felix he turned back on her again. You remember that don't you, Finn? Remember how Felix was all battered up that time?"

"Yeah, but I thought he had been sniffing around Nellie like he does and Swede just beat hell out of him for it and—"

"So'd everybody else think that."

"Well, why didn't you say anything Henry?"

"To Swede? Hell you know nobody coulda stopped Swede when he—"

"No, I don't mean say something to Swede, I mean tell the rest of us why Felix was all black and blue?"

"Oh, I dunno," Henry shrugged. "I guess because Felix was always after me, you know, all that burning in hell shit and plus it wasn't none of my business. Anyway like I said Felix ain't half bad sometimes like blessing Henry's Cabin and all."

"Why didn't Nellie say nothing?"

"Well you can figure that one out I guess, Finn. Like I'm telling you maybe she liked it."

Finn fell silent, staring down into the hole. Suddenly he got up and jerked out the shovel and the pick. He put them over his shoulder and walked away from the grave.

"Where you going?" Henry said.

"Let's go get him, get this over with."

"What about the grave? This ain't deep enough is it?"

"Deep enough for *si-wash.*" Finn strode off down the slope into the fog.

"But what about Felix," Henry called after him. "Saying them words and us getting everyone together for the burial?" Henry heard a sudden shuffling and a rattling of the pick against the shovel and then Finn's voice still angry coming from below the slope where he had stumbled.

"Goddamn fog. Goddamn lousy bastard." Finn came back to the grave and stuck the shovel in the dirt. "I forgot we'll be needing this later. Dirt comes out, dirt's got to go back in. Come on, Henry, let's go. You round up the others, tell them it's time. Then come to Yael's and help me get that bastard up here."

"Which bastard?"

"The dead one."

Inside his store Yael Feldstein rocked precariously on the shaking stepladder. He extended his short arm as far up the dusty shelves as he could reach and grasped a tin of salmon. Then he stepped down, walked behind the counter and opened the tin and dumped its contents into the trash pail.

It was not that Yael disliked canned salmon although he did prefer the smoked kind with a good bagel. What he needed was an empty can to spit in. He took a tin of snuff from his pocket, tapped on the top, opened it and placed a pinch in his lower lip. Then he sat on the stool at the counter and opened the big inventory ledger and continued his list of items for the summer ship. He had almost finished the figures when Finn burst in.

"Here's your pick. No sense waiting any longer. We're going to take him on up there and put him in the ground, fog or no fog, priest or no priest." Finn brushed passed Yael, stopped and turned. "Deputy or no deputy."

"Fine by me," Yael said without looking up. He brought the salmon can to his mouth, pursed his lips and allowed a long dark stream of tobacco juice to drip into it. "You can take one of them blankets to wrap him in." He looked up at Finn. "But I ain't helping you carry him. I carried him too long like it is." He went back to work on the ledger.

"Nobody's asking you to," Finn said and walked over to him. "Ain't you even coming up?"

"You crazy? Go out in this damned icefog? Catch a death of flu?"

"Hell, it ain't that bad Yael. Besides I figure since Felix ain't showed yet maybe you could say something."

"Say something?"

"Yeah. You know, some words. Something religious."

Yael smiled, spat again. "You got any idea at all what that goddamn Swede was? I mean religion wise? What the hell difference is something religious going to make to a heathen like Swede? Besides that I'm Jewish. Now you don't reckon Swede was a Jew do you?"

Finn thought about it. "Well, we oughta say something." He cut his eyes to the little man and continued. "You know, old Swede, bad as he was, he did leave some pelts, a lot of pelts up there cached with mine so I guess I can do with them as I please now. But then I guess if you can't see your way clear to go up there today and say something Yael maybe I can get Karl or somebody else to."

"Now I didn't say I wouldn't go up to the chapel," Yael said quickly. "I just said it was damned foggy and I was Jewish and I'd have to think about it." He spat again and moved his eyes across the ledger, working the debits and credits against the cache Finn had just mentioned.

"Well?" Finn said and smiled. "You thought enough about it?"

Yael stared at him, worked the snuff against his lip with his tongue. "Okay. But I ain't saying much. Maybe read something from the Old Testament, that's all though."

"Sure Yael, whatever you say will be just fine. Just dandy." Finn moved toward the coal room. "Tell Henry when he comes in I'll be in here with Swe—with the *deceased.*"

Yael didn't answer. Finn turned back. "Yael?"

"What?"

"Don't forget about that Bible." Finn picked up the blanket and closed the door to the coal room behind him. When Henry came in Finn had already wrapped Swede with the blanket and tied the bundle with a rope.

"I got a wheel cart from the cannery," Henry said. "It ain't much of a hearse but it beats dragging Swede up the hill."

"You see any of the others?"

"Yeah. I told Dago and Moon over at Heine's. They're coming. Karl too, closing up for the day at least until after the burial's done. And probably a bunch of kids. Maybe Chubby and some of the others will show too."

"Yael's going to say the words."

"Yael? What's he know about words?"

"He's a Jew ain't he?"

"Well I don't think Swede would like it," Henry offered. "He wasn't too religious anyway and he sure as hell didn't care that much for Yael. What about Felix?"

"Ain't seen hide nor hair of him," Finn said. "And from what you told me I don't think Swede cared much for Felix either. Besides what's the difference? Priest, Jew, what's the difference as long as we get words said."

"Yeah."

"Let's go. You grab the feet."

"Wait." Henry went to the coal box and kicked it twice to expel any mice lurking inside. Then he reached into the coal, dug around and brought out a quart of whiskey.

"Irish," he said and smiled. "Good Irish whiskey. May as well start the wake." Henry pulled the cork and took a long hit and held the bottle for Finn.

"I think I'll wait 'til this is done." He frowned at Henry. "You save me some though, hear?"

"Sure, Finn." Henry took another mouthful, held his head back, gargled then swallowed it. "Ahhh! Picks a man right up." He slammed the cork back in place with the palm of his hand and tucked the bottle up under the blanket by Swede's chin. "I'll just keep it here handy. Let's go."

In the front of the store Finn paused and called to Yael in the back office. "We're going on up now Yael. You coming?"

Yael didn't answer.

"He'll be there," Finn said. "Let's move."

Outside they placed the body on the cart and started up the street toward the chapel, each tugging on the tongue of the wagon. By the time they had reached the grave Henry had stumbled several times and a group of children from the orphanage had fallen in behind the cart, giggling and pointing. Nellie and Dago and Karl were already there but that was all. They were standing in the fog looking soberly at the hole in the ground.

"Ain't deep enough," Dago said. "Dogs'll dig it right up."

"Deep enough for *si-wash,*" Henry said slurring the words Finn had used. He looked at Finn for approval but stumbled and fell again.

Nellie stared at the bundle on the cart and then dropped her eyes to the grave.

"Help us put him in there," Finn ordered.

The men grasped the edge of the blanket and carried the body to the grave. Nellie watched as they held onto the blanket suspending the bundle over the hole. Henry removed the bottle from under Swede's chin.

"On three," Finn said and he looked around to see if the others were ready. "One…two…"

"Wait—" Nellie broke in.

Finn stopped counting and Nellie walked to the graveside. She stood over the bundle a moment as if she were about to say something and then turned her face toward Finn. He could see she was not in deep grief over Swede but he could not be certain what she was feeling because of her grin. And then he saw in her eyes something he had not noticed before, perhaps a bit of relief, perhaps an invitation, he could not be sure. He did know that everything else had suddenly disappeared around her, the mound of frozen clods, the others holding the blanket with the corpse, the kids, everything, and the fog was no longer an ominous gray mist. It had selected Hjalmar the Finn and Nellie Napiuk, encircled them in its diaphanous cloud, lifting their bodies above the mourners, above the grief in an erotic bonding Finn had only envisioned in his dreams. He stared at her from the gray hollow of his eyes and thought about her steambath and wondered if Henry had saved him some whiskey. Nellie stared back at him and wondered if the beaver tail above her stove were still warm. Then Finn dropped his narrow chin exposing the stained row of jagged teeth. Nellie grinned back.

"Goddamn fog." Yael huffed to a halt at the crest of the slope. He immediately opened the Bible and began to read a long passage from the Old Testament. The men had held onto the blanket as long as possible but the weight had become too much for them.

"*Three,*" Finn said before Yael had finished the passage. Finn continued to look at Nellie, ignoring everything else. The sudden release of Swede's weight by the others had caught Henry off balance and he tipped into the grave behind the body. Both thumped against the bottom at the same time, Henry landing on his hands and knees atop the corpse. He looked up when Yael scowled down into the grave at him.

"One at a time if you please," Yael said with scarcely a pause in the passage he was reading.

"Not necessarily," said a voice from the fog behind them. "Easy, Tinney. Sit, stay." Deputy Delbert Demara burst out of the fog and stood with his hands on his hips, legs astraddle. "What the fuck's going on here? Who's in this grave?"

"Well, one thing's for sure," said Henry still slurring the words. He stuck his head out of the grave and took a pull on the whiskey. "I sure ain't planning on staying in here but I reckon maybe Swede is. How about a drink, Delbert?" Henry tried to pull himself out but he could not get a knee up. Karl gave him a hand.

"Well, it's about time we got the law into this," said Finn. Yael kept reading.

"Answer my question," demanded Delbert.

"It's Swede," said Dago. "He's been murdered."

"Murdered?"

"Yes," said Karl. "It's that Keetuk again."

"You got proof this time?" Delbert looked from one face to the next around the grave.

No one looked up except Finn. "Proof enough," he said. "I don't think Swede could have put his axe in his own back."

Not amused, Delbert looked hard at him. "And where were you?"

"On the Mikchalk. Swede was running his trapline and didn't come back. I found him like that with the axe in his back."

"How the hell did he get down here?" Delbert said.

"Me. I towed him down the river, slid him on the ice."

"Oh yeah? Why?"

"I wanted to show you and everbody else," Finn said. "I just wanted to prove I ain't had nothing to do with it. Just like I had nothing to do with No-Talk. Felix seen us up at Ekok. And Marvin, they both seen us. Swede was already dead then and I guess that bastard Keetuk took some women from up there too, at least Felix thinks so. He was pretty shaken when I got there."

"Well, if it's so important to show me, how come you didn't wait to do the burying?"

"We couldn't keep him much longer Delbert. Yael here didn't want him stinking up his store that's all," Finn explained.

Yael kept reading.

"Well, if those are your alibis they're pretty weak Finn. In fact, one of them is so weak he's already dead," said Delbert.

"Marvin?" said Finn.

Delbert shook his head. "Nope not that one."

"Not Father Felix?" said Dago. He crossed himself. Yael stopped reading, shut his Bible.

"Felix?" Henry said. "You mean—"

"Yep. Deader'n a mackerel, as they say. Heart give out, I guess." There was a long silence. Delbert cleared his throat. "I found him laying in a clearing between the rivers and Black Point. Looked like someone had maybe chased him down—maybe that Keetuk, I don't know. I brought him down here on my sled."

Delbert paused and frowned at Finn. "What was that you said about women? What women?" Finn said nothing. "Well, I guess we'll have to dig into that one later. Killing's one thing, stealing women's entirely something else. That crazy bastard has done it up good this time. Hell, they may be dead too or worse." He sighed and surveyed the assemblage around the grave. "But it looks like you guys got this under control anyway. My job's just beginning."

"What are we going to do with Felix?" said Yael. "I ain't keeping no more bodies in my store."

Delbert walked over to the grave. The small group of mourners parted as he approached. He stood at the edge of the hole and looked in. "I already figured that out. Ain't no sense in digging another grave in this goddamn ground." He looked around at the faces and then stared into the fog. "We'll put him in here on top of Swede." Delbert spat on the ground, spun around and stalked off into the fog his hands still on his hips. "I'll go down and get him."

"Felix? On top of Swede?" Henry whispered and through a little smile he took a slow sip from the bottle. Yael sighed, opened the Bible, found a longer passage this time and started to read again. Except for the monotone of Yael's voice the only other sound was the fading foot-steps of Deputy Delbert Demara as he walked back down the slope. "Heel, Tinney," he said. "Heel."

# TEN

On his hands and knees in the darkness Finn poked the embers back into flames. The orange light danced over his naked body and across the low ceiling of the steambath. He closed the door to the woodstove and edged past the glowing metal. Then he took the place on the shortbench he had occupied each evening these past months since he had buried Swede and moved in with Nellie. She was already there on the bench flicking a goose wing across her naked back. She tossed a dipper of cold water on the hot river rocks which were stacked on top of the oildrum stove.

"Hey, come on." Finn bent over to avoid the rising steam. "You really like that don't you, that pain?"

Nellie began to slap him across the back and legs with the goose wing. Finn stood up, cracking his head on the low ceiling. "Now stop that." He rubbed the top of his long matted hair.

Nellie threw more water on the rocks and he bent over again to avoid the scalding heat. She giggled and began to whack him across his narrow butt with the goose wing. Finn grabbed the wing and twisted it from her hand, laughing with her and then he tossed a dipper of cold water across her bare breasts. She gasped and sputtered and laughed with him again then both settled back onto the bench and into the quiet truce which had ended their game each evening. It was time for talk, serious talk.

The dialogue had covered more of their lives than either had believed possible, happy parts as well as painful but each had needed it.

And just as the intensity of the fire in the drum stove had wavered each evening the subjects had ranged from trivial to serious.

"I seen Delbert today," Finn began. "Him and that mangy mutt down in Heine's Café. I can't understand why Karl let's him bring that goddamn dog in."

Finn cupped his hands over his nose and mouth, keeping out enough of the rising cloud of steam so he could continue talking. "When I asked Karl about the dog, Delbert asked me about you. He asked why you'd let an old fleabag like me move in. He said his dog was cleaner than me."

"What should he care?"

"Dunno. Got me thinking though, I mean about our ages and all. How old are you anyway Moon?"

"Thirty-seven." She thought for a moment about her age and the empty pouch inside the fur parka. Nellie wondered if it would always be empty.

"Hell, fifty-two ain't that much older. That pimp deputy ain't even thirty I bet. Bet he even sleeps with that damn dog."

"Thirty-two."

Finn paused. "How'd you know that?" He could not see her face in the darkness but he sensed she was grinning.

"He's jealous," she said.

Finn said nothing.

"He visited sometimes," she continued. "Sometimes when Swede was gone."

"You liked him?"

"He was a man. He was mean."

"Like Swede?"

Nellie didn't answer.

"Well, Swede's dead and buried and Delbert ain't gonna bother us. He's too busy chasing ghosts anyway."

"Ghosts?"

"Keetuk. And them women."

She nodded. "They're dead by now." Nellie thought about Mi'sha and Maruluk and the killing of Old Suyuk. And she discovered there was little sympathy inside her for them, especially for Maruluk.

"Delbert don't think so. Leastways he ain't found no bodies."

"You found nothing for Owens either," she said. "They're dead." Nellie slapped her shoulders again with the goose wing and felt the pleasant tingle after the sting was gone.

"Yeah, but I think he believes I done this one."

"To Swede?"

"Sure. And maybe to No-Talk too. He's looking but he ain't looking that hard. He's always asking me about it again every time he comes in. I don't like it."

"Then why do you stay? Why not just go back and meet Marvin like you've been talking about?"

"I will."

"When?"

"Soon."

"How soon?"

"Very soon."

There was a long silence and Finn moved closer to Nellie. He could feel the flesh of her leg moist and warm against his. "You know them pelts I told you about, Moon? The ones me and Swede cached there on the Mikchalk by my cabin?"

"Yes."

"I been thinking about all them pelts and—" Finn cleared his throat and shifted his position on the bench. "Well, they ain't just mine. I mean only mine. I been thinking a lot about them."

"And?"

"Well, I promised Marv I'd split them with him and I guess I ought to let him in on some of them, that is if we're going to be partners again and all, but—"

"But what?"

"Well, maybe in a way some of them belong to you too, Moon."

"What would I do with them?"

"I mean maybe you could sell them to Yael. Buy something, grub or something—a dress."

"I don't want Swede's pelts. I don't want anything of Swede's. You sell them Finn." Nellie took the soap and began to rub it on Finn's shoulders and soon his mind was off Starvin' Marvin and Swede and Delbert and even off the pelts.

"Well, whatever," he said. "I just thought when I come back down in the spring you might need something."

She stopped the soap and put her face close to Finn's ear. "Just you." She giggled again and began to soap Finn's front.

"Well if this ain't the cleanest I ever been." Finn put his face next to hers and began to do the same with the soap. Neither said anything as each lathered the other slowly until both were stark white in the darkness.

"Finn?"

"Yeah?"

"Do you like me?"

"Like you?"

"Yes, like me."

"Well what do you mean, like you?"

"I mean would you want me around very much of the time?"

"How much of the time?"

"Almost all of the time?"

Finn stopped rubbing the soap. "All of the time?"

"I said *almost.*"

"Well, I'd have to think about it I guess." He moved away from her and began to rinse off his body.

"Turn around," she said. "I'll rinse your back." She poured warm water over his hair and back. "We could cut this hair."

"Now goddammit don't try cleaning me too much. I already gave up snuff for you." He thought about the bottle of whiskey on the table inside Nellie's shack and her bed with the big goosedown quilt on it.

"It was a dirty habit," she said. "Go on inside. I'll be in soon."

Finn smiled in the darkness and then stood up abruptly, cracking his head again on the low ceiling.

"Shit," he said and rubbed his head again. "Same goddamn spot every time. Maybe it's trying to tell me something."

Nellie giggled and shoved his bare butt through the door which opened into the adjacent cooling room.

"Dry off and go in," she said. "Warm up the bed."

Finn dried off, put on his clothes and started to leave. Nellie called to him through the door. "And leave the whiskey alone."

Finn shut the outer door and hurried toward Nellie's shack next to the steambath. A few flakes of snow were beginning to fall and a cold wind had come down from the north. Finn rubbed the sore spot on his head and thought maybe he should just keep going until he got to Henry's Cabin and move in again with him or just keep moving until he was back upriver with Starvin' Marvin and then on to the Mikchalk and his own cabin where there were no low ceilings or deputies and where there would be plenty of snuff hidden under the floor planks. But he decided he should not leave without his Mackinaw. A man might as well be naked without a Mackinaw coat.

In the short distance between the steambath and Nellie's shack he had cooled off and was shivering when he got inside. He quickly slipped into his Mackinaw. The kerosene lantern was still burning on the table next to the bottle of whiskey. Finn reached for the bottle and uncorked it with his teeth, took the cork out of his mouth and started to tip up the bottle. Then he thought about Henry, passed out by now in his cabin and he thought about what Nellie had said in the steambath.

"Almost all the time," he whispered. "She said *almost.*"

He smiled and put the cork back into the bottle without drinking. Then he turned down the lantern to a glimmer, stripped again and got into the bed under the big goosedown quilt. He was still shivering when Nellie came through the door. He watched her cross to the lantern and hold up the bottle to the dim light to check its contents but he could not see her grin until she held her face over the globe to blow out the flame. He shivered for only a few more minutes after she got into the bed and pulled him to her.

When Finn came into Heine's the next morning Delbert was sitting at the counter talking to Karl but he stopped in the middle of what he was saying and looked down into his coffee cup. Tinney was curled up at Delbert's feet but the dog raised his head and growled low when Finn entered. No one else was in the café. After a pause Karl finally spoke but his voice was a little too bright for midwinter. "What'll it be Finn?"

"Coffee."

Karl set a cup on the counter next to Delbert's and moved back to get the coffee pot but Finn decided against joining the deputy. He ignored the cup on the counter and sat by the window in Nellie's favorite spot. It had started snowing hard outside and the flakes were blowing horizontally past the window.

"You antisocial this morning," said Karl. He brought the cup over to him.

"No," Finn said. "Just thinking."

"You think too much, Finn," Delbert said but he didn't turn around. Tinney lay with his head on his paws, keeping a steady watch on Finn.

"Cheer up, Finn." Karl filled Finn's cup. "This one's on the house. Besides thinking won't bring Swede back."

"Or Owens either." Delbert clicked his teeth softly but he still did not turn around. He sipped his coffee. Finn heard the teeth and stiffened.

"Well, if it's anybody's goddamn business that ain't what I got on my mind. I'm considering getting the hell out of this place if it's anybody's goddamn business. Going back up to the Mikchalk." He continued to look out at the snow.

"In this?" said Karl.

"When she blows over," Finn explained. "I'll be stopping at Ekok for Marvin." He turned his head toward Delbert's back as if talking to him instead of Karl. There was a challenge in his voice. "We're teaming up. That is if it's anybody's goddamn business. Partners."

Delbert turned around on the stool. He tilted his head to one side and leaned back against the counter on both elbows. "New partner, huh? You and Marvin this time? That's good, Finn. Now that's a real good idea except I wouldn't be in no big hurry if I was you."

"Yeah?" Finn had turned back to the window and continued to look out at the growing storm.

"That's right," Delbert continued. "Maybe you heard I ain't had much luck finding whoever done old Swede in?"

Finn said nothing.

"And maybe you heard how me and Tinney looked all up and down the Chiktok in every empty cabin we could find?"

Finn sat motionless.

"And about how I ain't seen hide nor hair of Keetuk—"

Finn added more sugar to his coffee.

"Or them women you say he's got. Maybe you heard about all that, huh Finn?"

"I never said he had them. Felix said that." Finn still did not look at the deputy.

"Which brings up another interesting point," said Delbert. "I guess I don't recollect anyone else talking to that priest about them women seeing's how when I found him he was already dead and all."

"So?"

Delbert moved over to Finn's table and stood over him, hands on his hips in his favorite stance. He tried to make himself tall but was scarcely a foot above Finn who remained seated still watching the storm. When he heard the deputy stop at his table Finn turned away from the window toward him but kept his eyes lowered. Slowly Finn worked his eyes up the small man's figure. There had been some changes. Finn noticed for the first time Delbert had tucked his pant legs into the tops of his boots and had made a lanyard for his revolver. Brass buttons had been sewn on his green Filson coat and he had also polished his badge and moved it from his lapel up to his beaver hat. Delbert had not even taken off the skintight black leather gloves to eat breakfast. Weak imitation of a Canadian Mountie Finn thought and he almost started laughing. When he looked up into Delbert's face though he saw the deputy was very serious and even the old dog had followed him over and was standing tensed at Delbert's heel, watching Finn closely through the strands of filthy fur over his eyes.

"So I think we just might need to have one of them official inquests into all this," Delbert said. "And like I said Finn I wouldn't be going anywhere if I was you. I'll let you know when you can leave. And if."

"What the hell's an inquest?" Finn said. "And what are you trying to say?"

"An inquest is a hearing, for your information and I ain't tryin' to say nothing. What I am saying is that I'm going to ask you some questions, under oath, so don't be leaving Snag Point."

"No problem." Finn turned back to the window as if he had just swatted a mosquito from his face. "You just say when Delbert. And if."

"When is tomorrow morning," Delbert said. "First thing tomorrow, eight o'clock sharp." He tugged at the gloves and worked his fingers deeper into the ends. "And where is at Yael's store. You be there."

Delbert turned and started for the door. "Heel, Tinney." He stopped and looked back. "Oh yeah, I meant to ask you Finn. How's the klootch? How's Moon doing?"

He smiled but Finn kept his back to him. When Delbert looked to Karl for approval he saw Karl had turned his back also and had busied himself at the counter. Karl said nothing when Delbert left without paying for his breakfast.

"Some day that Delbert he'll go too far," Karl said when he was gone. He took away his plate.

"What was he saying when I come in?" Finn moved over to the counter and sat.

"Nothing. He said most of the same to you."

"Most of it?"

"Yes."

"But there was more?"

"Yes. Just some small talk."

"Like what?"

"It doesn't matter Finn. He mentioned Nellie that's all. I pay no attention to Delbert and neither should you. I like Nellie."

"I think he does too. I think that's what this is all about."

"Perhaps. But I think he is also embarrassed about not finding those women. He has a big ego."

"He has a big mouth," Finn said.

"Yes. And he is the law for whatever that is worth."

"Well he's got nothing on me. I ain't done this to Swede and it's the truth about Felix. Why in hell can't nobody see that Karl? And No-Talk. Christ why would somebody knock off his own partner in the middle of the trapping season? I'm telling you Karl all this is getting me down. That crazy Keetuk and now Delbert."

Finn finished the coffee and sat sulking at the counter. When he decided Finn was through talking Karl moved away and started working at his stove. Finn got up to leave and dug in his pocket to pay for the coffee.

"Forget it," Karl said without looking around. "I told you this one is on the house."

Finn dropped a nickel on the counter anyway and walked over and opened the door. "They can't all be on the house, Karl." He turned up the collar of his Mackinaw and pushed his hat down on his head.

"Maybe I'll come down in the morning and watch," said Karl.

"Sure," said Finn. "Thanks." He closed the door and went out into the street and was almost instantly swallowed by the blizzard. When he heard Karl's voice screaming through the wind it was all he could do to turn and stand upright against it.

"Finn! Hey, Finn," Karl yelled. "Wait."

Finn lifted his earflaps and cupped his hands around the back of his ears so he could hear.

"I forgot to tell you," Karl called. "Yael said there was a game tonight at his store. A poker game."

Karl quickly shut the door leaving Finn alone in the street. By the time he had secured the earflaps and turned his back against the wind again, Finn's ears were stinging and Nellie's shack was only a blur in his eyes.

# ELEVEN

Hard Working Henry studied the cards he had been dealt, a deuce up and a Queen of Hearts down. It was not easy to focus on his cards through the haze of the whiskey and the dim light in the back of Feldstein's General Store but he liked the color of his hole card. Anytime Henry got a painted card in the hole it gave him enough courage to stay in for another hit even with a deuce showing.

"Check," he said and tipped up his pint of Irish whiskey.

Clockwise around the table and immediately to Henry's left Dago rapped his knuckles on the table indicating he too would relinquish his turn to bet. He turned to his left to look at Finn who had a ten of spades showing.

"This ten bets five dollars," Finn said confidently.

With a pair of tens back to back and no one betting so far Finn figured to make them pay to draw out on him. To his left it was Karl's turn now to call or fold and then on around to Yael who sat straight across from Finn. Yael was dealing. He had a Jack showing.

"Fold," said Karl.

"Call," said Yael without looking at his hole card. "And bump that ten." He made a big show of counting out single bills. It was Henry's turn to call but Yael ignored him. He looked across at Finn without blinking.

"One more time," stammered Henry and fumbling with the single bills he called Finn's bet and Yael's raise from his own kitty. There wasn't much left after he called the bet but Henry was determined to see the next card. It might be painted too like his Queen in the hole. He looked at her again. Henry was delighted that it was a heart. Even if he lost the hand, he loved to get the Queen of Hearts.

"Straight five stud—it is not my game," said Dago. He sighed and folded his hand flipping his cards face down into the center. Finn and Yael still locked eyes.

"Call the raise," said Finn without hesitation. He moved his hand to the stack of bills in front of him and without taking his eyes from Yael's put a ten dollar bill in the pot. Finn made a slight movement to take another bill but hesitated and instead shielded his hole card with his left hand and peeked at it just to make certain the other ten was still under there.

"Deal," said Finn. He would look at another card before raising again. Yael turned up a Jack on top of Henry's deuce.

"Oops, my Jack," Yael said and smiled across at Finn.

Finn watched the next card fall on top of his ten and then tried to look deadpan at the others. He did not know if it showed but his pulse quickened. *Another ten! Three of a kind, two up and one buried.*

"Twenty miles of railroad track," said Yael looking at Finn's two tens showing. He shook his head when he dealt himself a three. He was not happy about it and Finn saw it. With one of Yael's Jacks showing on top of Henry's deuce Finn felt pretty comfortable with his three tens.

"Tens bet twenty-five," Finn said.

"Don't blame you a bit," said Karl who was happy to be out of the hand. He was counting what money he still had on the table and thinking about Delbert not paying for his breakfast.

Yael studied the two tens showing in front of Finn and then picked up the empty salmon can by his money and let a string of brown saliva fall into it. With his head still bent over the can Yael cut his eyes up and across at Finn.

"Just call," he said and counted out the money. "I'll just call this time."

"Shit," said Henry. The Jack he had gotten on top of his deuce was the right color but it did not match his Queen of Hearts in the hole. He picked up his cards and threw them into the center but Henry saw his hole card, the lovely Queen of Hearts, slide all alone across the table and fall off the edge. Henry sulked.

"Take it easy, Henry," said Karl. He reached for the card on the floor and turned it face down in the middle of the table. But Finn had seen the color flash and he knew it was a face card though he did not know which one.

*Maybe another Jack!*

"Well just you and me I guess," said Yael.

"Deal," said Finn.

Yael flipped the next card to Finn and then quickly snapped one to himself. Finn's was a King. Yael picked up another Jack: two Jacks and a three showing. Finn started to worry a bit but then he thought about Henry's painted hole card, the card he had seen flash as it fell to the floor. If it had been a Jack that Finn had seen that would mean Henry had folded a pair of them.

*Why had Henry folded a pair of them? Why would Henry fold a pair of Jacks?* Finn decided Henry was just drunk. Or maybe he wanted to let Finn know something. *Good old Henry. He wanted me to know he'd folded a pair of Jacks. That was it.* Finn checked his hole card again. His bet. Three tens and a King. No Kings showing and none out as far as he could tell. *Hell I might pick up another one, a full house. Yael could have three Jacks but not likely, especially if the face card Henry flashed was the fourth Jack. That Henry, smarter than I figured. Folding a pair of Jacks and flashing one for me to see. He must know I got three of a kind or I wouldn't be staying in against Yael's pair of Jacks. The little fat bastard must have two pair. By god I'll have to get old Henry a bottle of whiskey for this.* Irish *whiskey.*

Finn thought about his poke, a little gold dust he had stuck inside his shirt, maybe two hundred dollars worth and he thought about the bills in front of him, maybe a hundred and fifty dollars now, everything he owned in the world except his cabin and the pelts. At least they were still secure in the cache near his cabin on the Mikchalk.

"One hundred big ones," Finn said. He tried to put confidence back into his voice but Yael was bearing down on him hard with those eyes set deep in the fat of his face. Finn decided the eyes looked like two mouse turds in the snow. Yael always pulled his head down so far when he played poker that his neck disappeared. With his colorless face and bald head shining under the kerosene lantern Finn decided Yael looked like a queball stuck in a pile of sourdough. It made Finn uneasy the way Yael just sat there without showing any sign of emotion. Maybe it was not a Jack that Finn had seen. Maybe Henry had just folded a bum hand.

"Call and raise a hundred," Yael shot back.

Dago whistled low. Karl and Henry sat motionless watching Yael count out the money. Finn leaned forward slightly and watched him also then sat back and sucked in a deep breath. *The sonuvabitch must have the other Jack in the hole—three of them. That goddamn Henry. Maybe it wasn't the other Jack he had flashed. What a dumbass.*

Finn studied Yael's hand: two Jacks and a three showing, the top card a One-eyed Jack. He watched Yael as he dribbled another string of tobacco juice into the can. Finn ached for a chew himself but he remembered Nellie and the promise he had made her. He rubbed the stubble on his chin and thought about her waiting for him and about how she would be if he won big tonight. He looked at the One-eyed Jack again. Just like Yael, he thought, that One-eyed Jack was just like his store with the twin facades, just like his dealings with the trappers, one side of his face showing and the other hidden. But Finn had seen the other side too often to be tricked this time.

"Call," Finn said. "And raise." He counted the remainder of his bills: forty-five dollars.

Yael smiled and started to count out the raise.

"Hold on, Yael," Finn said. "I ain't finished." He dug inside his shirt and took out the small leather pouch, suspended it tentatively over the center of the table and then released it with a thud onto the pile of bills. Yael's eyes glowed. He stopped counting the bills and looked at the pouch.

"How much?" Yael said.

"Six maybe seven ounces," said Finn.

Yael look at Finn for a moment and then got up and went into his office. When he returned he set a small assay scale on the table and stood over it.

"May I," he said politely and nodded his head toward the pouch.

"Sure," said Finn. "I trust you."

Finn worked his tongue against the inside of his bottom lip where the chew of snuff should have been. He barely managed to keep the confidence in his smile on the outside. Yael carefully tipped out the dust into the small pan on one side of the scale and with a long set of tweezers added tiny weights to the pan on the opposite side until the pointer on the scale settled in the center. The men around the table leaned over and strained to see the weight. The hypnotic luster of gold dust had silenced everyone except for the sound of their slow breathing.

"Six and a half," said Yael. "That's over two hundred."

He made a show of pouring Finn's dust back into the leather pouch and then took the scale back to his office. All the heads around the table followed him into the office and then back to the table. Yael did not sit down now but stood over his cards and without hesitation dropped another leather pouch, his own, onto the pile of bills. When Yael's pouch hit the table the thud was much louder than Finn's had been and it rattled the coins.

"Call…and raise a thousand," Yael said in a flat voice. He did not look at the others when he sat down. For awhile the only sound in the room was from Finn who sucked his teeth and studied the leather pouch.

"You know I ain't got that kind of money," Finn said.

Yael said nothing but stared at Finn who did not look back at him this time. He continued to study the leather pouch. Finally Yael spoke. "You don't need cash."

"What do you mean?" Finn narrowed his eyes but still did not look at him.

"Well you can call the raise if you want to but I'd need something." Yael picked up the can and spat again. "Some guarantee you could back it up. Something tangible like that dust there."

Finn understood. He sat motionless staring at the pile of bills and the pouches of gold. He thought about Nellie again and about the pelts and about what he had said to her. And he thought about Delbert and he wondered what the little bastard had cooked up for him tomorrow. Yael had been patient but now he shrugged his shoulders and began to scoop in the money.

"Might as well drag your dust back, Finn. No use getting silly about a little game of poker."

"Wait," Finn said. "You ain't buying this pot, Yael. How do I know there's a thousand there? And what do you mean a guarantee?"

"You know what I mean. And I think everyone at this table knows." They all nodded their heads. "And oh yeah, Finn, you can rest easy. That's more than a thousand there. That's four pounds of dust and nuggets." Henry let his jaw go slack when he heard this. So did Finn. "Over two thousand dollars worth. That's twice what I need for the raise."

Finn made a silent calculation of the pelts hidden in the cache on the Mikchalk. *Prime pelts, more than two hundred of them. They would average more than ten dollars each. Over two thousand dollars.*

He looked at the pouch of gold again and thought about Nellie once more and how they had talked about maybe getting out, going somewhere, anywhere, and how Swede had promised her that too but now he was dead. Swede had lied to her anyway; Finn had not. Even though he harbored no stale dreams about returning to Texas like he knew Marvin did, Finn had begun to think about a change of scenery. And though Nellie was not exactly a Stella Villard still she was not pushy. And besides she had said *almost* all the time not *all* the time. She would not consume him like some women might.

"I'll call," Finn said abruptly.

Yael smiled. He still had not looked at his hole card as far as Finn could tell. "Call my thousand the man says." Yael mocked him, pivoting his head from side to side as if checking with the others at the table to make sure he had heard right. He was whispering, his eyebrows raised. He leaned as far over the table as his belly would allow and glared at Finn. "Now just what the hell are you calling me with, Finn? How do you plan on backing your bet?"

"Give me a piece of paper," Finn said.

"Paper?" Yael chuckled. "I don't take no paper in a poker game, Finn."

"Just get it. And a pencil."

Yael shrugged his shoulders and retrieved a piece of paper and a pencil from the counter behind him and put them in front of Finn. Finn carefully drew a few lines on the paper showing the location of the cache near his cabin and then wrote down the number of pelts he and Swede had hidden there.

"Karl, you witness this, okay?" Finn said and then scrawled his name at the bottom. "And oh yeah," Finn continued, imitating Yael. "You can rest easy too. There's more than two hundred pelts, more like *two* thousand dollars worth."

Karl looked over the document and then nodded his head at Yael. "Looks okay to me. That is, if the pelts are there."

"Well now, which half you betting Finn? Yours or Swedes? I'm sure he trusts you though. Course he won't be needing them now anyway, will he?"

Finn said nothing.

Okay," said Yael still smiling. "I trust old Finn here too. But like Karl says how does Finn know there's really that much dust in my pouch?"

"Because he trusts you too," slurred Henry but he said no more because Finn scowled at him. He took a long pull on his bottle and offered it to Finn who ignored him and studied his hole card again.

"Maybe we should weigh it out," said Dago.

"No," Finn interrupted. "It's okay. Let's get on with it. I ain't worried. If he figures he's covered I figure I'm covered. Deal the last card and let's look at them."

"Sure thing, Finn," Yael said. "Old Swede would probably turn over in his grave though. That is, if there was enough room in there."

Yael was working it hard now but Finn decided it was only because he was nervous. He thought he saw Yael's hands shaking slightly when he dealt the last cards. Yael gingerly placed a six on top of Finn's two tens with the King and then he laid another face card beside his own two Jacks with the three. It was painted, just like Yael's two Jacks showing *but it was a Queen.* Finn wanted to smile but he did not for fear it would give away his hand.

Yael had gotten a Queen. The only thing that could beat Finn now would be the other Jack in the hole, three Jacks to Finn's three tens.

But Henry had folded at least one of the other Jacks; Finn had seen the up Jack in Henry's hand. And perhaps Henry had folded *both* of the other Jacks. Finn thought about it again and he was almost certain now—no he was *positive*—he had seen the other One-eyed Jack, seen it flash when Henry had tossed in his hand. *Good old Henry. There was just no way Yael could have three Jacks, no way. Henry had shown him that.*

The remainder of the dust in Yael's pouch equaled the other half of the pelts. The thought teased Finn's mind and that along with the money already in the pot was enough to caseharden his courage.

"Your bet," Finn said. "Looks like you got the power showing."

The pause—and then the words came flat.

"Bet the rest of it," said Yael.

But what was it? Too much pause, too much hesitation? Maybe not enough, the way the words just came out even like they always did when Yael won in chess. *"Check…and mate."* Flat. Was that how Yael had intended it? Not a command, not a request, just a statement of raw fact. *"Bet the rest of it. Check…and mate."*

Yael had said it as if it were already over. But Finn was not a man to be cowed by such cold confidence. Nor was he a man to cling too long to logic or sentiment. Swede was gone and Delbert was simply a threat which could be taken care of even if Finn did not have enough left for a bribe, even if he lost it all tonight. He could always let Delbert have Nellie back. But Nellie. That had become another matter. She would be under the big goosedown quilt by now Finn thought and the bed would be cozy.

Suddenly Finn wished he were there with her or anywhere else with her for that matter, anywhere but here. He felt like a wolverine with a leg in a snare, the harder he pulled the tighter it got until the only thing to do was to chew the leg off and leave it in the snare, try to get along with just three legs. But then maybe four legs were too many anyway.

"Call," Finn said. But there was no bravado in his voice and he said nothing, did nothing, made no effort to move or show any emotion whatsoever when Yael flipped over his hole card exposing the last One-eyed Jack.

# TWELVE

"Finn?"

"Unh?"

"Is that you?"

Nellie sat upright in her bed and listened. She was awake but she had not adjusted her eyes to the darkness inside her shack. The sounds she heard were familiar though, the sounds of someone preparing to leave her.

"You're leaving." It was not a question and she spoke it to the sound of boots scraping across the planks of the floor.

"Got to."

"Where?" she said but made no effort to stop him. "Marvin's?"

He did not answer. There was a long silence. "I lost them. Yael had three of a kind. He'll probably try to get the pelts out before spring breakup."

Nellie got out of bed and pulled her parka over her head. She fumbled the globe off the kerosene lamp, struck a match a touched it to the wick.

"Stay." She could never remember saying that to anyone before. "Why do you need more?" Then her eyes adjusted to the lamplight and she saw his face. He was staring at a heap of trail gear at his feet, showshoes, a packboard, new knives, food, coffee.

"I don't need more. I just ain't going to let him take these, Moon, that's all. I promised Marv. Yael just won't find them where I told him they were." He looked into her face. "And I promised you. Remember?"

155

"Yael won them from you?"

"Yes."

"He'll come after you. With Delbert."

"Delbert?" Finn laughed. "Now you don't suppose he'd tell old Delbert about two-hundred illegal pelts do you? What do you figure Delbert would say about that? What do you figure he'd do?" He laughed again. "Yael would never get them that way. Delbert would have to confiscate them. Anyway I'll just move them out of the cache that's all. Neither one of them will ever see them. Marv and I'll just wait and bring them down the river after breakup. Sell them on the beach this summer to someone else. Old Yael won't say nothing. I know too much about him and his goddamn fur buying. He won't say nothing about this either." He indicated the gear.

"Where did you get this?"

"Yael's storeroom." He bent over the packboard and began to lash the gear onto it.

"On credit?" Nellie said.

"Credit?" Finn shook his head. "After the game broke up I helped Henry get to his cabin and then went back, pried open the door, took what I needed. Simple." He continued to work on the packboard. "Sort of a payment for all the screwings he gave me over the years."

"He'll say you robbed him."

"Robbed him? *Took* some stuff maybe but not *robbed*. That'd be illegal." He smiled at her.

"He'll come for sure. And so will Delbert when you don't show up at the hearing. They'll come with Delbert's dogs. You can't outrun a dogteam on snowshoes."

Finn stopped working on the gear and looked at her. He had forgotten about the hearing. "Maybe. Even if Delbert does come with him that lardass Yael will slow the sled down. I got a headstart anyway. That is, if you'll cut the bullshit and give me a hand, help me get out of here."

"You know there's a wind. A hard wind from the north. I can hear it, Finn."

"Yep. A real screamer." He finished lashing the gear to the packboard.

"They'll find you sooner or later."

"Mmmmm."

"What will you do then?"

"Dunno. Have that hearing I guess." He smiled again.

"And me?"

Finn picked up the snowshoes and moved to the door. He pulled the latchstring but had to hold the door closed with his shoulder against the force of the wind. "Well, they'll probably come ask you about me and where I went."

"What should I tell them?"

"They already know about me and Marv. Tell them the truth."

"And what's that, Finn? The truth?"

"You mean about the gear?"

"I mean about us?"

Finn was not ready for this. He sensed it coming but he still was not ready. He thought for a moment and he looked around the inside of the shack. Nellie had put up new curtains and the bedspread had been patched.

"Well now let's see, Moon, if I recollect you said almost all the time right?"

He turned from her and moved out into the storm. The snowfall had diminished but the wind had backed into the East and was blowing fiercely, sending the tops of the drifts swirling like puffs of smoke into the darkness. Finn leaned into it and set his course straight for the river far enough up from the tide pools where he knew it would be frozen and solid enough to cross. It was too early for any hint of daylight but the fresh snow glowed when the clouds broke briefly and Finn could see black patches of trees toward the North. He knew the flats well enough so there would be no problem finding the Redstone River even in the darkness. After he crossed there he could cut through the trees and intersect the Chiktok River above Black Point and then up to Ekok staying on the ice where the snowdrifts were not so deep.

At first he had moved rapidly across the flats but the snowshoes had broken the crust and slowed him down so now he moved rhythmically as if learning anew how to work the webs, how to drag the tails of the shoes so they scarcely broke the crust of snow. He thought ahead about where the trail would snake across the flats and through the trees to the river and then he remembered it was the same route over which he had sent Felix. Finn tried to suppress the thought of Felix and how he must have met his end. He wanted to push the fear into his subconscious so he thought about more urgent matters.

How long had it been, a month? No, much longer. He and Marvin would have to hurry to move the pelts from the cache and establish another trapline if they were to get more beaver before spring breakup. It seemed to Finn that it never took long to forget and to grow accustomed to the ease of life away from the trapline. But there was never forgiveness, never margin for error when one did return and to hurry even with someone in pursuit was not a smart thing to do especially in the cold. The wise thing was to be cunning like the wolverine who was rarely seen and even when he was, the old natives would say the wolverine had already seen you twice. He was only teasing you, allowing you to see him as if to say that you had his permission to be there but you should not get too cocky about it.

Delbert was cocky. But Delbert did not know the rivers like Finn did. And even with dogs, he would have Yael with him and Yael would not budge from Snag Point until daylight several hours from now. Or it might take another full day for Delbert and Yael to mobilize. Finn could easily be in Ekok by then, join Marvin and then be on his way upriver and in five days they could be at Finn's cabin, move the pelts and wait for Delbert, try to talk to him, convince him to chase Keetuk and the women instead. And with the cache moved Yael would have to keep still. He could not say anything around Delbert, that is if he wanted to try to deal with Finn in the spring. Finn would have the upper hand then with the other buyers competing on the beach. Yael could just take his One-eyed Jacks and put them where the sun did not shine if he ever wanted to see those pelts. It would be a onetime deal shared with Marvin, and Nellie of course, and then he would get the hell out of there, leave Snag Point and the whole rotten mess. One final killing as they say.

*Killing?* he whispered. He did not like thinking it. When he heard himself say the word the old fear of being alone on the tundra tried to surface again.

*Push it back.*

Five days—that would be by snowshoe. That would be by way of the Chiktok and easier going on the frozen river.

*Easier. But that would be the long way.*

Finn stopped abruptly and looked behind him. That would be exactly what Delbert would be thinking. That would be exactly what Delbert would be expecting him to do, take the easier route. That would be exactly what Finn must not do.

He could not stay on the Chiktok after he joined Marvin. They would have to go on snowshoes through the trees and across the flats to the Mikchalk River in order to be at the cache ahead of Delbert. Even if Yael rode along, Delbert would still make good time with the dogsled on the ice and perhaps they would even catch up if he and Marvin chose to stay on the frozen Chiktok River. Finn knew he and Marvin would have the advantage in the trees even if Delbert did try to follow. Finn also knew that he and Marvin could cut two days off the trip if they stayed with it, put in full days. And kept away from the hotholes.

The hotholes: They were always a consideration. Theirs was a continuous presence in the winter on the hundreds of small frozen lakes across the tundra, the surface ice weakened by volcanic activity beneath the Alaskan Peninsula. Finn knew his way across the flats and through the trees, knew where the going was easy. He was confident that he knew where all of the hotholes were. And then Finn thought about Yael's poker hand and he remembered his confidence that Yael had not held three Jacks.

"Well, *most* of them anyway," he said aloud.

He had crossed the Redstone and was in the scrub spruce above Black Point. He would soon emerge on the bank of the Chiktok at the same place where he had urged Felix to cut through the trees. That seemed like years ago and Finn only thought about it to take his mind off Delbert and Yael. And Nellie. And then Finn remembered what Delbert had said about Felix dying like someone or some *thing* had chased him and all this tangled in Finn's mind, spun around in his head and when it sorted itself out he felt a tingling in his back between his shoulder blades.

*Push it back down.*

The deep snow in the trees and the fatigue from the long night without sleep had brought Finn to his knees several times but he had stood again quickly when he no longer heard his own trailshoes scratching through the snow. The silence caused him to stop his heavy breathing, hold his breath and listen for what he imagined would be a dogteam in the distance. But each time there had been nothing except the wind moving across the tops of the spruce trees.

*Keep moving.*

Finn stopped when he broke out of the trees on the riverbank and saw that the sky had lightened. He could see over the opposite bank and out across the tundra open all the way to the horizon. The storm had blown passed and the horizon was changing to chalkdust blue just south of a black mass of clouds lingering in the North dividing the sky into light and dark. Finn breathed deeply, sucking in the morning and a fresh attitude. He felt better knowing he was on the Chiktok again. He regained his wind and his easy stride after he set his course up the surface of the frozen river.

Finn did not realize how thin this sudden surge of energy had been until he saw the figure standing with a raised axe beside the cabin. He should have known how far he was from Starvin' Marvin's cabin by the sound, or the absence of sound, for when the axe fell he saw the two halves of the spruce round drop away from the cutting block and hit the tundra several seconds before he heard the sound itself.

*Marv,* he called. Finn rushed toward the figure, still just a silhouette poised with his hands on the axe handle, the head buried in the chopping block. When he finally reached the figure he was out of breath again but this time after he went to his knees he continued forward, collapsed chest down one cheek resting in the snow. Finn groaned, confident that his old friend and new partner would spring into action, warm bunk, hot stew, perhaps even a swallow or two of whiskey from some special cache.

"Marv," he whispered and then with a croak, "I made it."

Marvin fumbled in his pocket and without any move to turn Finn over or to help him sit up he brought out a penknife and started cutting the ropes which secured the canvas bag to the packboard on Finn's back. Marvin groped inside tossing its contents at random over the snow.

"You better have some coffee in here, you sonuvabitch," Marvin said. When he felt the cloth sack with the coffee grounds inside Marvin clucked with glee and disappeared into his cabin leaving Finn stretched out in the snow surrounded by the trail gear. After several minutes Finn decided if he lay there any longer he would have to place his mitten between his cheek and the snow to prevent frozen flesh or he would have to summon his energy once more to get up. The thought of Marvin's stew was not quite enough to urge him upward; the familiar pain of frostbite was. He pushed himself into a sitting position and sat there for a few moments longer stunned that this man, this pitiful incompetent that he had befriended *twice* now against his better judgement, would probably never know or understand the bond he and Swede had shared, the camaraderie so necessary on a trapline. Even if they could shake Delbert and Yael, Finn decided that with Starvin' Marvin it might still be a long spring, a very long spring.

"Well, how is it?" Finn had gathered his strength and all the gear that Marvin had scattered in the snow and now stood in the doorway of the cabin.

"Don't know. It ain't strong enough yet." Marvin stood at the stove watching the water boil in the old coffee pot. He had a rag wrapped around the handle and a death grip on it.

"Well, did you use it all?" Finn picked up the empty coffee bag and shook it.

"Nope."

"Then where the hell's the rest of it?"

"Hid it."

"*Hid* it. Gee-zus, Marvin, I ain't gonna steal my own coffee."

"I know. But just so's you don't go wasting it or giving it to some other fleabag old Marv will just dole it out as we need it, really need it."

"Well, we ain't gonna have time to worry about that none," Finn said. "So you just as well get it out and get your packboard and gear ready. We're leaving."

"This seems about ready now," said Marvin. "Get a couple of cups."

Finn moved into the cabin and shut the door. "I guess you didn't hear. I said we're going. Right now."

"Yeah sure. Right away." Marvin lifted the pot from the stove and retrieved two tin cups from the table. He poured the black liquid as carefully as he might a sacrament. He closed his eyelids halfway and sipped. When he opened them wide again the goodeye was glazed over as though he had discovered a true and wonderful elixir. But the glass eye, his *evil eye,* stared straight ahead as if it alone had heard what Finn had been saying.

"Leaving?" Marvin asked when he finally realized what Finn had said. "Where?"

"Oh come on, Marv, don't give me that crap. You know damn well what I mean. The Mikchalk like we talked about earlier. You and me, remember?"

"Oh yeah." Marvin held both cups, reluctant to give up even one of them. He brought the other to his lips, blew on the hot coffee and sipped delicately, savoring the aroma. "I remember." He frowned and set Finn's coffee cup down on the table. "Sit."

"Look," Finn said. "If I sit down I'll peter out. I can't rest now Marv. I'll never get up and they'll catch me here. Let's go."

"Catch you? Who'll catch you? What are you babbling about Finn. Sit down, drink your coffee. Let's talk."

Finn did not like the direction this was taking. It was definitely not working out like he had thought it would back on the trail. "Okay, Marv. I'll drink the goddamn coffee but I ain't listening to any of your bullshit. It's Delbert."

He removed his mittens, sat down and began to sip the coffee which was better than he had anticipated. He heard his stomach gurgle as it attacked the hot liquid and then he remembered he had not eaten since yesterday.

"Delbert?" said Marvin.

"And Yael. They'll be coming after me. Probably today."

"Why? Is it about Swede?"

"I guess, at least part of it. That is, for Delbert anyway. He had some kind of a goddamn hearing planned for me. He wanted to look into it he said and I jumped ship on him." Finn blew into the cup and eyed Marvin through the steam. "But that ain't the half of it. Look, Marv, it's a long story and I'm wearing down fast. I need something to eat and then we got to get up to the Mikchalk, get them pelts and move them and—"

"Wait a minute Finn, relax. I'll warm up the stew, you tell me what the hell's happening and then you can get out of here if you want to."

"What do mean I can get out of here? What about you?"

"I ain't going." Marvin took his cup back to the stove, refilled it and moved the stewpot over the heat. Finn's stomach was telling him not to worry about it but he wondered if this might be remnants of the same stew he had eaten months before.

"What do you mean you ain't going? You said you'd join me, Marv. Remember all that stuff about needing a partner again and getting out of Ekok here and getting a stake and maybe leaving for good and all that bullshit? Remember?"

"I remember." Marvin stirred the stew. "So what's this about Yael? Did you put Swede in the ground? And Felix, how'd his feet do? Did he make it down to Snag Point?"

"Shit." Finn shook his head. He could see Marvin was not going to budge without the full story.

"Okay," Finn said wearily. "I lost everything to Yael. Everything I had plus all the pelts in a poker game. I broke into his storeroom, stole all this gear, skipped out on the hearing. I moved in with Moon after the funeral and I think that pissed Delbert off the most and then I—"

"Moon?" Marvin turned around. "Moonface Nellie?"

"Yeah," Finn bristled. "So what? And Felix is dead."

"Dead? Felix?"

"Yes dead. *D-E-A-D,* dead and buried and I'm here now and what the hell do you mean you ain't going with me?"

Finn was trying to sound angry, get just enough edge to his voice to find out what was on Marvin's mind but he did not want to lock him to this decision to stay. And he wondered what Marvin's reaction would be to news about the death of Felix Manguson. Marvin and Felix had not been exactly best friends but when someone had been an acquaintance for over thirty years, even someone as twisted as Felix, Finn figured there would have to be some kind of reaction.

"Felix dead? Well who done this one?" asked Marvin. "He was always a little wacky but we did go back a long way." He stared at Finn. "All *three* of us."

"Yeah." Finn could see that Marvin was shaken by this. "You have to wonder if he'd been better off staying in Texas. Maybe we'd all been better off staying there."

"I don't think Stella Villard would have liked the idea much," Marvin muttered but Finn could see he was not talking to him. "Especially after all her railroad stock certificates disappeared like blown smoke."

It was the first time in thirty years that Marvin had made reference to the stocks. Finn sucked in a mouthful of the hot coffee and swallowed hard, scorching his tongue and throat. He could not agree with Marvin even if he wanted to. His voice was not working and neither was his mind. Everything was on hold waiting to hear what Marvin would say.

But Marvin was silent. He continued to stirred the stew searching for another mouse like the last time Finn had been at his cabin. But there was nothing foreign in the stew this time. He ladled out a bowlful and placed it in front of Finn.

"Well?" Marvin said. "Who do you think done it?" He looked at Finn hard with his goodeye and Finn wondered whether Marvin was talking about blame for Stella's lost fortune or about Felix's death. He decided he would take a chance on it being about Felix.

"I don't know who would have done him in but I got a pretty good idea," Finn continued. "Delbert found him on the flats above Black Point. Heart attack or something. He said something must have been chasing him."

Finn started to eat, mumbling around the hot food in his mouth which he could not taste because of his scorched tongue. He was silent for as long as he figured the solemnity of the occasion warranted.

"Now, about our deal," Finn said when he thought they had grieved long enough about Felix and Swede and lost fortunes and such.

"Look, Finn, I just ain't going, that's all," Marvin said. "Hell, it's already pushing spring, you got maybe a month of trapping at best and I just decided I don't want no part of it. I mean they're Swede's pelts and now Delbert and Yael are in the middle of it all and then there's Felix dying and all that. I ain't no good at it, never have been, never will be. And who needs it anyway? I got my place here, knock down a moose once in a while, catch a muskrat or a beaver on occasion. Who the hell needs it?"

"Well hell's bells, I need it Marv. I need a partner, don't you see. And what about you getting out and all that? What about all them plans Marv? And then there's Yael and Delbert, you know, showing them two bastards up. Just think about that. And shit there's enough there for us both and then some, maybe even enough for Moon to share in. That is if we can beat Yael back to it. Partners, Marv. *Partners.*"

"You and Moon," Marvin said shaking his head again. "I just can't get over it. Maybe you should'a brought her with you Finn. As a partner, a serious partner."

Finn stopped eating. "Well, I don't know how serious it is but I do know what I promised her. And I figure Swede owes her some of his share too."

"Swede?"

"Yeah. You got any idea how he treated her?"

Marvin shook his head.

"Well let's just say she deserves some of them pelts and I want to see she gets some. And if you come with me, Marv, you'll get your cut too. That's my promise just like I told you before."

Marvin was not one long on promises himself and did not put great stock in those of others especially promises made by Phineas Farrow alias Hjalmar the Finn.

"Promise? Hell, I'd given up on you long ago. How the hell was I suppose to know what was going on. I just figured you had cut a deal with someone else. And Yael? How do you plan on getting rid of two hundred and fifty pelts without old Yael?"

"Maybe on the beach, different buyer in the spring. No problem. You could even be there when I make the deal. You could even come down to Snag Point in the spring with me when the first freighter drops anchor. It's my problem with Yael and Delbert and I'll take care of that. They'll be cooled off by then anyway and I'll take care of Moon too. Don't sweat that. I promise."

"Spring?" Marvin thought about the freighter and he remembered it had been springtime all those years back when he and Finn had boarded one after deserting Felix in Seattle. And he thought about the photograph also taken in the bright sunshine of springtime but now lying in the darkness behind his tin plates over the stove.

Stella Villard. What would she be like now? What would she do or say if he stepped down from the train there in Texas. Marvin decided he would recognize Stella instantly even if there were a crowd. He would know her by the way she tilted her head to the side when she smiled. And she would look into his one goodeye which would be filled with remorse now and she would see that he was weary from his long ordeal in this alien place. But Stella's eyes would still hold the promise that Marvin had seen all those years ago. He was sure of that. A promise which had never been fulfilled due in large measure to Marvin's own belief in the schemes of Phineas Farrow.

"Promises," Marvin said. "What the hell good are promises?"

"Well, didn't I bring you the coffee? Didn't I?"

Marvin looked at Finn and took another sip of the coffee. It was good, he had to admit that. "Yeah, Finn, I guess you did."

"And ain't I back and ready to show you where me and Swede hid them pelts?"

"I suppose…"

"And hell, ain't I willing to show you where there's lots more? And how to set the traps right and all that?"

Marvin considered the pieces of the circle. It was still incomplete after all these years but perhaps he could no longer rely on himself to bring it all together. He took his glass eye out and placed it into his mouth, removed it and polished it on his shirtsleeve. Then he held it a long while staring into it as if seeing himself inside looking out. "Well, I guess you did," he finally said and returned the glass eye to its socket. "I guess you did all that, Phineas."

It was the second time this winter Finn had heard Marvin use his real name and he took note of the fact that this time Marvin did not turned away from him in that private way he always used when he reinserted the eye. Marvin looked at Finn for some time before he spoke again.

"Okay, let's give it a go." And then Marvin said another strange word, allowing his voice to resonate with the same hope Finn had heard thirty years earlier in the little town in Texas. "One more round—partner."

# THIRTEEN

Even though Finn was weary he was far out in front of Marvin pushing hard to put some miles between them and Ekok before dark. They had crossed the frozen Chiktok and moved through the scrub spruce along the riverbank above the village. They had emerged from the trees and onto the flats a scarce five minutes when Marvin called to Finn asking him to stop. Finn turned and looked back, waiting for him to catch up. When he saw Marvin was not moving he went back just far enough to talk without having to shout.

"Now what?" Finn said trying to balance anger and encouragement.

"I gotta go back," Marvin said.

"Back? Christ Marv you can't do that. Hell they may be in Ekok already or on our trail by now. Listen." Finn cupped his mitten to his ear almost hoping for the sounds of a dogteam.

"I don't hear nothing," Marvin said. "Besides I gotta go back anyway."

"But I thought you'd made up your mind. I mean about this spring and the freighter and getting a stake for passage and all?"

"I did. That ain't it. I just got a hell of a headache that's all."

*Headache?* Finn leaned forward on his snowshoes certain he had not heard correctly.

"Yeah. A headache."

"Shit." Finn dropped forward, resting his knees on the toes of the trailshoes. Then he lifted his eyes heavenward and shook his head. "I got a United States Deputy Marshal on my ass and a crazy native with

169

a sled full of double-bitted axes waiting out there somewhere to put one between my shoulders and *you* got a goddamn headache? *Gee-zus copped-up-Christ!*"

"Now don't have a fit, Finn. I'll be right back. I just forgot to do something."

"Forgot what?"

"It's my glass eye if you gotta know. But then you probably wouldn't understand. The glass gets cold see and that gives me a headache and I'm taking it back to my cabin that's all. Besides there's all that stew back there."

"Well, you can't pack that too, Marv. What do you plan to do with it? You can't pack all that stew and you can't eat it right now. Hell we got enough grub to get us up to my cabin, four, five days worth. And you got the coffee don't you? Well don't you? Everything else we need's already there in my cabin, beans, flour, sugar."

"Well yeah, but I need to leave this in it," he said and pointed to the glass eye. "In the stew. For thieves. You know that."

Finn remembered. And he also remembered how the eyeball had not prevented him from tossing out Marvin's sour coffee grounds last fall but he did not mention that. He did not want to say anything which would make Marvin have second thoughts about going with him.

"Well it is cold, Marv," Finn admitted. "It certainly is that." But Marvin was already out of earshot so he called after him. *It certainly is cold, Marv,* he yelled again and now confident Marvin could not hear him he whispered, "Milksop."

He watched in silence as Marvin disappeared into the trees along the river. An hour passed and Finn had almost decided to circle back to Ekok to check on him when he finally saw Marvin returning through the trees, a smile on his face and a black patch over the empty eyesocket. Finn had not seen the patch in all the years since they had come to Snag Point. When Marvin got closer Finn remembered the eyepatch was made of silk.

"That oughta do it," Marvin said and he stood confident as Finn inspected him. "Well, let's go."

"Silk? Now you didn't really have to dress formal." A stiff weariness had settled into Finn's body. He did not rise from his kneeling position but he knew they had to get some distance between them and the river, even a few miles. He knew he could not give Marvin time to think of another excuse to return so he pushed himself to his feet and adjusted the packboard once more to the highest, most comfortable position on his back. He started off again across the flats toward a thick line of trees two miles ahead with Marvin trailing behind.

Breaking trail over the tops of the frozen hummocks exhausted Finn further. The exposed muskeg proved solid enough but the footing was deceptive because the tips of the snowshoes teetered and then buried in the fresh drifts just beyond the dark tops where the frozen lichens showed. It took all of Finn's concentration on the hummocks and he could not look back to see if Marvin still followed.

For some time Finn had been resting in the corner of an abandoned cabin when Marvin finally forced the slab door open on its remaining hinge. Enough twilight remained so that Marvin could see the missing patches of sod roof through which a thin skiff of snow had fallen onto the floor.

"I never knew this one was here," Marvin said as he swung his packboard free of his shoulders and looked around. He sat on the floor near Finn.

"Not many do," said Finn. "This one was Old Eskaleut's. They say it was in good shape when he was alive and trapping out of it." Finn looked around at the decay and wondered if his own cabin would someday be the same. "No more though. Use it or lose it as they say, huh Marv?" Marvin did not respond to Finn's attempt to brighten the conversation.

"The old drumstove might still be okay," Finn continued. "Maybe we can fire it up. We can toss our blankets on the floor here tonight. I don't think we ought to be on the flats out there in the dark."

"Hotholes?" Marvin said.

Finn had not meant to get into that possibility so he ignored Marvin who waited for a long time before repeating it.

"Because of the hotholes?"

"Yeah," Finn admitted.

"I never been across this country, Finn. I always travel the river."
Marvin tried to sound casual about it. "You been across here?"

"That's why you ain't never got no furs come spring. Course I
been across there. Lot's of times. That's where the best trapping is, at
least for beaver," Finn explained and then added as if reminding himself of the danger, "Wolverines don't go in there though."

"Why?"

"Cause their smart that's why," Finn said but he immediately wished
he had not.

"Then why the hell are we going across there?"

"Cause we're smarter than they are that's why," Finn said and
quickly changed the subject. "Look at this." He sat up and drew into
the skiff of snow on the floor a large Y with his finger.

"What's that?"

"This is the main river, the Chiktok. It curves back to the left like
this." Finn traced the left branch of the Y with his finger. "And the
Mikchalk comes in up here on the right at the top." Finn was speaking
with authority now like a commander before an invasion.

"Yeah?" Marvin moved closer to see Finn's drawing in the dim
light.

"And here's Ekok," Finn continued. "Down here at the bottom
left okay?"

"Yeah. Got it."

"And my cabin's here just at the far right tip of the Y just where the
Mikchalk flows down out of Mother Goose Lake."

"Okay."

"Now if Delbert comes after me—and I'd bet a new fur hat that—
he'll stay on the main river until he gets to the fork, here, where the
Mikchalk comes in." Finn spiked the intersection with his finger. "Then
he'll probably just stay on the ice up the Mikchalk and try to take me
at my cabin."

Marvin nodded, catching some of the excitement. The authority
in Finn's voice was contagious and Marvin was being drawn back into
the game. He found himself regaining some of his ambition which
had lain fallow all these years since leaving Texas.

Marvin thought about Stella Villard again and he ran his hand inside his Mackinaw where he had tucked the leather folder containing the old photograph, his real purpose in returning to his cabin earlier in the day, and not the evil eye at all. He had not confessed to Finn how overpowering the dream of returning to Texas had become in the months since they had last seen each other. During Finn's absence Marvin had vacillated from strong commitment to total apathy on the subject of leaving. He had known Swede was dead but now Felix was gone too and the possibility of Marvin sharing in the cache of furs was just barely alive now that Yael Feldstein and Delbert were also involved. And then there was Nellie. Marvin could only guess at what plans Finn actually had for the furs and Nellie's share.

This renewed partner business between himself and Finn might not last. Spring was near. Marvin knew well enough how the bonds of winter in Snag Point often dissolved right along with the ice during spring breakup. He had seen it too often to ignore the possibility that this venture with Finn, this final lunge at the brass ring, could turn sour. Still the plan contained all the elements necessary for completing the circle Marvin had dreamed about. He would just need to focus. He would pay attention to Finn and try to be as much help as possible.

"Now we're right here," Finn droned on. "Just across the river and up from Ekok. What we'll do is cut through and stay off the rivers. We'll take less time getting there. We just have to beat him to the Mikchalk. It's the only way."

"How do you know Delbert won't cut through too?"

"Because he's got dogs and a sled, and dogs and sleds don't take to trees and because Delbert don't know that country like I do and because he's smarter than to try to cross them hotholes in the winter."

"Like them wolverines?" Finn said nothing. Marvin continued, "Seems like everybody and everything is smart enough to stay away from that country in the winter." Finn sat silent. "Except us, right Finn?"

"That's just what I want him to think," explained Finn. "That we're too smart to try to cross there."

"Well, whatever." Marvin wondered again about the plan but Finn had outlined it with such boldness that he did not question it further. "I'll bring in some wood."

"Be my guest." Finn gestured at the inside of the cabin. Marvin went outside and Finn heard him stomping around in the spruce for dry branches. When Marvin returned with an armload he saw Finn was already asleep in the corner, his head resting on his unpacked gear.

Marvin was feeling the pressure of the quick exit from Ekok himself and he was again wondering if he had made a wise decision and if Finn actually knew what he was doing or if he were acting in desperation. A fire would be good. It would cheer him up and give him time to think more about it.

He cracked several thumbsized spruce branches and lay them in the drumstove atop the birchbark which he had placed there. Finn was snoring loudly by the time Marvin had the old stove creaking and snapping and for almost an hour Marvin watched the flames glowing from the pinholes rusted through the sides of the oildrum as the light formed a changing orange and yellow pattern across Finn's face.

Marvin had never had the opportunity to stare into the face of a real general but he doubted if it looked like Finn's. Finally he open his pack and pulled out his own gear, a small tarpaulin, a blanket, a pan for melting snow, the coffee bag, some hardtack and dried fish. It would not be his usual evening fare, a longsplice made from the friendly stewpot in his cabin but it would have to do. He went outside again to scoop some snow into the pan to melt for coffee water.

This time the cold of the evening quickly worked its way under his Mackinaw so he buttoned it from the bottom all the way to his chin and turned up the collar against the fur hat. He adjusted the silk eyepiece. When he raised his chin to close the top button Marvin sought the moon in the clear night sky. It was something he always did when he went out on a clear night because when he discovered it, the moon always gave him comfort about the loss of his eye. If the night sky could get by for a billion years with only one eye so could he. But tonight when he located it Marvin saw it was in its final waning stages and it appeared someone had simply poked a hole in the night sky with the blade of a shovel.

A closing moon always depressed him but he knew it had to complete this cycle in order to return full and renewed. And if the moon had renewed itself countless times then surely Marvin G. Crush, alias Starvin' Marvin, should have no problem doing it at least once. And besides, he had the additional protection of the evil eye, something that even those with two goodeyes did not enjoy. Not even the moon had an evil eye for a backup. Marvin thought about the eye frozen by now in the stewpot, watching over his interests back in Ekok and he took great comfort in that. He placed his hand inside his coat and felt the warmth of the folder with the photograph of Stella and he took comfort in this too.

It was warmer inside his head now with all these thoughts and with the silk patch over the empty eyesocket. Marvin was glad he had dug the black eyepiece out. How long had it been? He had forgotten how nice it was with its warmth and its smoothness. When was the last time he had worn the damn thing? Surely not in the long years since he had landed at Snag Point, not since he and Finn had tossed their dufflebags on the dock at the Scandinavian Cannery and strutted around the village.

Everyone had stared at him then, not just because he was a stranger but because of the eyepatch. That had been fine with him. It had made him feel more mysterious and had given him an unexpected sense of bravado. He was not looking for any friends at the time. Finn would do for a friend even though Marvin suspected they would go separate ways in Snag Point. But when Marvin approached a woman with a child to ask about a place to buy a grubstake the baby began to cry so Marvin had darted into the nearest outhouse and inserted the glass eye. Wearing the patch was not something he had ever wanted to do again around the others. There was enough pretension already in the area but now as the thoughts of rejoining Stella were becoming stronger it just seemed like the thing to do.

Stella would not be frightened by the eyepatch. Nor would she think it pretentious. Indeed she would admire the dashing appearance it gave to Marvin's otherwise drab personality. Perhaps they would have another photograph made, just he and Stella. She would be seated this time, straight and proud on a velvet stool in front of the elder Marvin, suit and tie and tall and debonair and protective behind her with his strong hands cupped on her soft shoulders.

Still, there was that outside chance when he stepped triumphantly down from the train in Texas Stella might not recognize him with the eyepatch, especially after so many years. Marvin was certain he would know her immediately, perhaps a few wrinkles around the eyes and some graying but he would know Stella. He decided he would shave when he got back into Snag Point, do away with the unkempt beard that had been on his face for more years than he could remember. She would recognize him more readily without the beard. Definitely he would shave—that is, after he got his share of the beaver pelts.

The pelts. The money. Marvin tried not to think too much about Finn's plan. It was something he had given over completely to the control of Hjalmar-the-Finn, Hjalmar-the-Partner, Hjalmar-the-General and he would just have to take orders and try to be whatever help he could.

Marvin bent over and scooped up a full pan of snow and looked back up at the night sky but only the stars remained, much larger and closer now that the old moon had gone down. He searched in the North for the Aurora Borealis but there was no hint of that either, none of the distinct palegreen glow with its changing hues. He remembered Finn saying that he could hear the Northern Lights, a low crackling sound like frozen alder branches touching each other in a light wind. But that was Finn. Finn said a lot of things. Like knowing about hotholes.

Marvin went back inside the cabin and pushed the stubborn door closed, scraping the bottom noisily across the hewn floor planks. Finn snorted and rolled over but did not wake up and Marvin decided not to bother him. He took the blanket out of Finn's packboard and covered Finn with it and then turned his attention to melting the snow on the old stove. Even though the pan had been peaked with snow there was hardly an inch of water in the bottom when it finally melted, not even enough to boil coffee. It was too late anyway. Coffee would just keep him awake. And awake he would think about her. He needed rest to keep up with Finn tomorrow.

Marvin did not realized how late he had stayed up until he awoke the next day, blinking into the shafts of midday sunlight which spiked through the slits in the roof. Finn was still asleep but he was rolling inside his blanket and talking in his sleep, repeating a name and then he was breathing hard as if running. Suddenly Finn screamed and sat up. *Listen.*

"Listen to what?" Marvin said.

"Don't you hear them?"

"Hear what?"

"Dogs," Finn whispered, the fatigue still raspy in his throat.

Marvin frowned and cocked his head. "I don't hear nothing. The only thing I been hearing is you talking, saying things."

Finn looked at him. "Things like what?"

"Names. Or rather a name."

"A name?"

"Yeah."

"Well, shit. What name was it? Delbert? Henry? Yael?"

"Stella. You were saying Stella over and over."

"Well that's all you been talking about lately," Finn hedged. "Maybe she was just in my mind from all your yakking about her." Finn shrugged and stood up and began to lash his gear onto his packboard. Marvin was up too shuffling around in the shadows trying to arrange his snowshoes and gear.

"I swear I heard dogs," Finn said. "Out on the river. Cripes, Marv, why in hell didn't you wake me up earlier?"

"You're in charge of this platoon," Marvin scolded. "How come you weren't up at dawn? And if you were hearing dogs what the hell were you doing calling out Stella's name?"

Finn did not answer. He stood in the doorway, packed and ready to go except for lashing on his snowshoes.

"We got time for coffee?" Marvin asked.

Finn scowled at him and adjusted his packboard. "I'll wait outside."

Marvin finished his packing and started toward the doorway with his snowshoes under his arm. He paused at the door and listened, trying to convince himself that Finn had not heard a dogteam. "I don't hear nothing," he whispered and then louder to Finn outside, "I don't hear no dogs."

"Let's move," Finn called. "If they ain't here now they soon will be." He dropped the snowshoes and quickly slipped his boots into the bindings and secured the loose ends of the rawhide thong around the bottom of his trousers to keep the fresh snow out. "Even if they stay on the river we'll never get there ahead of them if we don't keep moving. You try to stay up with me, hear?"

Marvin nodded and fell in behind him, trailing closely as Finn made the tight twists through the trees. Twice they paused to drink at running springs Finn seemed to know about. Marvin was feeling more secure and toward late afternoon he offered some dried fish but Finn refused, saying they did not have time.

"We'll need to pass around the hotholes before dark." Finn paused at the edge of a clearing which dropped off into the cut made by a small creek. Steam rose from the shallow water which washed across the rocks. Drifts of snow and ice had attempted to choke the little rivulet but the warm water had simply cut through and proceeded on down the slope.

"This drains the whole area," Finn explained. "It never freezes never stops smoking even in the hardest part of winter. The old natives call it burning water. What they don't tell you is that some of it ain't burning and that's what makes it tricky."

"Why?"

"Because when it's this cold, burning water ain't burning. It gets a skim of ice over it and it ain't solid enough to support a man—or a wolverine. That's why they don't come through here. Beavers love it though. They swim around in here all winter, hundreds of them." Finn smiled and continued, "Except when I get them in my traps. This is where Swede was, checking our trapline. He must have had pelts with him when—" Finn stopped abruptly and turned his head, listening as if it had just occurred to him that Swede had met his end nearby and that they were not the only ones who knew their way through here. "Let's move," he commanded but his voice was weak and Marvin's confidence ebbed a little. Finn moved now with a quickened gait. "Stay close."

Marvin followed as closely as he could but Finn moved ahead as if more than imminent darkness pursued him. For more than an hour he did not look back at Marvin but instead called over his shoulder urging him to keep pushing.

They had moved out of this cluster of trees and onto a broad stretch of small frozen lakes and potholes and still Finn bore onward toward a group of small hills on the horizon. Marvin dropped behind several hundred yards but even in the approaching dusk he could easily follow Finn's trail by concentrating on his tracks in the brightness of the snow.

Finn had just reached another line of trees at the base of the hills when Marvin went through the ice. There was no panic. He did not even call out to Finn. It was as if this were just meant to happen. Marvin had been in Finn's tracks but Finn would never believe that. He would say that Marvin had gotten off the trail in some stupid attempt at a shortcut.

Marvin stood for a moment waist deep in the tepid water, too embarrassed to let Finn see him. Then he made a great effort to lift one snowshoe out of the muck on the bottom but even when he brought it to the surface, the thin coating of ice on the water would not support his weight. He put his leg back down. He could tell from the softness of the bottom the snowshoes had kept his body from sinking so he dared not risk unlashing them to walk out of the mud. His Mackinaw was wicking the water up his chest and his sleeves were already soaked and the coldness was quickly turning the damp wool into a crust of ice. Finn had finally discovered Marvin was not on the trail behind him and circled back to the edge of the hothole.

"Might as well join me," Marvin said. "Ain't half bad in here."

Finn ignored the black humor. He hunkered down just out of reach, not risking getting near enough to help.

"Warmest I been for a week," Marvin went on and even attempted a smile but his shivering was already out of control.

"Shut up," Finn said grimly. "I'm thinking."

And he was. But he was not thinking about the same thing Marvin was thinking about, a possible solution to this predicament. At least that was not the only thing in Finn's mind at the moment. In fact Finn was thinking that maybe it was not so much a shared as simply Starvin' Marvin's predicament alone.

Did Finn really need him? Maybe it was stupid bringing Marvin along anyway. He thought about the delay and wondered how close Delbert would be to Finn's cabin and the cache by now. And he was wondering if Yael had come with him.

Finn reconsidered it all. Perhaps he should let Yael have the damn pelts, let Delbert have Nellie. Who would know or even care a hundred years from now?

But Finn was also thinking about how quickly the cold would be getting inside Marvin's body and how soon he would be dead, his torso crusted over with ice in the center of a hothole, a comic corpse frozen into this final frontier, a monument forever to man's stupidity. Maybe others would benefit from it. Maybe somebody would look out across this flat someday and see Starvin' Marvin up to his waist in the center of this hothole and have the good sense to go back where he came from.

"Finn?"

"Shut up," Finn repeated. "I'm still thinking." He stood and moved cautiously around the periphery of the hothole with his palm over his mouth, sending heat from his breath into his nostrils. And then as if he had made a sudden and irreversible decision Finn abruptly turned and moved toward the trees.

"Hey, Finn," Marvin called. "You ain't going to leave me are you? *Finn?*"

"Get down in there stupid—to your chin," Finn yelled back. "And stay there."

*Wait!* Marvin was beginning to panic and the fear of being left alone to die set him in motion. But it was no good with the snowshoes and the soft mud. He fell forward up to his neck in the water and came to rest on his knees, his head just above the surface. He began to wonder which would be easier now, slowly freezing to death or just sinking below the surface and allowing himself to drown. Marvin preferred the latter; he would be in control that way. Freezing was horrible with its uncontrollable shakes and the pain in the toes and fingers and ears before the numbness came. He had seen it before, that pasty bruised look and the gaping mouth and eyes of a person who had frozen to death.

No, he would just sink slowly under the burning water. At least he would die warm. It was then he realized what Finn had meant. It *was* warmer under there, much better than trying to stay erect with the top half of his body exposed to the cold. At least he would not freeze to death as long as he stayed up to his chin in the warm water.

With some of the panic gone he turned his attention toward Finn who had moved around the edge of the clearing, finally coming to a stop beside a lone spruce tree, dead but still standing. Marvin watched him assess the tree, suddenly elated by the thought that perhaps Finn was not going to desert him after all. Then Finn disappeared into the forest and Marvin's heart sank again until he saw him return dragging dead limbs and branches.

Finn repeated this and in a short while had a large pile of dead wood around the base of the lone spruce. In a few more minutes Finn had the entire stack of wood ablaze. Smoke and sparks swirled upward along with Marvin's spirits. It warmed Marvin just to see the bonfire expand and work its way up the center shaft and along the dead branches until it leaped from the crest of the tree in a giant flare. When he had the inferno at its peak Finn hurried back to Marvin.

"Take off all your clothes," he commanded.

"My clothes?"

"Yes dammit all of them. Everything except the fur hat and hurry up."

Marvin decided against protest. Finn had not left him and he could argue later whether or not he had followed Finn's instructions to stay in his footsteps when the ice caved in under him. At the very least Marvin was sure that he would be accused of getting off Finn's trail. Right now Marvin would be busy enough trying to figure out how to get his pants off with snowshoes on his feet.

"You'd die sure if you got out of that water with them wet clothes on," Finn said. "They'd freeze solid on you. Now get it all off, boots, socks, everything. I'll dry them out as best I can before you try to come out of there."

Finn decided to explain the plan since he had nothing else to do while he waited. It would be a slow process getting all Marvin's wet clothes off and over to the fire to dry out. "Keep the snowshoes on so's you don't sink up."

"Maybe you ought to just leave me, Finn." Marvin struggled with the pants. He had one snowshoe and one boot free, balancing on the other leg.

"Well now, ain't you just pitiful?" Finn said. "Pitiful sorry you caused all this?"

"Well, I ain't sure you need me anyway. I ain't never been much good for nothing."

"Well, you let me decide that. I'll let you know if it comes to that."

Marvin tossed the wet pants and long underwear over to Finn and started to work on the coat and shirt. Finn began to ferry the garments over to the blaze, spreading each one out on forked branches he had stuck into the snow near the heat. It was almost dark by the time he had all of the clothes propped up to dry, the whole array in a stiff circle surrounding the bonfire like a coven of headless witches. Several times Finn went into the trees to bring out more deadwood for the fire and each time he circled back to Marvin to check on him.

"It ain't working, is it," Marvin said.

"Well, it's slower than I figured." Finn looked over at the fire and at the circle of silhouettes around it. "It's cold as a witch's tit out here. How about in there?"

"Well, it's warm enough but kind of lonesome." Marvin's voice trailed off and he stared across the blackness to the firelight. Then he remembered the leather folder with the photograph inside. What would it look like all wet and wrinkled? Even if the Mackinaw dried out what would the wet leather folder do to the photograph? He could not ask Finn to check on it. The photograph of Stella was probably ruined. The thought sent Marvin into a dark depression.

"Just take it easy," Finn said. "We're going to get you out of there just fine."

"I don't know about that. I'm getting awful tired. Maybe you ought to go on, Finn. I'll get out of here soon as I get some strength back and them clothes get dry. I can catch you later."

Finn could not see his face but he could tell by his voice that Marvin had no intention of doing what he just said. He had not heard Marvin this dejected since he had lost the sight of his eye all those years past.

"Yeah, fat chance of that," Finn said. "Hell you can't even stay on my trail let alone find me through them trees. Besides I ain't got no desire to try and haul all them pelts down the river by myself without a dogteam. You and me is the team and that's who'll be inside the harness when we hitch it to my sledge. You and me, partnering, remember?"

"I thought we was going to bring them down in the spring? I thought you said we was going to get some more and bring them down in the skiff after breakup?"

Finn tried to see Marvin's face in the darkness. He turned away and stared back at the bonfire trying to remember exactly what his plan was or if he had ever had a plan at all.

"You know something, Finn?" Marvin continued. "You just play it all by the ass of your pants just like you always did, just like this big idea about drying them clothes out. You know it ain't no good don't you? You know pretty quick I won't be able to move and you can just watch me sink under here and then you can leave, right?"

Finn did not turn around.

"And all that stuff about being partners that's all just so much bullshit ain't it? You just want somebody to help you get them pelts back down so's you and Moon can sell them off and then you'll just shaft me. When was you aiming to do that, Finn? When was the big shaft gonna happen?"

Finn slowly turned his face back to Marvin, finally understanding.

"Well, screw you Hjalmar-the-Finn. Screw you and the ship you sailed in on because I ain't going to let you do that to me. You can just kiss off because you and me is *done*. From here on in I take care of myself. I should never have listened to you all them years ago in Texas either. I should have known you'd screw up the whole plan and lose Stella's money. I sure as hell don't need another big deal like that one."

"That ain't going to work," Finn said quietly. "I know what you're trying to do and it just ain't going to work, Marv. Your chances of me leaving you here to die are about as slim as your skinny ass. Now just slip off one of them showshoes and balance on the other and hold the one you take off out to me."

Marvin grunted a string of obscenities but when he saw that Finn was not going to go away he sulked into the water.

"Hurry up," Finn said. "Hang on to the tail of it and I'll pull hard on the tip. When you feel yourself coming free from the mud, move fast up the edge of the snow here and grab onto my back. If the other shoe comes off don't worry about it. We can fish it out later. You just hang on and I'll haul you out of there. Worst you'll get might be a couple of frozen toes."

Marvin had gone from elation to despair so often this day that he finally gave up trying to make any sense out of Finn's plan. Without further protest he hunched into the water to remove the snowshoe. Balanced on one leg he grasped the tail firmly and held the shoe out to Finn on the edge of the hole. Finn grabbed the tip of the shoe with both hands and dropped his full weight away from the hothole. Suddenly Marvin emerged from the steaming water, slick and fuming and dripping, naked except for his beaver hat and the single snowshoe which was still attached to his bare foot. Marvin screamed when his other foot touched the ice and immediately Finn was on his feet and hunched over in a halfcrouch beside him. "Get on," he commanded.

"What do you mean?"

"I mean straddle my back stupid. I'll carry you over to the fire. There's a half full bottle of whiskey in my cabin and that ain't too far away now. That is if there ain't been nobody there and if you're at all interested."

It did not take Marvin long to decide that riding Finn's back was preferable to walking barefoot across the crusted snow even with one snowshoe on. He lurched forward with just enough momentum to come to rest on Finn's hip, the leg with the snowshoe still attached and dangling behind. Finn grabbed Marvin's long legs pony style and groaned as one knee buckled and then the whole arrangement teetered precariously but held as rider and mount wobbled toward the burning tree.

# FOURTEEN

Maruluk sat on the floor of Finn's cabin working the keen edge of her knife. With the skill of a thousand years in her wrinkled hands she moved it along the layer of fat between the skin of the beaver and its flesh. The curved blade of the *ulu,* the traditional Eskimo knife, had flashed its halfmoon shape in the light of the kerosene lamp each morning for these past months. And still they came. Each day another freshly killed beaver had appeared with the morning sun just outside the door of Finn's cabin. It was more than she and Mi'sha needed for food so Maruluk had dried the extra flesh with the salt she had found in the cabin and she had stretched the pelts on the round frames made of strong birch.

Maruluk smiled as she worked. Although her granddaughter had seen the appearance each day of the beavers as a mystery, Maruluk believe that the source was Raven himself. So each night she remembered to leave some of the dried meat outside the door.

Maruluk could not remember the journey here to Finn's cabin on the Mikchalk River. She remembered only that her arms had been separated with force from around Mi'sha as they clung to each other on the river ice above the village of Ekok. The old woman had opened her eyes for a moment and had seen the icefog as she was being lifted into the dogsled and then warmed in the caribou skins with Mi'sha. And then nothing. The remainder of the trip to the Finn's cabin was not there. When she finally awakened she and Mi'sha were alone in the cabin and a fire had been made in the woodstove. Maruluk had not seen the face of the spectral figure who had lifted them into the sled and saved them from certain death on the ice.

Had this too been Raven? Had it been Raven who had forgiven Maruluk for trying to blend the priest's words with the belief of the True People? Something or someone had saved her and Mi'sha. Just like Old Eskaleut had been saved from certain death and had been led to the original site of their village Tuluk-On-The-Bay she and her grand-daughter had been saved and perhaps even brought here to the Mikchalk for some greater purpose. Maruluk would not question it now. That was the way it was to be.

In the final moments before they had been rescued Maruluk had given herself fully back to the *Inua* and had called on these ancient spirits for help. Though she had not given up all hope the cold had settled into her mind and had numbed her thinking and she could not remember clearly. She was certain it had not been Finn. Even though it was his cabin she knew it had not been Hjalmar-the-Finn from Snag Point. There was only one other who had the power to do this. There was only one *Inua* defiant enough to bring them here and provide them with this protection. It had to be Raven.

"It's foolish," Mi'sha said. She turned from the small window near the door and frowned at her grandmother, seated on the floor in the light of the kerosene lamp. Maruluk did not look up but continued to worked the beaver skin with the sharp *ulu*.

"We can never eat all this. It's wasteful." Mi'sha looked around the cabin at the dried meat hanging on every wall.

"Perhaps," said Maruluk. "But the pelts should not be wasted."

"And if they find us here?" Mi'sha moved quickly to the bench beside the woodstove and sat with her back toward her grandmother. Maruluk did not answer.

"Why must we hide? Just tell whoever is doing this silly game to stop and take us back to our village."

Maruluk stopped her work and looked at the girl who still had her back turned. She returned to work on the beaver. "You said you would do this, Mi'sha. They would not accept us in our village now. Even after this long, Aiyut would still be bitter with what happened to Old Suyuk. Even if it was right he still blames us and the priest and his word. And now with you like this." Maruluk shook her head and continued? "Well, we were foolish to—"

"We?" Mi'sha said. "I never said we should do it. You said we should do it, everyone trusted you. You were the one who said Old Suyuk had to be punished. You were the one who wanted me to listen to the priest. You were the one who did nothing when the priest—"

"And I was wrong, Mi'sha," the old woman said. "You know this, I know this now. But we are still shunned and we will be shunned until we prove ourselves worthy of returning. What will we prove if we do not show our courage now? It is the old way and we can show them it is still the best way. We can prove that what is left of the past can still have meaning."

"But what do we prove by staying here? Why do we wait?"

"Because I believe it was Raven who brought us here Mi'sha just as he led Old Eskaleut. There is some reason we are not both dead. It must have to do with this child inside you. Something greater is moving here now Mi'sha. The old ways. We must wait and see. We will know when the time comes."

"Yes, wait. Wait and see," Mi'sha said bitterly. "Wait and see if the *kassaqs* find us stealing their food, find us living here. Wait and see what they do then. Wait and see where we can hide. You speak of the old ways, tired ways. I am sick of the old ways."

Maruluk flared at the girl. "Where would you have us go? What would you have me do? We can replace the salt and the sugar. We can sell the pelts. We can defy our people and return anyway yes. But how can we replace our pride? Where do we find this, Mi'sha?"

"What do I know of pride?" Mi'sha said and her bitterness turned darker. "Teach me about pride, old woman. Like the way you taught me to say yes to the words and the whims of the priest. Teach me again old woman." She paused and her eyes dulled and her voice became hollow. "But I was younger then. I was a hundred years younger."

Maruluk stopped, the *ulu* poised in the air. She could bring it down hard across her wrist she thought. She could mix her blood with that of the beaver in front of her. She could spill her blood, that of a land creature who could do such a thing as Mi'sha was saying, across the blood of a water animal. And this would be evil to mix the two.

This would bring down on Maruluk the wrath of the *Inua*. But it would also bring down the wrath on Mi'sha because she would then be alone. Except for Raven. Maruluk said nothing for a moment. She watched the girl pacing the cabin.

"I look around here, I see only reminders of them, belongings of the *kassaqs*," Mi'sha said. "And yet you tell me Raven is here. I feel the child of the *kassaq* inside me. And still you tell me Raven is here. Then ask him, ask Raven to take us somewhere, anywhere."

"I can ask him. I can call on Raven as I called on him when we were on the river ice. But he has chosen this way. If he wanted us to see him he would show himself. It is the way it is to be."

"The way it is to be? Like the influenza?" Mi'sha said and she saw the old woman wince.

Maruluk had heard her own words boil bitterly from the mouth of the girl, the same words she remembered speaking to the villagers during the epidemic, and still the people had died, all of Mi'sha's family had died. But they were Maruluk's people too, her family.

Mi'sha instantly regretted the words. Had Maruluk not been there for her? Had she not taken her in and been a source of great strength? And though it was difficult to erase all her bitterness about the priest, Mi'sha knew that Maruluk had only been trying to make things better for her and better for their village.

"But I don't understand," Mi'sha said and her words were softer. "If it is Raven why has he helped us? Why doesn't he show himself? Even with Old Eskaleut they say he appeared in the top of a spruce tree." She turned to her grandmother. "And we cannot stay here at the end."

"The end?" Maruluk's eyes widened. "What are you saying Mi'sha?"

Mi'sha walked to the window and looked out again. "I felt it move today," she said quietly.

"You frighten me when you speak this way," Maruluk said. "I do not always know your mind."

Mi'sha smiled. "Neither do I." She moved and stood above the old woman, gray and wrinkled and small on the floor, still bent over the beaver with the *ulu* in her hand like some ancient Shaman in a ritual.

Mi'sha threw back her hair and laughed. "You even cling to the slow-ness of the old knife."

Mi'sha reached in the shelf on the wall and retrieved Finn's long skinning blade. "Try this, try a new thing once." She gripped the knife at her side, the blade curved downward in a stabbing position near the old woman's head as she stood next to her. Maruluk looked at the glint-edged blade and then up into her granddaughter's eyes. The old woman shut her eyes and behind them she saw a film of blood cover-ing everything in the room. She waited for the steel to enter her and wondered where Mi'sha would chose to plunge it.

But when it did not happen the vision behind her eyes changed and Maruluk saw the blade buried deep in the pregnant belly of Mi'sha, draining the blood from both her granddaughter and her great grand-child onto the bloody carcass of the beaver on the floor, mixing the blood of all three in an evil taboo.

Maruluk snapped her eyes open. Mi'sha was standing limp, the skinning knife held loosely at her side. She dropped the knife to the floor beside the beaver carcass.

"Just once try a new thing, just once. It's what you told me to do," Mi'sha said. "Or don't you remember?"

"First you say you hate the *kassaqs* then you say you hate the old ways and then you offer me this *kassaq* knife. No Mi'sha, I do not know your mind at all." Maruluk shook her head. The girl had not seen fifteen summers and yet when she moved like this, when she thrust her shoulders back and placed her hands on her hips and mocked her, it frightened and angered the old woman. In the short time they had been here Mi'sha had changed. There was a hardness in her face, a maturity which had come with a cruel suddenness.

A new thing? Yes Maruluk had tried a new thing. She had tried the new ways, placed her trust in the words of the priest. And now in her guilt, Maruluk turned her eyes from Mi'sha. She looked at the *ulu,* perfect in her hand. She felt its smooth ivory handle engraved with the symbol of the *Inua,* the head of Raven and then she thought of the knife alone without her hand and how the blade was shaped like the halfmoon. "Do you not see that it is like the moon, Mi'sha? Bright and whole and full?" She held out the *ulu*. Mi'sha looked at it but quickly turned her eyes away.

"I see only half a moon," she said. "And the superstitions of our people. We can't live in the past."

"You look but you do not see. But you are right in one way. The ancient shape of the *ulu* is only half the moon but the hand itself makes it whole. See, Mi'sha? The hand guides it and the *Inua* is whole."

But Mi'sha would not look. Maruluk shook her head again. "Do you not see this, Mi'sha? It cannot be complete without the hand."

"But the hand must be without shame," argued Mi'sha. "It can't be shamed and still be whole. You said yourself we could use the pelts to buy the things of the *kassaqs*. You say you reject the priest now. Then why don't you reject these things too? I see only Raven's head on the *ulu* and I sense his trickery."

Maruluk was silent. She would not deny this. She knew well the trickery that Raven could do. But she also knew her own heart and the wholeness remained, even if Mi'sha and her own people did not see it. Mi'sha bent to the floor and retrieved the skinning knife. She took it to the shelf and thrust it back. "I have to go. These walls are too close."

"Where?"

"Don't worry." Mi'sha pulled on her parka and moved toward the door. "I'll be back. I need to walk, to be alone for awhile."

"Mi'sha?" The old woman's voice was soft again and the girl paused at the door. "You will not do something…foolish?"

Mi'sha turned and for a moment the harshness in her face disappeared and she was a child again. "I'll bring some water." She picked up the water pail, smiled and closed the door behind her.

*Outside, Mi'sha breathes in the fresh air and sets her course to the trail which winds through the spruce trees along the river's edge. The sun is up now but it is cold and clear and the whiteness of the snow hurts her eyes. She knows the path will end at the hole in the ice Maruluk had chopped the first day. And she knows that the skim of ice which forms each night over the hole will already be cleared. It has been this way each day and the trail through the fresh snow leading down to the river has been tamped. To*

*Mi'sha, even though there is a strangeness about it, there is comfort knowing they are being watched.*

*At first there was fear. Now it is not fear she feels but an urgent curiosity about the mystery. Mi'sha knows the stories and she has stayed awake at night and thought about them and has sometimes heard movement outside Finn's cabin. Once when she heard a noise she sat up in her bunk and looked out the window. In the moonlight she saw a shadow moving swiftly away with scarcely a sound. Where did it go, where did it sleep? The old woman would not talk about it the next morning.*

*"There is no danger," she had said. "Do not ask foolish questions."*

*At the river Mi'sha bends over and tries to dip the pail through the hole in the ice and into the water but because of her stomach she can not bend over far enough. She chuckles at herself and then on her hands and knees she crawls up to the hole and dips the bucket in. She pulls it back out and sets it on the ice and then, still on her hands and knees, she watches the rings formed by the ripples inside the hole. They retreat from the edges of the ice and return to the middle, collide with themselves and then return again to the edge of the hole and then repeat the cycle.*

*Mi'sha thinks of herself and her feelings now with the baby inside her, feelings which come and go like the bright rings of water, feelings of joy which turn to fear and then to sadness and then to guilt. Even now she wants to laugh and thrill at the thought of a baby, her own child and yet there is no one to share it with except Maruluk. It is better when she does not think about it at all so she turns her thoughts to the water again and the hypnotic motion of the rings. And then she sees Alexie Napiuk's face in the rings as though he is looking over her shoulder into the water. Mi'sha remembers her foolishness not a hundred years ago but only a few when Alexie had led the whole village of Tuluk-On-The-Bay in catching the fish for the winter. She chases him again across the tundra, flushing the flock of white and brown mottled ptarmigan into the air. The startled birds call to her, glide over the hummocks and land just out of reach. Then they are aloft again calling and gliding.*

*Come-on-come-on-come-on-come-on! they cluck over and over and Mi'sha laughs.*

*"Let me catch you, Alexie. You know you want me to."*

"Go away," he says. "Can't you see how you frighten the birds? How can I snare anything if you follow and squeal and act stupid, Mi'sha?"

"But who needs it Alexie?" she calls after him. "The fish racks are heavy now and you will be a hero Alexie. Maybe even an umialik, Alexie. They'll give you Aiyut's boat just as you dreamed."

And she chases him further.

"Let me catch you, Alexie."

And then Alexie stumbles and Mi'sha is on him, giggling in his ear but he pushes her off. She turns on her back and puts her hand under her kuspuk to hold her aching side. And soon her breathing is easier. She says nothing now because Alexie is quiet beside her on the warm muskeg watching the sky. Mi'sha turns her eyes and sees Alexie has turned also and is watching her move her hand under her garment.

"Your side is aching?" he says and he seems concerned in a sullen way. Mi'sha thinks he is scolding her.

"Yes, it was. But not now," she explains. "It's okay now."

And then he is quiet again and Mi'sha hears his breath through his nostrils. "You should go back then," he says and then he looks again at the sky.

"I could help you, Alexie," she says. "Teach me how."

"Girls don't know about snares," he says. "They only think about baskets and such."

"But I could learn," she says. "Things are changing, Alexie. Maruluk says things are much different now."

"True. But some things never change," he says. "Old Suyuk will never change. Aiyut will never change. No matter what I do he will never change." And then he thinks about all the racks filled with fish. "But maybe it's time the village had a change," he says and smiles. "A change of leaders."

"Maruluk says I must change."

"You?"

"Yes."

"Why? How?"

"I don't know. Except that I am growing." She feels the coolness of her face turn hot again as though she is still running. "Maruluk says the priest will tell me, show me. He has promised her this. And I have met with him but—"

*"You don't seem too happy about that, Mi'sha. Maybe it's a new way you don't want?"*

*Mi'sha says nothing. She rubs her side again under the kuspuk.*

*"It still hurts?" Alexie says.*

*"Not much," she says.*

*Alexie moves toward her now and she hears his breath in his nostrils. He reaches over and places his hand on top of hers under the garment. He follows the slow circling of her hand on her side. Mi'sha stiffens at first, stops the rubbing but then continues.*

*"You should not have run so hard after me," he says. "Unless you really wanted to catch me that bad."*

*"Just to learn the snares," she says and looks in his face. "Only something new, just to learn something new."*

*And then Alexie's hand leaves hers and he glides the tips of his fingers over the flesh of her stomach under the kuspuk. Slowly he moves the fingers upward toward her breasts trying to change the touch from that of a rough fisherman's hand to that of a ptarmigan feather.*

*"Something new?" he says. "Is this something new Mi'sha?" His hand moves over the soft mound of one breast which barely fills his cupped palm and then he explores the other. And he spreads his fingers and closes them gently around the erect nipple and then circles it slowly with the tip of a finger. Alexie's face is next to Mi'sha's now and his body is turned to her and she feels the stiffness of him. She sucks in her breath with short gasps each time his hand moves to another place on her body.*

*"Like the snares?" he teases and his nose is under her ear sending chills down her neck.*

*But now Mi'sha's breath is that of a rabbit in a snare and she feels herself choking, choking, gasping for air. And Alexie's voice has changed and it is like that of the priest repeating the new phrases from his book.*

*"No!" she says and abruptly she sits, her eyes wide. She pushes Alexie's hand from her and turns away rising to her feet. Then she flees across the muskeg, stumbling and crying, leaving Alexie with a bewildered look on his face.*

*And now Alexie's face in the bright rings of water changes for Mi'sha. With each new cycle the voices and the faces blend and distort as each in turn rebounds from the sides of the hole cut in the river ice.*

*First there is the face of Father Felix looking over Mi'sha's shoulder into the water and he is scolding her for allowing Alexie to touch her. And then the face in the rings is that of Maruluk telling her to listen to what the priest is saying because it is best. And then the face turns into Old Suyuk and she is somber and pleading and she twists her old features in agony as the tide slowly laps at her shoulders, then her neck and then her chin. And the crowd closes in around Old Suyuk with angry faces but each face is the same, each face is Mi'sha's face. And Mi'sha sees her own face laughing as Old Suyuk's feet sink in the mudflat so she cannot move. And the water is on Old Suyuk's lips filling her mouth and her final scream is muffled in a gurgle from her throat. And then there is nothing but water.*

*Mi'sha screams and turns away from the hole in the ice and covers her face with her hands. And it is then she hears the voice above her.*

*"Come away with me," it says. "Fly away with me."*

*Startled by this new voice Mi'sha tries to stand but her mukluks slip on the ice and she falls on her side.*

*"Careful," the voice says.*

*Mi'sha lies still for a moment, the veins pulsing in her neck. When she regains her feet she turns toward the voice but there is nothing there.*

*"Where are you?" she says and then she sees the shadow moving through the tops of the trees and she backs away.*

*"Do not be afraid," the voice says but this time it comes from a different place.*

*"Who are you?" she says. "Is it you, Alexie?" She has calmed herself and is more curious now than frightened. She moves closer to the shadows.*

*"Stop," the voice says. "You do not need to come in here to talk."*

*"Talk?"*

*"Will you come with me?"*

*"No!" she says. "Who are you? What do you want?"*

*There is a long silence.*

*"Where?" she says.*

*"Away from here. Away from the kassaqs, the trappers and the panners. Away from the old ways and the new ways and the greed."*

*"Who are you?" Mi'sha repeats and she strains to see into the shadows but the brightness of the sun on the snow makes her squint.*

*"You know," says the voice.*

*"If you are Raven I only know the stories."*

*"I know you. I have watched and I know."*

*"Then you know about—"*

*"I am not blind."*

*"Then you know what the villagers are saying," she says and laughs. "About me and Keetuk?" There is no response from the trees. "Are you still there?"*

*"Yes."*

*"Let me see you." She moves again toward the voice.*

*"No," the voice says.*

*She stops.*

*"Where are you?" she says. She remembers chasing Alexie and the game with the ptarmigan.*

*"Come away with me."*

*"But my grandmother?"*

*"She can come too."*

*"But they will look for us," Mi'sha says. "It would be stupid."*

*"They will never find us."*

*"Why?"*

*"I will trick them. I have many tricks. We will be safe but you must first trust me."*

*"How can I know you are speaking truth? How can I trust you if I can't see you?"*

*"You trusted him, even when you could see him."*

*"Alexie?"*

*"No, the priest. You trusted him."*

*"Is that you, Alexie? Stop this! Let me see you." Mi'sha waits and watches but nothing moves. "But he lied," she says. "The priest lied."*

*"And you followed him. You followed him into the lie."*

*"Yes. And I have shamed my grandmother and myself. But I have learned. And she has learned and now I know what I have to do."*

*Mi'sha moves toward the voice in the trees above the riverbank. She struggles through the deep snow in the trees as she searches for the voice.*

*"Come with me," it repeats but the voice moves away from her each time she nears it, teases her like the ptarmigan. Finally she breaks through the trees and stands at the bottom of a sloping wall of sharp granite rocks.*

*"Fly away with me," the voice says again and this time it calls from atop the bluff above the jagged rocks where she cannot see.*

*"Raven," she says. "I know it is you. Do not hide from me. Please wait for me, take me with you." She struggles again, this time over the sharp rocks and claws her way up the bluff until she stands where she can see the tops of the trees below her. But the voice is again above her, in the air this time and it resonates in her ears.*

*"I will give you wings," it says. "Lift them. You can soar with me away from here forever. Come with me, Mi'sha. Come with me. Come-on-come-on-come-on-come-on-come-on!"*

*Mi'sha looks out over the rocks below and then turns her face upward to the voice. She stretches her arms into the wind as if they are wings. "Yes," she answers. "Yes!"*

# FIFTEEN

"Finn?"

"Mmmm?"

"Is that you? You're back?"

Nellie sat upright in her bed and listened just as she had done on the night Finn had left her. She was awake but as before she could not adjust her eyes to the darkness inside the room. And like the sounds she had heard before, these too were familiar, the sounds of someone preparing to get into bed with her.

"Now why would old Finn just up and leave you like that, Moon?" asked the voice from the darkness.

"Delbert! Get out of my bed!"

"Aw, now don't get so excited, Moon. I won't stay long. And maybe we'll just forget about old Finn, huh Moon? Maybe you and I will just let him go on his merry way and not worry about him for awhile like we use to do when Swede was gone, remember? See Moon, old Yael and I were suppose to chase him today but I just couldn't go without saying 'bye to you tonight now could I, Moon?" Delbert had stripped and was under the big quilt and on top of Nellie, pinning her arms to the bed.

"Finn's not like Swede. But you are. Now get off and leave me alone." She easily rolled the little man aside and slipped out of the bed and into her *kuspuk*. When she had lighted the kerosene lamp she stood looking at the wall with her arms crossed. "Please leave," she repeated, trying to give her voice the right quality, a practiced blend of pleading and anger.

Delbert made no move to go. He lay on his stomach under the quilt with just his head showing. He had substituted Nellie's pillow for her body and held it trapped in a bearhug, his chin resting on it. For a long moment he too looked at the wall, his face at first showing the rejection but then slowly it relaxed into a deceptive smile, then a grin, an imitation of Nellie's.

"Well now, I guess it don't take old Deputy Delbert Demara long to figure things out. I understand, Moon." He braced himself on his elbows, then sat on the edge of the bed. He fluffed then straightened the pillow and stood beside the bed still nude and grinning. "I'll just smooth this out for you, Moon, so's you can get right back in there while it's still warm." He took the corners of the quilt and after a few hostile snaps above the bed, allowed it to flutter back.

"There now," he said stroking the quilt. "Old Delbert will just get out of here and back to his own business. You see, it's like I told you, Yael and I have some trail running to do tomorrow, nothing personal you understand, just some legal stuff with ole Finn and I'll be hanged if he ain't up and run off. Now you wouldn't know nothing about his plans would you, Moon?"

Nellie faced him with her arms still crossed. Her grin had returned but she continued to stare at the shadows in the corner.

"Would you, Moon?" Delbert moved in front of her trying to get her to look at his body. She diverted her eyes to the bed. She had seen him nude many times but even in the dim light there was not much the flickering shadows could add to Delbert's body.

"Please understand, Delbert. It's not you, it's just that Finn and I talked about—"

"Oh sure, I can figure it out, Moon. Inside *here.*" Delbert spoke sharply, pointing to his head and returning the grin in a way that frightened her. "It's just that all of me don't quite understand. Know what I mean, Moon?"

Moon understood. She continued to avoid looking at him.

"You see what I mean, Moon? You ain't looking, Moon. Now how are you going to understand what I mean if you don't look at what I'm talking about, Moon? Right down there between my legs, Moon? This part of me don't quite understand." He reached out abruptly for her face, grasped her cheeks between his thumb and fingers, the palm of his hand over her grin.

"See. And this part of me just never has liked being grinned at, *klootch*. Look at it!" He jerked her around, forcing her head down. "Apologize to it!"

Nellie could feel his grip tighten on her face, the teeth cutting the inside of her mouth and his fingernails digging into her cheeks like a wolf trap. She tried to talk but the words came out muffled into his hand. Finally in a futile attempt to ease the pain she sank to her knees before him and began to whine through her nose. Delbert's grin had become a snarl and he brought Nellie's face toward his groin.

"See," he said with a mocking kindness in his voice. "Look at it, tell it you're sorry, Moon. See if it understands."

Nellie closed her eyes and felt the blood from inside her mouth drooling down her chin. And then at the moment when he had her head held just right, Delbert quickly lifted a knee and brought it hard against her chin. Nellie felt her teeth come together, severing small chunks of flesh from inside each cheek. Her head snapped back and she collapsed on her side to the floor, blood seeping between her lips onto the planks.

Delbert stood trembling over her for a few seconds then he began to put on his clothes. He carefully secured the new brass buttons on his green wool jacket and then stood in front of her broken mirror and adjusted his fur hat. Even with the top portion of the mirror missing Delbert did not have to stoop to see his face like Nellie had to do. When he moved his head forward to inspect the badge he noticed how it caught the lamplight and instead of the polished silver it reflected a warm golden glow. Delbert nodded his head forward several times smiling at the reflected beauty of the badge. "Hey now, look at that, would you, Moon. Ain't that beautiful?"

Nellie lay with her face in the crook of her arm listening to him. By the time he had stomped his boots on she was alert again but because of the pain inside her mouth she could not bring back her grin. She refused to raise her head and allow him to see her without the grin. Delbert slipped on his Mackinaw and started toward the door, hesitated and went back to the lamp.

"I'll just crank this down for you Moon. So's you can get on back to sleep." Then he turned and stood over her again. In the last glimmer from the lamp Nellie saw his boots next to her face. She closed her eyes and held her breath, bracing for what she expected would be Delbert's parting shot, perhaps a boot in the ribs. Nellie waited until she could hold her breath no longer but no boot came. Instead she felt the pleasant sensation of a warm liquid that quickly saturated the back of her hair and began running down her face. But then it became a fierce stinging as it ran into Delbert's fingernail cuts on her cheek and then a pungent odor as it pooled under her face in the hollow of her arm. Delbert finished relieving himself, went to the cabin door and left without closing it. Outside the cabin she heard him call to his dog. "That oughta help keep her warm, Tinney. Good dog. *Heel.*"

Nellie did not know how long she remained on the floor. It was still dark in the early morning when she finally pushed herself up and relighted the lantern. She washed her face and soaped her hair a second time and then she counted a full four hundred strokes with the stiff brush. Still she did not feel clean.

Nellie sat facing the broken mirror. She lowered her head to see her face, wishing the cuts Delbert had left in her cheeks with his fingernails would be healed and that a smooth fairskinned complexion would be there. She wished she could be young again with her body slim and lithe, the breasts which sagged now once again firm and tipped up and shaped for the tiny mouth of an infant.

Nellie ran her tongue inside her cheeks where only a few hours earlier her teeth had been forced into the flesh by Delbert's grip on her face. She reached for Finn's bottle, which she had set on the dresser, and she held it up to the weak light from the kerosene lantern. She studied its amber contents. "He won't need it now with Delbert going after him," she said. "Why should I save it for Finn anyway."

She would probably never see Finn again she thought and Delbert was another matter she would have to deal with as best she could. She could always make up with Delbert if she needed to or she could spread the word about her rejection of him. But that could be dangerous.

At first the whiskey seared the open wounds in her mouth but then it filled her chest with its warmth and sent a small shiver down her back. She took another mouthful and let it flow quickly down avoiding the cuts inside as much as possible. Nellie made up her mind that she would finish the bottle before returning to bed, for even though she had secured the door and she knew that Delbert would not return tonight, she would need the help of the whiskey to fall asleep again.

She had reached for the bottle once more when she heard the first noises outside. She was almost certain that it was the sound of a moving dogsled and yet there was no sound at all from dogs. It could not be a dogteam, at least not the yelping dogs of Delbert's team. She put the bottle to her lips again and then she heard the muted sounds of voices outside her shack and the rustling of gear being unloaded and the crisp breaking of the snowcrust beside her doorway. The sounds were unmistakable.

But no voice called to her. And no one knocked on her door so Nellie quietly crossed to the lantern and blew it out with a quick puff of breath against her cupped palm. Then she moved to the window and peeked under the edge of the lifted curtain out into the darkness. She let her eyes adjust to the blackness and saw that it was indeed a dogsled and a team although these dogs had given no sound. There were also two figures bundled into the sled, immobile as if waiting for something to happen. And then Nellie heard the low whimpering moan from inside the sled and then another voice.

"Go ahead," one voice urged from the sled and then shortly thereafter Nellie was aware that someone was pushing at her door. It was not forceful nor threatening as Delbert would have done but only a gentle nudging against the creaking planks and a slight rattling of the steel bolt which announced that someone needed inside. Nellie moved to the door and put her ear close.

"Who is it?" she whispered but her words were strung together in a rush of breath. She cleared the whiskey from her throat and spoke again but this time she steadied herself and tried to make her voice sound deeper, calm. "Who's there," she said. "What do you want?"

"It is time," said the voice outside the door. It was deep and clipped and that of a man. Nellie stiffened. Another man this night was not what she wanted or needed. She drew in a deep breath, allowed her forehead to rest against the door and released the air slowly.

"Go away." She was aware that her voice was emotional and nasal and did not carry the strength she intended. She tried to forced the grin back onto her face even though it opened the cuts again on her cheeks and she knew it could not dissuade whoever was there through the planks of the door.

"Go away," she repeated and then held her breath when she heard no further attempts at the door. She pressed her ear to the splintered planks. The voice was still there but she knew now for certain that it was not Delbert's.

"It is time for the baby," the voice said but still it was not a request to enter. It was stated as if the fact alone could will the door open.

Nellie stared into the darkness of the room for a moment and wondered if she were dreaming. She wondered if she would awaken from another night with her fantasy, the dream in which she was carried by the same dogless sled each night over the soft summer tundra. In this dream there were always wildflowers growing just below the high ground, the earth lush with the longgrass perfect for basketmaking. In her dream Nellie always floated just above the muskeg toward the high bluff overlooking Tuluk Bay. But this bay was different. This bay was never cold and murky, never the whiskey color of Tuluk Bay. Nellie's bay was always the color of jade, deep and warm. And in her dream there was always the child. The baby would sometimes be asleep in the pouch she and Old Suyuk had sewn inside the squirrel skin parka. But more often now Nellie saw the baby curved against her perfect body, suckling the firm breast and drawing its life from hers and Nellie would awaken with a sudden jerk and cry into her pillow when she realized the child was not there.

"It is time for the baby," the voice said more urgently.

"Yes," Nellie whispered and the euphoria of the whiskey swept her away like the dogsled of her dream. "Yes, I am ready."

Nellie fumbled with the latch and then drew the door open and back against the wall. She stood there in the rush of cold air and darkness with her eyes closed and her head tilted back to one side and her arms spread to receive the child. But instead of an infant, something far different was thrust against her chest.

Maruluk stumbled through the door forcing Mi'sha against Nellie's body before she too fell to the floor. Immediately behind them stood the musher blocking the doorway, a shadow inside the furlined hood where the face should have been.

"*Keetuk,*" Nellie whispered. She knew it could be no one else. It was as if this man, this stranger who had spoken to her from outside her door had been there forever and knew all her fears and all her fantasies. But Nellie had time for neither fear nor fantasy now.

"You must help us," Maruluk said and began rocking gently back and forward on the floor. "This baby it is too soon."

Nellie was aware of the girl now and she felt her extended stomach pressed against her. She realized then what the old woman had meant. "But I can't help," Nellie protested. "I have no—"

"You have seen the *kassaqs.* You can save her and the baby. You have seen how," Maruluk said.

And then the whiskey and Delbert and Nellie's dream of a child and the sudden appearance of these people at her door were all swept away in a startling recognition: *This woman asking for her help was the Shaman, Old Maruluk.*

Then Nellie saw the face of Old Suyuk standing on the beach at Tuluk Bay and she felt a bitter anger rise in her throat. "Yes, I have seen the *kassaqs,*" Nellie hissed. "And so have you, old woman. Why don't you go to them? Why don't you call on their word for help?"

Maruluk said nothing.

"Ask the priest to help you old woman," Nellie continued. "Go up to the graveyard and ask him to step out of the grave and help you. Wasn't it he who set you on Old Suyuk? Surely there is some word or some book which you can call on now? Maybe his spirit will rise up and show you the way."

"Spirit?" Maruluk said and she realized what Nellie was saying. "The priest is dead?"

"Yes," Nellie said.

"*Raven,*" the old woman muttered.

Nellie waited for her to say more but she did not. It was as if this single word explained everything. Mi'sha stopped moaning when she heard this. She turned her head toward her grandmother to say something but she could not speak.

"Maybe this is the way it is to be old woman," Nellie said intending to mock Maruluk but she looked at the old woman and then at Mi'sha who pressed her head against her thigh and the words came out gently when she repeated them, "Maybe this is the way it is to be."

Then Nellie felt the quick closing of Mi'sha's hands against her hips and heard her soft moaning turn into cries of sharp pain. Nellie thought about Alexie alone now in their cabin at Tuluk-On-The-Bay, in the house of their dead parents and brothers and sisters and she decided that there had been enough death. Perhaps it was time to think of life instead because that too was the way it must be.

Nellie shook some of the whiskey fog from her mind and tried to think about what needed to be done. Instinctively she led the girl to the bed and sat her on the edge. Then she lifted her feet and forced her to lie flat. It was then she saw the blood on her gown where the girl's hands had clutched it. Maruluk stood watching and Nellie looked into the old woman's face and remembered how it had looked the day Old Suyuk had been forced into the mudflat. But Maruluk's face was different now. The old woman had resolution in her eyes but she was too exhausted to be of any help. The musher had simply moved inside and closed the door behind him. He stood silently against the wall, the hood of his sealskin parka still concealing his face in its shadow.

Nellie knew she would have to do something, at least make an effort to do what she could. She went to the stove and took the wash water she had used earlier and stood beside the door holding the pan with both hands. When the man moved to open it for her she did not look at him. "This is the father?" she asked over her shoulder. She tossed the water out into the darkness.

"No," said Maruluk. The old woman would not look at Nellie but sat on the edge of the bed and began to coo at the girl who whimpered between the sharp cries. "He is not the father. But it does not matter any more. This one will die. I know this one will die now and it will not need a father anyway. It comes too soon."

"Quiet, old woman," Nellie scolded. She moved quickly to refill the pan with water and place it back on the stove. "Why do you say that?"

"She threw herself down the bluff on the jagged rocks beside the river," Maruluk said. "She said she flew with Raven but I know this is not so. Raven would not do this. Mi'sha did not want the baby and she blamed herself. She meant to kill herself also and they both would have died but he—" Maruluk stopped and turned to the man.

Nellie stood near the bed but behind her she could feel the man tense in the shadows. "But why would Mi'sha do this?"

"Because of the father," continued Maruluk. "Because of who he is—"

*"Alexie?"* Nellie rasped and stopped cold. Maruluk shook her head and started to speak but she was interrupted by the girl.

*"No!"* The anguish in Mi'sha's voice silenced the old woman. She turned away from both her grandmother and Nellie and buried her face against the wall. "We don't have to talk about it again, ever."

Nellie put her hand on the back of the girl's head and sat on the bed beside the old woman. "It doesn't matter. Lie still now. You'll be okay."

Nellie stroked Mi'sha's hair gently with a warm rag, loosening the caked blood. She could feel the anger from both the girl and the man and together they filled Nellie's room. "Sometimes a man does not know." Nellie's voice was hollow and flat and without thinking she raised her hand and brushed the wound on her own cheek with the tips of her fingers.

Then suddenly he was there, standing over Nellie much taller than she had remembered and he had grasped the wrist of the hand she held against her cheek. Nellie could see in the shadow of his fur hood the eyes reflecting the lantern's flame as if they had become the source of the fire itself. The man's grip was firm but he did not hurt her and with his other hand he reached out and touched the open wounds on first one cheek and then the other and Nellie felt his touch as a strange source of both pain and comfort. Then she spoke the name without being asked.

"Delbert," she said but there was no bitterness, the word just there on her tongue in neither accusation nor apology, just the name of another man spoken as she might have said Swede or Felix. But when she felt the grip on her wrist relax she looked again into the man's eyes and she realized that by speaking Delbert's name she had loosed a fury. Nellie could not know it but it was the same rage that Mi'sha had set loose earlier on the trail that same day when in her pain the girl had cried out the name of the father of the child in anger and the musher had heard that too and he had understood without explanation just as he now understood Nellie without further words.

Then Nellie quickly added, "But not Finn, not Hjalmar the Finn," but she was not sure the man had heard or understood this and she wanted to explain further. When she reached out to touch his arm the man spun away from her and so Nellie turned her attention again to Mi'sha who was crying louder. "I should get the nurse," said Nellie rising from the edge of the bed.

"They must not know we are here," said Maruluk. "We are shamed enough without the *kassaqs* knowing. And what about him?" She gestured to the man in the room. "They would try to take him too. You know that. Please."

"And if the baby's dead?" Nellie looked at the old woman and then at the girl, fragile and weak, curled under the big quilt against the wall and Nellie knew she could not do much. She could only allow things to happen.

She turned back to the stove to bring more warm water and rags because it was the only thing she knew to do but she saw through the window that the sky had already turned gray and knew that soon people from Snag Point would be moving across the flats. She went to the window and tied a burlap bag under the new curtains shutting out prying eyes and darkening the room. It was then she noticed the man was gone as if he had vanished with the darkness.

"You will have to help," Nellie said. Gently she tugged the girl away from the wall and removed the quilt and her clothing. "She cannot have a baby with all this on."

For hours Nellie and Maruluk listened to the cries of the girl. The whiskey had worn off and the skin on the outside of Nellie's cheeks had grown taut with the dried blood from the cuts. She wondered if the cuts would leave scars but she did not have time to inspect them in her mirror and she did not have time to think about Finn or Delbert or why and where the man who had brought Maruluk and Mi'sha had gone. She knew only he had disappeared and Mi'sha's baby was almost here.

# SIXTEEN

At daylight Delbert stopped his dogteam on a nearby hummock just outside Snag Point. He could see the new curtains had been replaced with a burlap bag over the window of Nellie's shack and he suspected the door would be bolted. But Delbert no longer cared about Nellie or what she might be doing inside. He thought only about Finn, smug and secure wherever he was and about how everyone in Snag Point would soon know that Finn had just walked away from Delbert, ignored him as if he were a mosquito. What was worse they would also know about Nellie and would ask about the cuts on her face. He did not care if they knew about the cuts or even her chipped teeth but they would know about the other thing. Even if she did not tell them they would know about her rejection of him.

"What the hell you stopping here for, Delbert?" Yael said. He was sitting tucked inside a caribou skin along with the rifles and trail gear in the deputy's dogsled. "I'm financing this party so let's mush. The bastard's already got a day on us and you're just dragging your feet, Delbert."

"Yeah sure Yael only let's get one thing straight right now," said Delbert leaning over the handrail. "I'm the law here and it don't make a shit to me who you are. This party's mine and it will be done my way. Understand?"

"Law? What kind of law allows a man to be robbed of hundreds of dollars of trail gear and nothing done about it? Where the hell do you get off telling anybody about the law? Hell if I hadn't agreed to come along you'd have no idea which direction to go."

"Only one direction to Ekok," Delbert said. He stood on the back of the sled runners and called to the dogs. *"Mush."* Delbert brought the dogwhip around his head and cracked it on the hunched backbone of the lead dog. The animal cowered and snarled back at him but then in full awareness of what his master was demanding it lunged into the harness and started squealing in delight. "Come on, Tinney. You keep up too, boy. *Heel.*"

"But that ain't where he is by now." Yael turned around as far as he could in the sled and tried to talk over the squeals of the dogs. "He'll be heading to the Mikchalk," he said loudly and almost mentioned the pelts but he caught himself in time. Delbert ignored him anyway. He kicked hard at the snow with one free leg and rode the sled runner with the other.

"I said that ain't where he is," Yael screamed back but Delbert's team was yelping as they crossed the high ground above Snag Point with the cold morning air in their muzzles.

Even though they were still in sight of the village the dogs had been inactive too long and were already caught up in the exhilaration of the chase. So was Delbert. But he wanted to make one long sweep on the high ground above Snag Point just in case anyone in the village happened to be watching.

He kicked back hard against the snow with his free leg and then dropped off the sled runners and paced behind still holding onto the rail. He knew this would lighten the load some and with the extra weight of Yael in the basket the dogs would need all the help they could get. A steady pace was the secret and this time out he would need all the tricks he knew. There was no way he could come back this time without a quarry.

It had been one thing to lose a poacher once in a while or even to fail at solving a murder. He could always blame it on Keetuk and no one wanted to go after that crazy native even with Delbert along. All he had to do was suggest they get up a group to chase Keetuk and everyone would clam up saying it had been wolves or foxes breaking into caches or something inexplicable and mysterious.

But Nellie was different. Rejection by the town whore, a *klootch* no less, would be a defeat not easily explained. And if a fleabag like

Finn were allowed to come back and live with her then Delbert, the very law itself, would lose face. He would just have to get his man like the Mounties always did and charge him with something big. Stealing some trail gear from Yael was not big enough, murdering a man of God was. Delbert would charge Finn with the killing of Father Felix.

The very thought of such a religious desecration aroused Delbert's indignation. He narrowed his eyes into the brightness of the snow. The rush of cold morning air had caused his eyes to fill with tears, blurring and changing the string of seven rangy sleddogs into a matched set of fifteen proud strong Alaskan malamutes. And beside the sled pacing the whole procession Tinney became a muscular purebred German Shepherd, the tan hair on his belly blending into a sleek dark brown on his back and outlining his intelligent face.

Then Delbert envisioned himself on the sled. The drabgreen wool jacket became a scarlet colored tunic with black flaps over the pockets and a row of polished brass buttons ending just under the firm, carefully shaved, squared chin thrust forward in juxtaposition against the mustache, a brush of hair so carefully manicured that it appeared to be painted on his upper lip. And in his black leather gloved hand Officer Demara held a matching twenty-five foot braided black leather dogwhip, which he cracked over the heads of his charges, never actually touching them because that was unnecessary with such noble animals. He swung the whip out and around and brought it back over their heads with a quick jerk ending in a deafening crack, just a little noise to liven up the chase.

Delbert was still swinging the whip in great arches around his head and rocking the sled from side to side when the runners hit the edge of the escarpment on the high ground behind Snag Point. It teetered, tipped and then spilled Yael and the entire bundle of gear over the edge. The dogs, screaming and yelping, were pulled tumbling down the slope stopping in a tangled knot halfway to the bottom. Yael's body was just the right shape to continue rolling all the way down. He came to rest inside an alderpatch in a ball of caribou skin and gear and snow. Delbert had been luckier. When he sensed that the sled was going over he had snapped back and leaped clear in time to stand dumbfounded at the edge where he watched the whole disaster unfold down the incline.

"You stupid bastard," Yael called from below. He was on his feet, coughing and sputtering and ejecting snow from his mouth. "No wonder you never catch any criminals, you incompetent sonuvabitch."

Yael whipped the snow from his hat and started back up the slope cursing and grumbling and digging his toes into the snow for traction. Delbert said nothing although he knew exactly why the sled had tipped. Had he not mushed along this ridge a hundred times before on patrol? Had he not been on this same sled with this same team enough hours to become an integral part of it like the heart of the team itself? It was this fatassed Yael who had caused the accident, slowed him down. And now he would slow him down further if Delbert did not assist him up the bank.

Delbert was beginning to wonder if it was worth all the trouble to take Yael along. Down he went first to the dogs to set them free of the tangles of harness, then to the gear lugging it back up to the top. By the time Delbert had retrieved the team and the sled and all the gear his anger had subsided. So had Yael's who had stopped to rest three times and had almost arrived at the crest where Tinney lay belly down comfortably watching the drama below.

"Out of the way, you cur." Yael was on his hands and knees just below the dog and was not about to go around him.

"Heel, Tinney." Delbert stood near the dog who moved aside at the command. He reached over the edge and offered Yael his hand. Yael looked at the black gloved hand and then curbing his contempt took hold of it. Delbert had to lean backward to counterbalance him and when Yael suddenly mounted the edge of the embankment Delbert was caught off balance and fell backward pulling the fat little man on top of him. Yael lay there face to face with Delbert whose voice came out in a wheeze. "Get off, Yael. *Quick.*"

But Yael was paying no attention to Delbert's struggling. He was staring toward Snag Point a halfmile back along their path. "Well, I'll be a sonuvabitch," he whispered. "Look at that would you."

"Look at what?" Delbert squeaked and craned his head to see.

"It's burning. The sonuvabitch is *burning.*"

"What is? Get off lardass. *Get off!*" Delbert wriggled furiously trying to work his way from under Yael's weight.

"Wha—? Oh sure, let me help you up." Yael rolled off and offered his hand but Delbert refused. He pushed himself up and stood bent over catching his breath.

"Look." Yael pointed to the high ground overlooking the bay. "It's the church. Goddamn thing's on fire."

Stunned, Delbert stared at the burning church in the distance. It was a long while before he finally realized his role in Snag Point might demand more than simple bystander, perhaps even one as a leader in a situation like this. It was Tinney's excited barking at seeing people rush up the paths and fill the main street that finally galvanized Delbert. Hjalmar the Finn would just have to wait for now.

"*YeeeeeHaaaaaaa!*" Delbert screamed. "*Let's go, Tinney!*" He rushed to the sled and began lashing the dogs again. Yael fell in behind and lunged sideways into the basket of the sled just as the dogs moved.

"*Haw,*" Delbert called to the team trying to turn them back. "Haw you fleabags turn, *turn.*" He set hard on the brake digging the footspike into the snow. The animals finally responded with a wide sweeping turn and ran headlong toward the burning church. Yael had just regained his sitting position when they broke into the crowd which stood in a semicircle at the edge of the bluff.

"Stand back, stay clear!" Delbert yelled and rushed through the villagers, scattering adults and children alike.

Then Delbert realized that the villagers were doing just that: standing clear. There was not a sound coming from the crowd not even from the children, just blank staring faces listening to the soft crackling of the old building as the flames worked their way up one side. Delbert stood mesmerized by the faces as he looked first into one then another. There was Karl and Dago and Chubby and all the others, even Hard Working Henry who was weaving slightly with a peaceful look on his face, a glow that announced he had already had his first morning belt and was enjoying the warmth from this unexpected source.

"Well, ain't nobody going to do nothing?" Delbert screamed. Then he noticed the ladder leaning against the side of the church. He remembered reading something once about how fires worked and how real firemen always chopped holes in doors and walls and other places in a burning building. Delbert stepped quickly to his sled and pulled out his axe.

"Well, I ain't afraid," he said elbowing the villagers aside. "I sure as hell ain't going to stand here gawking and let her burn without doing something."

With an upraised arm and a palm toward the fire Delbert shielded his face from the heat and worked his way close enough to retrieve the ladder and drag it to the front of the building. The heat inside had begun to smoke and curl the white paint on the outside walls but the flames had not yet burst through. He stood and stared at the front of the church, not certain where to start. Then he noticed the single window at the peak of the gable end, a delicately wrought stained glass panel depicting the Virgin Mary and the Christ child. Delbert focused on it as the heat from the side of the building grew more urgent and intense on his face.

*Probably brought over from Russia, he thought, probably hundreds of years old, probably irreplaceable. But this is a crisis goddammit, an emergency.*

Delbert leaned the ladder against the building just under the window. The figures in the colored panes glowed alive with the flames which flickered behind them. Quickly he mounted the rungs of the ladder and rested his left side against the wall just below the stained glass.

Then he raised his axe and swung.

There came an audible intake of air in unison from the crowd below and Delbert was aware of this sound as the first of the three events which—even later after they had dragged him away from the blazing building—he remembered as having occurred almost simultaneously. The second event was the crash of his axe through the bottom pane, followed immediately by the third, the tremendous release of superheated air from inside the church as it erupted through the window raining shards of colored glass over the crowd and pushing the ladder and the axe and the fireman in one graceful pivot backward onto the ground.

When Delbert finally managed to sit up, the crowd that had dragged him clear was standing around him as they watched the final collapse of the walls of Father Felix's church. There was still no talking, only resigned acceptance that this building, like all the others which burned during winter when no water was available, would simply no longer be there.

Still, within the paradox of opinions concerning Father Felix and his influence on the village of Snag Point, this building seemed somehow special. Even Delbert wondered if perhaps he should explain how it had become necessary for him to destroy that window in order to save the church. But then his mind began to function in its official capacity again and he turned to the matters at hand. Like Felix himself, the building was simply gone, that was that. It was time to get on with the business of assigning blame.

Delbert looked into the faces around him and noticed Nellie was not there, making it easier to assumed his lawman's stance in front of the crowd with his hands on his hips and his chin elevated.

"Finn," he blurted. "It's Finn that's done this. He's done it for sure, set the church on fire."

A low rumble went through the gathering and Delbert looked over at Yael who had gotten out of the sled and stood at the edge of the crowd nodding his head and smiling.

"And that may not be all he's done either," Delbert mused when he was certain he had the undivided attention of the crowd. "Besides breaking into Yael's store and stealing him blind that may not be all…"

Delbert scanned the faces as he paced along the front ranks. He locked eyes with each person in turn and then magnetically each head followed him in a slow pivot as he rested his gaze on the unmarked white cross above the grave on the slope bearing the bodies of both Father Felix and Swede. Delbert looked back at the crowd and paused long enough to let this piece of drama sink in. He knew he would not have to explain in detail what he was thinking or what he had to do.

"And I aim to get him and have him tried for all of it," he whispered. "Now let's just break this up and go on about our business."

"Finn wouldn't have done all this, Delbert," offered Henry. "You know that." Some of the others nodded agreement. "I think it's Keetuk again, just like before. I'm telling you he's closing in on us."

"Now you just get on about your business," Delbert ordered. "I got knowledge about all this that I ain't at liberty to share and I got everything in hand so you go on now. All of you, git."

The group slowly dispersed leaving Delbert and Yael. Yael moved over and stood beside the deputy. "You know, Delbert, I decided I ain't going with you after all."

"I thought you was hot to catch him?"

Yael produced a tin of snuff and offered it. He would have to work Delbert carefully. When given an opening Yael Feldstein never missed an opportunity. And he never threw away One-eyed Jacks in a poker game. "Finn ain't going to let you catch him, you know that. And I'm just slowing you down that's all. Let's just admit it."

"Think so?"

"Right."

"What makes you so sure he'll resist?"

"He said so," Yael lied. "He told me that night in the poker game before he broke into my store. Finn said if you thought you was ever going to get him into one of them hearings you were just bucking a heavy tide. I think I know what he meant and that's why I packed this." Yael opened his fur parka and exposed a forty-five revolver tucked into his belt. "He'll get you first, Delbert. And he's probably got Marvin to help him."

Delbert thought about this and how it fit. He needed no real convincing but he had to be sure Yael would explain all this to everyone in Snag Point when he returned with Finn—or Finn's body.

"And you can't be slowed down none now," Yael went on. He eyed the deputy and thought about the pelts, his pelts, and how he would need time later to go up for them. Finn must not be allowed to reach them. But Yael knew he could not tell Delbert about the furs. As badly as he wanted to catch Finn, Delbert could never allow Yael to take all those illegal furs. Delbert would have to confiscate them as further evidence that Finn was a hardened criminal and Yael would never see them.

"You gotta get after him right now, Delbert, catch him on the river. I know he's going up to his cabin on the Mikchalk and you can't let him reach it. He's like a wolverine in that country. He'll get you first if you allow him to beat you there."

"You're right, Yael. Two on a dogsled's just added weight. Finn must have circled back and set this fire just to tease us, knowing we'd try to put it out, slow us down."

"You got it, Delbert. Crafty. That scrawny little sonuvabitch is crafty."

"Well, don't sell me short, fat man. Old Delbert's got a trick or two also. But standing here ain't catching him." He walked toward the smoldering ashes and found his axe where it had fallen clear. He tucked it under the caribou skin with the other gear. Then he stood on the back of the runners and turned to Yael. "If you see Moon tell her I'll be coming back."

Yael nodded.

"Soon. And tell her not to worry about me, okay?"

Yael nodded again.

"Come on, Tinney, we got work to do. *Mush.*" Delbert raced off toward the Northeast leaving Yael standing on the slope with the smoke from the remains of the church wrapping around his legs and moving across the flats toward Nellie's shack.

*And the smoke from the church moves quickly on the breeze rising over the edge of the bluff. It snakes its way above the drama being played out inside Nellie Napiuk's shack. It blends with the dark smoke from her oilstove and finally both trails move as one into the shadows of the trees behind the shack where a silent watcher has waited out this drama he has created at the church and now he stands poised with his dogwhip in his hand. His eyes follow the wavering path of Deputy Delbert Demara as he and his team move toward the Chiktok River. And then when the distance between them seems appropriate the watcher gives a single cry to his dogs and he moves out in pursuit. And inside Nellie's shack another voice sounds, that of an infant, and it echoes the sharp cry of the watcher who erupts from the shadows.*

# SEVENTEEN

Five miles below Finn's cabin a traveler moving upriver must make a choice, for here the Mikchalk River divides into two branches. In the spring it is swollen with melting snow but in the fall the river runs feeble. Shortly thereafter and until the cycle completes itself in the spring it is frozen and lifeless. It is during this time that the river becomes a pathway of ice and the traveler must take careful note of the subtle slope of the terrain. He must think beyond the confusing array of lifeless alders on the embankment and choose the right direction at the fork of the river. If he selects the wrong one he will not find the prime trapping area and the comfort of Hjalmar the Finn's cabin. Instead he will drift into a vast bowl of glaciers uninhabited and unexplored, an overwhelming chasm where the snow has been driven hard against grayrock walls, snow and ice and rocks which can without warning loose themselves in one treacherous mass.

Finn did not have to think about the right direction. Without hesitation he had moved ahead of Marvin as soon as he had cleared the trees and stepped onto the frozen Mikchalk River.

Although he could see ahead Finn was confident about the direction he was going, Marvin decided to stop where the river forked. He pondered his own choice, wondering which one would be right for him. The renewal of hope since Finn had rescued him from the steaming hothole had begun to wan even with the dried clothes at the burning spruce tree and a fresh start the following day. Finn's optimism had driven them both and they had made quick progress across the tundra avoiding further hotholes. They had intersected the Mikchalk River at the fork just below Finn's cabin.

Even with the delay Marvin thought there would be a good chance he and Finn would arrive ahead of Delbert and his dogteam. He knew he should not have hesitated in pushing onward behind Finn. There should have been no reluctance now to carry out the plan for moving the pelts, salvaging both Marvin and Finn's hopes for something better and he should not hesitate in moving rapidly to Finn's cabin and warming himself. But it was precisely this thought—the heat which would soothe the bite of the cold—which had given Marvin pause, for it would also release within Marvin's body the agony that comes with the thawing of frozen flesh.

Over the past few hours Marvin had recognized that his feet were far beyond frostbite and were nothing more than numbed lifeless clubs. He had commanded them to shuffle along and had seen them move the snowshoes but when Marvin had paused and tried to wiggle his toes he felt nothing. And now just as he had decided not to tell Finn about the feet he decided not tell him of his sudden decision to take the opposite direction at the fork of the river and drift into the glacier bowl.

He did not know what lay ahead but he knew it would not be the warmth of Finn's cabin. As long as the feet were kept frozen there would be little pain and he could simply allow the numbness to grow and consume the remainder of his body. Now that he had chosen the chasm instead of following Finn he was moving much faster, unaware that Finn had reversed direction and followed him and he was startled when Finn suddenly grabbed his arm from behind and spun him around screaming into his face. "Now what the hell?"

"I'm going this way," declared Marvin.

"Well, fine." Finn let his arm drop. "That's just dandy with me except that ain't the way to my cabin."

Marvin turned away and kept moving.

"I said that's the wrong way," Finn called. He shook his head at Marvin and tried to remember. Had Marvin not been here before? Had he not stayed in Finn's cabin dozens of times over the years? Maybe the cold had disoriented him.

"No direction," Finn muttered. "At least Swede and No-Talk could find the goddamn cabin. This one's got no sense of direction at all." Finn caught him again and followed a few paces behind as he talked. "Okay Marv, see for yourself but I'm telling you this ain't the right way."

Marvin did not reply. Finn took it for disagreement. "Hell, I ought to know where my own cabin is? Shouldn't I ought to know that, Marv? Hey, answer me that one?"

Marvin finally stopped without turning. He held his back rigid and spoke quietly as Finn listened speechless to the words and realized what they meant. "It's the feet. Frostbite's gone. I can't feel them at all now, Finn."

It was a long while before Finn moved beside Marvin and hunkered down in his favorite trail thinking position with his butt on the back of his snowshoes. He did not look up at Marvin's face turned into the distance, grim and pale. The black eyepatch devoid of any former mystery was crusted with frost from Marvin's breath.

Finn stared at Marvin's feet and then tested his own toes by wiggling them inside his boots. Suddenly Finn was overcome with a flush of guilt for having convinced himself his own feet were okay. As a gesture of apology, or celebration, he did not know which, Finn removed his mitten and took out a tin of snuff he had tucked inside his shirt to keep thawed. He tapped the lid with a fingernail before he opened it. Without looking up he offered it above his head to Marvin who ignored the gesture and continued to stand without speaking.

Finn turned his eyes up and studied Marvin's profile, stern and rigid as a block of ice. "Shut up," said Finn after a long silence. "Quit yakking so goddamn much. I'm thinking."

Marvin said nothing.

"Can't you see I'm thinking? Can't you see I'm figuring out what to do now just like I done at the hothole?"

Marvin remained silent, stiff as an axe handle.

"Can't you get it through your thick head for once that I can't think when you keep talking so damn much?" Finn stood and moved in front of Marvin to look into his face, his voice rising. "And I'm done offering you this, too."

He made a show of poking the pinch of snuff between his lower lip and gum. "Hell, I'm the only one around here who thinks of things like this anyway." He snapped the lid back onto the snuff tin. "The good things that makes for traveling out here halfway bearable."

Finn tongued the tobacco into the pocket of his lip and screamed directly into Marvin's face not four inches away from his goodeye. "So in the future, deadbeat, you just try to remember to bring your own. I'm talking about the next time we go out you hear? You understand, the *next* time."

Marvin switched his focus from the jagged peaks in the distance to Finn's eyes, which were beginning to water and fill from the charge of snuff.

"You listening to me?" Finn demanded again. He narrowed his eyes to their most threatening slits, the kind he usually reserved for a poker face to accompany a pair of deuces. Then he brushed past Marvin and began to retrace his trail back to the fork in the frozen river.

"Yeah," whispered Marvin. He tried to blink the fatigue from his goodeye. But Finn could not hear him. "I suppose I'm listening." With a shrug of resignation he hunched back into his trail position shifting the packboard. Then he turned around and began walking toward Finn who had slowed. When Marvin caught him he shuffled beside Finn for awhile before he spoke. "God, your breath reeks," Marvin said catching his wind. "When you're dipping."

"Well, yours ain't no pot of honey." Finn dropped a twisted stream of black saliva onto the ice. The intervals of silence lengthened with only the sound of scraping snowshoes as the two walked side by side.

"They'll hurt like hell you know," said Marvin quietly.

"Yep," agreed Finn.

"When they start to thaw."

"Yeah."

"I'll scream and cuss and, hell, maybe even need some whiskey."

"Probably."

The two passed the fork in the river and moved on up the ice toward Finn's cabin. There was more silence before either of the men spoke again though both were thinking the same thing.

"Any at your cabin? Whiskey, I mean," said Marvin.

"Probably."

Silence again and then, "They'll swell up and turn purple and blue and all shiny," Marvin said. "Puffy."

"Mmmmm…" Finn was trying to remain neutral because Marvin was talking to himself anyway.

"And I might lose a toe. Hell maybe two, three."

"Maybe."

*And gangrene!* Marvin wanted to scream. *I could even get gangrene and pass out and get a fever and die in agony! What the hell's the point? Freezing's better!*

But both knew this possibility; neither saw any need to say it. They did not speak even after they had seen Finn's cabin tucked into the familiar notch of spruce trees atop the riverbank, its back turned so it was hardly there at all to the Northwind. Finn paused and looked at it and drew in an extra breath. He released it slowly through his teeth warming both the air and his spirits.

Crude and desolate as it was, his cabin had remained a sanctuary against both the cold and those who would threatened him. Just seeing it and knowing it was secure after so many months lifted Finn's spirits. The pelts he and Swede had taken were nearby, also secure. They rested high above the ground in the cache they had built deep in the thick of the spruce trees.

But new elements had entered his plans. Though he knew this was not a good place to try, the presence of familiar surroundings gave Finn a surge of hope he might actually help Marvin's feet. Snag Point would have been better. But that was days away and Marvin would never make it back along the trail on frozen feet.

"Let's check it out," Finn said brightly. He unstrapped his snowshoes and kicked the toes of his boots into the snowberm and moved quickly up the side of the riverbank. Marvin followed but stumbled and fell back several times before he gained the plateau above the river. Finn had disappeared. Marvin was near collapse when he entered the darkness of the cabin where he waited for his goodeye to adjust, blinking away the brightness of the snow which had sapped his night vision.

There was a moment of terror for Marvin as the figure standing silently in the middle of the cabin became first an outline and then a blurred faceless spectre. When it did not speak Marvin paused and tensed with the realization that it might not be Finn but Delbert or Yael—or someone worse. He inhaled a sharp breath of musty air and was about to mutter the familiar feared name when instead the figure spoke to him.

"It don't seem right," Finn said. Marvin released his breath with a snort. "Something's not right, Marvin."

Marvin could see better now and he realized Finn was also tensed, inspecting the inside of the cabin and the fear came back to Marvin though not as strong now that he knew it was Finn.

Finn tried to place things where he had left them months ago realizing something was awry. He spoke flatly, "Someone's been here."

But it had been so long since he had left the cabin in search of Swede that Finn could not say why he knew this. Even so, inside the sanctity of his own cabin he did not feel the same fear that Marvin had felt only a concern that things they needed might not be there. Things like whiskey.

Finn moved quickly and took inventory of the shelves and the boxes in the corner by the woodstove. He was saving the fate of the whiskey for last in an effort to appease whatever gods might be watching, powers that might frown on him if he appeared too curious about such a thing as a bottle of liquor. Finn remembered the bottle had been left half full. When he thought about Swede again the familiar ambivalence swept over him as he remembered how Swede would have insisted it was half empty. But there was no warmth to the ambivalence this time when Finn remembered that Swede had left Nellie neither half full nor half empty, just empty.

"Flour's been used," Finn said without emotion. He picked up a large tin box.

Marvin watched him move about the room but he was not much interested in this part of the inventory.

"Some beans left though," Finn continued. "And salt. And lots of this." He picked up a strip of dried beaver flesh and sniffed it, turned his nose away. "Not too sweet but it's okay I guess. Whoever was here must have had a good supply of beaver. It's strung up all over the walls." Finn worked his teeth into the dried meat and began to chew on it.

"Wonder what they done with the pelts? From the looks of all this dried meat there must have been lots of pelts Marv. Course we don't need no more anyway, do we?"

Finn had said the magic word and he raised his eyebrows when he spoke and showed Marvin his teeth, a small piece of beaver meat still clinched between them. "Here, you sit and work on this awhile. I need to look around some more."

He helped Marvin sit on the edge of the bunk and gave him a piece of the drymeat. There was no mention of the stove and the good stack of firewood beside it. There would be time for that later after the cabin had been inspected and the whiskey checked out and maybe even a friendly snort or two and some talk. Talk first, have a little food and whiskey, talk some more, talk about a plan, talk about the feet maybe. A plan. And then heat the cabin.

Finn poked around the room some more and then went outside and Marvin heard him crunching around, circling the cabin. Then it was quiet. He thought Finn had wandered off to check the cache and the pelts.

Finn had considered it but he had only paused for a while at the edge of the cabin to look deep into the woods, black and somber and winterstill. He was remembering how he and Swede had made a small clearing in the spruce trees and built the cache two miles back from the cabin, hidden in the thickest part of the woods. They had erected it on stilts ten or twelve feet which was higher than usual and had carefully nailed sections of stovepipe around each of the four legs so squirrels and mice could not grip the logs and climb up to chew on the pelts inside. And they had hidden a ladder in the woods nearby for easy access to the beaver pelts. But no passerby, human nor animal could get up into the little cabin they had placed on top of the platform without the ladder.

Finn smiled when he thought about the cache and what it held. He felt a strong urge to go back into the spruce trees and to check it out, run his fingers thorough the prime fur and think about Nellie. But he remembered Marvin inside the cabin and he thought about Marvin's feet. He began to wonder how close Delbert would be. Finn was certain the deputy would be on his way by now. The smile left his face. He turned back to the cabin.

"I guess we'll be okay for now," he said as closed the door behind him. "Must not have been Keetuk that was here." He pried the lid from a rusted coffee can.

"How so?" Marvin was relieved that Finn had said the name so casually.

"Sugar." Finn held up the can so Marvin could see inside. "It's still here. The bastard always steals the sugar first. You can always tell when he's been around but then you should know that. First he takes your sugar and then your pelts, your whiskey and then god knows what else he'll do. But he always finds the sugar." Finn put the lid back on the can and sighed. "Guess I'll check out the bottle. Now let's see, where was it me and Swede hid it?"

Finn stroked the stubble on his chin and frowned as he crept about the room in a mock game of hide-and-seek, fully aware hc had a very interested audience.

"Was it here?" Finn jerked the tinderbox away from the wall. "Nope, guess not." He pushed the box back and straightened it very carefully into its former place. "Well, maybe here?" He dropped to his knees and lifted the oilcloth from the small table, peering under it. He looked through the legs of the table and across the room at Marvin sitting on the edge of the bed and grinned at him.

"Okay, okay," Marvin said. "Cut the crap and find it or I'm back down the river. This ain't funny."

Finn cleared his throat, realizing he had carried the game too far. He stood and walked to the slab bench next to the woodstove and pulled it away from the wall. Then he knelt and poked a finger into a knothole in a floor plank and lifted it. "Well, what do you know, look what I found." He raised the bottle of whiskey above his head and smiled as he inspected the contents. "Hell, there's more here than I thought. It's three fourths full or as old hammerhead Swede might have said, one fourth empty."

Marvin looked at the bottle and then at his feet and managed a small smile. "Now what?"

"Well, first I'm going to get a fire going and heat up some water." Finn was all action now, plan in motion. "Then while I do that you can have a few snorts of this." He handed Marvin the bottle. "Now go easy on it. I don't want you passed out because I'll be putting those feet in some warm water and I can't do it with you slobbering drunk."

Finn moved back to the woodstove and stuffed in the kindling and touched a match to it. It caught and the sight of the working flames calmed Marvin at first. But when he thought about his feet thawing and the inevitable pain he began to panic. He uncorked the whiskey and let the liquid lay on his tongue, cold at first from being next to the frozen ground but then pungent and stinging and warm as it glowed inside his gut.

Marvin thought for a moment when the first swill had filled his chest that he could feel his toes again but he knew this was not true. He knew when he finally did regain the feeling in his feet it would not be pleasant, not at all what the whiskey was now offering. But he would be prepared. He sucked another long swallow from the mouth of the bottle and continued to watch Finn who had built the kindling into a full flame that whistled and thumped up the rusted flue.

"She's really going now," Finn chirped. "How's she feel? Can you feel her over there yet, Marv?" Finn rubbed his palms together over the top of the stove. "I used to call her Mariann, this old stove," Finn confessed. "I called her Mariann all the time especially when I was here by myself. She's the closest thing to a woman I ever had up here. Warm and friendly just like a woman."

"Well it wasn't Mariann you was calling out in your sleep back there on the trail." Marvin was beginning to get loose now slurring his words. "It was Stella." He moved a hand inside his Mackinaw to the pocket with the leather folder. He had not chanced a look inside the folder since the hothole but he knew the leather had dried out with the coat as it hung beside the bonfire Finn had built. Marvin thought about the photograph and wondered if Stella's image would still be visible.

"Well, like I said, you had been talking about Stella so much I guess her name was just in my head. Besides a man doesn't call out the name of a *stove* in his sleep. That would be a little stupid. Hell, it could just as easily have been the name of that crazy native or anybody. I was tired. I been having wild dreams ever since Swede was done in but they sure as hell ain't been about Texas or any of that shit thirty years ago. That's your dream and that's okay by me. I got different fish to fry. You feel this heat yet?"

"Not yet but that's okay. I'm warming up inside real good." Marvin tipped up the bottle again and then held it out. "Better have a hit of this."

Finn tongued the snuff deeper into the pocket of his lower lip to get it out of the way for the whiskey. He started to cross over and take the bottle from Marvin's hand but instead he paused at the table between them and looked at Marvin still pale sitting on the edge of the bunk in the shadows. Finn made a quick calculation of the whiskey left inside and what Marvin might need. "Maybe just a quick hit."

Finn turned his back to Marvin and lifted the bottle and held it to his lips but instead of allowing the whiskey to flow, he plugged the mouth of the bottle with his tongue and pretended to take a long swill. Then he quickly brought it down, released a long sigh and handed it back. "Damn that's good. You feeling anything yet?"

"Sure," Marvin said and then, "oh, you mean the feet. Nope not yet but I'm sure feeling this." He lifted the whiskey again.

Finn removed the globe from the kerosene lamp on the table and wiped the carbon from inside, lit the wick and replaced it. Then he went outside with a dishpan and returned with it full of snow and set in on the woodstove. "This will take a while. You just relax, work on that bottle."

"Well, I sort of feel bad about this. I mean this being your whiskey and Swede's whiskey and all that." Marvin held the bottle up to the light and squinted at the amber liquid down to half now. He was feeling much better and he looked through the bottle and centered Finn's figure in the clear part of the empty half. "Funny how this stuff can change things. Ever notice that Finn? You ever look through one of these things when it's empty?"

Finn stood by the stove shaking the melting snow down further into the dishpan. He smiled at Marvin feeling no pain and turning philosophical.

"Like now," Marvin continued. "Like when I get you right in the center of this bottle, this empty half of it."

"Yeah." Finn was heartened by Marvin's changing mood. This was more like the Marvin G. Crush he remembered years ago.

"You're all warped, Finn, distorted and fuzzy. See?" He squinted again at Finn through the empty part of the glass. "And if you move it this way…." He tilted the bottle so that the whiskey ran up into the neck almost spilling out the mouth. "Well now your feet are all different colored with the booze and your legs are almost cut off. Or all angled, sort of awkward you know."

"Yeah sure." Finn shook the pan and looked at Marvin's feet still inside his boots. "Now don't go spilling any of it. We better think about getting them boots off pretty soon."

Marvin brought the bottle back down a bit and looked over the top of it this time at Finn. "Yeah." He put the jug back to his lips, this time sucking hard on the mouth in eager gulps.

Finn moved across the room and took the bottle from Marvin's grip. "Okay, that's enough for now."

"Well, you should have some too…." Marvin had a silly grin on his face and slurred his words badly. "You have another pull too partner, old Finn, old Phineas Farrow alias Hjalmar the Finn *the by-god-hootin'-rootin'-tootin'-wildass-trapper-Hjalmar-the-Finn.*"

"Okay, okay." Finn tilted his head back again and once more plugged the bottle with his tongue and pretended to drink. "Now you hold onto this. I'll see if that water's warm."

Marvin waited until Finn's back was turned and quickly took another long pull from the bottle. Finn heard the liquid gurgling down the neck but he kept his back to Marvin while he checked the dishpan.

"Yeah, that's plenty of whiskey for now. You just lay off it and sit tight cause this water's getting warm now." Finn poked the last of the snow down into the water listening to the bubbles as they continued to gurgle up the neck of the bottle. He figured it would be almost empty now so he turned and went back to Marvin who was slumped with his elbows resting on his knees, the bottle gripped loosely in one hand. Finn took it from him and set it on the table and said, "Let's get 'em off."

"Finn?"

"Yeah?"

"How the hell are we gonna get them pelts back down to Snag Point? Tell me again?"

"In the spring stupid. We'll have to wait until spring breakup and take them down the river. Now take off them boots."

"Yeah," Marvin said. "Spring breakup. Down the river. Cause I don't think I can carry none of them for awhile with these feet, Finn. You know, 'til these feet get okay."

"Yeah right. After them feet get okay. Now get the goddamn boots off."

Marvin looked up at him, a face full of confused drunkenness. Then he bent over the edge of the bunk to unlace his boots but in so doing he tumbled off and sprawled onto the floor. He lay there, eyes closed, moaning.

Finn did not move to help him. He returned to the dishpan and poked a finger into the water. He brought it out abruptly, shaking the heat from it.

"That'll do," he said to himself and then he returned and stood over Marvin. "You stupid ass." He bent over Marvin's feet and began to unlace the boots. The leather was still too stiff with ice to work loose so he brought cups of hot water from the stove and slowly poured them over the boots until he could work them off. Marvin was breathing deeply in a semiconscious stupor, the moans drawn out with each breath. When Finn struggled to remove the boots and socks the groans did not intensify as he had expected.

"Well, they ain't thawing yet," Finn said. "He ain't so drunk that he wouldn't have felt me tugging."

He lifted Marvin under the arms and dragged him back onto the bunk leaving his bare feet dangling over the end so he could pack the warm rags around them. He took the hot pan of water over and set it next to the bunk below the bare feet and then he brought over the lantern and knelt so he could inspect them.

Finn winced at the sight of the feet in the light. The toes were bluegray but above that the flesh turned waxy white up to the ankle bones. Finn shook his head and drew in a deep breath and spat into the shadows against the log wall.

"Damned idiot." He rose and went to the table and sat down heavily on the bench. He looked outside through the tiny window and down across the frozen river now growing black with the dusk. The wind had picked up, this time from the north but the cabin was cozy now that Mariann was going strong. It was only by the stiff jerking of the tops of the spruce trees on the opposite riverbank that Finn knew the wind was becoming stronger and that it would be a very cold night. He lifted the bottle of whiskey and pondered its remaining contents.

"Well, even this won't do you much good now, Marv," he said to no one. Finn looked over at the feet again and he thought about Marvin's one remaining goodeye and about his dream to return to Texas and about Stella Villard. He began to wonder if Marvin had been right. Maybe Phineas Farrow alias Hjalmar the Finn was indeed a jinx at least where Marvin G. Crush was concerned. Maybe Marvin had been right all along that the two should never have met in Texas.

But then Marvin G. Crush had been a grown man and he knew the risks involved in harebrained investments. And he knew the risks involved in a long trek across the Alaskan tundra too. Finn decided Marvin should have known all along about the dangers in threading his way around the hotholes. He should have stayed on Finn's trail then he would not be in this predicament now with feet frozen and far from any medical help and no dogsled or dogteam to whisk him back to Snag Point. That is, no dogteam except that of Deputy Delbert Demara who was surely near Finn's cabin by now.

And Marvin should have known the risks involved in introducing Phineas Farrow to Stella Villard with her stock certificates all those years past. Finn did not want to think about that now; that too was done. He and Marvin had bigger problems now. Finn needed to think about the frozen flesh of Marvin's feet. He needed to concentrate on how to warm Marvin's flesh properly so that it might heal. He could not allow himself to think about how warm the flesh of Stella Villard had been next to his own all those years ago in Texas. And Marvin need never know about that at all. It was as dead as Marvin's toes were, let it stay that way. If Marvin ever saw Stella again she could tell him if she wanted to. Finn tipped the bottle but this time he filled his mouth and swallowed. Then he held it up to the light to measure, and if Swede had been there to remind Finn, he would have agreed that this bottle was indeed three fourths empty.

# EIGHTEEN

*It is a cold wind that passes high over the small clearing slashed out of the thickest part of the spruce grove. It moves only the tops of the tallest trees and brushes the ridgepole of the small cache built above the ground on heavy log stilts. It lifts a wisp of snow from the sod roof and sets it onto the wind, the cold flecks finally melting against the face of a figure standing at the edge of the trees. The man tenses as if awakened by the sudden coldness against his cheek and then he hesitates and finally moves quick and alert and determined. He drags the dry branches from the surrounding trees and packs them around the four legs of the cache and returns to the forest for more until the pile is as high as his head, like a huge nest at the feet of some prehistoric creature. And then he huddles at one corner of the nest and in the blackness a small flame erupts, tries to live and then dies. Again the flame pierces the darkness, flutters briefly and is gone. Finally one small shaft of fire catches, holds, grows slowly as it is fed with birchbark and then it rushes up into the nest of dry spruce boughs and the heat forces the man to back away downwind. He stands watching from the edge of the clearing, the nest and the cache ablaze now, lighting the face of the forest and sending sparks high onto the cold wind. And then the figure moves away and disappears back into the trees to escape the stench from the stacks of burning pelts.*

Marvin rolled over on his bunk and tried to blink the booze from his head. He ran his tongue across his upper lip and swallowed hard twice but there was nothing left in his mouth to moisten his throat. He forgot the pain in his head when he realized he could now feel his

231

feet. He tried to sit but the room tilted away from him and the bunk came up and hit him in the side of the head.

Marvin had seen a blur of a figure standing in the early morning light at the window. He tried to make his voice form words but nothing would come except a whine, small at first, almost a grunt but then it gained volume when the pain surged from his feet. He wanted to reach down and claw at them, to tear the blanket off and see how bad they were but he could not raise his body without his head whirling. Adding to his agony was the stench of burnt fur which lingered in the room.

"Sickening ain't it," said Finn from across the room. "Damn near makes you want to puke, don't it?" He moved from the window and stood over Marvin who was working his shoulders left and right on the bunk trying to get his body into a comfortable position, trying to ease the pain by rocking first one way and then the other. It was useless.

"Sorry, partner. Wish I could do something. You'll just have to bear it 'til the circulation's back."

Marvin tried to sit up again but Finn pushed him back down. "Take it easy. Ain't no sense trying to get up yet."

"I want to see them." Marvin had found his voice but it was weak and thin. "Let me look at them."

"What good will that do. Seeing them ain't going to do one damn bit of good, Marv." Finn held his weakened partner against the bunk with one hand. "He's out there you know." Finn attempted to take Marvin's mind off the pain. It did not work.

"Goddammit I want to see them. Who's out there?" Marvin struggled again to sit. "And what the hell are you burning in here?"

"Delbert's out there and it ain't nothing in here. Whatever's burning's out there too."

"Delbert?"

"Yeah. I seen him across the river in the trees at first light. He's tied his team up over there somewhere and he's watching us. Dumbass. I seen the badge shining on his hat as soon as the sun hit it. I figured he would have been here sooner. Maybe old Keetuk caught up with him and they had it out or something."

"If Keetuk had caught him then Keetuk would be here not Delbert," Marvin offered. "Maybe it's better Delbert anyway."

"Yeah. If you gotta choose." Finn sighed and walked over to the window and peeked out again. "But I expect Keetuk's out there some-where too. He always seems to be. Life's just full of dumbass choices nowdays."

"Meaning me? Maybe I should have just stayed in Ekok. Maybe you should have left me back there on the river. Or back in the hothole." Marvin turned toward the wall whimpering each time he exhaled. Finn looked at him and was almost ready to agree that Starvin' Marvin was indeed the most stupid goddamn choice for a partner he had ever made and what was worse Finn had made that decision twice now but he stopped short of saying it.

He stared at the blanket covering Marvin's legs and he thought about how the feet had appeared two hours earlier when he put the last of the warm water over them. Huge blisters had taken the place of toes and blueblack flesh showed where the frozen waxy areas had been. Finn hesitated to think what they might look like now. Or what they would be like in a few days when the gangrene took over and began to work its way up Marvin's legs. Finn stopped short of considering Marvin's fate if he did not get what small medical attention would be available in Snag Point. Instead he went to the stove and began to heat up some water in the coffee pot and decided to wait for Delbert to make his move.

Across the frozen river from Finn's cabin Delbert sat crosslegged in the snow with the top of his beaver hat showing above a huge spruce deadfall on which he had propped his brass telescope. In the darkness before dawn Delbert had tied off his dogteam back in the woods. He was trying to determine what he would face inside Finn's cabin and he needed time to work out a plan. Delbert envisioned how the two men trapped like animals would put up one hell of a fight maybe even to the death.

"Pistols," he whispered to Tinney who lay asleep curled in the snow beside him. "Or maybe even rifles. They'll be waiting for me to make my move, planning to get me before I take them. And they'll have guns, pistols or rifles or both. But I just might have a surprise or two for them Tinney."

Delbert was remembering how it had been with the Royal Mountie in a book he had once read. The officer had trailed a killer by dogsled for hundreds of miles through the Canadian wilderness. He had finally caught him holed up in a deserted cabin and had brought him back alive after a fierce gunfight which had left the Mountie wounded. In the book the Mountie had sneaked around behind the cabin away from the window, kicked open the door and blazed away with his pistol taking a slug in the shoulder before shooting the killer's gun from his hand. Delbert remembered the Mountie lost a considerable amount of blood and had slumped twice from weakness over the back of the sled but managed to regain consciousness just in the nick of time to avert a takeover by the killer who was riding in the sled handcuffed to a siderail.

"It's almost the exact situation, Tinney," Delbert muttered through his teeth. The dog did not move. "What we have here is the same basic situation."

He tilted his head forward and squinted into the telescope and the small pane of glass in the front of Finn's cabin filled the lens. Delbert could see him. He was certain it was Hjalmar the Finn's angular nose and chin at the corner of the pane, the barrel of some kind of gun, pistol or rifle or maybe both, resting on the sill ready to blaze away at the first sight of Delbert and his dog, those criminal eyes glaring back as if Finn knew he were hidden here.

But Finn could not know that. Delbert had been too shrewd. He smiled thinking about how he had turned his fur hat around earlier so the badge would be in the back and would not glint in the morning sunrise when he peered over the log and into the telescope.

Delbert turned around and leaned back against the deadfall to talk to Tinney about the plan he had been framing as he had watched the cabin. But he forgot about the hat, still backward on his head and now turned with the badge toward the cabin. It glinted and sparked each time Delbert moved.

Had he wanted to, Finn could easily have kept watch on Delbert all day. He could have sat at the window and watched the sun flicker off the brass telescope and off Delbert's badge. But Finn was not interested in Delbert's whereabouts or his plan. Delbert would come; that much was certain. There was no use getting excited about it. Finn sat in the cabin and listened to Marvin's agony and drank the black coffee. And he thought his own private thoughts, made his own private plans.

Across the river Delbert unsnapped his holster and pulled his pistol out using the new lanyard which he had attached to his gun. He had looped the cord around his neck in the event he might drop the gun in a scuffle with a criminal. Delbert spun the cylinder, checking the cartridges. "We'll go across after dark, Tinney."

The dog still had not moved so Delbert poked him awake with the muzzle of the gun. "Hey, Tinney, we'll be moving out at dark when they can't see us cross the river. What we'll do is go down the river a bit and just ease across on the ice."

Delbert turned back toward the cabin and waved the gun as he spoke. "We can leave the dogteam and most of our gear until we have both of the bastards cuffed and disarmed and down to our size. We'll come around from the backside of the cabin Tinney over there away from the window. And then we'll just bust through the door."

He paused thinking through this critical moment in his plan. He would have to be alert and Tinney might have to disarm one of the men perhaps by grabbing an arm and shaking a pistol or rifle loose. "Now you get some sleep, okay?" He turned back to the dog. Tinney was already asleep again.

"Good dog," he said. "You rest up."

It was dusk and Finn had already cleaned the carbon from inside the lantern globe, trimmed the wick and refilled the kerosene when he heard the deputy and the dog breaking through the snowcrust behind the cabin. "Well, here they are," Finn announced flatly.

Marvin acknowledge this by rolling back over in the bunk and groaning. Finn lit the lantern and placed it on the table in the center of the room. He turned up the wick so there would be plenty of light when Delbert came through the door. Marvin pulled the blanket up over his head.

Outside Delbert and the dog had moved to the corner of the cabin next to the door. He had taken out his pistol and now held the muzzle up in the safe but ready position beside his face. Delbert had come through the deep snow in the trees and was breathing hard from his effort to sneak up on the cabin. In an attempt to keep the noise level to a minimum he had not worn his snowshoes.

"Okay," Delbert whispered to his dog who sat in the snow and cocked a curious ear to his master. "Get ready."

Delbert allowed himself a few minutes to stop his hard breathing but he could still hear his pulse thumping in his ears. When his breath had settled to normal Delbert took a step back from the door and crouched, his left shoulder lowered as a battering ram. He raised his pistol in his right hand ready for the imminent gunfight.

*Now!* he screamed and charged the door. Tinney remained seated in the snow watching with curious interest as Delbert folded up at the feet of Finn who had jerked opened the door at the moment he heard Delbert's scream. Finn stood above the deputy with a cup of coffee steaming in his hand.

"You use sugar?" He offered Delbert the cup. Delbert lay on the floor his head jerking left and right quickly sizing up the situation inside the cabin. He waved his pistol in the air.

"Now don't move," Delbert said. "Don't either one of you bastards make a single move." He pointed the gun above his head at Finn who did as Delbert ordered and stood motionless. Marvin groaned. Moving was the last thing he was interested in.

"Put that goddamn thing away, Delbert," Finn said and closed the door. "Before you hurt somebody. And turn your hat around. I hardly recognize you with it on backward.

"Just shut up. And let my dog in here. *Move.*" Delbert rose to his feet and gestured at the door with the gun. He glanced over his shoulder at the figure under the blanket. Then he moved with his back to the wall so that he could keep both men covered with the pistol. "Hurry up," he commanded.

"He's okay out there." Finn moved over to the table and set the coffee cup down. "I asked you if you take sugar in this. You ought to be more polite when you visit somebody Delbert."

"Is that Marvin under the blanket?" Delbert demanded.

"Yeah," Finn said. "That's Marvin alright but don't worry about him. He ain't going nowhere for awhile."

"Is he dead? You done in another one, Finn?" Delbert was incredulous.

"He ain't dead, Delbert. Just a touch of frostbite in his feet. Not dead though."

"Sit," Delbert said to Finn.

"I ain't your dog, Delbert."

"I said *sit.*" Delbert waved the pistol. Finn sat. Delbert moved cautiously over to the figure under the blanket. He took one edge and with his pistol poised he jerked the cover off Marvin who moaned and rolled onto his back.

Marvin had his goodeye shut and the pallor in his face was lighter than the gray stubble on his chin. His black eyepatch had twisted to one side and up into the strands of hair which were pasted with sweat to his forehead. Delbert surveyed him and then moved to get a better look at his feet. He shook his head and frowned as he inspected them and whistled low.

"Yeah," Delbert agreed. "I'd say he did get a little bit of frostbite alright. He sure as hell done that. Just look a them toes swollen up real good, purple as plums. Hell they're even turning black right here, Finn, look at them." Delbert poked at one foot with his gun and Marvin cried out. "Tender too, huh?"

"Come on, Delbert, leave him be." Finn moved toward the deputy but Delbert spun around and pointed his gun at him.

"Just you stay put. And don't give me any shit either. You and I have a little business to settle Finn and it don't include old Marv here. He ain't gonna be no trouble anyway looks like." Delbert pulled the blanket back over Marvin and moved beside the table next to Finn. "Turn around."

"What for. You going to shoot me?"

"Just do as I say."

Finn turned his back to the deputy who took a pair of handcuffs from the pocket of his parka. He pulled Finn's arms behind his back and snapped on the handcuffs.

"Nice fit." Finn turned and faced the deputy. "Now what?"

"Now we sit, now we talk, now I'll have that coffee. And now I'll let Tinney in. That is of course if it's alright with you? I wouldn't want to break no rules of hospitality." Delbert pushed Finn down on the bench and went to the door. "Come on in, buddy. Good dog. *Heel.*"

The dog came inside and sniffed Finn's leg. He growled low when he recognized the scent and then sniffed the other leg.

"He gonna piss on me or what?" Finn said.

"Well, he just might. If he takes a notion to. Don't you worry about it none because you got plenty of other stuff to worry about, Finn. A little dog piss on your leg is the least of your problems."

"Problems like what?" Finn kicked at the dog who snarled and moved next to the stove, curled up and went to sleep.

"Problems like burglarizing Yael's store." Delbert sipped the coffee. "I think you're right, Finn. It does need a little sugar. Got any left or did old Keetuk take it all?"

"Speaking of problems, Delbert, that might be one you'd want to think about yourself."

"How so?"

"Somebody's been here. If it ain't you and it ain't Yael then it was probably him."

"Him?" Delbert cocked his head, held the cup poised.

Finn nodded. "And it ain't been too long ago either. He may be out there right now Delbert."

Delbert said nothing. He blinked several times rapidly and sipped the coffee again. Finn went on. "But then there ain't any of my sugar gone and like you say Delbert, Keetuk always takes the sugar first so I guess it wasn't him. It's in that can there." He nodded toward the shelf. "Course I coulda laced it with strychnine. Some trappers do that you know." Finn showed his widest rows of stained teeth to the deputy who decided against the sugar.

"And then there's poaching too." Delbert leaned over and spoke into Finn's face. "Poaching's a very serious offense, my friend."

"What are you talking about?"

"Come now let's not be so innocent. Surely you been smelling what I been smelling all day, Finn. Surely you don't mean to tell me that you got no knowledge of that cache back in the woods there?"

Finn shifted on the bench and turned away from Delbert's face. "That's right, Finn, I found your cache early this morning back there in the woods. Course I must have got there a little late because all that was left was a big stack of black hides all crisp and burned, worthless."

Finn did not speak but he noticed Marvin had stopped shifting in the bunk and his groans had ceased. He wondered if Marvin had died.

"But you know, funny thing about them hides, a body could still count them. Even charred and ruined a body could still count them if he'd a mind to."

"Yeah?" Finn still did not look at Delbert. He kept staring at Marvin who had not moved or made a sound.

"And guess how many I estimate Finn?"

Finn said nothing.

"Just take a wild guess, Finn. Go on, a real wild one."

Finn remained silent but he noticed that Marvin had rolled over in the bunk and was facing the two at the table. He had his goodeye open for the first time in hours and he had moved the eyepatch back into place. Marvin was the one who answered Delbert. "Try two hundred and fifty," he said and then a single word hollow and lifeless, "gone?" He looked at Finn who stared back at him.

"Well what do you know, our patient's awake. How about that, Finn?"

"Shove it, Delbert." Finn did not look at him.

"Well, Marv's about right I think." Delbert puckered his mouth and squeezed his chin with his fingers. "I calculate about that number. And it seems odd to me when I count up the Swede's limit and your limit and maybe even throw in Marvin's here, though God knows he ain't never trapped a limit in his life, even counting all that up Finn I figure you're still a couple of hundred over. That's a pretty big offense boys *two hundred and fifty*. What do you say to that? Course they're all ruined anyway. Now I wonder who'd do a thing like that?"

"You probably did, Delbert." Finn turned to face him. "Or maybe it was your *other* problem that done it."

"Problem? Mine? And what would that be Finn?"

*"Keetuk,"* Finn said and the smile immediately left Delbert's face. "Like I said earlier he's probably been following you all the way up the river."

"Bullshit," Delbert said and then quickly, "what makes you think that?" He had moved to holster his pistol but decided against it. Instead he glanced at the window and then turned so his back was not to the door.

"I just think he's got it in for all of us," Finn said. "I think he done Swede in because we was taking the beavers and I think there's no way he'd let us out of here with all them pelts in the cache anyway. I think he was following you all along."

"Well, maybe so. I ain't worried about it though," Delbert lied.

"Well, it looks to me like all of us oughta worry about it Delbert. You know it ain't going to be any fun for you trying to get me and Marv back down the river let alone worrying about him chasing us."

"Shut up," Delbert said. He remembered the Mountie again but this was different. Delbert was not wounded and he still had all his deputy marshal wits about him. And he had Tinney.

"Well now, you are planning on taking us back down aren't you?" Finn said. "You got room in your dogsled. And you don't even have to think about hauling any of them pelts down now." Finn watched Delbert's face. He could see he was working out all of the facts and if push came to shove there would be no question what Delbert would leave behind in a rush to get to Snag Point. "You're not going to let Marvin lay here and die are you? And what about the hearing?"

"You just keep still, Finn. I ain't asking your opinions. And what's more it ain't going to be just a hearing now."

"Yeah?"

"Yeah. I'm charging you with burglary, poaching and murder. First degree. I'm holding you for trial and then we'll put you away for good."

Finn could tell by Delbert's voice he was very serious this time. There was the burglary and of course the illegal pelts but surely Delbert knew Finn had not been involved in any murder. The problem with the burned furs could be worked out with Yael. Finn decided it had to be something else. It had to be Nellie.

"Who'd I murder this time, Delbert?"

240

"Well we can start with No-Talk Owens and then we can throw in Swede and maybe them women who ain't showed up yet. And last but not least that priest."

"Now that's downright poetic Delbert, '*Last but not least that priest*.'"

"Justice is what it is, Finn, and it ain't poetic at all just serving time, long hard time."

Finn could see Delbert had thought it out. There would be no use arguing about it and besides there were more important matters to take care of at the moment. Finn rose and walked to the bunk and looked down at Marvin who was staring at the ceiling. The pain in Marvin's face had changed to a permanent look of defeat. The blanket had worked up and exposed his feet again. Finn forced himself not to look at them. He wanted to cover them again, to make them go away. He moved his arm but he could not grab the blanket with his hands cuffed behind him.

"What about him," Finn said. "You got to get him out of here and back down to Snag Point, Delbert. You got a sled and a team. You got to help him."

"It don't matter," Marvin whispered. "They're gone now anyway, burned up in smoke."

"We'll pack him out," Delbert said. "You know I wouldn't just leave him here. Why, that would be cruel and unusual punishment. That would be something you would do, Finn. I'm a lawman. You know I couldn't do that."

"Yeah, sure," Finn said. "Unless you had two hundred and fifty beaver pelts to haul out. Then you'd leave us both to die if you thought you needed the extra room."

"I don't think I'll make it," Marvin said. "I just got this feeling none of us is going to make it."

"Knock it off," Finn said. "Course you'll make it. We're all going to make it."

"He's out there waiting you know," Marvin continued in a whisper. "He's been there all along just biding his time and we all know it. He'll get us all before we get back down to Snag Point."

Marvin did not look at either of the two but continued staring at the ceiling. Finn had noticed a curious absence of fear in his voice, a strength he had never heard in the past especially when the topic turned to Keetuk. Marvin had always been philosophical about Keetuk but Finn had never determined if Marvin was serious or joking. He might be delirious now but he was not joking.

"We'll need to do something," Finn said. "If we aim to ever make it back down. We'll have to try to stop him before he can stop us."

Marvin struggled to prop himself on one elbow. He looked at Finn with his goodeye as cold and hard as the glass one he left guarding his cabin. "How? With Keetuk it's useless even to talk about it."

"Strychnine," Finn said. "Just like I said before. I keep it here for the squirrels and mice and put it on a foxbait once in a while."

"What are you talking about?" Delbert said.

"Strychnine. Poison, powerful stuff."

"I know that," said Delbert. "I mean what are you hinting at?"

"It's powerful alright," agreed Marvin with sudden interest. "It'd kill a man real quick."

"Yeah," said Finn. "I put some on a foxbait once and when I found the fox there was four ravens dead around him. The fox ate the bait and died and the ravens ate on the fox and they died too. Powerful stuff."

"That just goes to prove you should never eat a dead fox," said Delbert and he chuckled at his wit. "Now let's cut this bullshit and get settled for the night. We got a long trail tomorrow."

"Or sugar," said Finn. "Maybe you shouldn't eat anybody's sugar, Delbert? Or steal it like old Keetuk always does?"

Delbert nodded and so did Marvin but neither spoke.

"And sugar is white," continued Finn. "Just like strychnine, white and grainy." The other two nodded again. "And if you was to mix them up good and leave that sugar around for someone to *steal* and then if that someone was to eat some of that sugar, well somebody might find a lot of dead ravens around here. There might just be dead ravens all up and down the Mikchalk River, right Delbert?"

Finn smiled at Delbert who listened with confused interest on his face and then said, "Yeah but that would be illegal. I mean that would be *murder* or something. That is someone might get ahold of it like a human or something and it might kill him dead."

"Yeah," said Finn. "Dead." There was a long pause as each listened for sounds outside the cabin.

"Well, I could never go along with that," Delbert said but there was no conviction in his voice and Finn detected it immediately. "I could never allow that in a million years. Why, I'd be an accessory."

"Yeah, but what if someone else—not you of course Delbert—someone else just happened to take some of that strychnine from that little cloth bag tucked away over there," Finn nodded toward a small wooden box in the corner of the room and continued talking, "and what if someone was to mix all that strychnine with the sugar on that shelf right there? And what if that someone did it and you didn't even see him do it, Delbert? And then what if someone else just happened to break into my cabin—after we're gone of course—and was to steal that sugar just like he always does and then what if he ate some of it or *all* of it? Then what, Delbert?"

Finn smiled and winked at the deputy and then at Marvin.

"Well, then I guess I wouldn't even know nothing about it," Delbert said. "Would I?"

"Not a thing," said Finn. "And he'd probably just crawl off somewhere and die just like one of them ravens and nobody would ever find him. He'd just be gone. Forever."

"Yep, gone forever," repeated Marvin and he looked grimly toward the corner and then lay back down on his side so he could keep watch on the box.

"Well now, Delbert," continued Finn. "Maybe you and I oughta go on back across the river and bring over your dogteam. We could feed and bed them down over here by the cabin so they can haul us all downriver tomorrow."

"Yeah," said Delbert. "Only we ain't making it down in one day. There ain't no way I'm cutting across them hotholes, Finn, frozen feet or not. We're staying on the river to Ekok and then to Snag Point. With you two along that's probably more like three days."

"Sure, Delbert. Whatever you say," said Finn. "Now why don't you just unlock these cuffs and let me give you a hand out there? Marv will be okay here by his lonesome while we get the dogs across."

"I don't know." Delbert squinted at him. "I ain't sure I can trust you, Finn." He looked at Marvin who continued to stare vacantly at the box in the corner. He was certain Marvin would not be a threat and maybe this plan of Finn's would work. He could keep an eye on Finn and not worry about Marvin.

"Okay, turn around." Delbert took out the key and unlocked the cuffs. "Let's get them dogs."

"Sure, Delbert. Just let me have one quick look in that little box there, okay? I just need to move it over here closer to Marv you know just in case he might need something out of it while we're gone," Finn said and he winked at Delbert. "And the sugar. Old Marv might want to sweeten himself a cup of coffee while we're gone so I'll just need to set that tin of sugar close to Marv so's he won't have to get up."

"Just move real slow Finn." Delbert took out his gun again. "How do I know this ain't a trick? For all I know there might be a gun in that little old box instead of that bag you been talking about."

"Trust me, Delbert." Finn crossed and brought the box back to the table. Then he raised his palms toward Delbert and nodded at him to show there was no trick up his sleeve before he opened it. Delbert looked inside and convinced himself it did not contain a weapon. He holstered his pistol and feigned disinterest while Finn lifted a small cotton sack out of the box. Finn showed it to Marvin, nodded again and then returned it. Marvin watched him glumly as he sat the box beside the bunk and placed the tin can of sugar on top of it.

"Well now, I guess we got everything Marv might need while we're getting the dogteam across." Finn winked first at Marvin and then back at Delbert. "Let's go."

Delbert looked at him for a moment and decided Finn was not trying to trick him. In fact Finn had devised a plan that was so appealing to Delbert it might even be considered brilliant. If it worked Delbert could be rid of all his problems at once and he would not have to do a thing except take Finn back to Snag Point for trial and then send him away for good on the spring ship. Nellie would see Finn at the trial and learn how evil he was, killing Felix and all, and she would see how brave Delbert had been to bring him back alive when he could have just shot Finn. Marvin would do the dirty work with the poison in the sugar and surely Keetuk would raid the cabin as soon as the three were gone. He would find the sugar and then it would be all over for Keetuk too.

The thought of getting rid of Keetuk and Finn at the same time was enough to make Delbert smile. He could afford to act benevolent. He could even help nurse Marvin along, tuck him in the sled since he did not need the room for any illegal pelts now. He would get him back down the river at least as far as Marvin's cabin at Ekok. And then he would decide what to do about Marvin.

"Now you just relax, Marv," Delbert said. "You get a good night's rest. We're going to take care of you and get you on back down that river first thing tomorrow. Let's get them dogs, Finn." Delbert crossed to the door and held it open. "Heel, Tinney."

The dog growled and slinked past Finn. Delbert closed the door behind them and they went out into the night. Soon afterward Marvin opened the box beside his bunk and lifted out the small cotton sack.

# NINETEEN

It was still dark when Delbert roused Marvin and Finn from their blankets and forced them into the sled the next morning. Marvin had to be carried out of the cabin and he sat in the front of the moving dogsled between Finn's legs leaning back against him bobsled style. Delbert had handcuffed Finn's right wrist to the siderail of the sled. Even though the early morning air held a hint of spring and had warmed above freezing during the night the men covered themselves with a caribou skin.

If Marvin had been interested he could have watched the birches moving past in the predawn. They grew in stunted clusters from the embankment along the frozen Mikchalk River. The early spring melt had separated the barren limbs in gnarled relief atop the snow and they had become twisted black lines against the whiteness. But Marvin's world was already black enough for he had moved the silk eyepatch and covered his goodeye with it, exposing the empty socket where the other eye had once been. He had withdrawn into dark contemplation with only his head exposed above the caribou fur which almost concealed him and Finn. Because he had his fur hat on, the only things exposed to the morning air were Marvin's nose, his pale forehead, his empty eyesocket and the black eyepatch. All of this provided an unintended grim greeting from the front of the sled to anyone who might chance by on the frozen river.

But no one chanced by. And there was nothing to fill the passing hours for Marvin except a single thought. He had not allowed his mind to waver like Delbert's dogs were doing. The sharp pain which had worked up from his feet and settled in his groin had not permitted itself to be forgotten. Marvin had removed his mittens and thrust his hands down into his trousers gripping the insides of his upper thighs as hard as he could. He forced his fingernails into the soft flesh as he pushed both thumbs against his groin in an effort to stop the pain. He was trying to divert his mind from the throbbing deep inside his abdomen by moving the pain to the outside where his nails clawed at the skin.

It was not working. In the late afternoon and through the first night on the trail, after Delbert and Finn had bedded the dogs down and made a quick shelter with spruce boughs against the embankment, Marvin had noticed the throbbing had moved into his armpits. He knew his feet were numb again, almost painless, perhaps dead.

The second morning when he pulled back the blanket which Finn had wrapped around his feet, Marvin saw streaks of purple had traced the veins up the legs into that part of the flesh which had not been frozen. He did not show this to the other two but instead settled back under the caribou skin, retreated into his own thoughts, wild hallucinations behind the eyepatch.

Marvin floated to visions of Stella Villard waiting for him in Texas but then jerked back to reality with each crack of Delbert's whip and each call of a solitary raven which had followed them all the way down the river.

In those lucid moments when Marvin surfaced from his brooding he was certain the voice of this lone raven had never changed. Hour after hour he was sure it was the same bird each time for he had once lifted the eyepatch quickly and seen it gliding and flapping, gliding and flapping, calling in a eerie voice like no other raven he had ever heard. It had chilled him in much the same way the talk of Keetuk had chilled him even though Marvin feigned bravado when he spoke about the elusive native to cover his fear.

Marvin wondered if Delbert and Finn had also noticed the raven but he did not mention it to them. He lowered the eyepatch and did not lift it again until the dogsled came to a stop late on the second afternoon in front of Marvin's own cabin at Ekok. He was eager to get inside to check on his things to see if they were in order, especially the stew with the glass eyeball he had left in it. "Lift me out of here. Hurry up, I gotta check it out."

"Relax, I can't lift anything until Delbert unlocks these cuffs." Finn jangled the chain but Delbert ignored him and instead went to the front of the dogteam and released the dogs one by one. He tied them in the alders beside Marvin's cabin.

"Hey, Delbert, how about it? Let me loose," Finn said. "So's I can help lift Marv."

"I ain't setting nobody loose no more," said Delbert. "We're too damn close to Snag Point. I ain't trusting you no more, Finn." Delbert moved cautiously to the two sitting in the sled. He unlocked the end of Finn's handcuffs from the siderail but then quickly snapped it around Marvin's wrist.

"Now you're really partners, Finn. How's it feel? Maybe that's what we should'a done with you and No-Talk? Of course you'd probably just eat your way out of that." Delbert clicked his teeth several times. "Now grab on, let's get him inside."

Finn hesitated, aware that if they remained in the dogsled Delbert would have to take both of them into Snag Point. He was not certain the deputy would bother with Marvin again once he got him inside his cabin.

"Come on, Finn," Marvin pleaded. "Hurry up, will you? I gotta see inside." Marvin's voice left no room for arguing and besides they could not spend the night handcuffed together in the dogsled. Finn had no desire to drag another partner down the river to Snag Point. He stood and threw the caribou skin aside and worked his arms under Marvin's armpits as far as the handcuffs would allow. Delbert lifted the legs which were still wrapped inside the blanket but he turned his head aside when the feet got close to his nose. *"Whew* something's sure as hell rotten inside there."

"Shut up Delbert," Finn said but he too had smelled the rotten flesh and he could not stop himself from retching. "Just lift."

Finn moved backward toward the cabin and bumped the door open. He stumbled inside and almost dropped Marvin before he could reach the bunk. "There you are." He jerked their handcuffed arms from under Marvin's back and held them up and then gagged again.

"Come on, Delbert, take this cuff off him. You can leave it on me. Hell, you know he ain't going nowhere."

"I ain't worried about him going anywhere," Delbert said. "I'm worrying about what you might be thinking. And you sure as hell won't be running off with Marvin handcuffed to you so just get comfortable on the floor there. You can snooze a bit and rest up because we'll be underway early in the morning."

Delbert left the two and went outside to feed his dogs. Finn sat down on the floor and leaned back against the bunk with his wrist still attached to Marvin's on the blanket beside him. He was trying to keep his hand as still as possible and to figure out what he might say or do to make things better for his partner. "You hungry?"

"Nope," Marvin said. "Not yet."

"Well you know your stew's still there. Probably already thawed out with this warm spell. We could ask Delbert to heat it up and make a longsplice out of it with some of that dried beaver meat. What do you think?"

"You seen that raven following us?" Marvin said.

"Raven?"

"Yesterday and today. All down the river from your cabin Finn. One big old raven all by himself. He followed us all the way down. You didn't see it?"

"Naw."

"You heard it though," Marvin said. "Odd sound, not like a raven at all."

"I didn't hear no raven and I didn't see one either. You sure you ain't hungry?"

Marvin did not answer. Finn soon heard him breathing deeply but he wasn't sure if he was sleeping or unconscious. Finn rested his head against the bunk and tried to get as comfortable as possible. It would be a long night.

It was still dark outside when Finn jerked awake from one of his wild dreams. He heard Delbert snoring across the room and Marvin was breathing differently now with a small cough in his voice. The sound made Finn remember what he had been dreaming about only Marvin's cough was not as loud and not as terrifying as in the dream, a burst of sound from a huge black raven which had been chasing Finn and hovering just over his head as he ran. Its giant shadow had moved closer and closer on the snow behind him until finally just before Finn had awakened the shadow had passed and Finn thought its blackness had consumed him. But instead the shadow had simply moved over him, or *through* him, and it had left Finn on the tundra in bright sunlight with the snow suddenly gone and he had seen himself standing there transformed into something or someone he did not recognize. But Finn knew it was himself. The raven's voice had become a thin thumping sound inside his head now even awake and Finn could not rid himself of it. It was a rhythmic beat, slow and weak but steady and he thought it must have been something outside the cabin. Delbert must have heard it too because he snorted abruptly and stopped snoring.

"Finn?" Delbert whispered. "You still there?"

Finn waited a long time before he answered just to worry Delbert a bit. "Where the hell did you think I'd go, maybe drag Marv out for a stroll? How come you're awake?"

"I don't know." Finn detected fear in Delbert's voice. "But I think it's time to pack up and get out of here."

"Marv's still sleeping." Finn tried to shake the thumping from his ears. "Or unconscious." He wanted to ask Delbert if he was hearing the same thing but he said nothing. Delbert had moved silently across the room and found Marvin's wrist and unlocked the handcuffs almost before Finn knew what he had done. Marvin stirred in the bunk but did not awaken.

"Get up," Delbert ordered and kicked Finn's leg. He moved Finn across the room and pushed him back down onto the floor. He snapped the other end of his handcuffs around one of the cast iron legs on which the drumstove was mounted.

"Get it going," Delbert said and kicked the stack of kindling in front of Finn. "I'll get the team and the sled ready. We'll try out Marvin's stew before we leave." He went to the door and then turned back. "And make some coffee too," he ordered and shut the door behind him.

Finn balked at first but then rose onto his knees and opened the door to the stove with his free hand. He would do it for Marvin not for Delbert. He placed a handful of kindling inside the stove and put a match to it and soon had the fire going. Marvin was moving in his bunk and Finn could hear him. Now that the sky outside had lightened he could see the bunk and the figure as Marvin struggled to sit up.

"Well, top of the morning to you," Finn said. "How about some breakfast? Hotcakes and honey? Hot coffee? Maybe a little fresh churned butter and jam?" Finn's humor was contagious. Marvin moved his feet gingerly over to the floor and tucked the blanket around them.

"How are they?" Finn said.

"They don't hurt so much now. Maybe the circulation's back." Marvin smoothed his matted hair and straightened the eyepatch.

"Yeah, that's probably it." Finn stood as far as he could with the cuff still around the leg of the stove. He peered into Marvin's stewpot. "This seems about ready again. What do you say, you want to try some?"

"Scoop it out of there for me would you?"

"Sure." Finn reached for a bowl.

"I don't mean the stew Finn. My eyeball, it's there in the stew that's where I left it."

"Oh…" Finn nodded. He stabbed into the stewpot with the long wooden spoon.

"It should be in there. That's why nobody ever bothered it. That old evil eye was frozen in there."

"Sure, Marv. I'll see if I can get it." Finn wrinkled his nose and frowned into the stewpot as he sloshed the spoon around. "Oh yeah, I seen it that time." He moved the spoon around again and finally trapped the glass eye against the side. "Got it!"

"Toss it over then." Marvin cupped his hands to catch it.

"Alright, you ready? On three now—"

Marvin nodded.

"One…two…"

"Careful now Finn, throw it easy."

"*Three.*" The eyeball sailed across the room in a high arch and Marvin reached up for it, snatching it out of the air.

"Thanks. I'll be able to see everything real clear now."

"Sure." Finn turned his head away remembering Marvin liked privacy when he put the eye back in place.

"It's okay," Marvin said. "You can watch."

"Naw you go ahead." Finn kept his head turned.

Marvin popped the eye into his mouth and cleaned it off, warmed it, worked it around in his cheek while he removed the black eyepatch which he folded carefully. Then he reached up and took down his Mackinaw from the peg beside the bunk and placed the eyepatch inside one pocket. From the other pocket he removed the leather folder with the photograph and then put on his Mackinaw. He slowly buttoned up the coat and put on his fur hat.

"You all set?" Finn said. "Can I turn around now?"

"All set."

Finn turned back. Marvin looked much better with the glass eye in place and the coat and hat on straight.

"Hey, you're all spiffed up now. Hell, you'll be the best looking thing in town once we hit Snag Point. We'll get them feet all fixed up and you'll be as good as new. Then we'll get all this bullshit with Delbert out of the way and get on about our business."

"Business?"

"Sure. You know trapping and fishing and well *partnering* and stuff." Finn was almost believing himself again and his voice brightened. "Things are looking up for us, Marv. I think Delbert's even coming around a little bit. Maybe it's because old Keetuk's been taken care of. I think that's it. Keetuk's finally out of Delbert's hair and he's feeling pretty good about that, thanks to you."

"Yeah, things are looking up," Marvin said quietly and he turned his face toward the window. "Except I ain't going down to Snag Point with you."

"What are you talking about. Don't talk nonsense."

"I ain't talking nonsense. I'm talking longsplice. I intend to take this and make a very longsplice out of that stew." Marvin reached into a side pocket of the Mackinaw and retrieved a small cotton sack and held it up for Finn to see. Finn immediately recognized the sack and he started to say something to Marvin in protest, to ask him what the hell was going on and why the sack was still full and what he was doing with it. Instead Finn slowly sat back down on the floor beside the stove and said nothing. He waited for Marvin to speak again. When he did there was grim resignation in his voice.

"And I guess old Keetuk ain't taken care of either," Marvin confessed. "I guess he might just find your sugar back there in your cabin and it'll be gone if you ever get back up there to the Mikchalk. Sorry about that, Finn."

"But why?"

"I don't know. I guess I figured it'd just be easier this way than the other," Marvin continued in a monotone. He glanced at his feet and then back to the sack in his hand. "And I guess I wasn't sure it'd be Keetuk who'd get that sugar anyway. I guess I ain't even sure he really exists out there. Hell, nobody ever really sees him, Finn. And Delbert only talks about catching him. Nobody ever catches Keetuk. And if he don't exist out there nowhere what's the point in trying to catch him? And even if he does exist out there what's the point in trying to catch him?"

"What do you mean?" Finn said indignantly. "And quit whining about all this. Hell, he burned all our pelts, didn't he?"

"Well, I ain't even sure about that and you ain't either." Marvin eyed Finn suspiciously. "Even you said so. You said Delbert probably done it. And besides they weren't *our* pelts anyway. They were yours and Swede's and Moon's. They weren't none of mine anyhow."

"Well, you're half right. Keetuk didn't burn them. You're right about that part," Finn admitted. "But Delbert didn't burn them either." He paused a moment and looked over at Marvin who sat stiff and determined on the edge of the bunk. "I burned them."

"You?"

"Yes."

"You burned them?"

"Right. Sneaked out that night and torched them while you was passed out. It made a helluva a blaze too only it stunk like shit."

"But why? You crazy?"

"Just seemed like the thing to do. Just like you and that little sack you got there, it just seemed like the thing to do at the time."

"But all them pelts? Prime furs?"

"Well, to be honest with you there just wasn't no way we could have packed them out. I seen that. Not with your feet like they are Marv. And the only way I could see to get you back down and try to do something was to let Delbert catch us. But there was no way he could take you and me and all them pelts in the same load. He was bound to find out about them if Yael hadn't already told him. Sooner or later Delbert would know and he'd make a choice. He'd left you for sure. I just wanted to make sure there'd be no choice. He had to take you too. Of course, we could have asked Keetuk for a little ride. That is if we could have caught him. Right?"

"You done that?" Marvin muttered. "I don't believe it."

Finn chuckled and opened the door to the stove and poked at the flames with a birch limb. "It don't matter anyway. Besides, think how mad Yael's going to be." He laughed again.

"But all that trouble, all that work. Getting up there and all. All them plans you had for you and Moon." Marvin opened the leather folder as he talked and checked the old photograph for the first time since it had become soaked in the hothole. It was wrinkled and faded but he could still make out the face of Stella smiling at him across the years.

"All that never gave me much hesitation." Finn shrugged his shoulders and stared into the flames. "What bothered me more was it spoiled all your plans for leaving, getting out and all."

"She wouldn't have been there anyway." Marvin stared at the photograph. Finn turned and looked at him.

"You mean Stella?"

"Yeah. You never did see this did you Finn? This photograph?"

"No, I guess I never did."

"Well, it ain't much now wrinkled and all. I had it in my coat at the hothole but it don't matter now anyway. She never thought twice about me."

Finn thought about Stella and the months he had spent in Texas under her magic when he and Marvin first met and he thought about how his own attraction to her had become both magnetic and mutual but it was not something that anyone else had known, least of all Marvin

G. Crush. "That ain't true," Finn said. "That ain't true at all. Stella thought a lot of you."

"You're just trying to make me feel better. How would you know anyway?"

Finn turned away from Marvin and looked back into the flames. He thought about Marvin's feet and about the pelts up in smoke and he thought about Stella Villard's stock certificates and Marvin's interrupted career as a stationmaster. "She told me so," Finn lied. "Stella said to me once you had become a real important part of her life. I think she fell hard for you."

"Stella said that?" Marvin looked up from the photograph.

"That's what she said." Finn closed the stove. "I think she was on the verge of telling you too and then we had to leave so quick when everything went haywire and—"

"How come you never told me that?"

"It just never did seem like the thing to do until now." Finn turn back to Marvin who started to speak but fell silent so Finn continued. "Of all the bad things that happened back there, us losing her money and all, I think you leaving her musta been the worst part. How come you never wrote her or nothing?"

"I guess it just never did seem like the thing to do." Marvin stared at the sack in his hand. "Writing wouldn't done nothing. Action's what woulda counted and I think it's about time Marvin G. Crush took hold of something, did something."

Finn said nothing for a long while. He watched Marvin toy with the sack. "Well action's what Delbert's up to now. He's getting ready to leave out there so cut all this bullshit and give that back to me. Besides you'd be lonely if we left you here anyway so just toss it over."

"I been alone before." Marvin made no move. "Being alone is good practice," he said and then closed the leather folder and buttoned it inside his shirt. "For whatever's after this."

He shoved the sack into a side pocket of his Mackinaw. Finn did not respond. He had no further suggestions for Marvin G. Crush. Plans and schemes did not seem to be in order at this particular time. Marvin was determined to stay and Finn could smell the feet from across the room now. There would be no further talk, no further convincing. Marvin sat with his hand thrust deep into the pocket of his coat, still clutching the small cotton sack as he stared into a corner of the cabin.

When Delbert returned Finn said, "Seems like the circulation's come back. Marv's decided to stay."

Delbert thought this was a sudden change in Finn's attitude but he did not argue, pleased to be rid of the extra weight. "Fine by me." He unlocked Finn's handcuffs from the stove leg and peeked into the stewpot but decided against having any.

"Maybe next time," he apologized to Marvin as he led Finn to the door. Finn stopped and looked back at Marvin who was still sitting rigid on the bunk. He wanted to say some last clever remark to sum up all the years but decided silence summed it up best.

"You said next time you come up?" Marvin did not lift his head as he spoke to the deputy.

"Yeah, maybe next time," Delbert repeated. "I guess I ain't as hungry as I figured right now."

"You know, Delbert, if I just happen not to be here next time—"

"Yeah?"

"Well, I don't think I'd eat any of that stew if I was you."

Puzzled by Marvin's comment Delbert frowned and shook his head. "Let's go, Finn."

# TWENTY

Delbert and Finn had not been long on the river when two dogs behind the lead animal tangled their lines and twisted in a snarling heap, forcing Delbert to bring the sled to a stop. He got off the rails behind Finn who sat in the basket with his right hand cuffed again to the siderail.

"Goddamn mongrels." Delbert stomped forward to untangle them. Tinney followed but stayed clear of the dogfight. Delbert kicked and screamed at the dogs as they cowered and rolled over on the river ice with their bellies turned up. Finn watched the action with detachment until he noticed the ice under the animals was much blacker here than at Ekok. Maybe that was why the lead dog had been so hesitant and the others were tangling their lines and also balking. Or maybe it was the raven that had been following them all the way from Ekok, flapping and gliding, flapping and gliding, dropping down almost to the ice in front of the dogs and then soaring back up and calling out in a rasping voice. Finn wondered if it was the same raven Marvin had mentioned, and he watched it now perched on the top of a spruce tree above the embankment as if waiting for the procession to continue.

Finn shuddered, thinking about his dream and the giant raven which had been in it. He realized the thumping in his head was still there only louder. He wondered if Delbert had noticed the raven and if he too could hear the thumping almost like a drumbeat. But more important he wondered if Delbert had noticed the ice.

"It's thinning down here already," Finn said when Delbert returned to the back of the sled. The deputy said nothing but cracked the whip and pushed the sled before he jumped back onto the rails. Finn turned his head around and spoke again to Delbert louder this time. "I said it's thinning out down here, Delbert. That's why your goddamn dogs are quitting on you. The ice is starting to break up here closer to the bay."

"I know that, Finn. Tide works on it down here. Tide comes in, tide goes out, tide comes in again. What do you take me for, an idiot?"

Tempted to agree Finn just said, "Well, what do you aim to do Delbert, drive us right off into a tide pool? You know I won't be able to do much in a goddamn tide pool with my hand cuffed to the sled."

Delbert did not answer. Finn noticed he was watching the raven which had begun its antics again in front of the dogteam. Finn was about to point out once more the darkness of the ice and the fissures which now appeared along the edges of the river when Delbert abruptly stopped the dogs. He did not speak to the animals nor make any move at all for a long while. He stood there, tensed on the rails behind Finn, listening and watching.

"It's gone now, Tinney," Delbert finally said.

Finn did not have to ask what he meant. He too had noticed the raven was no longer there and he searched the tops of the trees for him but could find nothing. And then he discovered Delbert had stopped at the same spot where he and Felix had parted for the last time in the fall.

"We could cut through here," Finn suggested. "This ice ain't safe downriver from here. We could go through the trees and cross the flats and hit the Redstone up higher Delbert. It'd be better crossing up there."

Delbert did not answer. He continued to search the tops of the trees.

"Well at least unlock me, Delbert, in case we go through."

"Shut up Finn, I'm thinking." Delbert waited again for a long while and Finn fell silent too but he could still feel the dull thud of the noise in his ears.

"I think we'll cut through here," Delbert announced. "Across the flats and then hit the Redstone up higher. I don't think it's safe downriver from here. It'd be better ice crossing the Redstone up there."

"Hey, Delbert, great idea." Finn slumped inside the sled and decided maybe he would rather be at the bottom of the river than a captive audience in Delbert's jail cell. Delbert turned the team up the side of the riverbank and was soon threading through the line of trees which defined the river. Sensing they were near home, the dogs moved well now and had taken only a short time to work their way through the trees to the edge of the clearing but there they stopped. The lead dog stood stiff and hunched its back; Finn could see the fur lift along its spine.

"Now what?" Delbert screamed at the dogs to move on but they ignored him. The lead dog had backed into the middle of the team and the others bunched around him in a web of tangled lines. Finn thought it curious they were not fighting again. They seemed afraid to go into the clearing. Delbert stepped off the rails and into the snow, which was deeper here at the edge of the trees. He struggled, cursing and sputtering toward the ball of dogs which lay silent except for a few whimpers. He had just reached the dogs when he stopped and looked out into the clearing, recognizing it as the same one in which he had played his little game with Felix last fall, the one from which he and Tinney had packed the body back to Snag Point.

"What the hell's wrong with you fleabags?" Delbert demanded and shook the lead dog free. He tried to pull the others loose but to no avail. When he released the lead dog it quickly worked its way back into the huddle of animals.

"They're afraid of something," Finn suggested. "They ain't wanting to go out into the clearing"

"No shit?" Delbert said and scowled. "Now that's brilliant Finn." He stalked toward the animals. "They'll go out there. They'll go on out there or I'll kick hell out of them." He swung a leg around at the dogs but could not get enough force in the deep snow to do much encouraging. The dogs did not move. "Come on, Tinney. Let's go out there and check on it. We'll just have to show them it's okay I guess."

"You'll need these, Delbert." Finn started to dig the snowshoes out of the sled with his free hand.

"I don't need no snowshoes," Delbert said. "I ain't going that far. *Heel, Tinney.*"

Delbert lifted his feet high to clear the snow and with a swagger set his course toward the middle of the clearing, inspecting the trail in front of him. Finn saw him reach down and unsnap his holster. He pulled his gloves up tighter and straightened his hat. Tinney followed in the wake of snow as Delbert broke trail. Finn watched the legs move rhythmically in perfect time with the thumping sound still in his ears louder than ever. Finn took his free hand out of its mitten and tried to plug his ear with a finger but he could not stop the noise. He bent his head down to the cuffed hand and plugged the other ear but that did not work either. Finally he shut his eyes and rested his head on the side rail of the sled. Delbert moved steadily out into the middle of the clearing still searching for whatever had stalled his team.

Finn did not know how long he had kept his eyes closed but when he opened them again the noise inside his head had stopped. There was no sound at all now except his own breathing and when he held that there was only a soft whistling of wind across his ears. He squinted out into the brightness of the clearing, trying to blink Delbert into focus against the snow. He thought Delbert had gone out too far and crested over the rise at the far edge of the clearing but then he found him motionless, standing up to his knees in the snow in the middle of the opening. And behind Delbert on the horizon at the top of the incline Finn saw the dark string of dogs pulling another sled and driver along at a slow pace, musher and team moving in perfect unison across Finn's line of vision until they centered themselves on the silhouette of Delbert who stood stark and alone in the snow.

And then the team turned toward Delbert and stopped on the small hill beyond and some distance from him. Finn saw the other musher standing on the back rails of his sled facing Delbert. He could see the outline of the figure tall against the horizon, taller than he had imagined—much taller than Finn had ever remembered in his dreams—but he could not make out the face, only the outline of the fur-rimmed hood which arched over the man's head and covered with its black shadow everything but the eyes Finn imagined were shafts of flame.

Then Delbert was in motion. He spun around and began to run toward Finn and the sled, stumbling and clawing his way back along his trail in a desperate effort to escape. And Tinney was in front of him hunched and whining and outpacing him, his tail clutched between his legs. Still the dogteam and sled on the horizon behind Delbert had not moved. Finn's attention was locked on the musher and the team and then he saw the figure lean over and when he stood again he held high above his head a long-handled double-bitted axe.

When he saw the sun spark off the edge of the blade Finn's eyes widened and his shoulders shook. He stood, tried to turn and run but he could not move with his arm handcuffed to the rail of Delbert's sled. All he could do was stand and watch—or shut his eyes again. Finn decided to watch as long as he dared and he saw the sled and driver moving and gaining speed as it bore down on Delbert who still struggled frantically toward Finn who remained hunched over inside the sled.

And then the rest happened so quickly Finn could not absorb it all. He saw Delbert's eyes near enough now that the terror in them gripped Finn himself and he saw the musher too and the huge dogs, their mouths agape and their fangs bared just as they had been in Finn's dreams. And he saw Delbert stumbling and running with the dogteam alongside him and the sled at his heels and Finn envisioned himself there in Delbert's place. He saw Swede there too and No-Talk and Felix and Marvin and all the others. And then the axe was high above the musher's head, swinging round and round. The sled was alongside Delbert and then Finn saw the axe come round in one final fierce blow between Delbert's shoulder blades. It sent the small man sprawling forward onto the snow where he lay still.

But the sled did not stop. The driver did not look back. The team and sled now bore down on Finn, who remained standing as far as he could in the sled, jerking and pulling on the handcuffs. The axe was high again, circling above the musher's head and Finn saw his team gaining speed coming straight toward him. Delbert's animals slinked aside to allow the musher's charging dogs to pass next to Delbert's sled.

*"Keetuk!"* Finn whispered. He shut his eyes and ducked his head into the crook of his free arm and stood there waiting. He tried to remember one of the prayers Felix had given him but only that one word would come, a single word which embodied all his fears. *"Keetuk!"*

He heard the panting of the dogs as they brushed past. Finn prepared himself for the axe. He stood as tall as he could with his chest toward the oncoming musher. He was determined he would not take the blade in the back like the cowards Swede and Delbert. But he would keep his eyes closed.

And then the moving sled was there crashing and bumping into Delbert's and almost tipping it over and Finn felt the blow from the axe. But it was not as he had expected. It was not against his chest. Finn did not feel the sharp edge of the axe thump into his body but rather he felt his right arm jerked away with such force that it twisted him around in the sled causing him to lose his balance and fall to his knees. When he opened his eyes the musher and team had disappeared into the trees.

Finn felt his chest and looked at his hands and finally convinced himself there was no blood on them. And then he saw the side rail of the dogsled had been splintered, severed by a blow from the axe and the other end of his handcuffs had fallen free of it and dangled from his wrist. He held up the loose end of the handcuffs in disbelief. Not only was he still alive, Finn was free from the sled.

He sat down in the basket still trembling. He breathed deeply, closed his eyes again for a moment but then quickly opened them wide and looked around. He searched the darkness between the trees for any sign of the musher just to be certain he was not lurking there waiting to finish him off, waiting to play some grotesque game of cat and mouse with him. But he was gone. Delbert's dog was gone too. Then he remembered Delbert.

Finn looked out into the clearing and saw the deputy lying sprawled against the snow and he imagined what the body would look like, what the axe would have done to Delbert's puny back. He remembered Swede and how he had looked except there would be no axe to remove from Delbert. Finn was beginning to wonder why the musher had not done the same to him, why he had set him free, but he did not have time to dwell on this. He was happy to be alive and was already worrying how he would explain about Delbert when he got his body back to Snag Point. Finn did not relish the thought at all, going through all the explanations again except there would be no lawman to worry about now, at least not until someone sent in another deputy marshal and that could take months.

Finn pulled the snowshoes out of the sled and tightened the bindings around his boots. Then he stuffed the dangling handcuffs down into his mitten and moved out toward Delbert. The body was face down in the snow but Finn saw right away there was no blood on Delbert's back.

"He must have hit him in the side or something." Finn muttered and then knelt down and rolled the body over to inspect it. Delbert's eyes were locked open in a death stare looking up at Finn with that same terror still in them. And then Finn jerked back and stood up.

*Delbert had blinked!*

"What in the hell—" Finn said. Delbert blinked his eyes again and this time he whimpered. Finn stood stunned.

*The guy's not dead! The sonuvabitch ain't even dead!*

Finn knelt back down and rolled Delbert roughly from one side to the other searching for the axe wound and all the blood that he knew should be there but there was not a drop.

"Shit. He must have hit you with the broadside of the axehead Delbert. He just knocked your wind out, you noddy, you ain't even dead." Finn kicked at the deputy who continued to lie in the snow with a look of mute terror in his face. "Get up, Delbert. You ain't hurt. Get up and let's get on with it goddammit."

Delbert continued to lie on his back in the snow blinking vacantly at the sky. "Well I ain't waiting around here for you, Delbert. You can just lie there and rot for all I care. I'm going on into Snag Point." Finn reached down and searched Delbert's pockets until he found the key to the cuffs and unlocked them.

"Here." He dropped the cuffs onto Delbert's stomach. "You might need these for Keetuk. If he comes back."

Delbert's eyes widened even further at the prospect but he lay immobilized and speechless. Finn moved away from him working the snowshoes in the deep snow.

"And if you want me, Delbert, you can find me in Snag Point," he challenged. "With *Henry.*"

Finn shuffled across the clearing and was almost over the rise, which dropped off toward the Redstone River and Snag Point, when he turned back to look. He saw Delbert still lying in the snow, that look of terror still in his eyes for all Finn knew. And Finn decided it might always be there for as long as Delbert stayed around Snag Point, which probably would not be for long anyway. "At Henry's Cabin," Finn called back as loud as he could yell. "Or *Moon's.*"

# TWENTY ONE

Nellie Napiuk usually hated spring breakup, especially in Snag Point. It was the ugliest time of the year. She had moved along the boardwalk from Yael Feldstein's general store and passed the shacks next to the cannery and on up the side of the embankment high above the bay. She was trying to keep her balance walking on the rotten cannery timbers strung out as a pathway along the edge of the cliff. The timbers had been exposed by the melting snow and each time she stepped from one to the other the end sank into the mud.

Below the bluff, the warm weather had also exposed the human residue from the long winter. Nellie saw the empty tin cans and bottles and the garbage which had been tossed over onto the ice to be carried out to the Bering Sea by the first storm of spring. And she smelled the melting contents of the honeybuckets which had been tossed over during the winter and frozen below. The odor wafted up with the warmed earth on a steady thermal of rising air. She held her breath and looked over briefly to see if this tide would be big enough to lift the huge chunks of ice and perhaps clean away the debris and the smell. Even though Nellie held her breath while she looked, the stench made her choke so she moved back away from the edge and decided to seek a more pleasant place for her picnic. Her eyes settled on the crest of the promontory behind the village, the highest point where she could still find some dead grass exposed and unbent where the wind had blown the snowpack clear. It was the apex of the bluff, a place where the warm morning sun had also found the tops of the hummocks in a promise that the tundra was still beneath the snow and summer was near. Here Nellie would be able to settle down into the tall grass and make a nest so that she could see out across the bay. She would watch the tide change, watch the hulks of ice leave for the summer.

Nellie carried a small bundle of goods she had brought from her shack. Inside were dried fish and hardtack and a blanket to spread on the ground. She had stopped at Yael's and bought a can of condensed milk. And she had worn her squirrel skin parka. Yael had joked about it in the store.

"Nice parka, Nellie. Don't see many folks wearing something like that around Snag Point though. You moving upriver? Seems like that's where all the squirrels went."

She ignored him.

"Yep. Best place I know to get squirrels. Ain't a single squirrel around here now. That is except maybe Hard Workin' Henry and Delbert. Pretty quiet now with old Swede and No-Talk and Felix all gone. Finn's gone too, I guess. But then maybe you and Finn were planning on getting together upriver somewhere? Maybe up there on the Mikchalk?"

Yael studied Nellie's face for reaction. There was nothing, not even her usual grin now. "Catch a mess of them squirrels for me," he continued. "That is, if you do get up there. Course I don't really deal in squirrel fur. Now beaver pelts, that's another matter. You know come to think about it old Hjalmar the Finn himself told me about some pelts up there. Even said something about a big cache he and Swede trapped. Imagine that? Beaver pelts and a big bundle of them. Now I wonder what he and Swede planned to do with something like that Nellie?"

"I don't know anything about Finn," Nellie said. "But I'm not going anywhere."

"Well, where the hell is he then?" Yael dropped the sarcasm. Nellie saw he was angry and frustrated but she did not care.

"How should I know," she said. "Finn doesn't tell me about his coming and going. And if he did I wouldn't tell you."

"Yeah, sure. Old Finn does a lot of coming and going lately. Coming into my store with a dead body, going out of my store with a dead body, coming in to play poker and leaving without his poke of dust or a pot to piss in. Coming and going, going and coming." Yael mocked

Nellie's grin, trying to get her to grin back but she ignored him. "Except I think he came back in one more time when I wasn't looking. Leastways I had a lot of my trail goods walk away about the time Finn did. But then maybe it was all them mice back there carrying off snuff and coffee and things like that. Henry always did say they was big enough to haul away a case of whiskey."

Yael saw she was not going to cooperate and it occurred to him that perhaps Nellie knew nothing about Finn's whereabouts. "Well then maybe can I interest you in a new dress. I got a few left over on the rack there. I'd give you a helluva deal on one."

Yael gestured toward the rack of clothing, dusty and neglected, at the back of the store. Nellie continued to ignore him and counted out the coins to pay for the milk.

She might have told him Finn was hiding in her shack but that was not true. Nellie had not seen Finn and in the weeks since Delbert had staggered back into Snag Point, she had not seen the deputy either. Delbert had isolated himself in the jailhouse and no one could get him to come out. At Heine's Café Karl had told her Delbert had just been sitting around all day staring blankly at the walls and Yael had been heard screaming and cursing at Delbert inside the jail on several occasions. But still he had not come out. Yael had given up on the deputy and Hard Working Henry told Yael that he did not have a clue as to Finn's whereabouts either.

But Yael had not believed Henry. In the weeks since Delbert had returned to Snag Point, shaken and exhausted, Yael had been in a frenzy trying to find out about Finn and the pelts. But Delbert would do nothing, say nothing. He just stared at the blank walls of the jailhouse with a look of mute fear in his eyes. Yael had finally accused Henry of hiding Finn in his cabin or somewhere else and so it was no real surprise to Yael when Finn walked boldly into his store that same day, soon after Nellie had paid for the can of milk and left.

"Decided to come out of your hole?" Yael made an attempt to sound casual but he moved behind his counter for protection or to reach for his pistol or both. Finn did not care. He walked right up to Yael and spoke into his face.

"They're gone, Yael. The pelts. All ruined, burned to a crisp so just forget about that right up front. I can't make that square with you and since they were all illegal anyway you ain't got too much room to bitch."

"A deal's a deal," Yael said. "And poker's poker. How do you aim to make it up? And what about the gear you stole from my back room? Maybe I'll just walk over and get Delbert and have him lock you up. He'd be real interested to know you're here." Yael moved his hands to the top of the counter. Finn thought he detected a bit of weakness in Yael's position but he had played too much poker with him to relax.

"I can work that off," Finn said and immediately hated the sound of the offer.

"*Work?*" Yael threw his head back, his gut jiggling in deep laughter. It was the first time Finn could ever remember hearing Yael laugh like that.

"What's so goddamn funny?" Finn said. "And Delbert ain't interested in me anymore. I don't think Delbert's interested in much of anything anymore except maybe how to get the hell out of here. I ain't buying your bluff so you might as well take my offer."

Yael saw his position was indeed eroded. He knew Delbert would not be any help and in fact he too wondered why Delbert had stayed as long as he had. Deputy Delbert had obviously lost interest in doing his job.

"What did you do to Delbert? How did you pay him off Finn? With them pelts? My pelts?"

"I'm telling you the pelts are gone, burned up, worthless. And I didn't do nothing to Delbert. Keetuk did, scared the shit out of him I guess."

"*Keetuk?*"

"Yeah. Now what do you say? Put me to work."

"Why?"

"Why? I told you why. So's I can pay off that gear I took, so's you'll get off my back, so's I can get on about my business and so can you." Finn watched Yael's eyes and he thought about the One-eyed Jack. Finn decided he would take a chance anyway. Maybe he had a better hand this time than he thought.

"And maybe you'll stake me to another winter upriver," Finn said quietly. "Maybe we can make another deal."

Finn expected more laughter. When it didn't come, when Yael just stood there and stared at him and then picked up an empty salmon can dropping a drizzle of black saliva into it Finn decided the answer was simply no. He turned around and started to leave.

"Wait a minute," Yael said. "Maybe we can deal. *Work* it off you say?"

Finn thought it was a little too fast, too accommodating. He thought about the offer he had just made to Yael and he could not remember ever saying that word aloud before. *Work.* Saying it bothered him enough but thinking about actually doing it was different. Work had not entered into Finn's life all these years since he had left Texas.

But what really bothered Finn was that Yael had not resisted. Maybe he would make it too tough. Maybe he would trick Finn somehow and wind up owning him body and soul. Or maybe Finn would begin to fool himself and get use to this, maybe even get to liking it. That worried Finn most but he had no choice at the moment.

"Okay," Yael said. "I got a load of goods to move. Both ways, onto the spring ship and off the spring ship. You're mine for that, Finn, and then we'll see what's next. Deal?"

Finn did not answer. He just nodded and moved toward the door. "You seen Nellie?"

"Nellie? Oh, you mean Moon," Yael smiled. "Yeah, she was here right before you come in. Said she was going on a picnic. She went up toward the point there. Now ain't that something? A picnic right out there in all that mud and stench and all that—"

Finn turned away from Yael and went out into the sunlight and down the boardwalk past the cannery and the shacks along the cliff and past Henry's Cabin where he had been secluding himself now for these past weeks, just as Yael had suspected. But he saw no movement around the cabin now. He wondered where Henry might be but he knew it would not be hard to find him. Finn looked at the words slopped with broad strokes in white paint on the gray wall of the cabin. The paint had weathered the winter pretty well but he wondered how long Henry's Cabin itself could last precariously close to the edge of the bluff now that the spring storms had eaten away another ten feet.

Finn decided Nellie would probably be up there somewhere, up there away from the embankment and the grim view of the garbage being exposed on the beach below. He wasn't sure he really wanted to see her but it would be better up there where they could be alone than to bump into her at Heine's Café or in Yael's store or on the boardwalk where everyone could see them talking. He probably did not need to talk to her anyway except maybe to explain why he had not come by and why he had chosen to hide out with Henry rather than her.

And Finn guessed he needed to tell her about the pelts. That would be the hardest part. He saw the top of her head above the dead grass on the point, her black hair shining in the sunlight. When he got near enough Finn saw she was sitting on the blanket and had laid out dried fish and hardtack and was fumbling inside her parka with one arm pulled inside and the sleeve left dangling.

"Hello, Moon," he said to her back.

Nellie did not turn around. She kept working inside the parka. "It's no good, Finn." She did not look at him. Finn was a little perplexed that she had not even given him a chance to explain. He wondered if Henry had betrayed him and had already told Nellie about the pelts and everything that had happened.

"Well, hell's bells—at least let me tell you why I burned them, Moon." He sat down beside her on the blanket but Nellie still had her chin dropped and did not turn.

"Burned what?"

"All the pelts," he said. "See, Marvin got his feet froze and Delbert was catching us and we couldn't get all of them back anyway without his sled and then to make matters worse old Keetuk came poking around. Anyway I *thought* about you, Nellie, but Marv was fading fast and I had to—"

"I'll have to try the other," Nellie interrupted.

For a long while Finn was struck mute. *"Delbert?"* he finally sputtered. "Come on, Moon, don't be silly. Try the *other* one? You don't mean *Delbert?"*

Nellie turned around and looked at Finn and grinned. He liked seeing her grin again but he saw she had not been listening to him. She had been preoccupied with something else, something inside her parka, something inside the pouch she and Old Suyuk had sewn there years ago.

"No, stupid," she said. "I'm talking about the can of milk there. I'll have to try that other milk, the kind in the can."

Finn saw the can of condensed milk on the blanket with the other food. "Make sense, Moon. What are you talking about? What's going on?"

"I'm dried up, Finn. It's too late for me to do it this way and I was probably foolish even to try. I wanted to try with my own breasts, my own milk, but I am not its mother and it just won't work this way. Open the can."

She put her arm back through the sleeve of the parka and shifted the bundle around and now Finn could see the face of the infant tucked inside the parka against Nellie's breasts. Finn stared at the baby and then looked at Nellie and he backed away on the blanket.

"Please," she said and nodded at the can.

Finn sat still, silent for a long time and then he shook himself. "Where?"

"The can of milk, silly," Nellie said. "Open it. You have a knife?"

"No, I mean where the hell did the kid come from? It can't be—"

"Of course not, stupid. It's the girl's, Mi'sha's. She was here with Maruluk. She had the baby here. They came after you left. She hurt herself, fell on the rocks upriver and the baby came. They were afraid to go back to Tuluk."

Nellie stopped short of telling Finn about Delbert's visit. She saw no need to explain about Keetuk and the church. If Finn wanted to know he could find out about all that. Right now Nellie had other things on her mind.

"But what the hell are you doing with it, Moon?" Finn frowned at the baby and ignored the can of milk. The baby began to stir and clinch its fists. Nellie looked down at it, contentment on her face that Finn had never seen. She put her nose next to the baby's.

"It doesn't matter," Nellie said. "I told them I would keep the baby. I told them I would take care of it. Maruluk thought it would be better and Mi'sha was weak anyway. She finally agreed. They left with Aiyut and three other villagers who came down with pelts."

"Old Aiyut was here?"

"Yes. And he was still bitter. When he learned about Felix being dead and he saw Maruluk and Mi'sha and found out about the baby, well, he finally gave in."

"You saw your brother?"

"No," Nellie said and she smiled. "He wasn't with them. But I think Mi'sha will see him. They're back in the village by now. There is no way Mi'sha will not see Alexie and maybe I can see him too. Maybe someone would be kind enough to take me for a visit." She looked at Finn who was still frowning at the squirming infant. "Now open the milk, please. Look how it jerks and moves. It's hungry."

She smiled again and made cooing noises and the baby gurgled and snorted. Finn reached absently for the can of milk and took out his pocketknife.

"The sun's warmed it up good here, Moon. But how are you going to give it to him?"

"It's not a him, Finn," Nellie looked at Finn and then back at the baby. "It's a she."

"A girl?"

"Yes, but that's okay," Nellie said but Finn saw she was not talking to him at all but to the baby. "She'll be proud to be a girl."

Nellie looked at him and he saw the smile leave. And then Finn saw a determination sweep her face as Nellie looked back at the child. "And she'll smile whenever she wants to smile," she continued, again speaking to the baby and not to him. "A true smile and not one she puts on her face and removes to please someone else. Not a smile she forces to be there because her smile will be there anyway. And she won't fight."

"Fight? What are talking about, Moon. You ain't making sense again. Fight who?"

"Fight," she said, this time speaking to Finn. "Like Keetuk."

"*Keetuk?*"

"He was here too."

"In Snag Point?" Finn's eyes widened.

"He brought them in his sled all the way down from the Mikchalk. Maruluk said they had talked about our people, talked all the way down the river. She told him that things were changing with us and that this was the way it was to be. She's always said that Finn, as long as I can remember. But then Keetuk told her that we must not change, that we all must fight to stay the way we are."

Nellie looked at Finn and then again at the baby and she shook her head. "But if we fight to stay the way we are," she whispered. "Then we're no longer the way we are."

Finn nodded but he was not certain he understood. And besides his mind was elsewhere. *"Keetuk?"* he repeated. "Here in Snag Point?" He scooted away a little more and held the can of milk to his chest.

"Yes, but they were all at your cabin first. That's where he had taken them I guess. They were freezing on the Chiktok above Ekok when he first found them."

"My cabin? I should of known it was him."

"I knew he was going after Delbert," Nellie said. "And after you."

"He did come after us," Finn said quietly. "I saw him too. He caught Delbert and he caught me."

"I wanted to stop him but he left anyway," Nellie said. "And I thought I wouldn't see you or Delbert again. Why didn't he kill you? Or Delbert, like he did Swede? What did he do with Marvin?"

Finn said nothing. He was remembering the rush of dogs and the sled and the whistling of the axehead and the giant raven in his dreams with its shadow moving through him. And Finn was remembering Delbert and the terror in his eyes that would always be there.

"What he done to Delbert was worse than what he done to Swede. And he didn't do anything to Marv," Finn said gravely. "But maybe in a way I did." Finn was silent for a long while before he spoke again. "And I don't know what Keetuk done to me, Moon. I just know that right now I got to go and find Henry. You seen him today?"

"No. Now what about the milk, Finn? You said you'd open it for me."

Finn noticed he still had the can of milk clutched in his hand against his Mackinaw. "Oh sure." He opened his knife and cut the top of the can halfway around and bent back the lid exposing a jagged edge. "Now what? She can't drink out of this."

Finn tried bending the jagged edge back some more but his hand slipped on the metal and plunged into the milk. He jerked it out and saw he had cut the end of his finger.

"Dammit. Now I cut myself." He stuck his finger into his mouth and frowned at Nellie who watched this with amusement. Then she saw his eyebrows lift and he cocked his head. "Hey, it's pretty sweet." Finn sucked on the grimy finger. When he brought it out the finger was cleaner than it had been in weeks. "That's it. That's how you could do it, Moon. Look, just dip your fingers into this and let the kid suck the milk off."

"You could do it," she said but then she saw how dirty his fingers were. "Maybe not." She took the can and balanced it on the blanket. "You need a steambath."

Nellie began to dip her fingers into the can and the baby sucked eagerly at the sweet milk on them. Nellie puckered her lips and made clucking noises as she fed the child. Finn pulled his palm across the rough growth on his chin and looked at his hands and thought about the pinch of snuff he had tucked into his lip first thing that morning and how Nellie would have hated it. And he thought about Nellie's hot steambath and the soap and how the goose wing tingled when she slapped his back with it. But most of all Finn thought about Nellie's big goosedown quilt.

"I gotta find Henry," Finn repeated and made a move to get up from the blanket.

"You said you'd think about it, remember?" Nellie stopped dipping her fingers. She left one finger in the baby's mouth for awhile and soon she could feel the baby relax the grip on it and the lips become slack and the child was asleep. But when she tried to remove the finger the baby moved its head up again and sucked. Nellie smiled and left the finger inside the mouth while the child slept.

"Think about what?" Finn said but he knew what she meant. He craned to look at the baby's face and then stood up and moved off the blanket. Nellie looked up and he saw the contentment on her face was the same as on the sleeping child.

"About me being around. You said you'd think about it."

"You said all the time." Finn was trying to remember the conversation but all he could think about was the hot steam and the big quilt.

"I said almost all the time," Nellie corrected. "I could be around almost all the time if that's what you wanted."

"I don't know. I need to find Henry right now. A man needs a partner you know. I'm fresh out of partners."

Nellie said nothing. She looked at Finn and remembered what he had said about Marvin's feet and she understood. She knew it was not something Finn wanted to talk about. There was no need to explain about Marvin.

"Yes," she said. "Everyone needs a partner."

Finn turned around and started back down the slope toward the village.

"I could have the steambath hot tonight," he heard her call but he did not turn around.

Finn walked back along the embankment retracing his path atop the cannery timbers which had sunk even further into the thawing muskeg. They would be almost out of sight by the end of the summer and the water would then trickle up around their sides onto the top when someone walked across. Finn wondered how many years it would be before they were consumed by the tundra and someone would have to place fresh ones on top of them. To his right Finn saw the blackened hulk of Felix's church showing through the melting snow and he thought he might ask Henry about it when he saw him again. But Finn did not really care about that. Just as Marvin had found peace so might Felix, especially without the weight of an empty church on his soul. Finn forgot all about that when he noticed the spring ship anchored out in the bay. It was a threemaster and he knew then where he would find Henry.

The incoming tide had just slackened as Finn made his way down and under the dock at the cannery. It was a large tide and Finn wondered if Henry would risk being under there with such high water. The tide had lifted the last huge chunks of muddy ice from the highest part of the beach and was holding them in suspension waiting to take them out on the ebb for a final time.

"Did you see her, Finn?"

Finn heard Henry before he could see him. He was tucked under the dock as high as he could get, hunkered against a piling just above the slack water.

"Moon?" Finn said.

"Naw. I mean the ship. Did you see her out there? She's laying on anchor just off the point." The pitch of Henry's voice was high, a nasal tenor full of excitement.

"Yeah," Finn said. "I seen her."

"She's just coming around, Finn. Come on, get over here where you can see her. She'll be swinging on her anchor soon as the tide changes."

Finn leaned over to avoid the timbers and shuffled up under the dock next to Henry.

"She's a three master. Just like the one I come up on. Look at her. Ain't she a beauty?"

"Yeah," Finn said but he was thinking about all that cargo he would have to move for Yael now that the ship was in.

"This calls for a little celebration." Henry stood up as far as he could and groped in the darkness above his head. When he felt the timber he reached above it and retrieved a bottle.

"Ain't it a little early," Finn said. "She ain't going nowhere."

"This here's a flat one, see? This kind's better for under here, these flat bottles. They don't roll off the timbers." Henry held up the bottle, a pint of whiskey, real Irish Whiskey, or so Yael would have said. Henry uncorked it and held it up to Finn. "You first since you're back and all. You go first."

"Naw you go ahead Henry. You toast the ship."

"You sure? You won't take it wrong?"

"Course not. Go ahead."

Henry smiled at him and held the bottle up toward the ship in the bay. "Here's to you—" He started to tilt his head back and then stopped. "What's she called, Finn? You got any idea what her name is?"

"No, I can't make out the name on her but it don't matter. Just call her *Lady* or something, anything."

"Yeah that's it. It's gotta be a she of some kind. I could just call her Lady or something." He lifted the bottle and then stopped again. "Hell I could just call her Moon, huh? That's a woman's name. How about that? How about me just calling her Moon?"

"Sure, Henry. Whatever."

"Okay then, here's to you, *Moon.*" Henry threw is head back and let the whiskey bubble out of the bottle. "Now you Finn. Go ahead toast her."

Finn took the bottle and held it up, looked at the ship through the part of the glass that was empty. He put the bottle to his lips and took a deep swallow and handed it back to Henry.

"Once more." Henry held it up again and once more he stopped. "I think I'll go aboard her," he said quietly, the high pitch gone from his voice. "Meet the captain and all. You know talk to him. What do you think about that?" He tipped the bottle up and then passed it back to Finn.

"Sure, Henry. That'd be fine. That'd be just fine." Finn held the bottle up again and again he looked through the glass, half empty now or half full, he wasn't sure which.

"You ain't toasted her yet," Henry said. "Come on, you ain't done it yet. Say it, Finn."

Finn paused and looked at Henry and then back at the ship which had just begun to swing on her anchor. "Here's to you...*Moon.*" He lifted the whiskey, only this time Finn turned his back to Henry and he stuck his tongue up into the mouth of the bottle. He handed the whiskey back. "You know, Henry, we oughta stop all this someday."

\* \* \* \* \*